Praise for BC Powell's
"KRYMZYN"

"Thrilling and spellbinding, 'Krymzyn' drew me in from the very first page."

Roxanne Kade, author of "The Bloody Crescent"

"Unique? Original? Captivating? All of the above? Yes. This book is truly one of a kind!"

Ethan Gregory, One Guy's Guide to Goodreads

"This book has gotten into my brain, and I don't want to let it go. It was truly beautiful!"

Tiffany Williams, imabookshark.com

"Very original plot, dark and intriguing . . . a gripping book."

Mamta Madhaven, poet

"'Krymzyn' is a page turner . . . a strong start to a very promising series."

Lorena Sangui, Reader's Favorite

A Traveler's Fate

by

BC Powell

book three
The Journals of Krymzyn

Published by BC Powell
facebook.com/bcpowellauthor

Cover design and artwork by Ravven
ravven.com

First Edition

ISBN 13: 978-0990500780
ISBN 10: 0990500780

Library of Congress Control Number: 2020906977

Special Acknowledgments

To Ron Guyatt for the fantastic maps. To Ravven for another amazing cover. And a huge thank you to all the book bloggers and readers who support this series.

A Traveler's Fate

The Infinite Plane of Krymzyn

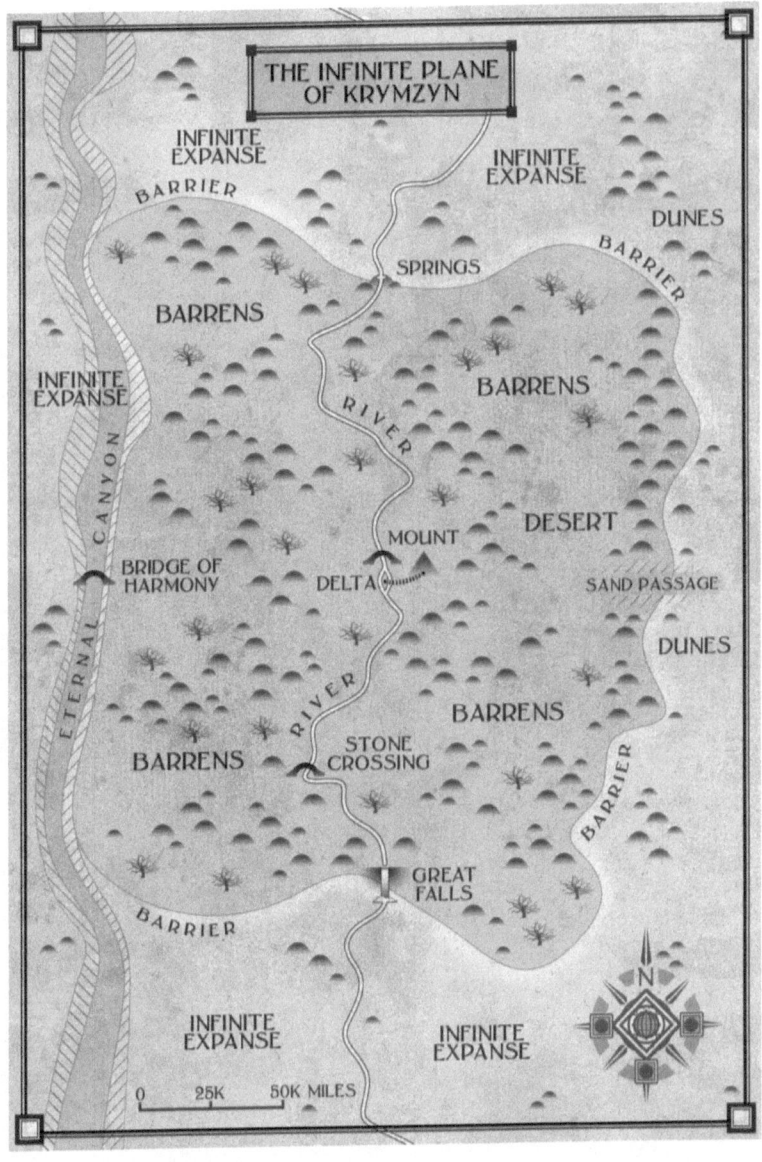

The Delta of Krymzyn

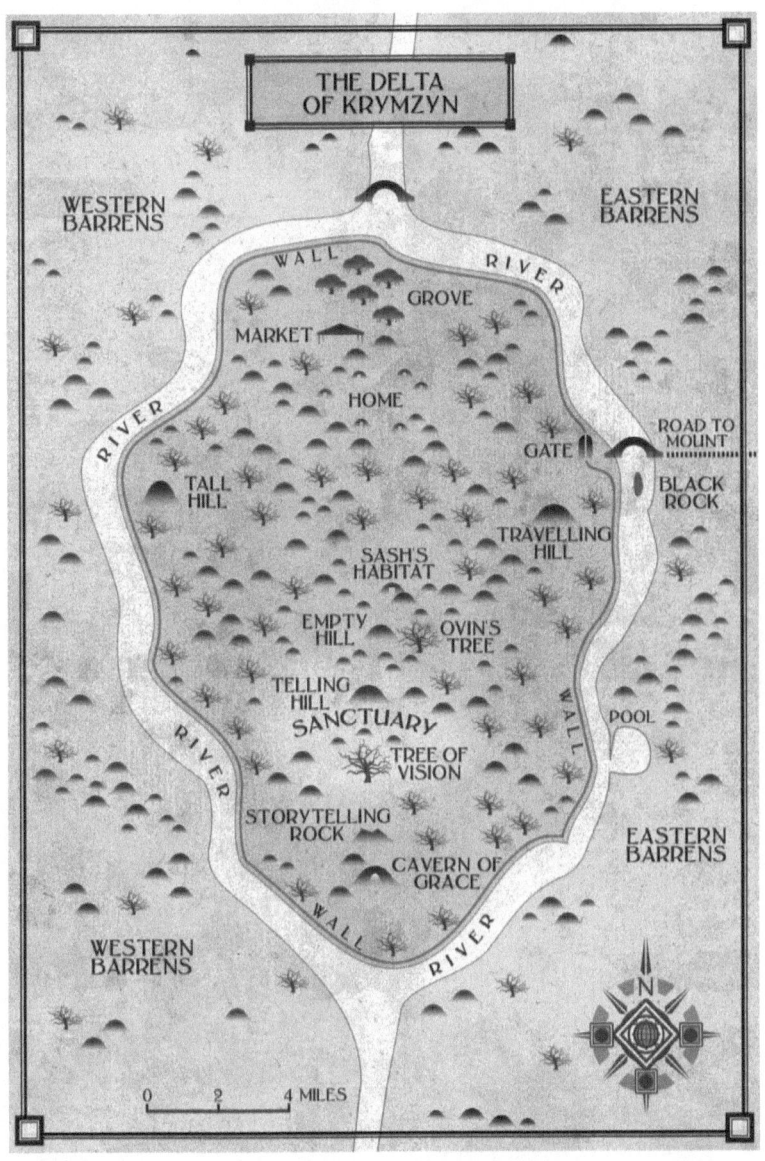

Prologue

Standing on a barren hilltop, the woman watches a streak of light arc across the horizon. One of her hands instinctively reaches for the spear stabbed in the ground at her side. Her other hand remains pressed to her stomach, protectively holding the curve hidden beneath her tight, black shirt. As she studies the luminescent shape in the distance, she decides it's moving far too fast to be one of her kind. And it's heading directly towards her.

It could be the man responsible for the child growing inside her, returning from the Desert sooner than expected. It could be a lone Traveler soaring across the stark wasteland for reasons unknown. It could even be the extraordinary Hunter on one of her solitary treks through the Barrens. The figure is still too far away to determine who it is, but the tiny hairs on the back of the woman's neck stand upright, prickling her skin.

She leaps into a shallow crevice concealed behind a ridge on top of the hill. As she lands in a crouch, lines of firm muscle crease the pants that hug her slender legs. A long braid of shimmering black falls down her back, a few white strands radiating the pallid light from the sky above.

The woman cautiously raises her head and peers over

the jagged rocks that conceal her. Less than a mile away, the beams of light disappear behind a hill and almost immediately stream over the top. On the flat ground in front of her, the speeding figure cuts sharply to the woman's left. Brilliant rays recede from the air and form the body of a young female—a Traveler of the Delta, the woman knows, from vibrant blue highlights in ebony hair. As the Traveler glides to a stop in front of a lone sustaining tree, long straight bangs fall over her eyes.

Did a glint of light from the stake lodged in the tree's bark catch the Traveler's attention? the woman wonders. *The stake is old and weathered. The Traveler should assume it's from a raid on a transport long ago.*

Fortunately, I didn't need to bind the upper branches of the tree. The few limbs that remain attached to the trunk reach straight up to the dark clouds, unable to bend downwards without ripping themselves from the trunk. The Traveler would undoubtedly tell others in the Delta of a tethered tree.

I would prefer not to kill her. An errant blow during a fight might harm the child growing inside me. But I won't hesitate to end her life if I must.

When the Traveler looks around her, the woman ducks her head below the ridge. After a few moments pass, the woman raises one eye to a narrow crack between two rocks. The Traveler finishes scanning the terrain, apparently wanting to make certain she's alone. Standing profile to the woman, her spear in the grip of one hand, the Traveler returns her attention to the trunk of the tree.

I know who that Traveler is, the woman realizes. *She's*

young, several inches shorter than I am. I've heard stories about her from the man who created my child with me. He helped train her to fight with a spear when they were children of the Delta.

The Traveler steps forward to the tree. Sparse gray leaves growing from gnarled branches dangle high over her head. Stopping just a few feet from the trunk, she squints at the stake. After reaching out a hand, she clenches her fingers around the shaft of the steel spike, pulls it from the bark, and holds it in front of her face. To the woman's surprise, the Traveler drops her spear to the dirt.

The Traveler glances over each of her shoulders, but the woman doesn't move. Confident that she's well hidden behind the ridge, she continues to spy through the rocks. The Traveler soon returns her eyes to the stake. With the fingertips of one hand, she twists the point of the spike to make sure the hollow tip is open.

Slowly tilting her head back, the Traveler raises the steel to her lips. Thick red liquid drips to the Traveler's mouth. As soon as she swallows, the Traveler rips the stake away from her face. Her entire body trembles from the rush of wild sap shooting through her veins.

A curious young Traveler, the woman thinks to herself. *Like others of her generation, she must long for something more than life in the Delta provides her.*

Lifting the stake over her mouth again, the Traveler throws her head back. Once consumed, the woman knows, wild sap unleashes an almost uncontrollable thirst. The Traveler continues to gulp until she has to gasp for breath. After she pulls the stake away from her face, she looks down at the ground.

As the wild sap pulses through the Traveler's limbs, tightening muscles contour her bare arms and stretch the fabric of her black pants. Raising her empty hand in front of her face, the Traveler clenches it into a fist. She takes several deep breaths, spreads her fingers apart, and presses her palm to her chest.

The Traveler slides her hand over the roundness of her breasts. She continues to move her hand down her torso and then outward around the curve of her hip. Her fingertips graze over the front of one leg before coming to a rest on the inside of her thigh.

She's aware of carnal sensations, probably for the first time, the woman surmises. *Physical desires have been awakened, replacing the spiritual that those of the Delta adhere to.*

The woman's flesh crawls when she spots a pale, brutish creature creep around a mound of rocks. From behind the Traveler, the Murkovin silently skulks towards the tree. The beast must have been in hiding when the Traveler arrived, the woman concludes, waiting to steal the sap-filled stake that belongs to her. He'll now crave the sap inside the Traveler's veins. He's taller than both the Traveler and the woman, much more muscular, but the woman fears no creature of the Barrens. Time has taught her the harsh lessons of survival in the wasteland.

The woman starts to spring over the ridge but freezes before her feet leave the ground. Still peeking over the rocks, she notices the stake slip through the Traveler's hand. Before it falls to the dirt, the Traveler stops it by tightening her fingertips on the shaft. Almost unnoticeably, she presses her palm to the butt of the stake.

She knows the creature is behind her. Will she have the strength, quickness, and cunning to kill the brute? But a more important question enters the woman's mind. *Why did I feel the need to rush to the Traveler's aid?*

When he's less than ten feet from the Traveler, the Murkovin rears back his spear. As he lunges forward, the tip pierces the air behind the Traveler's head. The woman anticipates the perfect moment for the Traveler to react, the exact point of the creature's assault when he's off-balance, his weight falling forward, and most vulnerable to a counter-attack.

The point of the spear is within a few inches of the Traveler's skull when she jerks her head down and wrenches her hips to the side. Ducking under the steel, she furiously spins. With a powerful upward thrust, she shoves the stake into the Murkovin's larynx. She rams it through his head until the sharp point shatters the back of his skull. Black blood mixed with gray light spews from the beast's head.

The Traveler's palm smashes against the underside of the creature's jaw. With a savage grunt, she lifts the Murkovin's feet off the ground. The brute writhes in agony until the final breath of life gurgles from his lungs. Heaving his body away from her, the Traveler sends the limp corpse sprawling to the ground.

The Traveler raises her hand in front of her eyes. Her body shakes as she stares at the Murkovin's blood dripping from her palm. With a sudden urge to query the Traveler, the woman leaps over the ridge and lands on the crest of the hill.

"You like the power you feel, don't you?" the woman calls out.

The Traveler snaps her head to the voice. In an instant, she jumps to where her spear lies on the ground, snatches it from the dirt, and whirls towards the woman.

"I'll kill you if I have to!" the Traveler shouts.

Maintaining her grip on the spear in one of her hands, the woman holds her arms out to her sides. "I have no quarrel with you. I'm with child and have all the sap I want." She tips her head towards the dead body by the Traveler's feet. "But that stake belongs to me."

"I have no use for it!"

"You drank the wild sap from it," the woman accuses. "Why would you do such a thing?"

"What I do is none of your concern!" the Traveler retorts.

She's having difficulty controlling her temper. She's not used to the effects of wild sap. She's dangerous while it's in control of her mind.

"Why are you here?" the woman asks.

The Traveler crouches and points her weapon at the woman. "I don't have to answer to you."

"This is my territory," the woman calmly replies. "It's a simple question to put my mind at ease. Are you hunting Murkovin? Are others nearby?"

"Of course not!" the Traveler barks. "We don't hunt your kind in the Barrens for no reason."

"Then explain why you're here."

Narrowing her eyes with distrust, the Traveler hesitates. "I have no duties this day," she eventually says. "I wanted to feel open space."

Still holding her arms out to her sides, the woman takes a few steps down the hill. She stops when the Traveler coils.

"And to satisfy your curiosity?" the woman asks.

The Traveler grimaces at her words. "If you come any closer, I'll kill you."

"As I said," the woman replies, lowering her arms to her sides, "I have no reason to fight you. Go on your way. You didn't drink much. If you take an indirect route back to the Delta, the wild sap will be purged from your veins before you return."

The Traveler takes two steps backwards. Without saying another word, she turns away, bursts into a sprint, and explodes into rays of light. After the beams of her body disappear in the wasteland, the woman walks down the hill to reclaim her stake.

Why did I feel the need to help her when I thought her life was at risk? I don't care what happens to anyone from the Delta. She's nothing like me, and I'm certainly not like her. Was it merely because I'm familiar with her from stories of when she was younger? Is that why I had the urge to protect her? Or is there more to it than that?

It may have been nothing but a coincidence that I was here when she found the stake. There's no doubt that these are strange times we live in and many changes are upon us. I should expect that odd things will happen—events far from the ordinary.

None the less, I can't help but feel that this was more than a random encounter. I'm certain that our paths will cross again.

Chapter 1

I rocket over a hilltop and soar at least thirty feet into the air. Flapping my arms by my sides, I try to keep my spear in the grip of one hand. I realize that I was traveling way too fast when I hit the crest. The drop on the backside of the hill is much steeper than I anticipated, always a risk when sailing through the Barrens.

The more I blend my light, the more I learn that distinguishing between two thousand and ten thousand miles per hour is a lot more difficult than I thought it would be. When I'm cruising through the Delta, I have familiar landmarks to help me judge my pace. But in the open space of the wasteland, it's like being behind the wheel of a sports car on an empty highway in the middle of nowhere. Excessive speed is inevitable.

I estimate that my speed was well over eight thousand miles per hour at the top of this hill, much faster than I should have been going in an area I'm not familiar with. Decisions aren't split-second at this speed. They're split-millisecond. And they're much less of a decision than they are a pure instinctual reaction.

Trying to maintain my balance through the descent, I concentrate on the layers of light flowing between me and the dirt. As gravity pulls the millions of particles of my body downward, I focus only on the beams pointing in the same direction that I am. If I get tangled in the rays that splay off to my sides, my landing could turn into a painful explosion of my molecules in many different directions. When they eventually slap back together out of my control, at the very least, it would result in a horrendous wipeout with several broken bones. Death would be more likely.

Of equal concern is the sheer face of rock on the side of the next hill in front of me. If I can't regain control in the half-second I'll have on the ground before covering that mile, the last painting I create in Krymzyn will be my body splattered all over the side of a cliff.

As soon as the particles of my feet graze the dirt, friction slows my speed with a jarring stutter. I start to topple forward and feel my molecules trying to implode. Fighting to maintain my running motion, I funnel as much of my body as I can into a few distinct beams. I rifle forward after regaining my balance, but a wall of rock instantly fills my vision.

Jerking my head to the left, I jam my focus into a series of light rays perpendicular to the direction I'm traveling. Like a fully stretched rubber band being snapped, my particles spring in the direction of my vision and complete a ninety-degree cut at full speed. I imagine a thunderous "whoosh" echoing off the side of the hill as my body sweeps into the light ahead of me, but I'm traveling way too fast for my own sound waves to enter my ears.

"Woo-hoo!" I shout, curving around the base of the hill.

My heart is racing from the surge of excitement,

something I'm getting used to in Krymzyn. I've never considered myself an adrenaline junkie, but nothing on Earth can begin to compare to the feel of blending my light. To be honest, I find it addicting.

With one hundred miles of flats between me and the road to the Delta, I glance around one last time to check for Murkovin. Not seeing anything but lonely hills and a few dead trees, I return my attention to the road and angle in from the south.

From the north, the vague shape of Tela sparkles towards the dirt path. She and I often find ourselves assigned to lead watch for transport caravans between the Delta and the Mount. Both of us have surpassed the speed of the other Travelers and can stay neck and neck with Larn, although I have to assume that even he'll be lagging behind us soon.

As I close in on the road, I make a gradual curve towards the center. Checking to the east, I spot the rays of Jeni and Velt with the blurs of their empty sap transports in tow. Farther behind them, Larn races down the road with his Apprentice Kale at his side. Bringing up the rear, Nuar jets in from the Barrens behind Larn and Kale.

Tela and I reach the hard dirt path at about the same time and both aim towards the Delta. With our particles lightly bristling against one another's, we race the final few miles to the bridge. I feel a slight bump in my motion from the last little hump in the road, my marker to let me know that the bridge is only a mile away.

Tela is still at full throttle by my side, so I don't slow yet. As we near the end of the road, the multi-directional array of reflections from the steel bridge becomes increasingly brighter. They're the same reflections that Larn once warned me will scatter my body in many different directions and more than likely kill me if I'm still in my blend when I reach them.

Less than one hundred yards from the bridge, I suck my particles in from the beams. With the sting of a hurricane-force wind hitting my skin, they reassemble into my body. A split-second later and slightly in front of me, Tela transitions from her blend to a sprint. The last rays of light seep into our bodies just fifteen yards from the end of the road. In our unspoken game of chicken, Tela wins again.

She coasts to a stop on the upslope of the bridge while I jog towards her from behind. When I stop by her side, I'm panting from a combination of excitement and overexertion. With her spear dangling from one hand, she rests her other hand on her hip. As she looks up at the sky, she inhales a few deep breaths, a definite clue that she was pushing her speed just as much as I was.

"You're becoming much more efficient at coming out of your blend," she says, still studying the clouds.

"I'm working on it," I reply through gulps of air. "No matter how many times I do it, I don't think it'll ever get old."

Tela looks at me. "Traveling?"

"Traveling," I reply with a nod.

The slightest smile curls the corners of her lips, a response from her that's becoming more and more common. "It never will," she says. "I promise you that."

Tela just confirmed what I've already come to realize. Travelers relish in our ability to blend our light. It's a stupendous gift that only a handful of people from each generation experience. We never take it for granted and immerse ourselves in the sensation as often as possible.

Even with the precautions that Larn put into place after the Murkovin blockade killed Beck, on a day off, a Traveler will almost always end up alone in the Barrens. The Murkovin lack the focus to keep up with us, and if we travel in an unpredictable route, they can never set a trap. With tens of thousands of miles of open space, we can unleash our mind-blowing speed. To paraphrase what Larn once told me, it becomes meditative when our bodies transfuse with the light of the world around us.

After Tela and I catch our breath, we both look at the road. Much farther from the edge of the bridge than where Tela and I exited the light, Velt and Jeni have already come out of their blends. Muscular like a heavyweight boxer, Velt effortlessly pulls his transport along the road. His short, spiky hair radiates the same cobalt blue that all of us Travelers have in our hair.

Walking beside Velt with her transport handles in her grip, Jeni has a natural bounce in her step. She's curvy and athletic, not heavy, not lean, with long, wavy hair tied in a ponytail behind her head. Other than Jeni being about three inches taller than Tela, the two are built almost exactly the same.

Nuar streaks in from behind Jeni and Velt and then transitions to a run. Her sleek stride is always calculated and graceful in its motion. With a pixie-like hairstyle that seems to match the delicate features of her face, she looks more like a tall, thin ballerina than someone who would be traveling across the badlands with a spear in her hand.

Finally, the beams of Larn and Kale recede into bodies. They jog past the others before slowing to a walk. At six foot six, trim and athletic, Larn towers over Kale. He immediately begins offering his Apprentice a few words of traveling critique.

Only about eighteen, Kale still has a boyish quality to his chiseled good looks. He's not as lean as I am, but not nearly as stocky as Velt. His long, straight hair hangs over his eyebrows, covers his ears, and falls past his neck in the back. As they all walk towards us, I look past them to admire the colossal Mount of Krymzyn in the distance.

"There's a very long flat space in the Barrens to the southwest," Tela says to me. "It's several thousand miles west of the Stone Crossing."

"What's the Stone Crossing?" I ask, turning my head to her.

"The only natural river crossing in Krymzyn," she answers. "It's about two-thirds of the way to the Great Falls. At some point, you should go there to test your speed in the flat area."

"Is that allowed?"

"We all do it," Tela says. "We rarely speak of it, but every Traveler does it sooner or later. Even Larn."

The others walk up the slight slope of the bridge to Tela and me and stop in front of us. After Larn finishes imparting whatever advice he's been giving Kale, he looks back and forth between Tela and me.

"Did either of you see anything?" he asks.

"Nothing," I answer.

"Not a thing," Tela replies.

"That's good," Larn says. "If this continues, perhaps we'll be able to reduce the number of Travelers needed for trips to the Mount."

"It seems weird to me," I comment.

"What do you mean?" Larn asks.

"We haven't seen any Murkovin since the blockade that killed Beck."

In the six weeks since Beck died, no one has seen a single Murkovin. It seems to me that they've purposely vanished from our sight. The Watchers haven't spotted any near the river during Darkness, and the Travelers haven't caught a glimpse of even a lone Murkovin when we're crossing the Barrens.

"It's not out of the ordinary at all," Larn says. "We can go hundreds of days without seeing a Murkovin. What *is* strange is how many encounters you've had with them during your short time here. You've already had more direct contact with Murkovin than most people have in their entire lives."

"But we saw so many for a while," I say. "It seems like they're trying to avoid us now."

"They normally avoid us," Larn explains. "They're solitary creatures for the most part. A few might band together, usually a male and female who create a child, or a small group that will try to work together. They occasionally attack us for clothing, tools, or sap, but they eventually turn on one another if their sap runs low. Most of the sustaining trees around the Delta have been dead for many Eras. Only if a few Murkovin happen to be near the Delta when Darkness falls will they try to enter."

"Unless Balt is trying to change all that," I counter.

"It's quite possible that they've turned on Balt by now. Their attacks on the Delta and the road didn't result in anything useful to them. Once they realize he has nothing of value to offer, there's no reason for them to let him live."

"I guess so," I say, although I certainly don't believe that Balt is dead. I can't help but feel that this is just the calm before the inevitable storm.

"Our duties for the day have been completed," Larn says to the group. "We don't have any trips to the Mount on the morrow, but we'll need to transport a few items from Market to the southern part of the Delta. We also need to take some of the children to the gate to spend time with the Watchers. We can all take the early part of the morrow to ourselves and then meet at Market. I'll summon you when it's time. I think Kale is ready to tow a transport."

With a determined look in his eyes, Kale nods his head in agreement with Larn's statement. Larn has been much slower with Kale's traveling progression than he was with mine. I know he feels guilty for rushing me into carrying a transport too early in my Apprenticeship, so I don't think he wants Kale to repeat my rather painful experience. The fact of the matter is, I was more to blame for my injuries the first time I traveled with a transport because I wanted to prove myself to the others as soon as I could.

"He'll do great," I say emphatically. "See you on the morrow."

After Kale and Larn tip their heads goodbye to us, Tela and I say our farewells to the rest of the group. We turn away and walk side by side over the arch of the bridge. Still thinking about how Larn had said that confrontations with Murkovin don't happen very often, I realize that I've never asked Tela what her experience with them has been.

"How many fights have you been in with Murkovin?" I ask.

"It's rare to encounter a Murkovin," she answers, "even as often as Travelers are in the Barrens. As Larn pointed out, you've had more interaction with them than most people ever do."

I notice that Tela gave me a logical response, but she didn't actually answer my question. "When they attacked us near the bridge, was that the only time you've been in a fight with them?"

"I didn't fight them during the attack," she says with her eyes focused on the Delta wall and her tone of voice seeming mildly annoyed by my question. "I tried to get you to safety and then helped Miel."

The people of Krymzyn—those of the Delta and Mount, anyway—will never flat out lie to your face. But that doesn't mean they won't answer a question with an ambiguous response or twist my question into a question for me. Even the Serquatine didn't blatantly lie when they lured me into the Springs. They encouraged me to jump in the water by telling me half-truths.

"So you've never actually fought a Murkovin," I say as a statement of fact.

"Very few people ever fight a Murkovin," she replies with her irritation much more obvious. "I have to go to Market to get a few things. I'll see you on the morrow."

Tela abruptly jogs away from me. When she reaches the end of the bridge, one gate in the wall swings open. She quickly disappears behind it.

For some reason, she didn't want to answer my question with a direct "yes" or "no," and I seem to have made her feel uncomfortable by forcing the issue. I feel bad for putting her on the spot that way. She's been much more open to idle conversation than anyone else in Krymzyn other than Sash.

Tela and I have fallen into the habit of strolling to our habitats together when our work for the day is completed. I'd define us as becoming good friends. The more time I spend with her, the more I feel the same way about her as I do my little sister on Earth. But the fact remains, she never answered my question. I can't help but wonder why.

As I step through the gate, I wave to the two Watchers on duty. Once my feet are on the crimson grass, I drop to one knee and sink my fingers under the blades.

"Sash," I say, "I'm on my way to our habitat."

A few seconds later, her voice speaks inside my mind. "I'm running a little late, but I'll be there soon."

Chapter 2

By the time Sash arrives at our habitat, I've already cleansed in the waterfall and had a few cups of sap. Sitting in front of my easel in the small cavern that serves as my studio, I work on a detailed painting of a Murkovin. The Swirls slowly move inside the crystal ceiling over my head, projecting their soft golden light on the blue quartz walls around me. Lost in serene concentration, I don't even hear Sash when she enters. She sneaks up behind me, throws her arms around my neck, and kisses my cheek.

"I'm sorry to be so late," she says in my ear. "I don't know why, but I had an urge to visit the children at Home."

"You don't need to apologize," I reply. "You know me. I can always keep busy."

"But I like our time together." She kisses my cheek again and then returns to upright with her hands still resting on my shoulders. "Do you want to go out for a walk in a bit?"

"I'd like to," I answer.

Sash and I often go for walks in the evening, or "end of day" as the people of Krymzyn call it. Every few days, we stroll to the Tall Hill to admire the view. Other times, we just walk hand in hand around the Delta. Assuming that's what we'd do this evening, I re-dressed in my black pants and sleeveless shirt after showering instead of slipping into the more comfortable shorts and tank top I usually wear in the evening.

"Why do you insist on painting Murkovin?" Sash asks.

"I like subject matter that's interesting to look at. The Murkovin are definitely interesting."

"They're hideous," she says.

I chuckle at her comment. "We have a saying on Earth. 'Beauty is in the eye of the beholder.'"

"Does that mean you think they're beautiful?" she asks, squeezing my shoulders.

"Not at all. But they are interesting to look at."

"Please don't hang that up in our habitat," she says firmly. "Even in here."

"Don't worry," I reply. "I wasn't planning to. But I *do* want to show you something that I hope we can hang up."

I lay my paintbrush on the easel tray, stand from my stool, and walk across the studio. Leaning against the far wall is a sheet-covered steel picture frame that Wren made for me. On the canvas inside the frame is the first full-color painting I've finished since being in Krymzyn. Turning to Sash, I grab the sheet with one hand.

"Ready?"

"You finished it?" she asks, raising her eyebrows.

"A couple of days ago. I just wanted to live with it for a while before showing it to you."

"I'm ready," she says.

With an imaginary drum roll in my head—I'd do it out loud, but it wouldn't have any meaning to Sash—I lift the sheet off the painting. Sash's eyes widen and the corners of her lips turn up in a smile. Focused on the canvas, she walks across the room to where I'm standing.

The painting of Sash kneeling beside Ovin's tree with her head bowed, one hand resting on the bark of the trunk, the other hand clutching a spear by her side, is deeply evocative to me. In my opinion, it's the most beautiful painting I've ever created, probably because of how I feel about the subject matter.

When Sash reaches me, she kneels in front of the painting. Her eyes study the painstaking detail I put into the blades of grass, the gray billows overhead, and every twig and leaf growing from the branches of the tree. The lighting in the painting intentionally draws the viewer's focus to Sash. At least a full minute passes while she examines my portrayal of her.

"Chase, it's . . ." She pauses and shakes her head. "It's amazing."

"I really hope you like it," I say.

"More than I have words to express. I like seeing the way you see me."

"That makes me happy," I reply. "I know things don't look the same to you as they do to me."

She stands up and turns to me. "The way you see things is beautiful."

"Thanks," I say. "If you don't mind, I was hoping we could hang this in the empty space between the tunnel entrance and the door to my studio. That way, we can see it from across the room when we're in bed."

"That's a perfect place for it. I'll talk to a Construct on the morrow about securing mounts in the wall for the frame." She reaches her arms around me and pulls me to her. "Thank you for making it for us," she says softly in my ear.

"You never need to thank me for painting. It's one of the things I love most in life."

"I know it is." We silently stand in each other's arms for several moments. "Should we still go for a walk?" she asks, leaning back from me.

"Absolutely," I answer.

"Let me have some sap first."

"Tell me when you're ready," I say.

She steps back and looks at the painting again. I can see by the appreciative glow in her amber eyes how much she truly likes it. When she walks to the main cavern, I return my attention to the canvas. I wonder if I'll always see things in Krymzyn the way they would look on Earth, or if my perception of this world will eventually change to the way it actually exists here.

"Darkness!" Sash shouts from the other room, startling me out of thought.

I rush to the main cavern. "Where to?"

I already know what her answer will be, but I always like to confirm where we're going. For the past few weeks, Darkness has been falling roughly once every day and a half. It usually lasts about two hours. That gives Sash enough time to take sap from three trees per Darkness while I stand watch over each location from a nearby hill. We've been working in a consistent pattern through her hunting region to make sure all the trees contribute equally.

"The Empty Hill," she replies. "It's the turn of Ovin's tree to provide for us."

After hurrying to the habitat entrance, we stop by the hooks on the wall. Sash takes down three packs of stakes, slings them over her shoulder, and we both grab our spears. I follow her through the tunnel until we burst outside. Since Sash is usually aware of Darkness several minutes before it falls, the sky is still blanketed by dormant clouds.

We sprint out of the gorge in front of our habitat, cut into the broader valley, and surge into beams at the same time. With Sash leading our way, we navigate to the Empty Hill. As we slide to a stop on the crest, rain begins to pour from a darkening, tumultuous sky. Sash drops two of the three packs of stakes to the ground and charges straight down the hill towards the awakened tree.

She effortlessly bounds, twists, and leaps through the violent limbs. In almost no time, all seven stakes are spiked into the bark and filling with sap. Using the shaft of her spear, she protects the stakes from branches that slam down at her from above. She's meticulous in her defense, careful to never damage even the smallest twig when she blocks a limb away.

I slowly turn in a circle, scanning the stormy countryside for any sign of Murkovin who might have entered the Delta. Other than rain splattering on the blades of grass, the hills and valleys are motionless and empty. About ten minutes later, I return my eyes to Sash. She's already ripping the stakes out of the trunk and slipping them into the cylinder on her back.

When the last one is securely in her pack, Sash presses her forehead against the trunk of the tree. The limbs that were lashing down at her are still waving vigorously in the air, but they stay high over her head. It's as though the tree is allowing Sash to peacefully pay homage to it by temporarily suspending its assault.

To my surprise, the rainfall thins, the undulating clouds slow until they're static, and scarlet light cuts through their edges. This is the shortest period of Darkness since before my sister Ally was here.

Sash glances up at the sky and squints at the clouds, probably wondering why Darkness didn't last longer. After turning away from the trunk, she walks towards the base of the Empty Hill. She only makes it a few steps before freezing in place. Locking her eyes on my body, her mouth gapes open and she drops her spear.

Chapter 3

"What's wrong?" I call out.

Sash doesn't reply, make the slightest move, or even blink. As she continues to gawk at me, I look down at my body. Amber light is sparkling in the veins running from my shoulders to my hands. I drop my spear to the ground and raise my hands in front of my face. Golden light glistens from the skin of my palms and fingers.

I finally realize that I've been given the sign of fertility, basing that conclusion on Sash's description of it to me long ago. Lowering my hands to my sides, I return my eyes to Sash. Like liquid amber is being injected into her body, luminescent gold spreads through the veins of her face, neck, and arms. I expect to see confusion or surprise on her face when she looks down at her body since she told me that Hunters are never chosen for the Ritual of Balance. Instead, she just smiles and walks up the slope of the Empty Hill.

"We've been chosen for the Ritual of Balance," she says, stopping in front of me.

"I didn't realize it would happen so soon," I reply.

"What do you mean?"

"I knew we'd be chosen," I say.

She nods her head, probably figuring out that the only

way I could know is from my Vision of the Future. "I did too," she confesses.

"How?" I ask.

"During your Ritual of Purpose, I had a glimpse of the future. It was of our child."

"Why didn't you tell me?"

"You know how I feel about revealing the future to others. I never want you to feel as though you're obligated to be with me because of something I've seen in the future. I want you to be with me because you want to."

"That *is* why I'm with you," I say. "What do we do now?"

"Are you happy?" she asks with genuine concern in her voice.

"I'm thrilled," I answer. "I mean, I kind of wish we had more time alone together before starting a family, but I couldn't be happier."

I wrap my arms around her.

"A family," she whispers.

My head spins with exhilaration. I knew this day would arrive at some point, but I thought it would happen in a year or two, maybe even farther down the road. I've only been permanently in Krymzyn for four months. As deep as our emotional connection is, in many ways, Sash and I are still learning about one another and adjusting to our lives together.

Leaning my head back, I look at her eyes. "Sash, I want us to raise our child. I saw it, all of us together when they're . . . I mean she . . . _Dammit_! I'm trying not to give away my—"

Sash covers my mouth with her hand. "In my glimpse, I saw her as well. I know our child will be a girl. But we have to accept what the future holds for our child no matter what that might be."

She pulls her hand away from my lips.

"You know how families are structured in my world," I say.

"All that matters is that we do what's best for the child. Krymzyn will want the same. We can talk about it later. Right now, we've been summoned for the Ritual."

"What do we do?" I ask.

"We go to the Cavern of Grace," she tells me. "Let's leave our things in our habitat and we'll go together. We learn the steps when we're mature enough, usually about the time we leave Home. The man and woman meet inside the Cavern, but our circumstances are obviously different. Since you don't know the procedure, I'll tell you what to do once we're there."

After gathering our things from the grass, we speed to our habitat. With our veins still shimmering amber, we quickly drop off our spears and the packs of stakes. Gliding over the hills to the south, we pass the Tree of Vision and the Storytelling meadow. We finally stop at one of the last hills before a mile-long field that runs to the southern wall of the Delta.

Sash leads me inside a narrow gully that's so uniform it seems almost carved in the incline of the hill. Rich crimson grass grows on both sides of the tall corridor. At the end of the gully, we reach a sheer wall of rock in the base of a steep hill. An arched marble door stands in the center of the wall. The veins that run through the black marble glow with the same golden light that's emanating from our skin.

"The door only shows light," Sash says to me, "when two people have been summoned for the Ritual. Only those with the sign have the ability to open the door to the Cavern of Grace. The woman usually enters first and waits for the man. The door leaves the light of her handprint on the surface to let the man know she's inside. We'll go together since you don't know what to do."

We step towards the door, but I don't see a knob or handle to open it. Sash presses the palm of one hand against the surface, so I do the same. Yellow light flares around our hands, gradually recedes, and the slab swings inward. After we pass through the opening, the door closes behind us with a loud thud.

As we walk through a narrow tunnel, the radiant amber from our veins reflects in the smooth, dark walls. We soon reach a small, high-ceiling cavern shaped out of glossy black stone.

Falling from the domed ceiling, flakes of colored light float down through the air. Like a gentle snowfall of every color imaginable, the points meander to the ground. The flakes end their descent with a gentle splash in a shallow pool of water that covers the ground. A myriad of color reflects in the circular walls of the cavern around us.

In the center of the cavern, seven thick vines hang from the highest point of the ceiling, each of them vibrant with a different color of the rainbow. Intertwined with one another, they form a single massive pillar roughly the size of a sturdy tree trunk. With her face bathed in multi-colored light, Sash turns to me.

"The Vines of Life," she says. "We need to take off our

clothing."

We both lift our shirts over our heads and slip our pants down our legs. After laying our clothing on the tops of two granite slabs that reside on either side of the Cavern entrance, we step inside.

"Wait here," Sash says quietly.

She walks through a nebula of swirling color. With each step she takes, ripples glimmering with brilliant reflections spread outward in the shallow water around her feet. When she reaches the Vines, she kneels in front of them, rests her hands on their base, and bows her head.

"Kneel behind me," she says, her voice echoing inside the cave.

I walk through the inch-deep water while the sparks of light in the air prickle against my skin. When each twinkling flake touches me, it sends pulses of pleasure through my nerves. After stopping behind Sash, I get down on my knees behind her. Resting on all fours, Sash extends her backside to me. I slowly run my hands over the curves of her hips.

"You're not allowed to touch me with your hands," she says. "Keep them at your sides and press your midsection against me."

Lowering my hands as she instructed, I lean my stomach against the firm curve of her rear. She reaches one hand between her legs and softly caresses me. Her fingertips feel as though they're reaching through my skin and deep inside my body. Once I'm fully erect, she takes me in a gentle grip and guides me into her warmth.

"Slowly move inside me," she says, returning her hand to the ground, "and then remain still."

A tranquil smile comes to my face as I slide inside her wetness. Once I'm as deep as I can go, I remain perfectly still. For the first few moments, I feel calm and relaxed. But out of nowhere, a sudden jolt hits me that literally lifts my knees off the ground.

Like being electrocuted by a power line that falls in a swimming pool, thousands of volts surge through me. With my muscles clenching out of my control, my body convulses until I realize that I've been forced to climax inside Sash. Excruciating pain swells in the center of my stomach and shoots outward through my extremities. I slam my hands to my gut and collapse on my side. Squirming in the shallow water, I try to focus my eyes.

"Sash!" I wail.

Oblivious to me, she bows her head to the Vines, whispers a few inaudible words, and stands to her feet. With a somber expression on her face, she looks down at me. The amber light in her veins slowly fades away.

"I'm sorry it has to be this way," she says. "The pain will soon pass. I'll wait for you in our habitat."

Chapter 4

Sash stares at me for several seconds and then walks to the cavern entrance. I can't even call out to her while I writhe on the ground. Each time I think the pain is about to recede, another wave of misery burns through me. I'm not sure how much time passes—maybe an hour, maybe a little less—but it seems like much more. I spend every second of it tucked in a ball with intense pain needling through my body.

When the agony finally recedes, I'm exhausted, cramped, and sore. Hopeful that this warped Krymzyn experience is behind me, I hesitantly stand to my feet. As I limp through the water to my clothes, my leg muscles feel like they're tied in knots.

I learned early in my visits to Krymzyn that casual sex between people doesn't happen in the Delta. The innate desire doesn't even seem to exist here. With the most extreme Pavlovian response I can imagine just programmed inside me, if a man is chosen for the Ritual of Balance, I now understand the negative reinforcement that's forever embedded in his mind.

After dressing as rapidly as I can, I exit through the dark tunnel. The door at the end of the passage swings open for me on its own. Since the granite slab is now absent of light, I look down at my arms. The amber that glittered in my veins an hour ago has entirely left my body.

Once I step out to the grass-lined gully, the door behind me slams itself shut. Feeling aches in every muscle, I jog out of the gorge. It takes me a few tries to merge with the light, but I eventually jolt into the beams.

When I reach our habitat, Sash is already lying on her back in bed. She's wearing shorts and a tank top with the bottom of her shirt lifted to just below the curves of her breasts. With both of her hands resting on her stomach, she gazes up at the Swirls in the crystal ceiling. I cross the cavern to the mattress and sit down by her side.

"How are you?" I ask.

"Our child grows inside me," she answers, turning her head to me. "I'm sorry you had to go through that. In Krymzyn, the woman experiences pain at childbirth. The man feels pain at conception."

"You could have warned me," I say tongue-in-cheek.

She smiles at me and moves her hand from her stomach to my knee. "I didn't want to scare you away. I prefer making love the way it's done in your world."

I return her smile. "I do, too. What happens now?"

"For the next seventy Darknesses, I do nothing but protect the child growing inside me. Then I give birth."

"You won't hunt during Darkness?"

"No," she replies. "But I'll spend time with the trees in my region each day to make sure they're healthy."

"Is that going to be hard on you?" I ask, knowing how much she thrives on fulfilling her purpose as a Hunter.

She returns her hand to her stomach. "What I feel

doesn't matter. My only purpose now is to care for the child."

"What happens after the child is born?"

"I take care of the child until seventy more Darknesses pass. After that, the child will be called for the Naming Ritual."

I hesitate before my next question, bracing myself for an unwanted response. "And after the Ritual?"

"The Keepers take the child," she answers.

"Can we talk about that?"

Her face instantly hardens. "I know what you're going to say, but I don't think you want to hear my response."

"I can't imagine us not raising our child," I tell her. "Love and nurture start with the parents."

"Do you believe the only way a child should be raised is by its mother and father?"

"Yes," I answer. "I mean, not really. It could be two men, two women, or even a single person. It doesn't matter as long as they love the child. They're still a family."

"In this world, everyone in the grace of Krymzyn is what you think of as family."

"It's not the same," I argue. "It's much more personal in my world."

Sash closes her eyes for a moment. When she reopens them, the amber orbs swirl with turmoil. She reaches a hand to my wrist, takes it in her grip, and lays my hand on her stomach.

"Please listen carefully," she says. "Children are raised in Krymzyn the way they are for a reason. We're all one, all responsible for each child, and the child is taught by all. Nurture comes from all of Krymzyn. That ensures that each child finds balance with everything around them."

"It didn't work out that way for Balt," I counter.

"He's an anomaly," she replies. "On rare occasions throughout our history, a person can't control their desire for sap and might end up in the Barrens. But it doesn't happen often. There's a purpose for Balt to be the way he is, even if we don't understand it, just as there's a reason for you to be in this world. The only thing that matters for our child is what's best for her. Do you want her to feel different from the other children?"

"Of course not," I say. "But I think the best thing for her is to be with us."

"But you don't know that," she insists. "You only know how things are in your world. We discussed it once before. Parents in your world aren't always nurturing to their children."

I dig my fingertips into my palms. "You and I will be great parents. The Keepers can educate her the same way a child in my world goes to school. I can't imagine coming back to our habitat at the end of the day and not having her with us."

Sash shakes her head. "You only feel that way because that's how things are in the world where you were raised. This is your world now. You made that choice freely. Even if it's difficult for you, you have to accept the ways of Krymzyn."

Unable to believe what I'm hearing, I look across the room and then back at Sash. "Are you saying that you want to just hand our daughter over to the Keepers?"

"I won't fight Krymzyn on this, Chase," she replies

resolutely. "Don't ask me to. I stood up for us dwelling together because I thought that was the best thing for both of us. But I don't believe the ways of your world are the best thing for a child born in Krymzyn.

"Eval told me," she continues, "that our daughter was in her Vision of the Future. I shouldn't tell you this, but I will. She said that our child will know I'm the woman who gave birth to her. Our daughter had blue eyes in my glimpse of her, so I'm sure she'll know that you're her father.

"I know it's difficult for you to understand, but the way a child is raised in Krymzyn is for the good of the whole. Knowing what we've both been through in our lives, would you want her to feel different from the other children because of how you want her to be raised?"

"No," I say. "But I don't think this will make her feel different."

Sash snaps upright in bed. "Think about it. How could it not make her feel different?"

While weighing Sash's words, I don't reply. Although there's a certain amount of truth to her logic, I can't help the way I feel. The last thing I want is for our child to be viewed as different, but I also can't imagine watching her grow up from a distance.

"Please don't ask me to defy Krymzyn on this," Sash implores to my silence. "We have to accept whatever Krymzyn wants for our child. If the ways of Krymzyn aren't the best thing for her, then we'll be shown that. Unless we are, the only thing we should care about is what's best for her."

I know I shouldn't, but I decide to tell Sash what I saw

in my Vision of the Future. "I saw us all together in my Vision. I saw you and me with our children. The four of us were playing together on the Tall Hill. They were older, up to our waists, and we were all happy."

"Children?" she asks with mild confusion.

"We're going to have a son as well," I say.

"No one is ever chosen for the Ritual of Balance twice," she reminds me.

"We will be."

"That was in your Vision of the Future?"

"Yes," I answer. "I saw us all together as a family. That was my Vision."

Sash peers into my eyes for a few seconds before speaking. "But you didn't see the path that will lead us to that Vision."

"Then what do I do?" I ask, trying to keep my temper in check. "Just stand aside and let our daughter be taken away from us?"

"She'll never be very far from us," she replies. "We'll find ways to spend time with her as a family, but she should be raised in the same way that other children in Krymzyn are."

With a growing sense of despondency and needing some time to think, I stand up from the bed. "I want to clean up and have some sap. I'll be right back."

I step to the table and gulp down several cups of sap. Trying to keep a combination of hurt and anger under control, I undress and walk to the waterfall. While standing under the water, for the first time since being in this world, I have doubts about my ability to accept the ways of Krymzyn.

It might be a selfish reaction, but I believe with all my heart that we should raise our daughter. Even harder for me to accept is that, also for the first time, Sash doesn't seem to have my back.

After I finish cleaning off, I slip on my shorts and return to bed. Sash is lying on her back with her hands perched on her stomach. I lie down on the bed beside her and look up at the Swirls. I decide that I don't want to push Sash on the subject right now, but as far as I'm concerned, this conversation is far from over.

"I just want you to know how I feel," I say. "I won't ask you to do anything that you don't think is right. All I want is what's best for our child."

"She'll know we're her parents," she replies. "We'll be in her life and spend time with her. We've both seen that, so we'll find ways to make sure it happens."

"Does anyone here keep track of the ratio between Darknesses and days?" I ask.

"Why do you want to know?"

"I just want to know how long a Krymzyn pregnancy lasts in Earth time," I answer.

"On average, Darkness falls once every day and a half," she says.

"Thanks."

It takes me a few seconds to work out that a pregnancy in Krymzyn lasts about three and a half months. Maybe the pure energy of sap has something to do with the shorter length, or maybe it's due to the biological differences between people in Krymzyn and on Earth. After our daughter is born, she'll spend another three and a half months with us before going to the Keepers.

Sash rolls on her side with her back to me, reaches a hand behind her, and clenches one of my hands in hers. After pulling my arm over her body, she presses my hand to her stomach.

"All you should care about is what's truly best for her," she says. "Not what you think is best."

"I will," I mutter. "Peace."

From my single word, the light from the Swirls dims until dark surrounds us. As minutes turn into hours, I know from Sash's breathing that, like me, she's still awake. But neither of us says anything. I finally close my eyes, finding a little comfort in the fact that I have seven months to figure something out.

Chapter 5

"You have sap!" the Murkovin hisses. "More than you need."

"Where did you hear that?" the woman asks, scrutinizing the creature standing forty feet in front of her.

"Word travels the Barrens," he answers.

The threat in the creature's stance is obvious to the woman. The muscles in his bulky arms are taut and his knees slightly bent. At least four inches taller than the woman, he must weigh twice as much. His stringy hair is tied behind his head, and his weapon is gripped in both hands. Like many of the spears wielded by their kind, his was carved from a sturdy tree branch and sharpened with a coarse stone. He's primed for a fight, the woman knows, ravenous desires gnawing at his mind.

"If you join us, you'll never thirst again," the woman tells him.

"Give us what you have!" he demands. "I'll spare your life and that of the child inside you."

He said, "us," the woman thinks to herself. *There's more than one.*

After removing a metal flask from a rope tied around her waist, the woman tosses it to the creature's feet. "Have some sap," she says evenly. "You won't be so shortsighted after your thirst has been satisfied."

"You should control your tongue!" the beast growls. "This is your final warning."

The woman hears almost silent footsteps creeping down the hill behind her. She doesn't need to look to know exactly where the creature is. But the woman bows to no one in the Barrens, even those too consumed by craving for rational thought.

Her eyes hastily scour the terrain in front of her while her ears stay tuned to her rear. She'll have to flee if there's more than two, she decides. Even though she's certain she could kill three or four, the risk to her unborn child would be too great. As the faint footsteps behind her grow closer, she concludes there's only two.

"You'll be safe, little one," she whispers.

Digging her feet in the gravelly dirt, the woman storms forward. After only three steps, she jolts to a stop. The Murkovin in front of her springs in her direction, but he's slow and clumsy as he charges across the rocky ground. Keeping her eyes fixed on him, the woman slips both of her hands to the end of her spear.

From behind her, the crunch of feet on gravel is only a few feet away. Swinging her spear low to the ground, the woman twists to her rear. The steel smashes into the ankles of the beast, sweeping the creature's feet out from underneath it. A loud female grunt gasps from the body when the Murkovin's back pounds to the ground.

With the end of her spear still in the grasp of both hands, the woman catapults her arms over her head. The female Murkovin on the ground frantically tries to roll out of the way. The shaft slams to the creature's forehead, leaving her stunned on the ground.

As the first Murkovin nears the woman, she snaps her face to him. The brute lunges the tip of his weapon at the woman's head. Throwing one hand up in front of her, she catches the shaft in her grip. The woman yanks the beast's spear by her side and pulls the Murkovin towards her. As he pitches forward, she jams her spear straight into his gut.

The man releases his weapon and tries to smack his fists against the sides of the woman's head. She ducks the blow, feeling the gust from his hands on the back of her neck. Careful to never put her stomach at risk, she hammers her forearm to the Murkovin's chest. Churning her legs, the woman drives him backwards.

Blood pours from the wound in the Murkovin's stomach, but his strength doesn't wane. He finally batters one fist to the woman's face. Ignoring the sting on her cheek, she spins away and yanks her spear out of his belly.

The Murkovin dives after her. As he tries to clench his arms around her thighs, she twirls out of his grasp. Flailing forward, the brute falls flat on his chest. The woman rivets her weapon into the back of his head.

Ripping her spear out of the man's skull, the woman leaps to where the female Murkovin still lies dazed on her back. The moment the woman's feet touch the ground, she plunges her weapon down at the creature. Glaring straight at the female Murkovin's eyes, the woman suddenly halts her downward jab. The tip barely pierces her forehead before coming to a stop.

Her eyes didn't look at me as I brought death upon her. Filled with worry, they looked up the hill at our side.

"I beg of you," the female Murkovin on the ground pleads. "For the sake of my child."

Keeping the point of her spear pressed to the Murkovin's head, the woman glances up the hill. Near the top stands a small girl, barely as tall as the woman's waist. Her frail body is draped in worn, shabby clothes, and unkempt hair hangs around her face. As the woman returns her eyes to the creature at her feet, her thoughts slip to the past.

The woman's *Mür*, the name a Murkovin child calls the man who provides the seed for birth, had been killed only days before the woman was born. But the female who gave birth to her, her *Ovì*, had done everything she could to protect her child. She'd not only provided sap for her, but had also taught her the skills to take it from trees. Her *Ovì* had shown her how to sharpen her teeth with rocks so they'd better rip through the bark of a limb. And her *Ovì* had trained her to fight with a spear, made certain she knew how to protect herself, how to commit everything inside her to the defense of her own life.

But while still young, having grown only as high as her *Ovì*'s chest, she had to watch as the woman who gave birth to her was slaughtered by two of their kind. Two treacherous creatures. Two cowards. Vile men who lacked the courage to take sap from a tree themselves. It was easier to stand idly by while others exhausted themselves in a battle with the limbs and then kill them for the sap in their blood.

On that hateful day, Darkness fell. Violent clouds roiled

over their heads while rainfall spattered on the dirt around them. Her Ovì fought through savage branches to rip a small limb from a trunk. When she returned to where the girl waited safely out of the tree's reach, the two knelt over the branch. Her Ovì's lips didn't touch the bark until she was sure that her child had her fill.

Two men were in hiding nearby, watching as the two females drank. Once the precious liquid flowed through their veins, the beasts attacked.

Her Ovì was still kneeling over the limb when, out of nowhere, a spear split open the back of her neck. When the girl spun to the sound, her eyes widened with terror. A hand slammed to her face, knocking her to the wet dirt. As she tried to scurry away, a muscular brute grabbed her by the hair. He lifted her off the ground and held her face in front of his.

"We'll deal with you later!" he snarled.

He smacked his fist against her jaw and dropped her to the ground. As she struggled to maintain consciousness, the two creatures knelt over her Ovì with their backs to the girl. They had no clue of the flourishing power inside her slender limbs, or the intense will of her mind.

Dizziness from the blow caused the dark clouds overhead to spin in her eyes, but the girl managed to lift her head from the ground. Through blurry vision, she watched the two hideous creatures tear open the veins of her Ovì's neck. Their repulsive mouths leeched to her Ovì's skin. Fighting the pain, she forced herself to stand. Tears for her Ovì rolled over the fresh bruise on her cheek.

The brutal winds of Darkness continued to shriek

through the hills. In the mud in front of the girl, pellets of rain splashed on steel. Her Ovì's spear, a weapon stolen long ago during a raid on Travelers, was still on the ground behind the two men. As soon as her hands clenched the shaft, the strength of vengeance shot through her limbs.

While the beasts slurped her Ovì's blood, she crept towards the creatures and cocked the spear over her shoulder. With all the power her young body could muster, she spiked the weapon straight into one of the Murkovin's skulls. When she drove his head to the ground, the other brute jerked his face to her.

Before he could make another move, she kicked a bare foot to his throat. Gurgling sounds spewed from his mouth as he clutched his neck. She tore the spear out of the dead body at her feet and screamed her wrath. Powering forward, she rammed the point straight into one of the second beast's eyes.

After his head hit the ground, over and over, she pummeled his face with the tip of the spear. The crackling of bone ricocheted from the ground each time the weapon found its mark. Only when his entire skull had been shattered, an unrecognizable muddle of flesh, bone, and blood, did the girl's rage subside.

She dropped the spear, turned to the corpse of her Ovì, and fell on top of her body. The girl's chest heaved with sorrow while the pain of a loss that could never be replaced twisted her insides. Mixed with the falling rain, her tears dripped to her Ovì's face.

Can I now inflict that same fate on another child? the woman silently asks herself.

She examines the female Murkovin's eyes. The creature's plea was not for her own life. It was for that of her child. The woman decides that these two lives may be worth sparing.

"If I let you live," the woman says, "you and your child owe your lives to me. You can stay with me and have all the sap you need."

"Our loyalty will be to you," the female Murkovin whimpers.

"Make no mistake. If you ever betray me, I'll kill your child in front of your eyes and then end your life as well. But if you prove that I can trust you, no harm will ever come to either of you."

The female Murkovin looks at her child and then returns her eyes to the woman. "We're at your service. We'll earn your trust."

"You bear no grudge that I killed that man?"

"He was . . ." The female Murkovin pauses. "He was not the kind of man whose death you mourn."

The female Murkovin's words confirm what the woman had already guessed from the actions of the man. Like many of the men in the Barrens, he was despicable. He probably drank his fill of sap before allowing a single drop to go down the throats of his woman and child. When physical desires overcame him, he took what he wanted from the woman. If she ever voiced her displeasure or tried to leave, he beat her until her tongue was silenced, and then beat the child to further destroy their will.

The only reason the creature at her feet would stay with the man was out of fear. Fear that survival would be more difficult without him than it was with him. Fear that an already dreadful existence could become even worse. And fear that he might find her if she left him and end her pitiful life.

There were good men in the Barrens, loyal men who cared for the women they spent their lives with and the children they created together. Her Mür had been one of those, so her Ovì had told her.

And many Murkovin women needed no man, creatures with the strength and will of mind to survive on their own. Like her Ovì before her, the woman was of that ilk. There was no doubt that her life had become easier after she'd met the former Watcher of the Delta, but she'd never needed him.

"I'll teach you and your child to defend yourselves," the woman says. "You'll meet others you can trust."

"Is it true that our kind our gathering?" the female Murkovin asks.

"It's true," the woman answers.

"And there's an endless supply of sap?"

"Nothing is endless," the woman says. "But with me, you'll have more than you need."

After pulling her spear away from the creature's head, the woman reaches a hand down. She pulls the female Murkovin to her feet and then turns to the hill. The girl still stands in the same spot as before with her eyes focused on the dirt at her feet, her hands folded in front of her, and her bottom lip clenched between her teeth.

"Come down here, child," the woman calls to her.

As the girl timidly walks down the slope, she stumbles on the loose stones. The female Murkovin dashes up the hill to her child's side. With the girl's arm in the gentle grasp of one hand, she helps her child make her way down the hill to the woman.

I made the right decision to spare their lives, the woman thinks. *She's protective of her child. She's loyal— exactly what I need.*

When the two stop in front of her, the woman kneels in front of the girl.

"You're safe now, child," the woman says. "As long as you're with me, no harm will come to you."

The girl doesn't reply, but the woman sees trust in her eyes. The woman rises from the ground.

"I have a large cavern," the woman says to the girl's Ovì. "You can both stay with me."

"Thank you for your mercy," the female Murkovin replies.

"We'll soon be moving to a different part of the Barrens," the woman tells her. "My unborn child's Mür will be here in a few days to help us move. You'll have comforts you've never known."

"How can I repay your kindness?"

"After I give birth, you'll help me care for my child. I have much work ahead of me to gather our kind."

"A fair arrangement," the female Murkovin says, bowing to the woman. "I serve you now."

Yes, you do, the woman says in her mind. *In more ways than you know.*

Chapter 6

As soon as we wake up the next day, Sash schedules a meeting with a man named Falk, the tallest Hunter in Krymzyn. Since I have the early part of the day off, I ask her if I can tag along. Although she doesn't stop me from joining her, she seems mildly irritated by my request.

We could easily travel to Falk's hunting region in a matter of seconds, but Sash tells me she wants to walk the five miles. As we stroll across the meadows and rolling hills, she doesn't seem interested in conversation. I decide to break the silence when we're about halfway there.

"Can we finish our talk from before we went to sleep?" I ask.

"There's nothing left to talk about," she answers without looking at me.

"So that's it? I don't get a say in how my daughter is raised?"

"You're in Krymzyn, Chase," she says evenly. "It is the way it is."

"But everything about me being here represents change in some way," I argue.

"As I've said several times," she replies, finally turning

her face to me, "the only thing that matters is what's best for her. You need to accept that."

Returning her attention to the landscape in front of us, Sash increases her pace. In her mind, this discussion appears to be over. Encased in uncomfortable silence, we walk the remainder of the way to Falk's hunting region.

Falk must be one of the tallest people in Krymzyn, which also means one of the oldest. At about six foot nine, he dwarfs both Sash and me. If I had to estimate his age, I'd say he's in his late seventies or early eighties based solely on his height. But his athletic build, smoothly rounded facial features, and wavy hair all give him the appearance of a man in his mid-fifties at the oldest.

Falk is utterly dumbfounded when Sash informs him that she was called for the Ritual of Balance. Based on what Sash told me in the past, it must be the first time a Hunter has ever been chosen. As far as I know, Ovin was the only Hunter to ever parent a child, but that wasn't from partaking in the Ritual. Her child, who resulted in the birth of the Murkovin, was referred to as "unsanctioned" in the story of The Beginning.

During the conversation between Sash and Falk, I notice that Sash never mentions who the man called to the Ritual of Balance with her was, and Falk doesn't ask. Since gossip doesn't exist in Krymzyn, my conclusion is that no one would ever ask or tell. As I think more about it, if the woman enters the Cavern of Grace first and never turns around, neither the man nor the woman would have any idea who the other person is. It seems to be another part of the anonymity of parenthood in this world.

Their brief discussion concludes with Falk telling Sash that he'll have the other Hunters fill a few extra stakes with sap each Darkness. They both agree that it should be enough to make up for Sash not being able to contribute while she's pregnant. Sash and I say our goodbyes to Falk, exchange momentary glances, and then leave in different directions.

Over the next couple of days, the silence that began between Sash and me on the walk to see Falk is always present. Knowing that Sash doesn't want to discuss how our daughter should be raised, I consider going to see Eval. She's been able to provide me with guidance in the past, but I ultimately decide against talking with her. My conclusion is that she'll just put a philosophical spin on the situation that's probably not much different than what Sash said to me after the Ritual.

More than ever, I miss my family on Earth. They're the ones I could always turn to for advice in a difficult situation like this one. With Sash and Eval ruled out, I don't have anyone else to talk to about my daughter. Tela is probably the person I've grown closest to on a friendly level in this world, but the subject is way out of her range of experience. And since the topic is closed with Sash, I have no choice but to internalize my feelings.

Ten days after conception, Sash begins to show. Given that pregnancy in Krymzyn lasts less than half the time it does on Earth, I guess it makes sense it would happen so soon. I first notice when I'm about to leave our habitat one day. I pause by the entrance to the waterfall cavern to say goodbye to Sash.

Unaware that I'm watching her, she steps under the fall

and raises her face to the spill. As the water splashes off the top of her head and glides down her hair, she tenderly runs one hand over the slight curve of her stomach. It's the most beautiful sight I've ever seen, and I want her to know.

"Sash," I say.

With her face still pointing up at the ceiling, her reply is sharp. "What, Chase?"

I stare at her for a few seconds before saying anything. "Never mind. I'll see you later."

I turn away and leave our habitat.

With each passing day, Sash's routine is essentially the same. I see her sometimes when I travel across the Delta, and she briefly fills me in on her day before we go to sleep. During the early part of the day, she visits the trees in her hunting region and checks the roots and limbs to make sure they're healthy. In the latter part, she usually sits on a hill near Home and watches the children.

When I complete my traveling duties each day, I meet Sash at our habitat. I paint, she exercises or meditates, and we sometimes go for walks. Even though we're right beside each other while strolling through the Delta, miles and miles of distance seem to separate us.

As the curve in her stomach becomes more pronounced, Sash picks up several loose-fitting black tops from Market. Two of the tables that reside under the enormous canopy at Market consist entirely of items for babies and pregnant women.

Displaying what would be called "nesting" behavior on Earth, Sash brings a steel cradle, small mattress, and various other items to our habitat. The supplies include several of what they call "swaddling cloths." Large enough to wrap an infant in, the rectangles of soft, white fabric are the Krymzyn equivalent of a baby blanket.

Every time I enter our habitat, I notice that the baby things are neatly arranged, but often in different places than they were the prior day. Sash becomes obsessive about finding the most functional layout. If I move something even an inch, she chastises me and then re-arranges everything in an entirely new way. My response is to disappear inside my studio and paint.

Whenever Darkness falls, I meet Sash on a hill overlooking one of the trees in her region. I scan the countryside for Murkovin while she sits on the grass and stares at the awakened tree. After each Darkness passes, I make a numeric entry on a hand-made calendar that I keep in my studio to track how many are left. As more and more days pass, I feel a growing sense of panic that I haven't come up with a new way to address what I consider a dilemma of mammoth proportion.

While standing on a hilltop during Darkness about halfway through her pregnancy, I glance at Sash. She's studying the tree with what appears to be intense longing in her eyes. The fire at the core of Sash's being—fulfilling her purpose in Krymzyn—has been temporarily extinguished.

I realize that maybe a big part of her withdrawal from me is the result of missing the interaction with sustaining trees while they're awake. And then it hits me. Maybe there's something I can do to help her feel that again, even if only vicariously. More importantly, maybe it will reopen the lines of communication between us that we've completely lost.

Over the next few days, a plan fully takes shape in my mind. I can't honestly say that it's the best plan I've ever come up with, but it's the only one I have. When the next Darkness falls, I meet Sash on top of the Empty Hill with a pack of empty stakes slung over my shoulder.

"What are you doing with those?" she asks over the howling wind.

"Role reversal," I answer loudly.

"I don't understand."

"I'm you, you're me," I say with the rain stinging my cheeks. "You can talk me through getting sap."

She vigorously shakes her head. "It won't work, Chase."

"I've watched you enough times that I think I can do it. Besides, Ovin's tree likes me. You told me so. That's why I picked this Darkness."

"The tree respects you," she replies with the volume of her voice a little louder and her tone a bit more incensed, "but that doesn't mean it will let you reach its trunk. Apprentice Hunters train for hundreds of days before ever getting one stake in the bark."

"They don't have you helping them," I say.

"You're not a Hunter!" she yells.

"Can I just try?"

Her eyes widen with exasperation. "Do you want Ovin's tree to kill you?"

"I don't think that will happen," I say, keeping my voice calm to avoid an all-out fight.

"Why are you so stubborn?" she snaps.

"That's hysterical! *You* calling me stubborn?"

"I can't allow this!"

"Don't worry," I grumble. "I won't hurt the tree."

Without waiting for a response, I grab one stake in my hand and drop the pack and my spear to the ground. I breeze past Sash and sprint down the hill. Watching the branches lash through the air in front of me, I plan my course of attack.

"Chase!" Sash yells from behind me. "Stop!"

Ignoring her command, I duck under the first limb I reach, leap over the next, and cut safely around the third. The fourth branch proves to be my downfall. After it slams into my gut, the branch throws me backwards towards the Empty Hill. As soon as my rear hits the ground, another limb swoops down at me. I roll to my hands and knees, scamper across the slippery grass, and dive just out of the branch's reach.

Lying flat on my stomach, I lift my head to look at Sash. Shaking her head, she's still standing at the top of the Empty Hill. She's also trying to hide a smile. It's the first one I've seen from her since I returned to our habitat after the Ritual of Balance.

"Don't worry!" I call out to her. "I got this!"

"Think more moves ahead!" she shouts. "You have to anticipate what every branch of the tree will do."

As she steps down the side of the hill, I jump to my feet and turn towards the tree. Charging under the branches again, I realize that all I've done by embarking on this quest is to anger the tree. I base that conclusion on the fury of the branches that whip in my direction and the ferocity of their blows. I try to get out of the way, but I can't even dodge the first one. The tree seems to know every move I'm about to make.

One branch barrels into my chest at the same time another one takes my legs out from underneath me. Sprawled on my back, I look up at a third bough plummeting down from high above. Even though I'm able to cover my face with my arms, a few gashes rip across my skin on impact. Once the branch whipsaws away, Sash grabs me under my arms and pulls me to safety.

Kneeling beside me, she wipes blood away from a cut on my forehead. I suck in several deep breaths and lock my eyes on hers. She smiles at me with so much caring that my pain fades away.

"You see the tree move," she says. "You react to the tree. But you don't *feel* the tree. That's what a Hunter does."

Sash stands up and walks to the outer edge of the branches' reach. Resting one hand on her stomach, she reaches the other out towards the tree. Every limb continues to slice the air except one. It slowly sways down towards Sash until coming to a stop with the tip resting on her palm. The blazing red-leaves on the end curl around her outstretched fingers.

Sash bows her head and stands reverently with the tip of the branch embracing her hand. Fierce limbs sail back and forth over her head, but they never come close to her body. For the remainder of Darkness, I sit on the grass and watch Sash commune with the tree.

When the dark clouds finally come to a halt and the rainfall ends, Sash kneels to the ground. As she lowers her hand to the grass, the tip of the branch slips from her touch. A few twigs on the end dig into the grass and the tree returns to slumber. Under crisp scarlet rays that dissect the idle clouds, Sash stands up and looks at me.

"Come feel our daughter kick," she says.

I jump up from the grass and dart to her side. As she slips an arm around my waist, I reach a hand under her shirt. After my palm is resting on her stomach, several gentle kicks from inside Sash thump against my hand.

"Hello, baby girl," I whisper.

I'm immediately filled with wonder and awe at the new life growing inside Sash. I lean forward and kiss her lips.

"Why did you do this, Chase?" she asks after our kiss.

With my hand still pressed to her stomach, I gaze at her eyes for several seconds. "I thought it might improve your mood," I finally say. "Everything has been so weird between us since the Ritual. I can't take it anymore. I've been in a bad mood and you've been distant. I thought the way you're feeling might be because you miss the trees during Darkness."

"I do miss them," she replies. "But that's not why I'm so quiet."

"Is it because you know how I feel about raising our daughter? You're mad at me about that?"

"No, Chase," she says. "I'm not angry with you."

"Then what is it?" I ask.

She closes her eyes for a few seconds and then reopens them. "It's because I feel the same way you do. Every day she grows inside me, I feel closer and closer to her. I never want to let her go, but I can't do anything about it."

"We could talk to Eval," I suggest.

"No," she replies. "She can't do anything about it."

"She agreed to us living together."

"That was different," she explains. "That only impacts you and me. The way a child is raised is for the balance of everyone in Krymzyn."

I look at the sleeping tree. "It takes a _village_," I murmur.

"What does that mean?" she asks.

"It's a saying on Earth," I answer, returning my attention to Sash. "It means that everyone who's around the children of a community should feel responsible for their upbringing. Everyone is part of shaping their lives."

She nods her head. "I still believe the best thing for her is to be raised the same way that other children in Krymzyn are. I never want her to feel different. But I know how much it will hurt me not having her with us."

I can't say that I'm surprised by her confession, but I wish I'd recognized what was going on with her sooner. The clues were all there. She's been overwhelmed by maternal instincts in the same way that a pregnant woman on Earth would be. But like many of the emotions she's experienced from my world, she has no basis for comparison and no way to express them.

"I'm sorry I've been so quiet," I say. "I've been feeling sorry for myself. I should have been more aware of what you might be going through."

"It's not your fault," she replies. "It's all new to me. I don't always know how to explain my feelings to you."

I draw in a deep breath. As hard as it is for me to accept, Sash was right when she said that I chose to be in Krymzyn and have to abide by the customs here. I've selfishly wanted to raise our daughter the way she would be on Earth, but it's time for me to let go of that line of thought.

"I told you that I saw us together as a family," I say. "And what you said was right. I don't know the path that will get us there, but I do know that you and I can help make that path if we work together.

"We'll take days off," I continue, "and spend every moment of them with her. The same way you take Maya away from Home sometimes, we can do that with our daughter. Instead of going for walks at the end of the day, you and I can go to Home and spend time with her. We'll say it's important for *my* balance because that's how it is in my world. I don't think anyone can say no to that."

She reaches a hand up and rests it on my shoulder. "I think that's a good plan. Thank you, Chase."

"You don't need to thank me," I say. "I should have said something sooner. I was too caught up in my own feelings."

She squeezes my shoulder. "I'm sorry I didn't explain why I was behaving the way I was. I worried that talking to you about it would only make it worse for both of us."

"It always feels better to talk with you about things."

"It does feel better," she replies, "thanks to your awful attempt at getting sap."

I smile at her. "I have a lot more respect for what Hunters do after that."

"I'm sure the tree admires you for at least trying," she says.

"I'll stick to traveling from now on."

We both slip our arms around each other. As soon as our bodies press together, I feel a kick against my stomach from our daughter.

"I think she approves," I say in Sash's ear.

Chapter 7

While skimming over the dirt road from the Mount to the Delta, my motion unexpectedly flutters. The muscles in my arms strain while trying to keep a transport full of newly-made tables and stools under control. As Darkness descends, the light overhead seeps into the edges of the clouds. Like someone else is jamming on the brakes, my speed is instantly cut in half.

"Seventy," I whisper.

The weeks since my unsuccessful attempt at taking sap from Ovin's tree have flown by. They've also been a complete one-eighty from the early part of Sash's pregnancy. After the lines of communication between Sash and me reopened, we immersed ourselves in our time together. She even let me help her arrange, re-arrange, and then re-arrange yet again all the baby things in our habitat.

We've come to grips with our daughter dwelling at Home by making plans for how we can always be active in her life. Although we can't change the ways of Krymzyn, as Sash proved after my Ritual of Purpose, she can bend them. But when all is said and done, I've accepted that our child should be raised in the same way that other children in this world are. Sash was right in her proclamation that it's the only way our daughter won't feel different.

With a combination of tickles and stings, the molecules of my body sail through the rain that begins to fall. I glance over my shoulder at Larn and the streaking Kale with his transport in tow. From one side of the road behind them, Jeni angles in from the Barrens.

If we'd still been on the Mount when Darkness fell, we would have stayed there until it ended. Fortunately, since we're past the halfway mark, we'll continue to the Delta as fast as we can. Our protocol in a situation like this to leave the transports inside the gate, speed to where our respective Hunters are so we can keep watch during Darkness, and then return to the gate when Darkness is over to take the transports to Market. Since it's close to the end of the day, I'm hoping Tela will take care of my transport for me so I can be with Sash.

As I return my attention to the path in front of me, Roen and Tela zoom to the road from the wasteland. After covering the last few miles to the river, we all come out of our blends. Knowing our priority during Darkness is getting to the Delta, no one breaks their stride while sprinting over the bridge.

Trailing Tela and Roen by twenty yards, I cross over the steel arch in the center of the bridge. On the downslope, tremendous waves from the river occasionally smash against the sides of the bridge and spray around me. Cavu swings both gate doors open for us just before we reach them. I pass through the gate and then slide to a stop beside Tela and Roen.

After dropping the transport handles to the ground, I snatch my spear from the back of the wagon. Once the rest of the Travelers make it safely inside the wall, we all rip our boots off our feet. A mighty clang rings out over the squall when Cavu slams the gate doors shut.

"Get to your Hunters," Larn yells to the group.

As everyone starts to speed away in different directions, I reach out a hand and grab Tela by the arm.

"I need a huge favor," I say. "After Darkness, will you take my transport to Market? Sash will be having the baby and I want to stay with her."

"Of course," she replies, but her face wrinkles with confusion. "Why would you want to be with her for that?"

"It's just the way it is in my world," I answer, wanting to keep the explanation as brief as possible. "Thanks, Tela. I owe you one."

"You don't owe me anything. I'm honored to help."

As Tela runs away, I sink to one knee and jam my fingers into the ground.

"Sash," I say. "We just got back from the Mount. I'll meet you at the tree farthest to the east."

A few seconds later, I hear her voice. "I'll stay in our habitat, but you should keep watch until Darkness is over."

"I'll be there as soon as it ends," I tell her.

I spring from the ground and run across the slick grass to the south. The moment a few shafts of dull light pop into my vision, I burst forward in them. After a short travel over the rolling hills, I stop on the top of one that overlooks the easternmost tree in Sash's hunting region.

While I scan the stormy hills, my hands tremble around the shaft of my spear. A combination of excitement and anxiety is causing my heart to pound harder and harder.

With my twenty-fourth birthday only a few months away, I'm about to become a father.

"Come on!" I shout at the clouds.

The dark masses ignore my impatience. Another hour of storm agonizingly ticks away. Wind whips through the valleys and rain descends from the sky, but the only other movement around me is the glaring tree in the meadow at the foot of the hill.

"That's enough!" I yell at the sky.

This time, Darkness seems to adhere to my will. As soon as the first rays of light cut across the sky, I race to our habitat and charge through the tunnel. When I enter the main cavern, Sash is relaxing on the bed with her back leaning against a pillow that's wedged between her and the wall.

"How are you?" I ask, kneeling in front of the bed.

"I just had the first contraction," she tells me. "I'll keep count of how far apart they are."

"Can I get you anything?"

"Not right now," she answers.

"I'd like to stay with you for her birth," I say. "If you want me to leave, just say so. It's up to you."

"I want you here," she replies.

For several hours, we sit side by side on the bed. With one arm around her, I try to comfort her through the contractions. As they grow closer together, I can see on her face how much pain she's in, but she never complains or makes a sound. After what I guess is about six hours, Sash tells me it's time to deliver.

"Will you get a knife from the shelves, please?" she asks.

"There's also a small metal clamp there. Bring that, too."

After helping her stand, I cross to the other side of the room and grab the clip and a knife. When I meet Sash by the entrance to the waterfall cavern, she's already stripped out of her clothes. Her skin is radiant in the golden light of the Swirls, and the amber in her eyes is electric and alive. She takes the metal clip from my hand and clamps it to the end of her hair, but has me keep the knife.

I follow her to the center of the shallow stream in the waterfall cavern. Facing the fall, Sash crouches over the water. She asks me to stay behind her, so I drop to my knees on the spongy rock. After kissing the back of her neck, I clench the knife between my teeth.

Although her breathing becomes sharper and faster during the next contraction, she doesn't make any other noise. I softly stroke her hair and rub her shoulders until her muscles relax.

"One more," she says between slow, deep breaths.

A few moments later, her body tenses and the pace of her breathing increases. She lowers her hands to the water beneath her while I stabilize her with my hands. She pushes so hard during the contraction that she lets out a loud shriek.

As her body jerks forward, she grunts from the pain. Her muscles remain tense for another few seconds while she continues to groan. She finally falls back against me, takes a few long breaths, and then raises her hands. Our baby girl is safely in their grip.

Her lustrous blue eyes are already open and focused on Sash. Instead of crying as I'd expect a newborn to do, she's quiet and calm with an expression of what seems to be curiosity on her face. Still panting from the delivery, Sash lays our baby her on her back in the gentle flow of two-inch deep water and reaches a hand back to me.

"Give me the knife," she says.

I remove the blade from between my teeth and lay the handle in Sash's palm. Using the fingers of her other hand, she makes a small loop in the umbilical cord and holds it over our baby's stomach. After the knife slices through the cord, she takes the metal clip out of her hair and clamps it to the small stub still attached to our daughter's belly button.

On her knees in the stream, Sash cups water in her hands and rinses off our baby's body. Running her fingers through our daughter's short, thick black hair, Sash finishes bathing her. The baby never cries out or makes the slightest sound, but appears to be alert the entire time.

"She's so beautiful," I whisper.

"She really is," Sash replies.

"Do you feel okay?"

"I'm tired," she says, "but relieved it's over. I'm glad you're here with me."

I rest my hands on Sash's waist. "I wouldn't have missed it for anything in the world. Shouldn't she be crying or something?"

"She's breathing and looks healthy," she answers. "I guess she doesn't feel the need to cry right now."

Sash lifts our daughter out of the stream and cradles her in her arms. Gripping Sash's waist, I help her stand to her feet.

"Do you want to hold her?" she asks.

"Of course," I answer with a grin.

Carefully supporting her head, Sash holds the baby out to me. I slip one arm under her body and the other behind her neck. After gently clutching her to my chest, I look down at her face. Her eyes immediately find mine.

"Welcome to the world, baby girl," I say and then look at Sash. "It's weird not having a name for her."

"I like the way you call her 'baby girl.' I guess that's what it has to be for a while."

Sash steps to the fall and spends several minutes washing off in the water. Every few seconds, she glances in my direction to check on our daughter. Despite how exhausted Sash looks, there's a fiery intensity in her eyes and a slight flex in her muscles. She's like a tiger in the wild watching over her cub, ready to leap to her defense if needed.

After Sash finishes cleaning off, she retrieves the knife from the stream. We walk together to the main cavern. Baby girl stays in my arms while Sash puts the knife away and dresses in shorts and a tank top. Sash then spreads one of the baby blankets out on our bed.

"Lay her down," Sash says to me.

I carefully place our daughter on top of the blanket. Seemingly mesmerized by the Swirls, baby girl gazes at the crystal ceiling. Sash folds the corners of the blanket around her and securely wraps her inside. While our daughter lies on her back looking up, Sash stacks a few pillows on the mattress. Using the pillows to prop herself up, Sash sits down on the bed. Once she finds a comfortable position, she picks up our daughter and cradles her to her chest.

I change into shorts, sit by Sash's side, and reach one arm around her shoulder. Baby girl's eyes slowly sway back and forth between us. After Sash lifts her tank top to expose one breast, she guides our daughter's mouth to her nipple. Baby girl instantly locks her lips to it.

"How are you feeling?" I ask Sash.

"A little sore," she says.

I softly kiss her lips and then ask, "Do you want some sap?"

"I would, thank you. And bring a cloth."

I get up from the bed and soon return with a cup of sap and a cloth. I hold the cup to Sash's lips for her to sip from while our daughter continues to nurse. When the cup is empty, I set it by the side of our bed. Baby girl pulls her mouth away from Sash's nipple, apparently full for the time being, and looks up at her mother. A few drops of blood roll down the underside of Sash's breast.

"You're bleeding," I say. "Is something wrong?"

"It's the blood stored in my breasts," she answers. "That's what she was drinking."

"You don't make _milk_ . . . a special liquid for the child?"

She shakes her head. "Our breasts fill with blood. That's how babies get their sap. I'll wean her to pure sap several days before her Naming Ritual."

I look away in thought for a moment. "That explains it," I mumble.

"Explains what?" she asks.

I return my eyes to Sash. "I could never figure out why the Murkovin drink blood."

"If it's what I needed to stay alive," Sash says, "I'd drink it, too."

Sash uses the cloth to wipe blood off her skin and clean

our daughter's lips. After pulling her shirt back down, she leans back with baby girl in her arms. Our daughter's eyes begin to droop a little, but they still bounce back and forth between Sash and me.

"She has your eyes," Sash comments. "They look exactly like yours."

Wanting to see our daughter as she truly exists in this world, I press my palm to the floor beside the bed. I close my eyes and whisper, "Please show me what she looks like."

After a few moments, I reopen my eyes and stare at our daughter. In the space between her face and mine, vibrant blue blooms from her eyes. The texture of her skin fades away, replaced by a semi-opaque, translucent film. Swirling molecules of glowing white matter shape her skull and skeleton. In the center of her head, a stunning starburst of color slowly rotates, every hue as pure and rich as I could imagine.

"She has your spectrum," I say. "She's perfect."

Chapter 8

Marking each Darkness on my calendar as it passes, I begin a new count of seventy. I also make notes of milestones in baby girl's development process. Her hand-eye coordination, motor skills, and mental alertness increase much more rapidly than anything I've ever seen or heard of in an infant, not that I have a lot of experience in that area. But I've always been under the impression that babies don't do much for the first few months.

From day one, baby girl's eyes follow Sash or me whenever one of us walks across the cavern. If either one of us says something, she immediately turns her head to the sound. At two weeks, if we lay her on her stomach, she raises her head and uses her arms to push her chest up. At four weeks, she grasps things with her hands.

She soon becomes attached to the Krymzyn version of a baby rattle—a tiny steel shaft with padded material wrapped around hollow balls on either end that are filled with metal pellets. The toy provides our daughter with hours of entertainment. As though she's a mariachi musician with a maraca in her hand, she shakes it in distinct, rhythmic patterns.

At six weeks, she begins babbling incessantly in her own

private language. Like many new parents, I conclude that she's magically gifted in a way far superior to any child ever born. Sash takes the wind out of my sails by explaining that her maturation process is the same as any other child in Krymzyn. Children simply develop much more quickly in this world, and our daughter's behavior is within the norm— except for two things.

The first anomaly is something that neither of us can explain. Baby girl never cries. She softly moans when she's hungry, but the sounds never escalate into anything more. If she wants something, she reaches a hand towards it and grunts, but a tear never once falls from her eyes.

The second difference from other infants in this world is easily explained by me being her father. When baby girl looks at Sash or me, she almost always smiles. I've never seen the other children in Krymzyn smile, even when they're playing a game. Just like the adults here, the kids are always serious and focused.

In a strange way, our daughter's smile doesn't always look like one of happiness or contentment. It's often subtle and accompanied by a knowing expression on her face. The corners of her lips curl up slightly while her sparkling blue eyes look at Sash or me in a captivating way. It's as though her smile is saying, *"I know something amazing, but I can't tell you about it yet."*

Other than having my blue eyes, baby girl's resemblance to Sash is striking. When I sketch my first portrait of our daughter, it doesn't take much imagination to think that it might be a drawing of Sash at that age. And the more our daughter grows, the more uncanny her resemblance to her mother becomes.

Sash spends every day doing nothing but taking care of baby girl. As far as I can tell, she never once lets her out of her sight. When my duties for each day are finished, Sash and I take our daughter for walks around the Delta. Taking turns with her draped over our chests in a baby carrier, we stroll to the top of the Empty Hill, or sometimes to the top of the Tall Hill.

We sit in the grass, hold her in our laps so she can look at the world around her, and listen to her "coo." If she points a hand up at the clouds or towards a tree, we tell her what the words are. She can't repeat them yet, but she seems to enjoy translating them into her gibberish.

At the end of each day, our daughter always sleeps with us in our bed. Even though we have a cradle for her, Sash never once considers putting her in it. Cuddled between Sash and me, we shower her with affection until she falls asleep.

Only once does Sash correct me for doing something that she considers wrong. At the end of one day while Sash bathes in the fall, I walk around the cavern with our daughter in my arms. After stopping in front of the painting of Sash at Ovin's tree that hangs near the tunnel entrance, I point to the image of Sash.

"Mommy," I say to our daughter.

"Sasasa," she replies in baby-babble.

"That's right," I say, smiling with pride. "Her name is Sash. But to you, she's Mommy."

"Chase," Sash calls to me from the other side of the cavern. When I turn to her, she's slipping into her sleep clothes. "I don't think we should teach her terms like that from your world."

I nod my head. "Sorry. It's just habit."

"I know you mean well, but I don't think anyone else will understand."

There's no anger or reprimand in her voice. She's simply staying on top of what we both agreed to. Our daughter will be raised in the same way that the other children in this world are.

"I'll remember from now on," I say.

I return my eyes to baby girl. She peers straight into them and all the way to my soul. As has happened with Sash several times in the past, I feel tingles in my stomach and chest as my daughter uses her Krymzyn sense of awareness to reach inside me. I lean my face down and kiss her forehead.

"I love you," I whisper.

"Mugaba," she says in gibberish.

*　　*　　*

Over the next few days, Sash and I discuss several ways to spend time with our daughter after she's living at Home. I suggest one idea not only because it will give us an excuse to visit her, but also because it won't exclude the other children. Sash tells me that she thinks it's a brilliant idea. I've already seen that the children here play Red Rover, so it's reasonable to think that they might like another game. I'm going to introduce them to soccer.

After my duties have been completed one day, I stop by

Home to see Marc, the senior Keeper. Stressing that it combines physical exercise with mental focus while teaching the children to work together, I explain the game to him. He decides that learning a new game from another world could be beneficial to the children in several ways. In the ultimate Krymzyn justification, he declares it should help them achieve balance.

Since I'm already there, I ask Marc for a tour of Home. I've never been inside the caverns, only to the field in front of the entrances. The interconnected habitats lie under a mile-wide range of rounded hills that run across the central portion of the Delta. He leads me through the door on the eastern side of the field. Another entrance is located on the western end of the hills.

As soon as we step inside, I notice how much larger the tunnel is than the one leading to mine and Sash's habitat. With a ceiling at least ten feet high, the tunnel is wide enough for four adults to comfortably walk side by side. Instead of a solid granite top like in our tunnel, the rounded ceiling is made of crystal with Swirls inside lighting our path. When Marc closes the door behind us, I see another noticeable difference. On the inside of the door is a large steel bolt to lock it against the outside.

"We lock the doors during Darkness," Marc says. "We always make sure the children are safe from Murkovin who might enter the Delta. The Keepers stand watch in the tunnel until Darkness passes."

Carefully examining the six-foot-six Marc, I move my eyes from his spiky, black-and-gold hair to his square face with a strong jaw, and then finally down to his toned, burly shoulders and arms. One thought jumps into my mind. His demeanor is always gracious, but if it came to a fight, he's someone you wouldn't want to tangle with.

"Is this the only tunnel?" I ask.

"There are two that join," he answers. "This one is a long semi-circle from the eastern entrance to the western door. Another tunnel leads from the center point of this tunnel to a back entrance in the hills above us."

He leads me farther into the tunnel until we reach an opening to a cavern. The cave is about twice the size of my entire habitat. Large pillows are neatly arranged in a circle on the floor. In the center of the room stands a monolithic black marble stone about four feet tall.

"We call this school," he says. "The children sit on the pillows while Keepers provide education in science, mathematics, and a variety of other subjects."

"What's the rock for?" I ask.

"That's the Stone of Education," he explains. "Keepers have the ability to focus our thoughts on the Stone so that images are projected for the children. It helps them learn anatomy, physics, and many other areas of their studies. Would you like me to demonstrate?"

"Please do," I excitedly reply.

"I remember hearing a story from the Disciples of another world," Marc tells me. "It might have been the one that you come from, or a world that's very similar. Do you have large bodies of water on a circular planet?"

"We do," I answer. "We call them oceans."

"That's right," he says. "I learned the word once before. I was fascinated by them since the only above-ground water in this world is the river. They told us tales of large vessels called ships that sail on the oceans. Let me show you how I envisioned them."

He focuses on the Stone and his eyes glaze over with intense concentration. Almost immediately, rays of golden light shoot up from the top of the rock. As the beams slowly rotate, a three-dimensional image forms in the air, much like the holographic displays I saw during the story of The Beginning. The only difference is, the picture from Marc's mind gradually turns from gold to full color.

In the image he creates, calm swells roll across the surface of an aqua sea. Cutting through the water is a three-masted schooner with a few "Krymzynesque" changes compared to sailing ships on Earth. The hull and masts are made entirely of steel, while the huge, billowing sails are woven from the same black fabric that's used to make our clothes.

"That's incredible!" I exclaim.

The image fades away and the light rays recede into the stone.

"Is that what a ship looks like?" Marc asks, turning to me.

"Right on the _money_," I say, still in awe of what I just saw.

"_Money_?" he asks.

"The expression means it looked exactly as it should," I answer, not wanting to launch into an explanation of currency on Earth.

"I'm pleased I could show it to you."

He steps into the tunnel again and I follow him deeper

under the hills. We stop by two openings to caverns that are located directly across from each other.

"A Keeper's room," he says, pointing to one, "and a child's across the tunnel from it. When they first arrive, infants sleep in cradles in the Keepers' rooms. Once a child has grown enough, he or she is given their own room. But their primary Keeper is always in the room across the tunnel from them while they sleep."

I poke my head into the child's room. "Awaken," I say.

The Swirls illuminate an oval-shaped room that's not much larger than my bedroom was on Earth. Although there's no door to the cave, a curtain hangs by one side that I conclude can be drawn shut for privacy. A mattress lies on the ground by one wall with two pillows on top. A broom and bucket for cleaning reside in a rounded corner. A table and stool stand against one wall, and shelves containing personal items are carved in the same wall. The sound of a waterfall filters through an opening at the far end of the cavern.

"Does each cavern have a fall?" I ask.

"Of course," Marc replies. "Once they're tall enough, the children are responsible for keeping themselves and their caverns clean. We have small gates that lock across the entrances to the waterfall caverns. Until they're old enough to safely go in there by themselves, the children aren't allowed near the water unsupervised."

I start to turn away, but the golden light reflected on the wall across from the bed seems to slowly dance across the granite surface. As I examine the lights more closely, an image gradually develops. The unmistakable shape of the Tree of Vision comes into focus with its branches calmly swaying back and forth. The Tree eventually dissolves into random patterns of light, but they soon shape a large hill. Several small pools form on the slope with ripples of light defining their surfaces. A golden silhouette of a Serquatine soars out of one, dives over a small waterfall, and splashes into the next pool below.

"The Swirls of Home are unique," Marc says to me. "They can cast their light through the crystal in such a way that different images of Krymzyn appear on the walls. No one can explain it, but it only happens in the children's rooms."

"I hope they don't show them Murkovin," I comment.

"Never," he says. "It's always creatures or places pleasing to the eye."

We walk past several more bedrooms before reaching an enormous cavern with a vaulted ceiling roughly twenty feet high. Padded mats cover almost the entire floor of the room. Scattered across the mats are a dozen balls ranging from baseball-sized to basketball-sized and made of the same leathery, black material as my clothes.

About two feet under the ceiling near the back of the room, a single steel beam extends from wall to wall. Two ropes hang from the steel beam to the floor. Both of the ropes have a series of knots tied from top to bottom, much like the climbing ropes I used at school as a child. On opposite sides of the cavern stand a small jungle gym and a set of monkey bars.

Marc explains that the inside exercise room is used when Darkness comes during the middle of the day. He also tells me that several more pieces of exercise equipment, including swings, are located in a broad, grassy crater that's centered in the hills above us. The back entrance to Home that he referred to earlier is in that crater. I've never traveled directly over the hills we're under, so I didn't even know something like that existed.

The next cavern we stop at isn't as large as the exercise room, but still more spacious than my habitat. Marc calls it the common room, a place for the children to play or relax. Similar to bean bags, stuffed seating pillows are piled in the center of the floor. Several small tables and stools stand near the outer edges of the room. Neatly arranged in shelves lining the walls are a variety of toys, all made of either steel, padded fabric, or a combination of the two.

They include concentric steel circles stacked on a small pole that an infant would use, and a complex rolling marble maze about three feet wide. A huge metal box on the floor under the shelves holds what looks like a combination of an Erector Set and Legos, all the pieces made of steel.

After leaving the common room, we pass by another series of bedrooms. Near the end of the arcing tunnel, we reach the last room of Home. It's currently occupied by all the Keepers and children.

"This is the sustenance room," Marc whispers to me.

A dozen small, steel tables are spread out across the room with four stools at each one. Two Keepers and two children are seated at several of the tables. Profile to us with her long, black hair hanging down her back in a single braid, Maya sits alone at another table. Since Marc is her primary Keeper, I assume that he'd be sitting with her if I wasn't here.

At two of the other tables, infants sit in steel high chairs no different than those on Earth. Seated on a stool beside each of them is a Keeper. Pitchers and cups stand on top of the occupied tables, and more utensils are stored on shelves carved in one of the walls.

As everyone in the room sips from their cups, they're silent. The children—excluding the infants—all have distant, almost hypnotic looks in their eyes. I try to get Maya's attention with a wave. Although the eyes in her thin face are looking in my general direction, she doesn't seem to notice me. Marc tugs my shirt and pulls me away from the entrance.

"I don't want to interrupt them," he says quietly.

"Why isn't anybody talking?" I ask.

"During sustenance, the children learn to meditate. It's a chance for them to share their thoughts with the world they live in and develop their senses of awareness. We teach them to appreciate the sap the trees provide for us. As the energy from the sap flows inside them, they share their gratitude with Krymzyn. Always remember that sap feeds more than just our bodies."

"It really does," I say. "I guess I should work on developing my sense of awareness more."

"It's a lifelong process," he replies. "You didn't have the advantage of starting as a child."

We walk to the end of the tunnel and step outside through the western entrance to Home. After thanking Marc for the tour, I bid him farewell. Instead of immediately traveling to my habitat, I walk across the field and digest everything I just saw. I pause when I'm about halfway across the meadow to look back at the hills over Home.

I guess I've always thought of Home as one step above

an orphanage. I couldn't have been more wrong. It may be a different way of raising children than what I'm used to, but there's no doubt that it's a nurturing and safe environment. More importantly, the children are cared for by Keepers who dedicate their entire existences to the education and well-being of the kids.

In Krymzyn, a person's connection to the world around them is just as important as their relationship with other people. One of the most important lessons at Home, so I just learned, is teaching the children to open their senses of awareness. Maybe not having that foundation is why my mine only seems to reveal itself through Sash.

Even though I've accepted that it won't happen, part of me still clings to the idea of having our daughter live with Sash and me. But after what I just saw, I might finally be able let that go. Baby girl is a child of Krymzyn, not a child of the world I come from. Since Krymzyn is where she'll live her life, I now believe the best thing for her is to be raised at Home.

Chapter 9

With black veins pulsing under their pale skin, a male and female Murkovin race down a hill. They both lurch forward at the bottom of the slope, but only the female ignites into the light. The male stumbles on a rock, crashes to the ground, and slides on his stomach across the gravelly dirt.

"That one is useless!" the former Watcher of the Delta sneers.

"Give him more time," the woman replies. "He'll learn."

Standing on top of the hill that the two creatures ran down, the woman and former Watcher return their attention to the female Murkovin who successfully blended her light. The fluorescent shape soars across miles and miles of flat land, makes a broad arc, and then returns in their direction. As she rises the slope towards them, her beams evaporate into the body of a young woman in full sprint. She slows near the crest and coasts to a stop in front of them.

"Well done," the woman says to the female Murkovin. "Your progress is impressive. We'll travel greater distances on the morrow."

"Your guidance has been helpful," the creature replies.

"Return to camp," the former Watcher orders. "You've

earned your sap for this day."

After nodding to the man and woman, the female Murkovin jogs down the hill towards the nearby encampment. The man and woman focus again on the Murkovin who fell. Now walking up the hill towards them, the muscular creature wipes blood-soaked dirt from his scratched arms.

"We have fifty who can blend their light," the former Watcher says to the woman. "We need five hundred."

"I'll take care of it," she replies.

"I'm sure you will," he says. "There's no one better for this task than you."

In the Barrens, the woman knows, his statement is true. Few of her kind ever master the skill of blending their light. Over time, she'd developed the patience and self-control needed to teach others. Immense distances separate the Murkovin, keeping many of them isolated in remote areas of the Barrens. She'll soon change that.

The woman first learned to travel by sheer accident when she was still a girl. Or maybe it was fate. After the horrific Darkness that took the life of her Ovì finally ended, she pulled her Ovì's corpse to an area of flat, soft ground. Using only her hands, she clawed and scraped the wet dirt. By the time she dug a hole large enough for a body, her fingers were bloody and raw. Handful by handful, she covered the corpse with dirt.

She found two long lengths of tattered rope inside her cavern. After returning to the sustaining tree, she threw both strands over the highest bough. Struggling across the muddy ground, she dragged the bodies of the two men she'd killed to the base of the tree. She tightly bound their ankles with the ends of the ropes and used all her strength to hoist the corpses high in the air. Dangling upside down from the tree, the bodies would be a warning to others. Any creature who stepped foot in her territory would meet certain death.

When the task was completed, she returned to where she'd buried her Ovì. While standing over the grave, she felt an emptiness she'd never known. For the first time in her short life, she was alone in the expanse of wasteland.

Many creatures of the Barrens found death at violent hands, some of them children. The small had always been easy prey for the strong, especially if their *Mürs* and Ovìs had been killed. While staring at the mound of dirt, her heart sank with sorrow that her Ovì was gone, but her hands began to quiver with rage. The fury she'd felt when the two creatures had defiled her Ovì rekindled inside her.

She whirled away from the grave and sprinted across the wasteland. As she charged down a hill, an interwoven web of light unexpectedly flashed in her vision. She wasn't sure what was happening at first, but when she jolted forward, she knew.

With fervid determination in her mind, she transformed her anger to focus. She narrowed her vision to a few isolated beams and blasted into the light. Glittering wisps of white trailed behind her as she sailed across the dreary wasteland.

Before half the day passed, a wall of undulating colors spread across the distant horizon. The dirt under her feet tinted with red. The girl was filled with wonder that she'd journeyed to the western edge of the Infinite Expanse. Her speed would need to have matched that of a Traveler of the

Delta to cover so much ground in so little time.

Using nothing but instinct, she withdrew her particles from the beams. As they reshaped into her body, she tried to slow to a sprint. She tripped on the uneven, rocky ground and tumbled forward. After sliding to a stop on the red dirt, she wiped blood off the gashes in her face and arms. She vowed to practice the transition as many times as it took to achieve perfection.

Since that day, her speed had more than tripled. No other Murkovin could come close to keeping pace with her. Even a Traveler of the Delta would fall well behind her when she sailed across the open space. Only the gifted Hunter could equal the woman's speed.

The woman refocuses her eyes on the male Murkovin walking up the slope. He reaches the top of the hill and stops in front of the man and woman. Still breathing heavily, the brutish creature bends over and rests his hands on his knees.

The former Watcher snaps his spear up and lodges the point under the Murkovin's chin. As he lifts the beast's head with his weapon, the Murkovin has no choice but to return to an upright position.

"You said you know how to travel!" the former Watcher growls.

"I've done it before," the Murkovin argues.

"You're a liar! Sap is wasted on you!"

As the former Watcher's eyes narrow, he presses the weapon firmly against the Murkovin's neck. The woman realizes that he's wrestling with the urge to rip open the creature's throat.

"Stop!" the woman shouts.

She throws a hand up, grabs the weapon, and jerks it away from the Murkovin's neck. The former Watcher glares at her. The woman steps in between them and removes a flask from her belt. After she hands it to the Murkovin, he gulps down the sap inside.

"You were looking off to your sides when you saw the beams," the woman says to the Murkovin. "You need to keep your focus directly in front of you. I'll work with you more on the morrow. I promise that if you listen to what I say, you'll be traveling by the end of the day."

"I've done it twice," the creature replies. "I know I can do it again."

"That's the most important part. Believe in yourself. Go back to camp now. Drink all the sap you need and get plenty of rest. We'll resume on the morrow."

The creature nods his head and then holds out the flask to return it to the woman.

"Keep it," the woman says.

"Thanks," he replies.

The Murkovin jogs down the hill in the direction of the camp.

"Your benevolence is wasted on them," the former Watcher says quietly to the woman. "They need discipline."

You weren't born in the Barrens, she thinks to herself. *You don't know what it's like to be raised in the wasteland.*

The woman shakes her head. "They need confidence. That's how they find the focus to travel."

"Sap gives them focus," he grunts. "But as long as we end up with five hundred who can travel, I don't care how you do it."

"You're in a foul mood," she says.

The former Watcher drops his spear to the ground, slips his arms around the woman's waist, and lifts her off the ground. "I was away from you for too long."

The woman leans her face to his and kisses his lips. She longed for his touch while he was in the Desert, the feel of his muscular arms around her body. But more than anything else, she missed the adoration in his eyes when he gazes upon her.

After their kiss ends, he lowers the woman's feet to the ground. He turns to look down the side of the hill and drapes one arm around her waist. At the bottom of the slope, the female Murkovin whose life the woman had spared sits on a rock. Resting on her lap is an infant boy, the child of the woman and former Watcher.

The female Murkovin's child kneels in front of the boy and holds up a small rock. The boy grabs the stone in one of his hands. Scrunching his eyes, he briefly studies the rock and then drops it to the ground.

"Are you sure we can trust them with our child?" the former Watcher asks.

"If I didn't trust them," the woman answers, "they'd already be dead."

"I don't doubt that," he says, returning his attention to the woman. "How is the cavern?"

"It's perfect. Large enough for the four of us, but far enough away from camp that we have privacy."

"I know you can take care of yourself, but I feel great comfort knowing that several of those who have been with us for so long are close by."

"As do I," she replies.

Their new habitat had proven to be more than she'd hoped for. Large and spacious, the cavern contains a small waterfall at one end that spills into a shallow pool. Plenty of tiny grubs burrow inside the granite ceiling, casting their soft purple light from the maze of holes they leave in the rock. A small connected cave that's big enough for the woman's servant and the servant's child to sleep in allows the woman privacy with her child at each day's end.

Within a two-mile radius of their cavern, five healthy sustaining trees grow. All are bound by rope and have stakes with tubes attached to them stabbed in the bark. The tubes lead to sap transports, some old and weathered, some newly created in the Desert. During each Darkness, sap flows freely into the transports for all of those at camp.

The woman and former Watcher were fortunate to find an area with so many small caves inside a circle of hills. With plenty of trees close by, they have sustenance and dwelling space for fifty of their kind. Thirty Murkovin currently reside at the camp, including three who had been loyal to the woman and the former Watcher since long before he left the Delta for the last time.

Another Murkovin, the tallest the woman has ever known, lives in a cavern just a stone's throw away from hers. He'd been an ally of the woman's since long before she met the former Watcher, and he's the only creature of the Barrens the woman has ever trusted without question.

The camp lies only one thousand miles north of the Desert, close enough to the hidden canyon deep in the sandy expanse that the woman can visit as often as she wants. With the woman's traveling speed, she can make it there and back in a single day. Several times, she'd taken her child to the Desert to see his Mür.

"How goes it in the Desert?" she asks the former Watcher.

"We've completed one hundred transports. We'll use fifty to store more steel sap. Fifty are for you to use."

"Are they ready now?"

"You can have them picked up at any time," he answers.

"I'll send ten people who can blend their light back with you. Once they know the location, they can make several round trips."

"Are you sure they can be trusted?" he asks.

The woman looks in the direction of the camp. "All of those at camp now can be trusted."

"Do they know I'm from the Delta?"

"No," she replies, returning her attention to him. "None of the new ones know. Those who've been with us since the early days know to hold their tongues."

"I want the people of the Delta to think I'm dead and the creatures of the Barrens to believe I'm one of them. Never use my given name."

"We never do," she confirms.

"How many camps have you set up?" he asks.

"We have a total of forty. Between twenty and forty Murkovin are at each camp."

He shakes his head with frustration. "That's all?"

"We need more transports," she says. "We don't have enough for more camps yet. But the more camps we set up, the more Murkovin we'll find who can travel and bring them here for training. Our numbers will soon increase much faster."

The former Watcher moves to the front of the woman and grips her waist in both hands. "You're our face in the wasteland. You know we need as many Murkovin as we can find."

"We'll find them all," she says confidently.

Wrapping her arms around him, the woman leans forward and kisses him again. After their lips part, the former Watcher smothers her in a tight embrace.

"I couldn't do any of this without you," he whispers in her ear.

I know you couldn't, the woman thinks to herself. *And this part of the plan, I couldn't do without you.*

Chapter 10

After the sixty-ninth Darkness since our daughter's birth comes and goes, I ask Larn if I can take the next few days off. He grants my request without asking for an explanation, but I'm sure he knows the reason why. I want to spend as much time as I can with baby girl while she's still living with Sash and me. And even though it's not customary in this world, I want to go to her Naming Ritual. Sash had explained to me that the only people who usually attend are the Keepers, children, Disciples, and mother and child.

Over the next two days, Sash and I spend every waking moment with our daughter. Breaking its consistent pattern, Darkness delays its next fall, allowing us a little extra time with her. We take her to the Tall Hill several times to play in the grass. Sometimes, we just lay her on her back and lean over her face to tell her how much we love her. She often swings her eyes back and forth between Sash and me and reaches her hands up to our faces. The almost omniscient smile on her lips seems to say, *"I love you, Mommy. I love you, Daddy. Everything is going to work out for the best."*

We're awoken to the seventieth Darkness in the middle of the Krymzyn night. Sash silences the screeching of the Swirls and ends their flashing red light by calling out,

"Peace." Lost in slumber, baby girl never wakes up.

While I go outside to keep watch for Murkovin from a nearby hill during the storm, Sash stays in bed with our daughter. I return to bed after Darkness, but neither Sash nor I close our eyes. Instead, we lie in bed with baby girl nestled between us and watch her sleep. Despite the revelation I had after my tour of Home, the sadness I feel is so overwhelming that my gut twists inside me. Based on the dampness in her eyes and her hand always resting on baby girl, I know Sash feels the same way.

When the new day arrives, we drink our sap and feed our daughter from a cup. Knowing this is our last morning with her, Sash and I are somber and quiet.

"I don't even want to think about coming back here without her," I say.

Sash's eyes redden and it takes her a few seconds to speak. "Neither do I. We'll go to Home later and talk to Marc about visiting her. We can stay for a while to make sure she's alright."

"Sure," I reply, but her suggestion brings very little comfort to me.

As we're getting baby girl dressed in shorts and a tank top, three sharp, consecutive clangs of a bell resonate through the hills outside. A fountain of royal-blue light rises from our daughter's palms—the sign for the Naming Ritual.

Since it will take a while for the Keepers and children to reach Sanctuary, Sash and I meander across the Delta towards the south. Secured in a carrier strapped to the front of Sash's chest, baby girl attentively watches the countryside pass by us.

When we reach one of the hills overlooking the Tree of Vision, Sash and I sit in the grass. Our daughter can't sit up on her own yet, so Sash props her up on her lap. While we wait for the others to arrive, baby girl babbles excitedly, often pointing at the enormous Tree of Vision in the crimson meadow below us.

The Keepers and children eventually cross over the top of a nearby hill. Two of the Keepers have infants in carriers strapped to their chests, and the Keepers and older children are all panting. I assume they ran at least part of the way since it took them less than three hours to cover the fifteen miles from Home. I'm surprised they didn't summon Travelers to help transport the children, but Sash tells me that it's a tradition for them to walk to Naming Rituals as a group.

When they reach the bottom of the hill, the Keepers and children form a row in front of the Tree. On one side of them and also facing the Tree, the seven Disciples gather in a small semi-circle. A gigantic branch suddenly snaps into the silvery bell hanging from the towering steel pole. Before the first ring subsides, the limb pops into the bell again.

"It's time," Sash says softly.

After Sash returns our daughter to the carrier, we both stand from the grass. I pick up our spears and we walk down the hill. With our backs to the Tree of Vision, we stop in front of the group of Disciples. Eval takes a few steps forward to stand directly in front of Sash.

"You've preserved our balance by bringing a new child into our world," Eval says graciously. "All of Krymzyn is grateful to you."

"It's my honor," Sash replies half-heartedly.

"It's now time for the child to receive a name. Please present her to the Tree of Vision."

Eval and Sash bow to each other. After Sash lifts baby girl out of the carrier, she removes the straps from her shoulders and tosses the carrier to the grass. She turns to me and holds baby girl up in front of my face. Completely ignoring me, our daughter points at the Tree of Vision. Her hand quivers with excitement.

"Bugachee!" she exclaims.

"That's right," I say quietly. "Big tree."

I lean to her and kiss her forehead. She's so enamored with the Tree that she doesn't notice my display of affection. Trying to maintain a brave face, I look at Sash. The sorrow darkening her face sinks my heart to new depths of sadness. Sash holds my gaze for a moment and then cuddles our daughter to her chest.

As Sash walks across the meadow towards the trunk, outstretched branches calmly wave over her head. Like burning embers dancing against a dark sky, the yellow leaves flame in front of the gray clouds. When she reaches the base of the tree, Sash sinks to one knee. She lowers our child to the ground and rests her on her back in a grassy triangle between two enormous roots. Baby girl reaches both of her hands up towards her mother. Sash tenderly takes them in her grasp while whispering something.

It's a struggle for Sash to stand. She begins to rise but then crouches back down and rests a hand on our daughter's head. After she finally stands up and walks away from the Tree, she locks her eyes on mine. As they fill with dampness, she clenches her bottom lip between her teeth.

When she reaches me, Sash takes my hand in hers and stands by my side facing the Tree. As though they blow in on winds from four different directions, the four letters in our daughter's name float into my ears.

"A . . . V . . . E . . . N."

"Aven," I say to Sash. "What a beautiful name."

Without ever looking away from our daughter, Sash nods her agreement. Sash's eyes are so glassy and distant that I wonder if she's having one of her glimpses of the future. Eval addresses the Keepers.

"I present to you for your care, Aven, child of Krymzyn," she announces.

Marc takes a step forward from the group and bows to Eval. Except for Sash, everyone's eyes follow him as he walks towards the Tree. Oblivious to everything else, Sash continues to stare at our newly-named daughter.

Marc makes it less than halfway to the trunk when a giant limb on one of his sides rears back, pauses briefly, and then lashes in his direction. After jerking his head towards it, he ducks to the ground. Lowering its aim, the branch smacks against his body. It lifts him off the grass and catapults him towards the Disciples. He pounds to the ground on all fours and frantically scampers out of the limb's reach. Another bough crashes to the grass behind him with so much force that shockwaves ripple through the ground underneath my feet.

"Is that supposed to happen?" I ask Sash.

Hypnotized by our daughter, Sash shakes her head. "No," she murmurs.

Still sprawled on the ground, Marc looks up at Eval with utter confusion contorting his face. Eval turns away from Marc and studies the Tree. All the branches have returned to an almost dormant state with just the slightest side to side motion disturbing the air. After Marc stands to his feet, he has a brief conversation with Eval that I can't hear. Once they're finished talking, Eval addresses the Tree.

"On behalf of the Keepers," she calls out, "I claim the child Aven for all of Krymzyn."

Eval preemptively scans the branches before walking towards the trunk. She makes it about twenty feet inside the reach of the limbs when they all start thrashing up and down. I've always believed that tremendous strength and athleticism lurk in Eval's tall, trim frame. The quickness and agility that erupts from her body as she spins away from the limbs and dashes to safety confirm that observation.

Sash abruptly squeezes my hand so hard that it feels like she might crush my bones.

"Stay by my side," she says. "No matter what happens, show no fear."

Tugging me along by her side, Sash marches directly towards the trunk. Deciding they're the last things we need right now, I drop our spears to the ground. When we enter the realm of malevolent branches, Sash ignores them and stays focused on our daughter.

As I glance back and forth at our sides, multiple limbs slash across the meadow towards us. Without ever slowing our pace, we keep striding straight in the direction of the trunk. I grit my teeth and tense my muscles in anticipation of the branches hammering against our bodies. When they're only a few feet from us, they veer sharply away. A few leaves lightly brush across our skin.

Although the limbs continue to whip through the air, we reach the base of the Tree without any more coming near us. Sash releases my hand, leans down, and gently scoops Aven from the ground. Cradling our daughter in her arms, Sash looks up at the branches of the Tree. One by one, they ascend towards the sky and peacefully sway in the air.

"What does this mean?" I ask Sash.

"It means that Krymzyn wants us to raise our daughter," she answers.

"Are you sure?"

Sash smiles at me. "Absolutely."

Under serene branches, we return to where everyone else is standing.

"I'm not sure what to make of this," Eval says to Sash.

"Aven will dwell with us," Sash tells her. "At the beginning of each day, we'll take her to Home. The Keepers can educate her in the ways of Krymzyn, but at the end of each day, she'll return to our habitat."

"Do you know for a fact this is what the Tree wants?" Eval asks.

Sash nods her head. "During Aven's Ritual, it was shown to me in a glimpse of the future."

"What will you do if Darkness comes while you're asleep? You can't abandon a child or your duties."

Sash looks at me briefly and then back at Eval. "I'm aware of Darkness before it falls. Chase and I can both travel. One of us will take her to Home so the Keepers can protect her during Darkness. As it is now, I can fill one pack of stakes before the other Hunters even reach their first trees. We'll make it work."

"This is the way children are raised in my world," I add. "They live with their *parents* . . . the man and woman who create them, but go to school during the day."

"I'm familiar with the paradigm," Eval replies. "That's how Murkovin children are raised, although they have no school and receive little in the way of education other than what's needed for basic survival."

Sash speaks in a determined voice. "Aven will have all the experiences that other children in Krymzyn have when she's with the Keepers. But I believe the Tree has made it clear that, for whatever reason, Chase and I are responsible for raising her."

"Do you see any issues with this arrangement?" Eval asks Marc.

"My only concern is that Aven will feel different from the other children," he answers. "She may not understand why she has to leave Home at the end of each day."

In a timid voice, Maya interjects herself into the conversation. "We won't let her feel different. If she's sad to leave Home, we'll remind her that she'll be back soon. All of us will be there waiting for her."

Marc and Maya's words slam into my head so hard that a brick wall might as well have fallen on me. I've only had the perspective of how children are raised on Earth. I've mistakenly had the belief that Aven would be heartbroken living at Home. Added to that has been my concern that the other children might feel sad if they see her leave at the end of each day with parents they don't have. I can't believe how misguided my views have been. Their way is the only way they've ever known in this world, so it's the only way that makes sense to them.

"If you have room for her," I say to Marc, "maybe she could sleep at Home sometimes when she's a little older. That way, she can spend more time with the other children. It's common in my world for friends to have sleepovers."

Sash gently rubs her elbow against the side of my arm. I'm certain that it's a sign of approval for my suggestion.

"As you saw during your tour," Marc replies, "we always have spare rooms. Much of the time, fourteen children dwell at Home as well as several Apprentices who aren't mature enough yet for a habitat of their own. There's plenty of space. We already have a cavern prepared for Aven that no one else will use."

Still apparently debating the situation in her mind, Eval addresses Marc again. "Do you think Sash's plan for Darkness will work?"

"It shouldn't be a problem," he answers. "Kyra will be Aven's primary Keeper. If Sash or Chase can summon her when they're on their way, she can wait for them by an entrance to Home."

Eval silently deliberates the plan and then returns her attention to Sash. "Although I have my concerns, I believe Krymzyn has made it clear that this is how it should be."

Sash nods her head. "As I said, we'll make it work."

"Do you want us to take Aven with us for the remainder of the day?" Marc asks Sash.

"No. We'll bring her to Home first thing on the morrow."

He bows to her. "We look forward to caring for her."

"I'm grateful for your help," Sash says.

The Keepers and children turn away and walk up the side of the hill to the north. As Maya climbs the slope, she looks over her shoulder at me.

"I'll take care of her," she mouths.

I smile at her and nod my head. Except for Eval, the Disciples all stroll towards a hill on the eastern side of the meadow. Eval waits until they're out of earshot to speak to us again.

"I don't believe the reason for this happening is clear yet, but I'm certain there's more to it than we know. I don't need to remind you that a child's safety is of the utmost importance. A child can be at great risk during Darkness. The branches of sustaining trees don't differentiate between children and adults. If a Murkovin enters the Delta, a lone child is easy prey."

"We'll never let her out of our sight," Sash replies.

"I guess this explains a lot," I say.

"What do you mean?" Eval asks.

"The reason we can both travel. Why Sash senses Darkness before it comes. It all makes sense now."

"Your points might be valid," Eval says. "None the less, it's important for you to remember that your contributions to the balance of Krymzyn are as critical as anyone else's. You can't let having her with you interfere with your purposes."

"We would never let that happen," Sash tells her.

Eval's eyes drift to Aven and she speaks in almost a whisper. "She looks exactly as you did at your Naming Ritual."

After Eval looks at Sash, they stare at each other for several seconds. As I've noticed a few times in the past, they seem to silently share something deep and meaningful. Even though they never mention it or show an outright display of affection, the innate bond between mother and daughter is clearly in focus. Eval is the first to break the silence.

"I suggest you use the remainder of the day to fully plan how the two of you will manage the situation."

"We will," Sash replies.

"Don't hesitate to see me if I can help you figure anything out."

"Thank you," Sash and I say at the same time.

Eval bows to us and then walks away. While Sash loads Aven in the baby carrier, I grab our spears from the ground. With Aven secure on the front of her chest, Sash takes my hand in hers. We walk up a hill in the direction of our habitat.

"We can move the table from my studio to where it used to be," I say. "I can set up my easel in front of the painting of you at Ovin's tree."

"Why?" she asks.

"So that Aven has her own room."

"We can keep her cradle by our bed for a while," she replies. "I don't want you to lose your space for painting."

"It's fine. As she gets older, she'll need her own room. When we have another child, they can share it."

Before either of us can say anything else, Aven slaps her hands to Sash's cheeks.

"Mama!" she shouts.

Sash and I stop dead in our tracks at Aven's first real

word. After Sash smiles at our daughter, she opens her eyes wide at me with feigned exasperation.

"Do you remember what we talked about?" she asks.

"I only said 'Mommy' that one time," I say in my defense.

Aven turns her face to me and reaches out a hand. "Dada!"

Sash lowers her eyebrows. The pretend mad in her glare is replaced by genuine. "I told you that I don't think we should use those terms."

"The thing is," I say, "I never once said 'Daddy' to her."

"Are you sure?"

"Positive," I answer.

"Then how would she learn that word?" she asks.

"I have no idea."

Sash looks down at Aven's face again.

"Mama," our daughter says in a soft voice that melts my heart.

"I guess it's meant to be," Sash whispers.

After we return to our habitat, Sash and I discuss how to rearrange everything so that Aven has her own room. While we're in my studio taking inventory of items that can be moved to the shelves in the main cavern, I go to my calendar to make a notation of Aven's Naming Ritual. With so much of my recent time devoted to Sash and our daughter, I didn't even realize that today is my twenty-fourth birthday on Earth.

Sash and I spend the rest of the afternoon walking around the Delta with Aven. We eventually end up on the Empty Hill and sit in the grass. With Aven resting on my lap,

I lean to Sash and kiss her cheek.

"Happy _birthday_," I say.

"What does that mean?" she asks.

"Do you remember when I explained how we track years on Earth?"

"I remember."

"Every three hundred and sixty-five days from the day of their birth, a person has a _birthday_. It's to celebrate another year in that person's life."

"That's an odd number," she says.

"That's how long it takes for the Earth to revolve around what's called our sun. You saw the sun in the Infinite Expanse with me. I explained to you what it was."

Sash nods her head to let me know that she remembers. "But why are you saying happy birthday to me?" she asks, 'birthday' now translating and part of her vocabulary.

"Today's my birthday. You told me that you had a vision that showed us being born at the same time, so it's your birthday, too."

She leans to me, kisses my lips, and then nuzzles my cheek. "Happy birthday, Chase."

"Thanks," I reply. "It couldn't have been better."

Chapter 11

Sash and I wake up early the next morning, but not by choice. About an hour before we usually get out of bed, Aven launches into non-stop babbling. Mixed with her usual gibberish is an occasional "Mama" or "Dada," but most of the time, she points at the tunnel entrance and shouts her third comprehensible word.

"Go!"

Although there's no way to explain it, she seems to know that she's off to her first day at Home. Based on how animated she is, she couldn't be more excited about it. After dressing ourselves, Sash and I get Aven into a tiny pair of black pants and sleeveless V-neck. I chuckle at the thought that she looks like an infant model about to be paraded down the runway at a punk fashion show.

As we all drink sap together, Sash and I encourage Aven to say her name. Her only response is to wrinkle her forehead and study our faces. Before we head out the tunnel, Sash summons Kyra to let her know that we're on our way. Wanting me to get used to traveling with Aven, Sash straps the child carrier over my chest and we all leave our habitat for the day.

I've never exercised so much caution while traveling as I

do carrying Aven. Giving a wide berth to any trees and steep hills along the way, I steer through the widest valleys leading to the north. I doubt I ever exceed a thousand miles per hour, a much slower pace than I'm accustomed to traveling.

We reach the broad meadow in front of Home to find Marc and Kyra already waiting for us. I've met the forty-something female Keeper several times in the past in conjunction with my duties as a Traveler. Her long, straight hair is almost always tied in a bun on top of her head, probably to keep young hands from grabbing it. With a medium build, round face, big eyes, and little bulb on the end of her nose, she has a pleasant, soothing appearance.

When I pass Aven off to Kyra, Aven instantly pinches her cheeks. In a gentle, caring way, Kyra establishes a few boundaries by pulling Aven's hands away and telling her that it's not alright to do that. In response, Aven squeezes Kyra's cheeks again.

As Sash and I have already learned, Aven can be a handful in several ways. Much like her mother, she's extremely strong-willed. It's not uncommon for her to resist a bath in the waterfall cavern by trying to squirm away from us, or avoid going to sleep at night by chattering loudly in the dark, sometimes for hours and hours.

Based on her mysteriously calling me "Dada" and seeming to know that we were on our way to Home, she also must have some type of mystical clairvoyance. After witnessing Sash's glimpses of the future and adapting to the more magical aspects of Krymzyn, I'm not at all fazed by her sixth-sense. I can't say the same about how she explores how far she can push someone before they react, but that's just what young children do.

Like all new parents, Sash and I experience major changes in our lives. And like all new parents, we gradually adapt. It was easier when Sash's only duty was to care for Aven. Once we're both back to fulfilling our purposes, we juggle our schedules, alternate pick-ups and drop-offs, and dedicate our evenings to our daughter. Although it wears us out at times, the simplicity of life in Krymzyn makes parenthood easier than I assume it would be on Earth.

Since I often start my duties in the northern portion of the Delta, I'm usually the one who drops Aven off at Home. Sash typically picks her up at the end of the day, although we sometimes meet at Home and spend the evening with Aven and the other children.

While watching the children play in the common room or quietly having their sap together, I get a better sense of why people in Krymzyn are the way they are. Although they're always taught to be polite and respectful to one another, interaction with others isn't encouraged the way it is on Earth. Communing with the entire world around them is much more important to them.

If Darkness falls while Aven is with us, Sash insists on being the one to transport her to Home. Considering how much faster Sash's traveling speed is than mine, I don't blame her for wanting to take on that responsibility. She's also a better fighter than anyone else in the Delta. But to be honest, it annoys me at times because I feel like she doesn't trust me with the task. The one time I bring it up with her, she simply replies, "I'm faster."

As I noticed during Aven's first few months of life,

children develop much faster in Krymzyn than they do on Earth. In the weeks after her Naming Ritual, Aven's vocabulary increases from three words to twenty. Cup, sky, sap, and other words that I'd expect to be among a child's first in this world soon come out of her mouth. Like many small children, she has trouble with certain consonants, especially combining them. She pronounces "tree" as "chee," and "clouds" as "cowds."

At four months old, Aven sits up on her own. She's also easily engaged in simple games. Sash brings a few toys to our habitat from Home, all of them educational in one way or another. Aven's favorite is a set of interlocking steel rings with twist-open hinges. She adores unclasping them, putting them back together again, and then shaking them wildly to make as much clamor as she can.

Our lives are really turned upside down when, at five months old, Aven begins to crawl. Even though it's only a couple of inches deep, I panic that she'll somehow drown in the stream inside the waterfall cavern. Then I worry that she'll climb down the crevice that the water spills away through. Sash alleviates my fears by showing me that the crack in the rock is only a few inches wide. None the less, we tell Aven to never go in the waterfall cavern alone. In another sign of her stubbornness, she ignores the rule and often tries to crawl in there by herself. Fortunately, since she's never alone in our habitat, Sash and I can rush to stop her.

Our concern hits new heights when Aven crawls to our spears at the end of one day and yanks them off the wall. With the help of two Constructs, we completely childproof our habitat. The first thing we do is have the Constructs install new spear clasps. They set them in the wall so that they hold the spears horizontally and high enough that they're well out of Aven's reach. They also install a gate over the entrance to the waterfall cavern with a latch several feet above her outstretched arms.

We eventually move Aven into my former studio. Although we sometimes let her sleep with us, she spends most nights in her cradle. I find that I can get her to sleep faster by singing lullabies from Earth, so that becomes a regular part of our routine. Once Aven's asleep, we close a curtain over her doorway that the Constructs installed so that Sash and I can have a little much-needed alone time. We usually fall asleep in an instant.

The older Aven gets, the more pronounced the resemblance between mother and daughter becomes. As Aven's hair grows longer, her raven waves are identical to Sash's. Their subtle smiles, the intensity in their eyes, and their facial expressions are all mirror images of one another.

Despite there being no precedent in the Delta for her to draw from, Sash proves to be a patient and caring mother. She never loses her temper with our daughter, even when Aven tries to push us to our outermost limits. Sash can usually get her to back down with nothing more than a prolonged stare. Whenever that happens, Aven gazes straight back at Sash. Because their eyes glass over during the stare-off, I often wonder if they're sharing some type of unspoken communication, much like I've seen with Sash and Eval.

Eval stops by our habitat every few days, usually under the guise of making sure we're adapting to our daughter dwelling with us. She always ends up sitting on a stool with

Aven on her knee and playing a game with her. The caring of a grandmother may be foreign to this world, but it's unmistakable in Eval's interaction with Aven.

Although Larn always asks how Sash and Aven are, he's less willing to partake in customs that aren't natural to this world—like being a grandfather. Several times when our duties for the day are finished, I ask him if he'd like to stop by our habitat to see Aven. He never accepts my offer and always has some vague excuse for why. I eventually stop asking out of fear that it makes him feel uncomfortable.

Tela is the exact opposite of Larn. At least once a week, she comes to our habitat when our work for the day is completed. After the first few visits, Aven squeals with delight whenever Tela shows up. They play games together and sometimes go for evening walks with Aven in the carrier, giving Sash and me a little breather.

The only comparison I can come up with for the relationship that develops between Tela and Aven is that of an aunt and a niece on Earth. Considering how close Tela and I have become, the long-time friendship between Sash and Tela, and Tela's interest in customs from my world, I can't say that I'm surprised.

At six months old, Aven pulls herself up to a standing position by placing her hands on a stool. She never stays erect for very long and eventually wobbles and falls to her rear. She sticks her bottom lip out and lowers her eyebrows, making an adorable pouty face when it happens. But never once does she cry or shed a tear.

Sash and I cheer loudly when, at seven months old, Aven takes her first step. Over the next few days, we take her to the top of the Empty Hill and help her walk across the soft grass. Before we know it, she's trotting back and forth between us with a smile on her face.

Once our lives finally settle into a consistent routine, I decide to make good on my promise to teach soccer to the children of Krymzyn. Under an enormous willow in the grove of thread trees, I find the Weaver Nina to ask her to make a few balls and a net for the goal.

On a trip to the Mount, I want to ask Wren if he can make the goal frames. Tela accompanies me to the broad clearing where the Constructs work. Surrounded by blue-needled pines, the Constructs are putting away their tools at the end of the day when we arrive.

Near the center of the meadow, I spot Wren cleaning up his workspace with his short, curly hair aglow with the magenta of a Construct. When he lifts a large, marble mold from the ground to the top of one of the table-like slabs, I'm impressed by his strength, especially considering how lanky he is. He notices Tela and me walking across the clearing and stops what he's doing.

I quickly explain the soccer goals to him, including how Nina will fit the netting over the frames. He asks a few questions about their size and how they'll be used and then declares it won't be any problem to make them. After he tells me that he'll have them ready in ten days, Tela and I bid him farewell.

As we return to the road, I realize that I forgot to ask Wren for spikes to secure the goals to the ground. I turn back to him and instantly bite the insides of my mouth to keep from bursting out with laughter. With his head tilted to one side, his eyes dreamily follow Tela while she continues to walk away. Completely lost in his trance, he doesn't even notice that I'm looking at him.

"Wren," I say. He's so fixated on Tela that he doesn't hear me, so I call out again a little louder. "Wren!"

When he looks at me, his cheeks flush red with embarrassment. "I, uh," he mumbles, "was just making some calculations."

"I'm sure you were," I reply, still trying to keep from laughing. "I forgot to ask you for something else."

"What's that?"

"Spikes with a hook on the end to secure the goals to the ground. Eight inches should be long enough. Nina will make rope loops for the corners of the goals that they can go through."

"That won't be a problem," he tells me.

"Thanks, Wren."

After he nods his head to me, he returns to putting his things away. I jog after Tela, wondering why Wren would look at her that way since that type of attraction doesn't exist here. I've never seen a person in Krymzyn look at someone else with an apparent crush, but that's exactly how Wren was looking at Tela.

I can't say that I blame him. Tela is smart, helpful, and very pretty. Her big, round eyes have an underlying intelligence in their gaze, and her round face is naturally cheery. The bridge of her medium-sized nose might be just a little too wide for her face, and her eyes a hair too far apart, but they're the kind of imperfections that only enhance her overall beauty. Full, red lips over a smoothly curved chin complete a face that most guys would find alluring.

As I think about it, I decide that Tela and Wren would actually make a great couple, although I doubt there's any possibility of that happening. She was blind to his admiring eyes, and romance isn't part of life in Krymzyn. When I catch up to Tela, I slow to a walk by her side.

"Wren is sure a good guy," I say, studying her face for a reaction.

"He's very skilled," Tela replies in a typical Krymzyn response.

"You two are about the same age, aren't you?" I ask, thinking that if I'm twenty-four now, Tela must be around twenty, and Wren is twenty-one or twenty-two.

"He's a little older than I am," she answers, "but we were at Home together for a long time."

"Were the two of you close?"

"All of us at Home at that time were very helpful to one another. Did you know Sash was the one who taught me to blend my light?"

"I didn't," I say.

"I think I told you once that I learned to travel soon after the first time I met you on the Tall Hill. Sash had recently ended her Apprenticeship and had her own habitat. She came by Home at the end of one day and took me to the Traveling Hill. I remember her exact words. She said, 'Stop pretending that you don't know how to blend your light and do it. If you don't believe in yourself, no one else will.'"

"That sounds like something Sash would say," I comment.

As we near the gate where the other Travelers are

waiting for us, Tela and I stop walking and face each other. Her eyes light up when she resumes the story.

"We ran down the Traveling Hill side by side several times, but nothing happened. Sash refused to let me give up. Larn happened to pass by and stopped to watch what we were doing.

"On the fifth try, I saw the beams, jolted forward, and streamed my particles into them. I was so stunned that I was traveling that I lost my focus while crossing the meadow. I flipped through the air several times and broke both of my legs. The strange part was, I didn't care. I didn't notice the pain because I was so excited that I'd traveled at such a young age. Sash knelt beside me and told me how proud of me she was.

"I spent the next few days at Home in bed. Sash came by to see me several times each day. Nina was an Apprentice Weaver and made special pillows to prop up my legs. Wren sawed the legs off a table, set it by the side of my bed, and made sure I always had a full cup of sap. Even though he was small, Cavu refused to leave me alone in my cavern while I slept. He sat by my doorway with a training spear across his lap to watch over me."

"Wow," I say. "What a great group of _kids_ . . . children."

"We were very different from our elders," she says. "We took a much greater interest in each other's lives."

"Do you miss having that?" I ask. "I mean, do you ever get lonely? Everyone here is so solitary, but you seem to like it when you spend time with us."

Deliberating her response, she looks up at the highest branches of the steel trees. From what she just told me, I understand a little better why her relationship with Aven seems so natural. She eventually lowers her eyes to mine.

"I don't know that lonely is the right word," she says. "I've always felt like I want to have experiences that don't exist here. I honestly don't even know what they are. Just something more than what the norm in Krymzyn is. You've told me a lot about your world and it all sounds interesting to me. I think that's why I enjoy having you here so much. I discover new experiences with you, like getting to spend time with Aven."

"I'm glad you feel that way," I say. "People spend a lot more time with other people in my world than they do here."

We both turn towards the wall and resume our walk down the path.

"What are you doing with the day off?" Tela asks.

Larn decided we could finally reduce the number of Travelers needed for excursions outside the Delta. In all the months that have passed since Aven's birth, we've only seen two Murkovin. They were both far in the distance and didn't pay attention to us. As a reward for our hard work over the time since the attack on the road that killed Beck, half of the Travelers have the next day off, including Tela and me. The other half will take the following day off.

"I haven't decided yet," I say. "Sash and I have spent a lot of time with Aven lately. I don't think Sash can take the day off, so I'll probably just sleep and paint. How about you?"

"I was thinking of going to the Barrens," she answers. "You know how it is."

"Yeah, I know. I haven't had a chance to let loose since

Aven was born. Maybe that's what I'll do."

"I have an idea," she says excitedly. "On the morrow, you and I could go to the flats in the southwest Barrens that I told you about. We can race across the flats to get our count."

"Our count?" I ask.

"We count in our heads while we travel between two large rocks. They're exactly two thousand miles apart. The count is kind of like how you explained what seconds are in your world."

"That sounds like fun," I say, "as long as you don't try to annoy me by snapping your fingers and counting out loud."

She scrunches her nose at the reference to something she did when I explained time in my world to her. "You don't think it would be . . . *awesome* if I did."

We both chuckle at her sarcastic imitation of my slang. As was the case with Sash, once a sense of humor developed in her, Tela's has continued to blossom.

"Will we have time to make it there and back in one day?" I ask.

"As fast as you and I are traveling, we'll be back by sleep time. Maybe we'll break Larn's record in the flats."

"What was his count?" I ask.

"I'll tell you after we get ours."

"Let's do it," I say.

After we return to the Delta, I find Sash sitting on top of a hill that overlooks the outside playground at Home. In the meadow at the bottom of the slope, the older children are playing on a giant jungle-gym. Aven is sitting in a swing with safety straps used for infants and toddlers. With her hands clamped to the steel ropes that suspend the swing, Aven glides through the air each time Kyra gently pushes her from behind.

"Hi beautiful," I say to Sash, sitting on the grass beside her.

"How was your day?" she asks.

"It was great," I reply. "How was yours?"

"It was nice. The trees are all well, so I came here a little early."

"Your trees are always healthy," I say. "I may be a little late getting back to our habitat on the morrow. Can you pick up Aven?"

"Of course. Why do you think you'll be late?"

"Larn gave a few of us the day off. Tela and I want to go to the flats to get a count on our speed. Do you know what that is?"

"I do," she answers. "Larn owns the record, but I wouldn't be surprised if you surpass it as fast as you've been traveling."

"Have you ever done it?" I ask.

"I did it once on the way to the Infinite Expanse."

"What was your count?"

She looks at the children in the meadow. "I'd rather not say. It's something that Travelers do. I'm a Hunter, so I shouldn't even be able to travel."

I know there's no pushing the issue, her humility always intact, so I don't even try. "Do you mind if that's what I do? We've had a lot of time with Aven lately and I want to get out of the Delta for a while."

"Not at all," she replies, returning her attention to me. "I know what Travelers like to do on a day off. I'm very excited for you to get a count."

"Thank you," I say. "Something strange happened on the Mount."

"What was it?"

"Well . . . I think Wren has a thing for Tela."

She tilts her head to the side. "A thing?"

"Like what I have for you," I say, resting a hand on her leg. "Like how it was when you and I went to the Tall Hill for the first time."

"You call that a 'thing'?" she asks rhetorically. "Why do you think Wren feels that way about Tela?"

"Just the way he looks at her. It's the same way I look at you."

"That's odd," she says. "No one here would ever look at another person that way, except maybe the Murkovin. And you and me."

"That's what I thought, too. But I think I'm kind of rubbing off on people. Like, their senses of awareness pick up things from my world through me."

She nudges me with her elbow. "Does that mean you have a thing for Tela and Wren is getting it from you?"

"I'm serious," I say. "I've seen it in others. Cavu blushed once when you complimented him. Tela makes jokes now and even laughs sometimes."

"Maybe they're just mimicking your behavior," she reasons.

I shake my head. "That's what I thought at first, but it's more than that. I see it mostly in people close to our age, but I saw it in Tork once as well. He got really angry about the tunnel under the river and slammed his spear against a wall.

It's like he couldn't control his anger, so he reacted the way someone from my world might."

"That is strange," she says. "Maybe you're right. Maybe the more they're around you, the more they feel things through their senses of awareness that you would feel in your world."

"That's what I think. I just can't figure out if it's good or bad."

"It's neither. It's just the way it is." She suddenly snaps her face up to the clouds. "Aven needs to stay with the Keepers for a while." She springs from the ground, looks down the hill at the meadow, and cups her hands around her mouth. "Darkness is coming!"

As I jump to my feet, the Keepers guide the children towards the back entrance of Home. Kyra lifts Aven out of the swing and then briskly carries her towards the door. Looking up at Sash and me, Aven waves her hand.

After Sash and I return her wave, I start to sprint down the hill in the opposite direction. When Sash doesn't catch up to me as she usually would, I stop and look behind me. With her feet planted to the ground and her eyes glued to the meadow, she doesn't move until Aven is safely inside Home.

Chapter 12

In a desolate part of the northeast Barrens, the woman stands in a bitter storm. Rain stings her head, bleeds down her body, and splashes to the mud at her feet. A canister that once belonged to Travelers of the Delta hangs from a rope looped over one of her shoulders. Her spear is planted in the mire at her side, close at hand should peril befall her.

Studying the top of a rocky hill in front of her, the woman is well aware that a group of her kind lurks behind the ridge. Not wanting them to view her as a threat, she waits for them to make the first move.

A few steps behind her stands a female Murkovin, a newly appointed commander as those entrusted with overseeing new camps are called. Soon after the former Watcher had left the Delta for the last time, the female had joined their ranks. Possessing great skill at blending her light and expertise with a weapon, the female commander had gained the woman's trust over countless days of loyalty.

When a male Murkovin climbs over the top of the hill in front of her, the woman doesn't move. With a worn, wooden spear in the clutch of his hands, he leaps onto a boulder. A second Murkovin, this one female, steps to the side of the rock the first creature stands on. From the corner of her eye, the woman spots a man creep around the base of the hill on her left. On her right, a muscular female jumps out of a shallow gully. The woman focuses her eyes again on the top of the hill. From behind the crest, several children peek over the jagged rocks.

"We mean you no harm," the woman calls out over the wail of the storm.

"This is our territory!" the Murkovin on the boulder shouts. "What have you done to our tree?"

"We bring you a better way to take sap," the woman tells him.

The woman lifts her spear out of the mud and points it behind her. The beast's eyes follow the line of her weapon to a large sustaining tree with its upper limbs all bound by rope. Long before the woman found the tree, the lower limbs had been ripped from the trunk. Like many trees of the Barrens, the bark is riddled with scars from countless jabs of spears.

In a clan like this, the woman knows, one Murkovin at a time will drink from the tree while the others defend against the violent upper branches. During each Darkness, they typically fill a few crudely-made wooden containers to store sap for a later time.

The woman has now embedded four steel stakes in the bark. They were designed to look like Hunters' stakes, but the blunt ends were left open when they were crafted in the Desert. With tubes running from the hollow ends to a transport, she can provide them with a greater supply of sap than they've ever known.

"Each Darkness," the woman explains, "the transport will fill with sap. Since the limbs are bound, you no longer need to fight the tree. You'll have a large supply of sap for when you need it, even during long periods of light."

The man on the boulder aims his eyes at the woman. "Why have you done this?"

"We want to bring peace to the Barrens," she replies, sinking the tip of her spear into the ground at her side. "It starts by ending the fight for sap."

The woman removes the canister from her shoulder and throws it up the hill. Dull glints reflect from the worn steel when it splashes to the wet ground in front of the boulder.

"That will quench your thirst until Darkness passes," the woman says.

The man springs from the rock and lands in a crouch. After grabbing the canister with one hand, he drops his spear to the mud. Never taking his eyes off the woman, he unscrews the cap and swigs down one long drink. As he extends his hand with the canister to the female behind him, he grabs his weapon with his other hand. The female takes a few small sips, steps backwards to the top of the hill, and hands the canister to one of the children.

They only had a little each before giving it to the children, the woman thinks. *This is the kind of clan I need.*

The commander behind the woman removes two flasks from her belt. She tosses one to the creature on their right and the other to the Murkovin on their left. They both snatch the metal containers out of the air. While they drink from the flasks, the woman raises her eyes to the turbulent clouds overhead. The dark billows gradually grind to a halt as rays of gray light split their edges.

The creature at the top of the hill walks down the slope

towards the woman. The muscles in his arms are taut, she notices, but his gait is steady and slow. Although the woman remains in a relaxed and peaceful stance, her muscles sharpen in preparation for an unexpected attack. As she hoped he would, the Murkovin stops a few feet in front of her with his weapon idle at his side.

"What do you want in return?" he asks.

The woman briefly studies the man's long, worn face, as well as the many battle scars on his arms. The man has faced the harshness of life in the Barrens, but proven he has the strength and will to survive.

"I want our kind to live in peace," she answers. "How many Murkovin dwell near here?"

The man looks off to each of his sides and then returns his attention to the woman. "Almost forty within fifty miles of here."

"All in clans like yours?"

"Most," he says. "A few are loners."

"Do you get along with each other?"

The man clenches his jaw. "We leave the others alone. A few create problems, especially during long periods of light."

"How many sustaining trees grow in this fifty mile area?" the woman asks.

"Three that are still alive."

"It must be difficult to get what you need for survival," the woman says. "But imagine a new Barrens, one with sustaining trees never farther than a few miles apart. The trees are all bound by rope and provide more sap than you could ever consume. Imagine items made of steel and well-sewn clothing. Imagine the ground covered by grass, not the sparse patches of weeds we have now. And more than anything else, imagine our kind living in peace."

The man shakes his head. "How can that come to be?"

"It starts with a better supply of sap. When we have all the sap we need, there's no need to fight amongst ourselves."

"But you can't change what grows in the Barrens," he gruffly replies.

"Not now," the woman says, "but one day in the not too distant future, we can bring change. Camps like the one we hope to establish here have already formed across different parts of the Barrens. Some have several trees in a small area with as many as forty of our kind dwelling nearby. They have steel tools they use to improve caverns. They work together, not against one another. The time of killing our own has passed. An era of unity is arriving."

"That doesn't explain how you'll change the landscape of the Barrens."

"A plan is in place," the woman replies. "The first step is dwelling in peace."

"You're not answering my question!" the man fires back.

A clever man. He'll eventually be able to take over as commander for this camp, the woman thinks to herself before speaking out loud again.

"There will be a great battle one day. When it's over, those who adhere to the new ways will control the balance of Krymzyn. But until you and I gain each other's trust, I can tell you no more."

The Murkovin glares at the woman. "You want us to fight this battle for you."

She was ready for the man's response, the same one

she'd received at many other camps they'd set up. The woman doesn't hesitate with her reply.

"You can choose to join us in the fight for a better life, or you can choose not to. You have no idea how many of our kind there are and how many want to take part in these changes. No matter what you choose to do in the future, we'll help bring peace to this area. We require nothing in return."

Considering her proposition, the Murkovin takes a few steps to the woman's side and examines the tree fifty feet behind her. Knowing that she'll need a final plea to convince the man to join her, the woman focuses her eyes on the top of the hill again. The female Murkovin is still standing on the crest with three small children partially hidden behind the rocks.

"I have a small child," the woman says to the man. "Even if it costs me my life, I want him to have a far better existence than the one I've known. I believe you think the same way as I do."

After a few moments pass, the man turns his head to the woman. "What if someone from the Delta sees one of these camps? They could bring others and attack."

The woman shrugs her shoulders. "The people in the Delta don't care what we do as long as we stay away from them. The camps we have now are in the southwest and northeast Barrens, well off the paths that Travelers use. We'll eventually have camps in every part of the Barrens. At the speed that Travelers cross our land, it's unlikely they'd even notice a group of our kind. They leave the trading posts alone as it is now, so it shouldn't be a problem. Have you ever seen a Traveler near here?"

"No," the man answers.

"And you probably never will," the woman tells him. "As a precaution, the other camps always have a guard keeping watch. If a Traveler were to stop, the guard would see them and call others. The Traveler would be surely be killed. And if you work with those around you, dwell together in peace, you'll have numbers against those of our kind who believe they can take what they want from others."

Returning his attention to the tree, the man ponders all that the woman told him. The woman addresses the commander standing a few feet away from her.

"Bring the other transport," she says.

The commander runs towards a hill on the other side of the tree. After briefly disappearing behind it, she returns with a large wagon in tow. The back of the cart is stuffed with steel tools, several long lengths of rope, a large bolt of black fabric, metal pitchers and cups, and a dozen steel spears. When the commander parks the wagon beside the woman, the woman reaches into it and pulls out a steel axe.

"Everything in the transport is for you," the woman says and then holds up the axe. "Have you ever seen one of these?"

"Not made of steel," he answers. "Only the kind made in the Barrens."

"This one works much better."

The woman tosses the axe straight up towards the sky. The man's eyes follow the steel as it revolves in the air. After it reaches its apex and begins its descent, the woman holds out one hand. The handle slaps against her palm. In one fluid motion, she clenches her fingers around the handle, cocks the axe by her head, and hurls it towards the tree. Slicing deeply into the bark, the blade locks in the trunk. When the man looks at the woman again, the woman believes she sees respect in his eyes.

"Everything you've told me makes sense," he says. "When the time comes, how many of us will you want to join the battle you spoke of?"

"Just a few from each camp," the woman answers. "But only if they're confident in our plan."

The man nods his head. "It's a fair arrangement."

"You won't regret your decision," the woman says. "You and I will go speak with the others in the area. If the loners you mentioned give us any trouble, I'll take care of them. The woman with me will remain here for a while to help with anything you need."

Sizing up the commander, the Murkovin scrutinizes her from head to toe.

"She's trustworthy," the woman says, "and as skilled with a weapon as anyone you've ever met. I assure you of that."

"And what of you?" the man asks the woman.

"I'll come here from time to time. If you have any problems, tell me. I'll resolve them. Can any of you blend your light?"

"None in my clan," he answers. "A young man who dwells nearby can."

"When we go see the others, make sure I know which one he is. We need to reach as many parts of the Barrens as possible." The woman points her hand at the hilltop where the children are. "Call the others and have your fill of sap.

Drink until you're more satisfied than you've ever been."

The man yells to the rest of his clan to join him. The female commander takes out several cups from the back of the wagon and trots to the tree. From the spigot on one end of the sap transport, she fills the cups one by one.

The woman watches the female Murkovin and three children climb down the slope. Thin and pale, the children are clothed in faded rags hastily sewn together. Their plight will soon change, the woman tells herself, and they'll know she's the reason why.

I don't like being away from my child for so many days at a time. But it will all be worth it soon enough.

Like many of the other camps we've established, these people respect my boldness and trust my words. I bring them something they've never had—hope for a better future. And when that better life comes to fruition, their loyalty will belong to me.

Chapter 13

At the beginning of my day off, I say goodbye to Sash and take Aven to Home. Before I set my daughter on the ground, she reaches her arms around my neck and hugs me. Her thick, black hair has grown long enough that it hangs over her ears and past her neck in the back. As she presses her cheek against mine, a few strands tickle my face.

"Wuv-u, Daddy," she says.

"I love you too," I whisper in her ear. "Have a wonderful day."

After I lower Aven's feet to the grass, Kyra takes her hand and guides her still wobbly, sometimes unsure gait into the caverns of Home. Part of me feels guilty for not spending the day with my daughter, but in the year that I've permanently been in Krymzyn, this the first time I've gone out to do something just for fun with anyone other than Sash or Aven. Even though I was a bit of a loner on Earth, hanging out with friends or family for a day at the beach or an evening movie was always important to me.

When I arrive at the Delta entrance, I find Tela already waiting for me by the gate. I stop by the rack against the wall to grab a pair of soft, leathery boots and then walk to where she's standing.

"What took you so long?" she impatiently asks.

"I had to take Aven to Home," I answer.

"You should have woken up earlier."

She tries to scowl at me but can't stop a smile from coming to her lips.

"Very funny," I say. "Maybe you should have slept later."

"If I'd slept any later, the day would be gone," she quips.

Still smiling, she hands me a Traveler's canister full of sap. After I hang it around my neck, we both slip our boots on our feet. Walking side by side, we exit the Delta through the high-arched gate and cross over the bridge.

"We'll go towards the Mount for a few miles before heading south," Tela explains when we reach the road past the bridge. "We'll never stay close to the river for very long. If we see Murkovin, we don't want to get trapped in between them and the water."

"Like they could catch us," I say.

"I know," she replies, "but it's protocol for when we take children to the Infinite Expanse."

"Is this the same route we use to go to the Great Falls?"

"Essentially," she answers. "Remember landmarks along the way so you can use them to find your way in the future."

I've noticed that my memory has improved dramatically since being in Krymzyn, maybe a byproduct of living on nothing but sap, or maybe an enhancement Krymzyn made to my brain when I was brought here permanently. Although my memory hasn't increased to the "instant recall from years ago" level that people born here have, I distinctly remember major hills or recognizable rock formations in any part of the

Barrens I travel through. With an area two hundred times greater than the surface of Earth, it would be impossible to navigate the wasteland without the photographic imprints in my mind.

"Lead the way," I say.

As she jogs up the road towards the Mount, she looks over her shoulder at me and smirks. "Try to keep up."

"Try not to break your legs," I reply, laughing to myself.

After we blast towards the Mount for a few miles, Tela cuts off the road to the south. Like a pair of fighter pilots locked in a high-speed aerial display, we fly over hills and streak through valleys. Cutting back and forth in front of one other, we blaze across the empty wasteland. Sometimes we sweep beside the river, sometimes we shoot deep into the Barrens, but we never maintain a predictable path.

Drifting into a mesmeric state, I relax to the tingling sensation of blending my light. Shadowy hills, flashes of light from the crests of waves, and the blurred shapes of occasional trees pass by me. During my time here, I've grown accustomed to the luminous maze that fills my vision while traveling at unthinkable speeds. Other than briefly seeing Aven in her true form after she was born, and the one time in the Reflecting Pool with Sash, it's the closest I ever come to seeing Krymzyn as it actually exists.

Hours fall behind us as we speed through the Barrens. Interrupting my meditative calm, Tela suddenly rockets past my side. As she slows on her approach to a hill near the river, I trail close behind her. When I see her transition to a run, I slip my particles from the beams. After gliding to a stop on top of the hill, we both drink from our canisters.

"Where are we?" I ask.

"Two-thirds of the way to the Great Falls," she answers and then points a hand at the rapids. "This is where we cross."

I glance at the river, thinking how amazing it is that we traveled roughly sixty-five thousand miles in half the day. The river where we are is only about a quarter of a mile wide. The rapids are huge and leap from the surface of the river around a rocky bridge. As I start to return my attention to Tela, I do a double-take to look at the bridge again.

"We're not going over that, are we?"

"That's the Stone Crossing," she replies.

The only way I can imagine the natural bridge could have been created is if hundreds of enormous boulders fell from the sky and randomly fit together in a way that just happened to form a gradual arch over the river. Nothing but pressure from the weight of the rocks pressed together seems to be holding them in place. The top surface is about ten feet wide and more or less smooth, but seams between the rocks can clearly be seen. The sides and bottom of the bridge are an irregular array of rough edges. My first impression is that it's about as stable as a house of cards.

"That thing will collapse if we step on it," I say.

"People have been using the Crossing for millions of Eras," she tells me. "I doubt you and I will cause it to fall."

As soon as she finishes speaking, a towering wave swells from the rapids on the north side of the Crossing, pauses in the air, and then crashes down on the entire surface of the bridge. A booming clap echoes around us as the water splashes off the rocks.

"You're right," I say. "We'll just be swept down the river by a wave."

"Keep watching," Tela replies, "and count in your head."

Seconds tick away in my mind while I study the rapids. When my count reaches sixty, another enormous wall of water soars into the air and plummets back down on the rocks.

"Sixty," I say.

"That's how long we have to get across."

"Is it always sixty?" I ask.

"Always."

"Do we travel over?"

"Never," she says. "Too many reflections from the rapids and big waves shoot across the bridge. Your particles will be taken out over the water and may never return to your body. It's a lot safer to run."

"That seems like a relative comparison," I say.

"What do you mean?" she asks, tilting her head to the side.

"What I mean is, I'm pretty sure nothing about this is safe."

She rolls her eyes at me. "After everything that's happened to you in Krymzyn, this is what you don't feel safe about?"

"I guess you have a point," I chuckle.

We both sip from our canisters a few more times before returning them to our shoulders. As I follow Tela down the hill to the edge of the Stone Crossing, several more gigantic waves rise from the rapids and smother the rocks. I count between each of them, always ending at sixty.

"We'll go after the next one," Tela says.

With our spears locked in our hands, we crouch in what I think of as long-distance runners' starting stances. I'm not concerned with how long it will take to sprint over the bridge. I could turn a quarter-mile on Earth in well under a minute, and my running speed is probably twice as fast in this world. But I'm a bit worried about my footing on the rocks since the top of the bridge is uneven and filled with cracks. My heart rate doubles by the time the next swell shoots up from the rapids and pounds down on the bridge.

"Now!" Tela shouts as the leftover water from the wave spills over the sides of the Crossing.

We both sprint forward and onto the bridge. Through the soft material of my boots, I feel the roughness of the stones as my feet slam against them. With Tela's muscular legs propelling her over the rocks, she pulls ahead of me at the middle of the Crossing.

As I race down the back half of the bridge, my foot slips in an uneven gap between rocks. I stumble towards the side of the bridge and throw my arms out to keep my balance. Ravenous rapids churn below me while I tightrope along the edge of the Crossing. Trying to keep enough speed to make it across before the next wave, I veer towards the center of the bridge. I regain my balance and stabilize my path as a new wall of water rises from the river.

Tela reaches the end of the bridge and coasts to a stop on the rocky bank. After the new wave crests, it collapses down on the bridge. Water splashes from the top of the Crossing and onto my back at the same time I feel firm ground under my feet. I slow to a jog, stop beside Tela, and gasp for air.

"See," Tela says, breathing heavily. "That wasn't so bad."

"Maybe not for you," I pant.

"Do you need to me to carry you the rest of the way?" she asks.

"Like that would ever happen," I mumble.

After we grin at each other, I follow her into the Barrens on the western side of the river.

Chapter 14

We travel due west for about an hour and stop an on elevated plateau. The hill itself isn't very tall, no higher than a ten-story building. The western incline below us is at roughly a forty-five-degree angle to the flat ground below. The smooth, glossy surface is made of reflective rock that reminds me of black onyx. At the base of the hill, a flat, empty plain stretches to the horizon. The dirt is dull, lacking in any luster, and I don't see a single tree in sight.

"The light that reflects from the side of the hill carries across the flats," Tela says. "The beams are as pure and strong as you'll find in Krymzyn. If you can focus all your particles in just a few of the brightest rays, you should be able to increase your usual speed by about thirty percent."

"Do we start the count at the bottom of the hill?" I ask.

"No," she answers before pointing to a distant rock. "Start at the Flying Rock."

As I squint across the plain, I spot a towering lone rock in the distance. Extending from its sides near the top are what look like enormous stone wings spread out in mid-flight.

While once gazing at the stars with my father on Earth, he told me that under the right conditions, the human eye is capable of seeing a flashlight from thousands of miles away. If a person is standing on a mountain on Earth, they can see a solid object three hundred miles in the distance since the curvature of the Earth doesn't interfere with the line of sight. The "infinite plane of Krymzyn" is flat, and its atmosphere is crystal clear. As is the case now, I'm often amazed by how far I can see here.

"Are the wings natural?" I ask.

Tela nods. "When the rock was formed at The Beginning, they were left on its sides."

"How far away is it?"

"About two hundred miles. It's much larger than it looks from here."

"Where do we end our count?" I ask.

"The Stone Fist," she answers. "It's the only other tall rock formation you'll see across the plain. It's exactly two thousand miles from the Flying Rock."

"How do you know how far apart they are?" I ask.

"Someone measured it once."

"How?"

She returns her gaze to the Flying Rock. "The Flying Rock is exactly two hundred and twelve miles from here."

"How do you know that?"

"I just calculated it."

"You can look at something and know exactly how far away it is?" I ask in disbelief.

"Of course," she replies, turning her face to me again. "Can't you?"

"I can only estimate," I answer.

"We know the exact distance. I look at something and

instantly know how far away it is."

"This place never ceases to amaze me," I say. "So how did someone measure the distance between the two rocks? You can't see that far, can you?"

"Of course not," she answers. "But long ago, a Traveler calculated the distance by stabbing spears in the ground. He could see each one from a few hundred miles away. He worked his way across the plain and added the distances."

"Why would he do that?" I ask.

"So that Travelers could get their count and compare speeds. It's been our tradition ever since."

"It doesn't seem very Krymzyn-like," I comment.

She shrugs her shoulders. "Travelers have always been a little different."

"I guess that's why I became one," I say.

"You are from another world," Tela replies. "That's about as different as you can be."

I smile at her. "It sure is."

"Drink all the sap in your canister," she says. "You want as much energy as you can have."

We both guzzle our sap until the canisters are empty. Once Tela is finished, she lays her canister and spear on the ground.

"What are you doing?" I ask.

"Leave your things here. We'll come back for them."

"Is that safe?"

"It's never been a problem in the past," she answers. "There aren't any trees around here, so there shouldn't be any Murkovin. They can't catch us anyway."

"I guess not," I say. "Should we take our flasks with us?"

She nods her head. "Let's keep them with us. They don't slow us down much and we'll want more sap when we're finished."

I toss my spear and canister to the ground beside Tela's things. She and I walk to the edge of the slope and look down at the bottom.

"Everything you've got," she says.

"You, too," I reply.

"Ready?"

"Let's do it."

We explode down the side of the hill. When the beams burst into my vision, they're pure and brilliant white. With little or no reflection from the ground at the base of the slope, reflected light shoots straight across the plain. As soon as my body jolts forward, I funnel all of my particles into the most powerful beams.

I immediately sense how much faster I'm traveling across the wide-open space. My running motion is smooth and constant while I narrow my vision into the light leading my way. With the energy of so much sap pumping through my veins, my particles soon sting from the speed I unleash. Before I know it, Tela and I pass the Flying Rock and I begin my count.

Freeing my mind of any other thought, I let the numbers flow through my head. Out of the corner of my eye, I see the streaks of Tela's body right by my side. With flat, even ground and no hills to navigate around, we blister across the flats.

When the Fist of Stone begins to take shape in the distance, we're still neck and neck. The enormous rock pillar looks exactly like an arm with a clenched hand on top. The creases in the round top of the gigantic stone perfectly shape four curled fingers with a thumb pressed against the inner two.

Making a mad rush towards the finish, I burn forward with everything I have. As the Fist of Stone flies towards me, it's nothing but a blur. Tela and I torpedo past it in a dead heat.

I exit from the beams and slow to a jog. When I finally come to a stop, I drop my hands to my knees and inhale like a vacuum. Sucking down air, Tela trots to my side, rests her hands on her waist, and looks up at the sky. After catching my breath, I return to upright and look at Tela.

"That was incredible!"

"What did you have?" she asks, lowering her eyes from the clouds to me.

"Three-eighty-one," I say. "What about you?"

"You won't believe it," she replies. "Three-eighty-one."

"I do believe it. It looked like we crossed the finish at the same time."

"It looked that way to me too." She raises a hand in the air and takes a step towards me with the biggest, brightest smile I've ever seen from her. "We beat Larn!"

I slap her hand with mine. "What was his count?"

"Three-ninety-two," she answers. "He had the fastest time ever."

"Do me a favor, "I say. "We traveled two thousand miles in three hundred and eighty-one seconds. Divide thirty-six hundred by three-eighty-one and tell me what it is."

"What are those numbers?" she asks.

"It's the number of seconds in what we call an _hour_ on Earth divided by the number of seconds we traveled."

"Nine-point-four-four-eight-eight," she says without even thinking about it.

"You can just round it off."

"I did," she replies evenly.

I shake my head, once again in awe at how fast people's minds in Krymzyn can calculate things. "Anyway, multiply that times two thousand."

"Eighteen thousand eight hundred and ninety-seven-point-six."

"Unbelievable," I say. "Almost nineteen thousand miles per _hour_."

"What does that number mean?" she asks.

"Distance compared to time in my world. We use it to calculate speed."

Tela cocks her head to the side. "The people in your world are obsessed with measuring things, aren't they?"

"Yeah, I guess we are. It's mind-boggling how fast we were going."

"The fastest ever," she says. "Except probably for Sash."

"I know she's faster than us, but she's not a Traveler. Her count doesn't matter. She even said so."

"Larn will be proud of us," Tela remarks.

"I'm sure he will," I say, knowing that he'll share the same belief that many great athletes on Earth have—records are made to be broken. "You said that's about thirty percent faster than we'd normally travel?"

"Approximately," she replies.

"Wow," I say. "Even when we're not on the flats, you

and I are killing it with our speed."

"Killing what?" she asks.

"Just another one of my stupid expressions," I answer. "It means that you and I go really, really fast."

"*Awesome* fast!" she exclaims.

"You got that right," I laugh.

After I raise my hand, we slap another high-five with so much force that we fall against each other. Without even thinking about it, I loop one arm around her and pull Tela into a friendly hug.

"I'm thrilled we did this," I say. "I can't tell you how much fun I'm having."

She awkwardly puts her arms around my waist and squeezes me. "Me too. It's much more enjoyable doing this with you than it is alone."

"And now you've had your first hug," I say as we take a step back from each. "It's a custom between friends and family on Earth. I think I explained it to you once."

"I remember," she says thoughtfully. "You told me about hugs and kisses."

I smile at her. "Before you know it, you'll know all the Earth customs."

"I like learning about them," she replies.

"We should do this again sometime."

"We definitely will," she says.

We each take one of the two flasks from our belts and drain the contents. Even though our travel time across the plain was relatively short, it took us about six hours to get to the starting point. I definitely feel how much energy I've expended, especially from reaching the speeds we did across the flats.

After we return the flasks to our belts, we run past the Fist of Stone and travel towards the plateau. Our pace on the return over the empty plain is about half of what it was during our race. We reach the area where we rested before to find our spears and empty canisters right where we left them.

"Instead of going back to the Stone Crossing," Tela says, "we'll travel to the north and use the bridge above the Delta. It's faster from here, and you can learn your way back from this part of the Barrens."

"Sure," I reply, not at all disappointed at missing out on another frenzied dash over the Stone Crossing. "Lead the way."

Chapter 15

Less than an hour into our return trip to the Delta, Tela swerves sharply to the west. She disappears inside a narrow valley as I continue to the north. I glance in her direction several times, but she doesn't reappear. I whip through a u-turn and follow her trail.

Slowing my speed to search for her, I enter the same valley that she did. In a flat area surrounded by low hills at the end, I spot her standing in front of a black-barked tree. I come out of my blend and run up behind her. She looks over her shoulder to make sure it's me.

"What's going on?" I ask, stopping by her side.

"I saw a bright reflection," she says, returning her attention to the tree. "That's why I stopped. Look at that."

I focus my eyes on the tree twenty feet in front of us. The lower branches have all been cut off the trunk. A web of black rope secures the upper limbs in place. In the lower half of the trunk, six steel stakes like the Hunters use are anchored in the bark. Parked at the base of the tree is a sap transport that seems to be brand new. Steel tubes lead from the ends of the stakes to a small opening in the top of the transport.

"Have you ever seen anything like this?" I ask.

"No," she replies, shaking her head. "I've seen a stake stabbed in a tree, but never tubes and a transport."

After Tela scans the hills around us, she walks to the transport. I follow close behind her with my eyes peeled to our sides. When we stop in front of the transport, Tela bangs the tip of her spear against its side. Based on the dull thud and slight echo, it seems to be about half full.

"Where would they get all this?" I ask.

"Raids on Travelers. Hundreds of old transports stolen by Murkovin over thousands of Eras are scattered across the Barrens. Constructs use the tubes for a variety of tasks, and those are Hunters' stakes. They probably cut off the ends to feed the tubes. All of this could have come from the attack that killed Miel."

"It seems kind of elaborate for Murkovin," I say.

"They're not stupid," she replies. "They just lack purpose."

I whirl to a grunt behind me. Jerking up my spear, I knock a steel tip away from my face. A Murkovin elbow slams to my jaw and knocks me to the ground. Before Tela or I can react, another beast pounds into her back. She staggers forward and falls on her knees beside the transport.

I start to swing my spear up, but the Murkovin stomps his foot down on the shaft. A third beast roars in from my side and thrusts his lance at me. Releasing my grip on my weapon, I try to roll out his reach, but his spear gouges my shoulder.

The Murkovin behind Tela jabs a weapon at her skull. Dipping her head under the point, Tela blindly rams her spear backwards. The point slices into the creature's stomach, releasing a stream of blood. As Tela jumps to her feet, she yanks her spear out of the collapsing beast.

The other two Murkovin snap their heads to Tela. Lowering her body in a crouch, Tela grips the shaft of her weapon with both hands. When the two Murkovin lunge their spears at her, I spin my body on the ground. My fists hammer against the back of one's knees while my feet strike the other one's shins. As they stumble from the blows, Tela catapults out of her coiled position. She smacks the shaft of her weapon into the gut of one and then batters the steel to the other one's face.

"Run!" she shouts.

Tela grabs the back of my shirt and drags me to my feet. A surge of pain from the wound in my shoulder shoots down my left arm. Leaving my spear behind, I sprint away from the tree with one hand clamped over the gash. Directly in front of us, three more Murkovin charge over a hill.

"This way!" Tela yells, slashing to our left.

As I try to follow her, I slip in the dirt. I crash to the ground and glance at the tree. Two of the three Murkovin we fought are in pursuit. The one Tela wounded is still writhing on the ground behind them. The three who came over the hill are bearing down on me but still thirty yards away. I leap to my feet, churn my legs, and gallop behind Tela up a steep hill. She slows her pace to check over her shoulder.

"Keep going!" I shout. "I'm right behind you."

As soon as she crosses over the crest, she incinerates into the beams. Desperate for the light rays to appear in my vision, I fly over the top of the hill. The moment I hit the downslope, I jam on my brakes. Less than ten feet in front of me is the edge of a cliff.

I slide across the dirt until stopping just a few inches from the ledge. A sheer face of rock plummets below me to a ravine that's twenty feet deep and twice as wide. Tela's body is sprawled face down at the bottom with her mangled limbs at her sides. On the far wall of the canyon, fresh blood is splattered on the rocks. Since she went into her blend going over the crest, she never would have had time to stop and must have slammed into the far wall.

The ravine is too deep for me to jump into, so I frantically look up and down the canyon. Far in the distance to the north, the gorge shallows while gradually rising to the hilly terrain. I rifle in that direction at the same time the five Murkovin storm over the top of the hill. Zeroing in on the blooms of light, I blow forward into the beams.

Skimming along the edge of the ravine, I keep an eye on the height of the sides. After less than thirty seconds of traveling, I decide they're low enough for me to jump over. I suck my particles out of the light and leap over the edge.

When my feet hit the ground, I lose control and tumble across the dirt. Another bolt of pain seers through my shoulder. Rolling to a stop, I look back at where I just came from. Two shapes of light torpedo along the ledge of the ravine. I spring from the ground and fire into my blend in the direction of Tela.

In the dirt ahead of me, I spot her body and pull my particles out of the light. While running towards her, I glance at the top of the cliff. Three Murkovin are standing near the ledge with their eyes fixed on me. As I begin to slow, two of them heave their spears in my direction. I duck under one and spin away from the other.

After throwing myself to the ground beside Tela, I check the ravine behind us. Two apparitions are sailing straight in my direction. I scoop Tela's limp body from the ground and clutch her against my chest. Sprinting away from the beasts, I look up at the top of the cliff again.

The three Murkovin are running along the ledge above me, but I assume they can't travel since they didn't follow the other two who can. As I stream into the light to the south, two smears appear on my sides.

Angling in front of me, the Murkovin try to cut off my path. I intensify my focus on the beams and tighten my hold on Tela. Flooring my internal accelerator, I blast ahead between the two beasts. They fall out of my peripheral vision as I streak farther along the winding ravine.

Through the particles of my body pressed to her, I can feel Tela's heartbeat. It's rapid but weak, and her breathing is erratic. I don't know if I should have moved her with all the injuries she has, but it was my only option. Her best hope for survival now is if I can find a place to stop. Her life depends upon me getting sap on her wounds, and I have to figure out a way to get some inside her.

The sides of the canyon tower increasingly higher as the ravine cuts deeper into the landscape. At least five hundred miles go by before the sides begin to lower and the ground under my feet starts to rise. When I look behind me, the Murkovin aren't in sight. Although I doubt it's much, I've been able to put some distance between us.

They should anticipate that I'll head northeast to the Delta. If I was wrong about the others not being able to blend their light, they could already be blocking my route. Even if I can navigate around them, I'm not sure Tela will live through the hours needed to reach the Delta. I glance up at the sky to check the direction of the light rays from the clouds. Since they always point to the north, I'm able to confirm my bearings.

The sheer ravine wall on my right gradually dissipates until it's a smooth slope. I shoot up the side and curve around the bottom of a hill. Hoping they won't expect me to double back on the opposite side of the canyon from where they first saw us, I snake between the hills to the northwest. Although I check in every direction, I don't spot the Murkovin in pursuit.

Staying on low ground and using the hills to hide me, I slow my speed to look for a place to stop. As I arc around a slope, I descend into a shallow gully at the bottom of a hill. With the base of the hill on one side of me and a low, steep wall on the other, I should be out of sight from the ground above. Attempting to put as little stress as possible on Tela, I slowly and carefully grind to a stop.

After laying Tela's body on the ground, I press my fingers to her neck. Although her pulse is still there, it's nothing but a faint blip against my skin.

"Tela," I say, gently patting her cheek. "Can you hear me?"

Still unconscious, she doesn't respond. I unclip a flask from my belt and dab a little sap on my fingertips. Hoping that some of it will be absorbed into her bloodstream, I rub the sap on her gums and under her tongue. I only use a tiny amount because I don't want the liquid to choke her.

Scanning her body, I assess her injuries. Her left shin is broken with a sharp point of bone sticking out through her blood-soaked pants. Obviously fractured as well, the ankle of her other leg is twisted so that the foot is at a forty-five-degree angle to her leg. Cuts, abrasions, and blood cover her face and arms, but I'm even more worried about the lump sticking out of the back of her neck. I don't need to be a doctor to know that her neck is broken.

"Stay with me, Tela," I whisper. "I'll figure something out."

Chapter 16

I need to work on Tela's injuries right away, but I don't want to do it in the open. Looking up the ravine to the north, I notice a mound of boulders piled against one side of the gully wall. The rocks seem to have rolled down the slope of the hill over time and accumulated at its base. As I study the boulders, I think I see a crease wide enough for a body to fit through. I return the flask to my belt and run to the pile of rocks.

Between the boulders and the side of the ravine lies a narrow crevice no more than three feet wide and five feet tall. I climb over a few rocks to get to the opening and lean my head inside the gap. Although it's too dark to see very far, there's a small, natural tunnel inside. The faint sound of dripping water echoes off the walls.

"A cavern," I say to myself.

I climb out of the opening and run back to Tela. After sliding my arms underneath her neck and legs, I gingerly lift her in my arms. As I walk to the pile of rocks, I search the terrain around us again. I don't see any Murkovin by the time I reach the entrance, so I decide this is our best hope for a place to hide.

To fit us both through the small opening, I have to drop

Tela's feet to the ground. Gripping under her arms, I stabilize her head against my chest and then step backwards into the tunnel. As I drag her through the passage, I have to duck at times because the ceiling is so low. At several points, the walls on the sides are tight enough that they scrape against my arms. After maybe thirty feet, I reach a small cavern.

"Awaken," I say.

When no light appears, I peer around the inside of the cave. It's too dark for me to make out any detail. I can't blindly work on Tela's wounds.

"Where can I get light?" I mumble.

As my last word bounces off the cavern walls, a purple glow spreads across the cavern. I look up to see hundreds of tiny holes in the black shale ceiling. The light seems to come from deep within the rock and radiate from a hollow maze that's woven throughout the top of the cave.

Light, I think in my head. *That's the trigger.*

The entire cavern is no bigger than a small bedroom. The floor has a slight downward slant from the tunnel entrance to the back wall. A few rocks are scattered around the edges of the oval cave, but the center is bare. At the far end of the cavern from the tunnel, a foot-wide trickle of water drizzles over the uneven rock wall. The water forms a tiny pool at the base, no more than a puddle really, and then drips into a long, thin crack in the ground.

I lay Tela down in the center of the cavern with her head pointing towards the tunnel and her feet towards the water. The eerie purple light casts a deathly pallor on her face. Resting on my knees beside her, I take her two flasks off her belt and set the one that's empty aside. I have one almost-full flask left that I remove from my belt as well.

Since blood is still running down my arm from the wound in my shoulder, I decide that I better deal with that before trying to help Tela. I won't be much good to her if I pass out from losing too much blood. After sparingly pouring sap on my palm, I rub it on the wound. The burning pain recedes and the bleeding soon stops.

Wanting to save all I can for Tela, I take two small sips from the flask. We used a lot of energy traveling to the flats and racing over them, but we also drank a considerable amount of sap. That's probably the only thing keeping Tela alive right now.

Beginning on the leg with the bone sticking out of her shin, I rip her pant leg off at the knee. Trying to remember everything Larn did when he set the compound fracture I had in my arm, I start by pouring sap over the wound and softly rubbing it on the bloody skin around the gash. Bracing the back of her leg with one of my hands, I apply steady pressure with my other hand to push the bone back into place. The crackling sound turns my stomach, but Tela doesn't move.

Based on what Larn did to me, if I can get the bone close to where it belongs, the sap will do the rest of the repair. Once her leg is as straight as I can get it, I pour a little more sap over the shredded skin. The bleeding stops as I rub my hand over the wound, and a thick scab begins to form on her leg.

Since her broken right ankle didn't pop through the skin, it should be a little easier to set. After removing the boots from both her feet, I slide her pant leg up to the top of her calf. While pressing one hand to her ankle, I slowly straighten her foot. It's impossible for me to determine exactly where the fracture is with her ankle swollen to the size of a grapefruit. All I can do is spread sap over the puffy area, push the bone to where I think it should be, and hope for the best.

Once I finish with her legs, I empty the first flask by rubbing the liquid all over the cuts on her face and arms. One of her shoulders is badly bruised, probably from the impact with the canyon wall. If it's dislocated, I don't want to try to set it now. I worry that getting her shoulder back into place might make her neck worse than it already is.

From the second flask, I dribble a small amount of sap onto my hand and spread it over Tela's black-and-blue shoulder. Wanting something to brace her neck, I slip the empty canister from around my neck, set it aside, and take off my shirt. After folding it several times, I slide it under Tela's head.

Kneeling at the top of her head, I coat the back of Tela's neck with a liberal amount of sap. With both my hands, I slowly press my fingers against the lump that's sticking out of the spine at the base of her skull. When I pop it back into place, her body jerks stiff and then immediately goes limp. Shivering from the thought that I might have killed her, I lower my ear to the center of her chest.

"Thank God," I sigh, still hearing a faint heartbeat.

I return to upright and gently slide my fingers up and down the back of her neck. Although there's a little unevenness, the large bump is gone and her spine feels relatively straight. Using my fingertips, I align the remaining inconsistencies in her vertebrae as best I can. Finally, I grip the sides of her head and gently pull it towards me in an attempt to straighten her neck through makeshift traction. I hold her head in the extended position for a full minute and then rest it on the folded shirt.

Still on my knees, I scoot around to her side. I shake the flask and estimate that only about two sips remain. I drip a little more sap into Tela's mouth and rub it on the insides of her cheeks and gums.

"Tela, wake up," I say several times.

Her eyes don't open and she doesn't make a sound. Thinking back again to when Larn healed my broken arm, he poured half a canister of sap on the break. I drank the other half. I've used far less than that on Tela's entire body.

Considering how severe her injuries are and the large amount of blood she's lost, she'll never live through a journey back to the Delta. If I go on my own and come back with help, the round trip will take at least ten hours. I can't risk leaving her alone for that long. If she doesn't die from her injuries, the Murkovin could find her. The only solution is to get more sap as fast as I can.

The wild sap of the Barrens didn't change Balt into a Murkovin overnight. His transition seemed to be gradual, leading me to the conclusion that it takes a while to fully change a person. As much as I don't want to, my only option is to use wild sap. Fortunately, I know exactly where to get it.

Chapter 17

"I'll be back soon," I say to Tela. "Hang on a little longer."

I raise the flask that still has a little sap in it to my lips. One large gulp drips into my mouth. I clip all four flasks to my belt, carefully take Tela's empty canister from over her shoulder, and find mine on the ground. After standing to my feet, I drape the canisters around my neck.

As I step into the tunnel, I stop to look back at Tela. If she regains consciousness, I don't want her to wake up in the dark. But if a Murkovin pokes around the rocks, they might see the light.

"Dark," I say, trying the opposite of the word that ignited the purple.

The light fades away, leaving a dull silhouette of Tela on the ground. I feel my way through the tunnel until I reach the end. Before stepping through the seam in the boulders, I listen for any sounds. Not hearing anything, I slither outside to the gully.

After surveying the hillside above me and the ravine ledge on the other side, I break into a sprint to the south. Almost immediately, I stop and spin around. Nothing is moving behind me, but I wanted to make sure that no one was in hiding and waiting for me to show myself.

Keeping my traveling speed to a minimum, I eventually reach the canyon that I escaped through with Tela. I find a spot to cross to the other side and then return to the area where we first saw the transport. On a hilltop about a mile away from where Tela fell over the cliff, I search the wasteland for any sign of Murkovin. Far in the distance to the east, I spot a single blur of light, but it's heading away from me.

Sprinting from large boulder to large boulder and pausing behind each one, I descend the hill and cross the uneven ground to the outside of the low hills surrounding the tree and transport. Careful not to disturb a single rock or make a sound, I climb to the top of a knoll on the southern side of where the tree stands. When I reach the crest, I peek over a rocky ridge.

On the far side of the tree, three Murkovin sit together on the side of another hill. I'm certain it's the same three who were standing on the ledge when I rescued Tela from the canyon. Two are dressed in ragged, black clothes, and the third only in a pair of pants. All of them have steel spears in their hands.

The body of the Murkovin Tela wounded is no longer by the tree. I don't know if he died or was taken somewhere to heal, but I don't care. What I need right now is a weapon, but there aren't any spears on the ground by the tree. At the very least, mine should be there and probably the wounded creature's as well. It occurs to me that maybe the Murkovin haven't gone to the canyon to retrieve the spears they threw at me and are using the two that should be by the tree.

I creep back down to the bottom of the hill, run around it, and then jog up the slope of another hill to the edge of the deep canyon. Tela's spear is still lying on the dirt at the bottom as well as the two Murkovin weapons that were thrown at me. I have no intention of fighting the beasts, but I'll feel better if I have one with me. More importantly, a spear will help the plan that's taking shape in my mind.

I run along the ledge of the canyon to the north. When I reach the same place that I jumped from before, I spring into the gully. I travel to the spears, snatch two from the ground, and return to the area by the Murkovin camp. This time, I stop outside the northern side of the circle of low hills. If the Murkovin haven't moved, they should be sitting on the other side of the hill that's in front of me.

While examining the base of the hill, I see several boulders large enough for a person to hide behind. Staying low to the ground, I jog to one of the rocks and stab a spear in the dirt behind it. I adjust the exposed tip so that only a few inches of steel stick out above the top of the rock, but enough to be seen from the hilltop.

Taking the other spear with me, I quietly climb the slope and look over the top. With their backs facing me, the Murkovin are still sitting in the same spot they were before. After backing a few feet away from the crest, I crawl fifty yards to my left. Along the way, I gather a few baseball-sized stones.

I climb into a shallow wash that's been formed by rainwater running down the hill. Once inside, I decide it's deep enough that the Murkovin won't see me from where I hope they go. I slide on my stomach to the very top of the hill and check to make sure the creatures are still in the same place. Finding that they haven't moved, I scoot a few feet down from the crest and sit upright.

One after the other, I rapid-fire the small stones at the boulder that I left the spear behind. Loud, clacking sounds ring out when each rock hits its mark. As soon as the last one leaves my hand, I flatten my body inside the narrow wash.

I inch my way up to the top of the hill again. Through a crack between two rocks on the crest, I watch the shirtless Murkovin scurry to the top of the hill. He locks his eyes on the tip of the spear that I left behind the boulder and then waves an arm for the others to join him.

The two Murkovin climb the hill to where the shirtless one stands. Spreading out a few feet from each other, they step down the slope towards the spear. When they're halfway to the bottom, I slither over the top of the hill to the other side. I rise to a crouch and quietly but hastily make my way down the slope. As I near the bottom of the hill, I glance back at the top. The Murkovin haven't reappeared and should still be on the other side looking for someone who isn't there.

I dash across the small flat space to the tree. After stopping with my back to the front of the transport, I grab one of the handles with my empty hand. With my other hand, I clamp the spear to the second transport handle. Once I'm sure I can keep everything in my grip, I take off running. Never once looking back, I scorch into the light.

I weave through a short valley and then bank to the south. Staying away from high ground, I angle towards the west. I look over my shoulders several times but don't see anyone behind me. When I reach the end of the long canyon

I escaped through with Tela, I cross to the other side.

In case I'm seen, I don't want to stop anywhere near the cavern that Tela is hidden in. I weave through the hills until I'm about two hundred miles southwest of the cave. I coast to a stop in front of a deep wash carved in the side of an enormous hill. I drag the transport inside the rocky walls to conceal it as best I can.

Kneeling between the handles, I fill the empty canisters and flasks from the release valve at the front of the transport. When the last one is full, I consider drinking some for myself. After a brief internal debate, I decide not to have any wild sap until it's absolutely necessary.

I speed back to the gully where I left Tela and come out of my blend roughly half a mile from the entrance to the cavern. While jogging the rest of the way, I glance around for Murkovin. Even though I want to get back to Tela as fast I can, I stop near the pile of boulders and wait a full minute to see if anyone else appears. Once I decide that I'm safely alone, I squeeze through the opening in the rocks and hurry through the tunnel to the cave.

"Light," I call out when I enter.

As purple shimmers across the walls of the cavern, I drop my spear to the ground and fall on my knees beside Tela. Holding my breath, I rest my ear on her chest to listen for a heartbeat. I slowly exhale with relief when I hear a weak but steady thump.

Using an entire canister of sap, I rub the liquid on her legs, arms, and shoulders. The swelling around her broken ankle has gone down a little and her other leg hasn't bled anymore. The sap I already used on her seems to be having the miraculous healing effect that it should.

I rub more on the back of her neck and spread tiny globs over the insides of her lips. After rubbing my sap-soaked fingertips under her tongue, I try to figure out a way to use the spear to open a small hole in her body and inject sap into her bloodstream. When a faint moan vibrates from Tela's throat, I abandon that idea.

"Tela," I say. "Can you open your eyes?"

"Chase," she murmurs.

"You need to drink sap."

Her eyes open into tiny amber slits. I hold the canister to her lips and drizzle about a teaspoon into her mouth.

"Swallow," I say. "You have to get it down."

She clenches her jaw and strains her neck muscles while struggling to get down one gulp. As it goes down her throat, she trembles from the pain.

"Your neck is broken," I say. "Don't try to talk. If you think you can swallow another sip, blink twice."

Her eyelids slowly close, open again, and then close once more. When they re-open, I press the steel to her lower lip. Barely tilting the canister up, I dribble a little more sap onto her tongue. She gags trying to swallow it, so I lift the back of her head two inches off the ground. Her body convulses from the movement and she squeezes her eyes shut, but she manages to swallow the sap. I lower her head to the pillow again.

"I think that's enough for now," I say. "Get a little strength back first. We'll try again later."

With her eyelids half closed, she tries to focus her eyes on me. "Don't leave," she whispers.

"I won't," I say. "I'm right beside you."

After she closes her eyes, I lean my face down so that my lips are beside her ear.

"You're safe," I say. "I won't let you die."

She pushes the back of her hand against my leg. I tenderly take it into my grasp and hold it until she falls asleep. After her hand goes limp, I lay it on the ground.

After crawling to one side of the cavern, I lean my back against the wall. For several hours, I sit and watch Tela sleep. Every half hour, I check to make sure that her breathing and heartbeat are still there. Each time I find they are, my mind is put a little more at ease.

Although I fight to stay awake as long as I can, complete exhaustion finally sets in. Unable to avoid the inevitable any longer, I close my eyes.

Chapter 18

I'm disoriented when I wake up and have no idea how long I slept. The gloomy purple light is an instant reminder of where I am and the desperate situation we're in. After scooting over to Tela, I lay one hand on the center of her chest. It's hard to tell with her sleeping, but her breathing seems to be a little stronger than it was the last time I checked.

My body aches as I stand to my feet, just one sign of how depleted I feel. I peek into the tunnel to make sure no one has come inside and then sit back down beside Tela. Looking at the full canister resting beside her head, I decide not to drink any wild sap until I know more about how she's doing.

"Tela," I say in a hushed voice. "Wake up."

When she doesn't immediately respond, I repeat her name several times and lightly run my fingers over her cheek. Her skin is crusty with a mixture of dried blood and sap. She finally blinks her eyes open, but they're glassy and distant.

"Where are we?" she asks in a weak, raspy voice

"Try to drink some sap before you talk."

I pick up the full canister, twist off the top, and slip a

hand under her neck. As I tilt her head a few inches forward, she gnashes her teeth. When she opens her mouth, I drip a little sap onto her tongue. She chokes at first while trying to swallow, but soon forces it down. Over and over, she agonizingly gulps the small amounts that I trickle into her mouth. Her cheeks flush from the fresh energy in her blood.

"No more," she whispers after about a quarter of the canister is gone.

I lower her head to the pillow. "I can't believe you're alive."

"What happened?" she groggily asks.

"When we tried to get away from the Murkovin, you went over a cliff and crashed into a canyon wall."

She shudders and closes her eyes, probably from the memory of going over the cliff returning to her. "I hit my blend before I saw the cliff. I couldn't stop in time."

"I barely stopped or we'd both be dead."

"Where are we?" she asks, reopening her eyes.

"I found a hidden cavern," I answer. "I didn't think you'd live through the trip back to the Delta."

"How bad am I?"

Not wanting her to panic, I try to keep my voice even and calm. "One of your legs has a compound fracture. The other ankle is broken. I set them both while you were passed out. Your neck is broken. I did as much as I could to fix it. I think your right shoulder is dislocated, but I didn't want to work on it until you were stronger. Tell me if there's anything else that feels injured."

Her eyes wander around the cavern while she inhales a few shallow breaths. "I think my left ribs are cracked."

"Do you feel like they punctured your lungs?" I ask.

"No. They're just sore."

"Then we can deal with that when we fix your shoulder. I don't know if I should have, but I've been using wild sap on you. I didn't have any other choice."

"Where did you get it?" she asks.

"I stole the transport we saw," I answer. "I tricked the Murkovin into thinking I was on the other side of the hill from them. When they went to look for me, I took it."

"You're very resourceful," she murmurs.

"Thanks," I say. "Right now, let's just worry about getting you better."

Like she did before she went to sleep, she rubs the back of her hand against my leg. "Thank you for rescuing me."

"You don't need to thank me, but you're welcome. Besides, you saved my life at the tree."

"It was stupid of me to stop," she says.

"Don't blame yourself. I would have stopped if I saw what you did."

"Thanks," she whispers.

I sympathetically smile at her. "I want to do some more work on you while you're awake. How does your neck feel?"

As soon as she starts to lift her head from the pillow, her body tenses and her eyes water. "I can't move my head."

"Don't worry about trying now," I say. "The inflammation needs to go down first. Just stay still, try to relax, and let me know if anything I do hurts too much."

I stand up and cross the cavern to the small spill of water. Bringing handful after handful of water back to Tela, I wash the bloodstains off her face, arms, and legs. Using the tip of the spear to rip the fabric, I cut her pants leg off above the knee on the leg with the broken ankle.

After rubbing sap on both her legs and checking that the bones seem to be straight, I find two football-sized stones on the side of the cavern. With the fabric I just cut from her pants and the strip I tore off the other leg when we first arrived here, I cover the two rocks. I place them under her knees to prop up her legs in a more comfortable position.

Kneeling above her head, I gently massage several handfuls of sap on the back of her neck. Using my fingers, I again try to align any inconsistencies in the vertebrae of her upper spine. Any time she flinches or cries out, I stop for a few seconds to let her recover. I then carefully extend her neck in a round of traction while she talks me through the amount of tension that doesn't cause her too much pain.

Once I finish with her neck, I scoot to the side of her body. I pour the last of the canister on my palm and slip my hand under her shirt. As I gently rub it over her broken ribs, Tela lets out a soft groan.

"Am I hurting you?" I ask.

"My ribs hurt," she answers quietly, "but it's helping."

I slide my hand out from under her shirt. "We should set your shoulder before any more time passes. Do you feel up to it?"

"I think so," she tells me. "I need more sap first."

I open one of the flasks and help her drink about half of what's inside. After spreading the rest over her bruised shoulder, I use both hands to force the joint into place. She hoarsely wails and her body stiffens.

"I'm sorry," I say. "It had to be done."

"I know," she replies, choking back tears.

"I think that's all we should do for now."

"I need to sleep," she whimpers.

"Not yet," I reply. "I don't want to make a decision without talking to you about it first. Do you want me to go to the Delta and bring back help?"

After staring at the cavern ceiling for a few seconds, she moves her eyes to me. "I don't want to be alone. If the Murkovin find me, they'll kill me."

"I worry about that, too," I say. "I'd carry you back, but I don't think you're stable enough. It might do permanent damage."

"I shouldn't be moved," she confirms. "Are they looking for us?"

I nod my head. "I think so, especially after I stole their transport."

"They might gather others and block our route to the Delta."

I turn my face towards the puddle of water while evaluating our situation. I'm sure Tela's mind is foggy, but everything she says makes sense. I agree that she shouldn't be moved yet, and it had already occurred to me that the Murkovin could try to set a trap. More than anything else, I don't want to leave Tela alone. I would never forgive myself if I went to the Delta and came back to find her dead. Accepting that we're stuck here for a little while, I look at Tela again. She's struggling to keep her eyes open, but I need answers to a few more questions before she sleeps.

"I haven't had any wild sap yet," I say, "but I doubt I have enough energy left to blend my light. How long will it take for it to affect us?"

"You'll feel it right away," she answers.

"Feel what?"

"Extreme emotions. Anger almost to the point of rage, a sense of power, and some other things I don't understand."

"Those things are all common in my world," I say. "I should be able to control them."

She clenches her jaw. "It's hard. It twists your thoughts in a strange way. I'm already fighting it."

"How long until it turns us into Murkovin?" I ask.

"We'll be fine for several days. It takes eight or nine to completely change someone if all they have is wild sap."

"That should give us plenty of time." I want my next words to instill as much confidence in Tela as they can, so I pause for a few seconds to choose them carefully. "This cavern is well hidden and we have more than enough sap. We'll stay here until you're ready to be moved. If the Murkovin show up near here, I'll lure them away and come back to get you."

"That's a good plan," she says.

"I need to go out and get more sap. It shouldn't take long. I hid the transport a few hundred miles from here."

"Why so far?" she asks.

"So if the Murkovin find it, they'll search for us there and not here."

Her eyelids sag. "You really are clever."

"I have my moments," I say. "I just want to do everything I can to help you."

"Please don't be gone long."

"I won't," I reply.

"Will you wait until I'm asleep?" she asks.

"Of course."

After her eyes close again, I hold her hand in mine. I know it doesn't have much meaning to the people of Krymzyn, but I guess the need to show compassion the way we do on Earth will always be with me. Seeming to appreciate the gesture, she softly squeezes my hand.

Just a few seconds later, she's fast asleep. I lay her hand on the ground, check to make sure that her head is in a comfortable position, and then sit down by the tunnel entrance. I feel a little better about Tela's injuries since the wild sap seems to have the same healing power as the sap of the Delta. Tela once told me that it took three days to heal her broken legs when she was younger. I hope that the wild sap can do the same.

With no other choice, I unscrew the top from a full flask. The sap from the Delta energizes me instantly while also having a calming, almost euphoric effect. When I take one large sip of the wild sap, a flamethrower ignites inside me. Without making a conscious decision to do, I drain the rest of what's inside.

As a wave of rabid power flows through my limbs, the muscles in my body involuntarily flex. Trying to relax, I close my eyes. Every part of my being yearns for more sap.

I open my eyes and stare at the steel containers while a battle rages inside my mind. Should I give in and drink more? Or should I try to get some level of control over it now? Several times, I reach for a flask but stop myself before my hand wraps around it. Using the excuse that I need it to blend my light, I finally give in and swig down a second flask.

It does little to quench my thirst.

After another heated mental debate, I win the next fight for control of my brain. I pick up the canisters, flasks, and spear, and then take a few steps inside the tunnel. Pausing for a moment, I look back and call out, "Dark."

When I reach the end of the passage, I don't stop to scan the outside. Clenching my spear in both hands, I boldly jump straight out to the gully. If any Murkovin are nearby, I'd rather kill them now than play a game of cat and mouse. As I did before, I run a few hundred feet down the ravine and then stop to look behind me. The last thing I'll let those cowardly bastards do is trick me into leaving the area so they can have their way with Tela.

While traveling to the south, I have trouble concentrating on the beams. My attention is constantly distracted by the hills that pass by me. To make matters worse, the milky light of the Barrens fades, the clouds tumble into one another, and rain pounds down from the sky. With my blood simmering with a fresh desire for sap, I madly search for a sustaining tree. I'd rip a limb from a trunk in a heartbeat to gratify the incessant hunger gnawing at me.

I spot a tree near the base of a hill and slide to stop. I can't figure out why the limbs aren't moving, but then I notice thin strands of black string hanging from the branches and blowing in the gusts of wind. It's nothing but a thread tree like the ones that grow in the Delta.

After gushing into the few beams that I can find, I finally reach the transport. A shallow, fast-moving stream is now flowing through the wash. I climb over the rocks, jump into the water, and throw myself down beside the transport.

Once my mouth locks to the spigot, I open the valve and drink until I'm nauseous from gluttony.

As I sit up, warmth spreads through my body. Like lit fuses sizzling inside my blood, heat spreads outward from my stomach to the tips of my fingers and toes. With the water still rushing around me, I lean over to fill the canisters and flasks with sap. Realizing that the water has risen almost to the spigot, I bolt upright.

The cavern could flood! I shout in my mind.

My heart pounds faster and faster while panic tightens my chest. I search for my spear, but it's hidden somewhere under the water. Deciding to leave it behind, I sling the canisters around my neck and clip the flasks to my belt. I leap to my feet and bound out of the wash. Slipping and stumbling across the wet dirt, I lurch into a few dull rays.

Heading straight for the cavern, I swish over the bleak hills. I soon descend into the gully and tear my body out of the beams. Sloshing through knee-deep water, I lope towards the pile of rocks. The newborn river has risen almost to the bottom of the tunnel entrance.

When I make it to the crevice, I spring out of the water. As I jam my body through the entrance, my shoulders scrape against the sharp rocks. I barrel through the tunnel with the crash of water in front of me growing louder and louder.

"Light!" I shout once I reach the opening to the cave.

"Chase!" Tela calls out.

I storm through the entrance, drop to my knees beside Tela, and lock my eyes on the far end of the cave. What was once a trickle of water down the wall is now a thick, tumultuous spill. The pool is substantially larger than it was before I left and has risen to Tela's waist.

After grabbing Tela under her arms, I drag her to the higher ground near the tunnel entrance. To keep her body as far away as possible from the spreading pool, I turn her sideways. I place the rocks under her knees again and slip the pillow under her head. She glares at me with flaming amber eyes.

"I could have drowned!" she hoarsely snarls.

"I'm sorry," I say. "I came back as soon as I could."

Her eyes drift away from mine and stop on the waterfall. "I need sap!" she demands.

I open a flask, lift her head with one hand, and hold the steel to her lips. She downs sip after sip until the flask is half empty. After a few deep breaths, she looks at me.

"I'm sorry," she says. "I shouldn't have yelled at you. It was the wild sap. Darkness makes it worse."

"Don't worry about it. I feel it, too. Go back to sleep. I won't leave you again."

I reach out a hand and brush long strands of hair away from her face. She used to have bangs that hung just over her eyebrows, but she's let her hair grow out over the past few months. Her longer hair seems to make her look more mature—more womanly—and I'm not sure that I ever realized how truly attractive she is.

"Thank you for all you're doing for me," Tela whispers.

She immediately passes out. I lean my face down to hers and gently kiss her forehead. After scooting to the mouth of the tunnel, I stare at the swirling pool. It appears to have grown as much as it's going to, so I don't think there's a threat of the cavern completely flooding.

Once I'm confident that the pool won't reach Tela, I walk to the end of the tunnel to make sure the temporary river hasn't risen to the entrance. Water surges through the gully, slams against the rocky banks, and sprays mud in the air. It doesn't seem to have grown much since I got back from the transport, but I decide to monitor it a little longer. If the tunnel floods, Tela and I could drown inside the cavern.

Darkness goes on and on and on. It might be the longest I've experienced since being in Krymzyn. The terrain around me is dark and lifeless, an endless stark landscape of black and gray. I take an occasional swig from a flask while looking out at the dreary landscape. There's no color or detail to anything around me, just murky outlines of vacant hills. What could possibly have made me want to live in Krymzyn? It sure as hell wasn't for this glamorous life.

Even on the Delta, we live like wild animals in caves and drink tree sap to survive. That brain tumor must have really fucked with my mind. I've broken bones, been stabbed by spears, and watched people slaughtered in front of my eyes. I've been chased across a desolate wasteland by creatures that belong in a horror show. I know I came to Krymzyn to be with Sash, but I'm not sure she was worth it.

She wanted to give our daughter away to the goddamn Keepers. What kind of person thinks that way? I sacrificed my life on Earth to be here, abandoned my family and friends, and that's the thanks I get? Take my daughter away from me? If the Tree of Vision hadn't intervened, Sash would have gone through with it. Having a daughter is the only good thing that's happened to me in Krymzyn, but Sash wanted to take her from me.

I think I finally realize where her true loyalty lies. It sure as hell isn't with me. Everything she does is for the great and powerful Krymzyn, the elusive lie of balance that the zealots on the Delta preach all the time. Sash tried to brainwash me into thinking like the rest of the cult.

I grit my teeth, clench my hand into a fist, and hammer it against the rocks. As much as I want to find the assholes who attacked us and bash their goddamn brains in, I can't risk leaving Tela alone during Darkness. While the relentless storm wreaks havoc on the wasteland, one thought echoes in my head.

Why did I ever want to live in this godforsaken world?

Chapter 19

When Darkness finally ends, I return to the cave. Sitting beside Tela, I lean back against the wall. The fall isn't as powerful as it was during the storm, but it's still stronger than before the rain. The pool has receded enough that the edge is several feet away from Tela's side. As I stare at our dismal surroundings, I think the same thought over and over.

What the fuck am I doing here?

I eventually close my eyes and try to sleep. Every time I nod off, I almost immediately jerk upright with cold numbness prickling my skin and shortness of breath. I tell myself that the momentary anxiety attacks are because of the dire situation we're in, but in the back of my mind, I know it's the wild sap. None the less, every time it happens, I take a couple of swigs to restore the feeling of warmth.

Empty hours and more empty hours agonizingly tick by. I occasionally walk to the end of the tunnel to check the ravine, but soon return to the cavern. Sitting with my back against the wall, I never doze off for more than a few minutes during the entire Krymzyn night.

When Tela finally stirs a little, I reach a hand to her and lightly press my fingers against the artery on the side of her neck. While I measure her heart rate, she opens her eyes.

"Your pulse is stronger," I say.

"I feel a little better," she whispers.

"How's your neck?"

She starts to turn her head to the side but winces after moving no more than an inch. "It's stiff. At least I can move it a little now."

"That's a good sign," I say. "What about your legs?"

She tries to raise the leg with the compound fracture, but grabs my arm and immediately gives up. "They hurt a lot. I don't think the wild sap heals as quickly as sap from the Delta."

"At least it's doing something," I reply. "The bone in that leg was sticking out of your skin."

She frowns. "When I broke my legs before, neither one was a compound fracture."

"It may take a while to heal, but you seem more alert now."

Her eyes roam around the cavern. "How did you know how to get light?"

"It was an accident," I tell her truthfully. "I just happened to say the word 'light' out loud. I don't even know what makes it."

"Grubs," she says, returning her eyes to me. "Tiny creatures no bigger than a small twig. They burrow in the ceilings of caverns in the Barrens."

"You owe your life to them. Without their light, we were in bad shape."

Still holding my arm, she tightens her grip on it. "I'm alive because of you."

I smile at her. "Do you feel up to working on your neck?"

"I guess we have to. Do we have sap?"

"A few canisters and flasks," I answer. "Should we see if you can sit up?"

"Let's try," she says.

As I help her sit upright, she moans and bites her bottom lip. I grab a full canister of sap and hold it to her mouth. While I support her neck with one hand, she gradually drinks about half of what's inside. I start to pull the canister away, but she raises a hand to it and pushes it back to her mouth. It takes most of the canister to get her craving fully in check.

I scoot behind her and hold her head in my hands. Gently rotating it to the sides, I only turn her head about an inch in each direction the first few times. Once her muscles seem to loosen, I try to twist her head a little farther.

"No more!" she yells.

"I didn't mean to hurt you," I say.

"You need to be more careful!"

"You need to watch your mouth!" I snap.

After a few moments of uncomfortable silence, she leans back against my chest. Her voice is much softer when she speaks again.

"I'm sorry. I'm having trouble with the wild sap."

"I feel it, too," I say with my anger subsiding. "I'm sorry I talked to you that way. I shouldn't have."

"It's really hard to control sometimes."

I tenderly grip her shoulders in my hands. "Don't feel bad. We just have to stay aware of what it's doing to us. If we pay attention, we can keep it in check."

"Thanks, Chase," she says softly. "Do you think you can help me clean up a little while I'm sitting up?"

"Sure thing."

After making sure she can stay upright on her own, I rinse out an empty canister in the fall and fill it with water. She sits perfectly still while I wash her legs, arms, and face. I pour another canister of water over her head and comb my fingers through her hair. It takes two more refills before the knots, sap, and dried blood are all washed away. Just like in the Delta, her hair dries in a few seconds.

I help her lie down on her back again. As I adjust the pillow under her head, she asks me to spread sap on her injured shoulder and ribs. I rub it on her shoulder first and then reach my hand under her shirt. While lightly gliding my fingertips over her ribcage, the side of my hand accidentally grazes the underside of her breast. The sensation triggers a momentary flutter in my stomach.

"It feels good when you rub sap on me," she says.

I stop my hand on the firm muscles of her stomach. "I'm glad it helps."

"Will you hold me while I fall asleep?" she asks quietly. "It helps me feel safe."

I pull my hand out from under her shirt and set the canister aside. Facing her, I stretch out on the ground with my head resting on one of my arms. After I drape the other arm over her body, she slips her hand inside mine.

"What happened to your shirt?" she asks.

"It's your pillow," I answer. "It's all I had to support your neck."

"I'm sorry I'm putting you through so much," she whispers.

"Don't beat yourself up. This could have happened to anyone."

"But all I do is drink sap and sleep," she replies.

"That's what you need to heal."

She caresses my hand with her fingertips. "You're taking such good care of me. I don't know what I'd do without you."

"I'll never let anything bad happen to you," I say. "After you're asleep, I'll go get more sap. I promise I won't be gone long and I'll come straight back if Darkness falls."

"Thank you."

Her breathing gradually lightens and her hand goes limp in mine. I stay beside her for another few minutes to make sure she's in a deep sleep. After drinking an entire flask of sap, I leave the cavern.

Under idle clouds, I sail through the valleys and hills to the transport. The first thing I see when I stop is my spear lying in the dirt at the bottom of the wash. I snatch it from the ground, refill the canisters and flasks, and then climb the steep slope to the top of the hill. It's the highest peak for hundreds of miles around me.

Turning in a circle, I look for any motion in the bleak wasteland. Far to the northeast—at least five hundred miles away in a direct line between me and the Delta—a shape of light gleams over a hill. A few moments later, another one shoots across the trail of the first. The Murkovin must still be searching the Barrens for us.

"Stupid fuckers," I mumble. "You're looking in the wrong place."

While the two Murkovin crisscross in the distance, I sit down on a large rock. The people in the Delta must think that Tela and I are dead. I wonder if they'll even care. It took them a long time to pretend as though they accept me, but I still get sideways glances and voices laced with distrust. They'll just write us off as casualties of the eternal struggle for balance, bloody road-kill on the ambiguous path of the self-righteous.

Sash is probably using the same kind of philosophical bullshit they all drown themselves in to put me behind her. She already tried to betray me once, and now she can do whatever she wants to with our daughter. If I make it back to the Delta, one thing is for certain. Things are going to change.

But I'm not even sure I want to go back. Life in the Barrens seems simple and uncomplicated. I have no responsibilities other than to take care of myself and help Tela get better. My needs are what count in the Barrens, not some random purpose for the good of Krymzyn assigned to me by a goddamn Tree.

With the transport nearby, I have all the sap I want for the time being. I'm sure I can bind a tree the same way the Murkovin did and drain every drop. Maybe Tela will also want to stay in the Barrens. Unlike Sash, she appreciates everything I do for her and the sacrifices I make.

Once Tela has finished healing, we can tie up a few trees, kill any Murkovin in the area, and have an endless supply of sap. This part of the Barrens can be our own private kingdom, the two of us in complete control. I could even sneak into the Delta, grab Aven, and bring her back here to live with Tela and me. Aven adores Tela.

The little cavern filled with purple light can be our home. We could use thread from the tree I saw to make some fabric, and use the fabric to make a couple of beds stuffed with leaves. After Aven is asleep at the end of each day, Tela and I can take our clothes off, wash each other's bodies in the fall, lay down in our bed and—

"Stop it!" I bellow out loud. "That isn't you talking."

*   *   *

At the end of the day, I spend several hours battling insomnia for the second night a row. I finally give up trying to sleep and walk outside to the ravine. After climbing to the top of the hill that the cavern is under, I survey the surroundings. There's no movement in the valleys and hills, and I don't hear the slightest sound. As I anticipated, the Murkovin seem to have no idea that we're in the opposite direction of the Delta from where they attacked us.

When I estimate that the new day has finally arrived, I return to the cavern. I feel a wave of relief that Tela wakes up as soon as I'm inside. The more I'm alone with my thoughts, the more poisoned they become. Working on Tela's injuries is oddly soothing and helps me pass the otherwise vacant time. Instead of sinking into a mire of contorted thought, I can focus on helping her heal.

After we drink our sap together, I repeat the process of applying it to Tela's wounds. She surprises me by saying that she wants to try to walk. I help her to her feet and stand in front of her. With both of her hands gripping my shoulders and me holding her by the waist, she takes a few steps across the cavern. She decides that she's strong enough to go outside.

I turn my back to her and she wraps both of her arms around my waist. We cautiously inch our way through the narrow tunnel. At the end of the passage, she has to squint her eyes until they adjust to the light.

With my arms around Tela's hips, I lift her off the ground. She clings to my neck as I slowly climb down the rocks. When I reach the center of the gully, I lower her feet to the dirt. She hangs onto my shoulders while I grip her by the waist.

"I'll stay in front of you," I say. "Tell me if it hurts too much,"

"I'll let you know."

As I take a step backwards, she uses me as a crutch while gingerly taking one step forward. On her second step, she stumbles and falls against me. Tightening my grip on her waist, I return her to upright. As we continue up the gully at an extremely slow pace, Tela limps with every step. We stop after no more than twenty feet.

"I just want to stand for a bit," she says. "I'm stiff from lying down so much."

She braces herself with both of her hands on my shoulders.

"You did great," I say. "How do you feel?"

"My left leg hurts more than my right. My neck and back are really sore."

"I guess that rules out a race," I jest.

Tela smiles. "For now, anyway. Maybe later."

"I'll give you a big head start. Besides, my traveling speed isn't as fast as it was."

"There's not as much energy in the wild sap," she informs me, confirming what I'd already guessed.

I want to address the most important subject since she's doing better, but I also want her to feel comfortable with any decision made. It's getting harder to keep my thoughts clear and the almost constant desire for sap under control.

"You seem well enough for me to carry you back to the Delta," I say. "But like I said, my traveling speed is slower. It'll be even worse carrying you. I doubt I'm any faster than the Murkovin right now. If they cut us off, you're in no condition to fight. But I'm willing to try if that's what you want to do."

"Do you think they quit looking for us?" she asks.

"No," I answer. "The transport is hidden in a gully at the base of the tallest hill in sight. The last time I went for sap, I climbed to the top and saw two Murkovin traveling in the distance. They were searching for something between here and the Delta. I'm sure it was us."

She looks off to her side in thought for several moments and then back at me. "How long have we been here?"

"I think this is the third day. It's hard to keep of track of time out here."

"Let's give it another day or two," she says. "Maybe I can travel by then. They also might stop looking for us. There's less risk if you don't have to carry me."

"Are you sure we have that much time?" I ask.

"I'm sure."

180

I nod my head. "Then a couple of days it is."

Tela raises one hand to the side of my face. "Your eyes are purple."

"Halfway between blue and red," I reply. "Yours are kind of dark orange."

She lowers her hand to my shoulder. "Halfway between amber and red. I think I should get back to the cavern now."

"Do you want me to carry you or do you want to walk?" I ask.

"I'll walk with your help," she answers. "Just be ready to catch me."

"I won't let you fall."

"I wouldn't mind washing in the fall as long as I'm up," she says.

"If you're up to it."

With our arms around each other and me supporting most of her weight, we return to the cavern. After I guide her to the small fall, we both stand in the shallow pool. Facing the trickle of water, she rests one hand against the wall to help her stay upright. I hold her waist in my hands and support her from behind. Using several handfuls of water, she rinses her face and arms.

"I don't want to try to clean my hair right now," she says. "I'm too sore."

As I help her turn around, she unexpectedly puts her arms around me. She presses her body to mine and lays her head on my shoulder. I slip my arms around her.

"It feels good to hold onto you," she says.

"We've been through a lot together," I reply.

"You must be annoyed. All you do is take care of me."

She raises her face from my shoulder and looks at my eyes.

"Not at all," I say. "I enjoy being with you."

"Me, too," she smiles. "I need to get off my feet."

I walk her to the center of the cavern, help her lie down on the ground, and prop her legs up on the rocks. With her head elevated on my shirt, we share a canister of sap. Once we've both had our fill, I stretch out on the ground beside her.

"I don't feel like sleeping yet," she says, "but I was too tired to stay on my feet any longer."

"What do you want to do?" I ask.

"Will you tell me more about your world?"

"Sure," I say.

For the next few hours, we talk about life on Earth. I've shared tidbits with her over time, but with nothing else to do right now, I can go into more detail. She's fascinated by my description of cities, skyscrapers, automobiles, and airplanes. We talk about my family on Earth, and she asks questions about how people date and fall in love.

When her eyelids begin to droop, Tela takes my hand in hers and pulls my arm over her waist. I scoot closer to her so that my body gently presses to hers. After a few minutes pass, she drifts into slumber. Enjoying the calm I feel from being beside her, I listen to the water drip over the rocks by our feet.

My eyes eventually begin to close, so I call out, "Dark." Curled up beside Tela, for the first time since drinking the wild sap, I fall into a deep sleep.

Chapter 20

Another four days pass with essentially the same routine. After I treat Tela's injuries, we go outside for a walk. Although her motion is understandably limited at first, she gradually gains enough strength to jog up and down the gully. We spend most of each day seated on the hillside beside the cavern comparing the life I had on Earth to her life in Krymzyn. Whether it's on purpose or just by coincidence, neither of us ever mentions Sash.

Whenever Darkness falls, we sit side by side in the cavern and share flask after flask of sap. Near the end of each day, I help Tela wash in the tiny waterfall. Maybe because it comforts her after all that she's been through, or maybe because it's what happened after the first time I helped her clean off in the spill, we always end up standing in a long embrace.

Twice each day, I travel to the transport to replenish our supply of sap. Every time I go, I sit alone on the crest of the hill for a few minutes. While looking out over the somber badlands, I become increasingly dismayed with my decision to live in Krymzyn. Trapped in a shroud of toxic thought, I convince myself that Sash tricked me into coming to this world for her own needs.

She used me to understand the emotions from Earth that she was feeling and never once cared about how difficult it was for me to give up my life in my world. She proved that by wanting to give our daughter away. She's a master of control, a manipulative puppeteer with everyone in Krymzyn dangling from the ends of her strings. When those thoughts send me plummeting into a chasm of rage and self-pity, my only salvation is to chug down a canister of sap and race back to Tela.

At the end of each day, Tela and I lie down side by side. She eventually tells me that she's tired of sleeping on her back and wants to try on her side. After I place my rolled-up shirt underneath my head, she curls up beside me with her head resting on my bare shoulder. She gently nuzzles my neck and I lightly stroke her hair until we fall asleep.

Eight days after the attack at the tree, I wake up early and go to the transport for sap. When I return to the cavern, I scrape my arm against one of the rocks in the tunnel opening. I look down at the cut in my forearm.

Dark purple blood—almost black to the eye—oozes from the wound. My skin is pale and the veins underneath it pulse with the same putrid color as the blood that's dripping from the cut. Stained with the dirt of the wasteland, my body and pants are filthy. I close my eyes and run a hand through my grimy, stringy hair.

"How could I let this happen," I whisper in a brief moment of lucidity.

As soon as I'm inside the cavern, I call out, "Light." The purple glow illuminates Tela still asleep on the floor. I set the flasks, canisters, and spear on the ground and cross the cave to the fall.

Using water cupped in my hands, I douse my head and scrub my hair. Pouring handful after handful over my face and body, I wash until my skin feels clean. After slipping out of my pants, I rinse them off and toss them aside. I lean down and take the boots off my feet. Since they're caked with dirt inside and out, I clean them in the small pool. Holding them in one hand, I stand upright again and rest my forehead against the rocks.

"Are you alright?" Tela asks, startling me.

I turn my head to her. She's sitting with her back against the wall and an open canister in one hand. Since nudity doesn't seem to be a big deal in Krymzyn, I don't try to cover myself.

"I'm fine," I answer. "I just realized how dirty I am."

"You've been spending all your time helping me," she says.

"I don't know how you could stand to be around me."

"It's not hard." She slowly lowers her eyes from my face down to my feet. "It's no wonder you're so fast. You have the perfect body for a Traveler."

"Thanks," I say. "How are you feeling?"

She looks at my face again. "The best I've felt since we've been here. I want to see if I can travel."

"Let me finish washing off and then we'll go outside."

I quickly rinse my face and body one last time. Feeling refreshed, I redress in my pants and boots. When Tela finishes drinking her sap, she slips her boots on her feet. I reach my hands down and pull her to her feet.

"We really need to get back to Delta," I say. "We're out

of time."

"I know what we need to do," she replies with obvious irritation.

"You've been drinking wild sap for eight days. I've been drinking it for seven."

"Did you hear me?" she snips. "I already said that I know."

I bite my tongue to stop from verbally lashing out at her. After all I've done for her since we've been in the Barrens, she has no right to talk to me that way. With the veins in my forehead starting to bulge, I step past her to the tunnel and pause by the entrance to grab my spear.

"Let's see if you can travel," I say without looking back. "If not, I'll carry you."

"Chase . . . I'm sorry."

I glance over my shoulder at her. "This is why we have to get back. It's getting harder and harder to control."

"I know," she replies evenly. "Will you help me outside?"

With Tela's hands clenched to my waist, I guide her through the tunnel. At the end of the passage, I help her step down the rocks and into the gully. Loosening up before she tries to travel, she slowly rotates her head and shakes her arms by her side.

Outside in the light, I clearly see that the once blue streaks in her hair have faded to icy-white strands. The centers of her eyes are red and dissipate outward to dark orange. The veins under her skin are the same purplish-black as mine. When she finishes stretching, she jogs up the gully to the north. I run by her side and stay at her pace.

"What do you think?" I ask.

She turns her face to me and widens her eyes. "Go!" she shouts.

With her legs flexing into contoured lines of muscle, she sprints ahead of me. It takes me a few seconds to realize that she was challenging me to a race. After Tela runs about twenty yards, she blasts into the light and disappears around the curve of the gully. I charge forward, enter the beams, and arc around the bottom of the hill.

Tela only travels a few miles before coming out of her blend. As she coasts to a stop, I exit the light and jog to her side.

"How did it feel?" I ask.

She rubs the back of her neck with one hand. "The initial jolt hurt my neck, but I felt fine once I was traveling. I didn't want to go very far to be safe."

"I'll carry you to the Delta if you think it's too much," I tell her.

"I think I'll be fine," she says. "My left leg still hurts, but it's not bad. If I start feeling too much pain, you can carry me the rest of the way."

"What if the Murkovin come after us?"

She squints her eyes while thinking and looks to the north. "You said that we're west of where they attacked us, right?"

"A few hundred miles," I answer.

"We can travel due north," she says, returning her attention to me. "We can go way past where the Delta is, cut across the Barrens to the river, and follow it back down to the bridge north of the Delta. If they're searching for us between here and the Delta, they'll never see us."

"That makes a lot of sense."

She smirks at me. "I have my moments, too."

"You sure do."

A few raindrops splatter on top of my head. The billows above us roll into motion and the light fades away. My blood instantly simmers with the insatiable appetite unleashed by Darkness.

"Let's get to the cavern," I say.

We both take off down the gully. Although Tela sputters forward a few times, she never fully blends with the murky rays. She finally gives up trying to travel in the dark, so we have to settle for running to the cavern.

"It's hard to focus," she shouts over the wind.

"Believe me," I yell. "I've already learned that."

By the time we're halfway to the cave, we're wallowing through knee-deep water. Afraid that she's still too weak to make it through the rising river on her own, I grab Tela's arm and swing her onto my back. With her arms clutched across my chest, she locks her legs around my waist. I loop my free hand under one of her legs.

The force of the water pounding against the back of my legs almost knocks me down several times. Using my spear to help me stay upright, I finally make it to the tunnel entrance without falling. After I lower Tela's feet to the ground, she clings to my shoulders from behind as we hurry through the cramped passage. Inside the cavern, we plop down on the ground and ravenously share two flasks of sap.

"How much do we have left?" Tela asks.

"One full canister and two flasks," I answer.

"That should be enough to make it back to the Delta."

"Do you want me to go out for more?" I ask.

"No," she says, shaking her head. "We can stop at the transport before heading to the Delta if you think we need to. Where is it?"

"Two hundred miles southwest of here."

She looks down at her empty flask. "I'll miss the warm feeling."

"You can always go the Dunes," I tell her.

"It's not the same."

I take the last swig from my flask and stand to my feet. After stepping through the expanding pool, I raise one leg at a time under the fall to wash off the mud. With the rain outside fueling a powerful rush, my pants and boots are clean in no time. Tela stands and crosses the cavern to me.

"Since there's a real waterfall right now," she says, "I want to clean off before we leave. We can head to the Delta as soon as Darkness ends."

"All yours."

I walk to the other side of the cave and sit down by the tunnel entrance. With her back to me, Tela steps to the spill, tilts her head forward, and lets the water run through her hair. After reaching her hands to the back of her head, she lightly massages her neck. Her fingertips slide to the top of her shirt and grip the fabric.

Slow and supple in her motion, she lifts the shirt over her head. When it's off her body, she rinses it clean and then throws it to the dry ground beyond the shallow pool. Somewhere in the back of my mind, I have the decency to look away. But with the primal desires of Darkness clouding my thoughts, I can't find it. Like a wild animal locked on its prey, I'm captivated by her every move.

She turns around, closes her eyes, and leans her head back to the water. Beads of water glitter with violet as they trickle down her chest, slither over her full, round breasts, and drip off her rose-colored nipples. Her skin is ivory and smooth, her stomach flat and taut. Lowering her face, she opens her eyes and notices my gaze. A slight blush reddens her cheeks.

Tearing my eyes away from her, I focus on the ground between my feet. The cavern is so small that I can't help but notice that she slips her pants down her legs. After washing them off, she tosses them to the floor by her shirt.

Aphrodite might as well have cast her spell over me. Enchanted by the thought of Tela naked in the fall, I can't stop my eyes from drifting to her. The sensual curves of her hips lead to shapely, muscular legs that could belong to a powerful sprinter. Between her legs, a narrow triangle of fine, black hair glistens from the water running through it. Intoxicated by every detail of her body, I raise my eyes over her torso, up her shoulders and neck, and then stop them on her face. She's staring straight at me. Her puffy red lips curl into a faint smile.

"Your hair is darker," she says.

"What do you mean?" I ask.

Never taking her eyes off mine, she walks across the cavern. When she stops in front of me, she reaches a hand down. I take it in mine and she helps me stand to my feet. After letting go of me, she raises her hand to the side of my head. She combs her fingers through my hair and then rests her hand on the back of my neck.

"It must be from the wild sap," she says. "It's black now instead of dark brown."

"That's a good thing," I reply. "I'll finally look like everybody else in Krymzyn."

She rests her other hand on my shoulder. "You've always looked good the way you are."

"Thanks," I say. "You're not bad to look at yourself."

Assuming we're about to hug the way we've done at the end of her other showers, I lightly grip her waist in both hands. It's obviously different this time since she doesn't have any clothes on, but I don't seem to care. Instead of embracing me, Tela rises up on her tiptoes. She inches her face towards mine until our lips meet in a kiss. After our kiss ends, we look at each other's eyes.

"Now I've had my first kiss," she says.

"How was it?" I ask.

She pulls my face back to hers. Any innocence that may have existed in our affection for one another up to this point is obliterated when we kiss again. I open my mouth a little, she opens hers, and our tongues swirl inside each other's mouths. A wildfire sparks in my veins.

She presses her breasts against my chest while I slide my hands from her waist to the curves of her rear. Cupping her firm cheeks, I dig my fingers into her flesh. The growing firmness inside my pants pulses against her belly.

One of Tela's hands roams down my chest and over my stomach. When it reaches my waist, she unfastens the top button of my pants. With our tongues still probing each other's mouths, her fingertips trace down to the second button.

"Wuv-u, Daddy," whispers inside my head.

A knife plunged into my heart couldn't cause me more pain. With gut-wrenching guilt overwhelming me, I break our kiss and take a step backwards. I grab both of Tela's wrists and jerk her hands away from me.

"We can't do this," I say, letting go of her wrists.

Her face wrinkles with confusion. "Why not?"

"Sash is the only person I can be with this way."

"But you looked at me like this is what you wanted."

"I know," I reply. "I'm sorry if I led you on. You're so beautiful in so many ways that any man would find you desirable. But I can't do this because of how I feel about Sash. I lost sight of that for a while."

"Why is it different with her?" she asks.

"I tried to explain it to you once. I love Sash in a way that I can't love anyone else. It's different than how I feel about family or friends. I can't betray that."

"She'll never know what happens," she says bitterly.

"I'll know," I reply. "And so will you. I could never live with myself. I don't think you could either."

She balls her hands into fists. "I want to have this experience, Chase. I want to have it now."

"You only feel that way because of the wild sap."

"I don't care what it is!" she fumes. "I like the way it feels when you touch me. Why did you hold me when we slept if you didn't want this?"

"In my world," I calmly tell her, trying not to let the situation get any more out of hand than it already is, "friends can hug or hold each other. I care a lot about you. That doesn't mean anything else has to happen."

"It felt like you wanted more to happen when we were kissing," she sneers.

"We shouldn't have let it get that far. I think we're both confused right now. We need to get back to the Delta."

Her eyes flame at me for several seconds. "Have it your way," she finally says. "Let's go."

Wanting to avoid looking at her again until she's dressed, I turn away. Even though I seem to be able to temporarily suppress the corrupted thoughts of the wild sap, I'm never sure how long my self-control will last. After leaning down to pick up my shirt, I slip it over my head.

"Let me know when you're ready," I say without looking at Tela.

"Don't worry," she replies with so much festering anger in her voice that it shoots ice through my veins. "You'll know."

I spin in her direction. As I throw my arm up in defense, Tela slams a rock against the side of my head. Trying to fight off the dizziness, I stagger to the wall. The second time she smashes my skull, she knocks me out cold.

Chapter 21

I regain consciousness with jackhammers pounding inside my head. Lying face down on the ground, I reach a hand to the side of my skull. A big lump has risen from my scalp, and the hair around it is sticky with blood.

"Hell hath no fury," I mumble. "Even in this fucked-up world."

With a hand pressed to the side of my head, I roll over and sit up. Darkness must have ended because the waterfall has diminished in strength. The spear and flasks are gone, but one canister is still lying on the ground. Tela is nowhere in sight.

"Tela!" I shout.

The only response is my own voice careening off the cavern walls. I pick up the canister and feel somewhat appeased because she left me the one that's full. After rubbing a handful of the red liquid on my head, I drink about half of what's left inside.

Wobbling as I stand to my feet, I steady myself against the wall. As the sap gradually kicks in, the beating in my head recedes enough that I can walk. I hang the canister over my shoulder and step into the tunnel.

"Dark," I say, putting an end to the dreary purple aura.

I skulk through the passage and slide my body through the crevice at the end. Static clouds hang over the terrain. The ferocious flow of water that was in the gully earlier is now nothing but a feeble stream. Once I'm out in the basin, I look up and down the ravine.

"Tela!" I angrily yell.

Turning in a circle, I wait for her to show her face. When she doesn't appear, I surmise that she's already on her way back to the Delta. I wrestle with the idea of returning to the transport for more sap, but I'm so incensed at how Tela blindsided me that all I want to do is catch up to her and give her a piece of my mind. I run up the ravine and splinter into the light.

Consumed by smoldering fury, I have difficulty thinking clearly and focusing on the beams. Tela's idea about going far to the north and coming back down to the bridge by the Delta never enters my mind. I blaze a path straight to the northeast, aiming in a direction that should bring me to the river right around the Delta.

After several hours are behind me, I pause for a brief rest on top of a hill. While draining the rest of the canister, I scour the landscape in every direction. Any clarity that I felt after Tela and I kissed is now long gone, replaced by outrage at how she stabbed me in the back. I gulp down the last of the sap, rear my arm back, and heave the canister as far as I can. As the steel bounces across the rocky ground, two murky shapes flash over a hilltop a few miles to the south of me.

The first thought that enters my mind is that I'd like to ram my spear down the ugly fucking Murkovin's throats.

Then I remember that I don't have a weapon with me. I whirl around, bolt down the hill, and surge into the light to the north. I weave through a few small hills before reaching a long, flat open space. Maxing out my speed, I jet over the land, expecting to leave the Murkovin behind. A shape of light appears at my side.

The creature arcs in front of me and partially solidifies the particles of his body. When he suddenly reduces his speed, I realize he's trying to force me out my blend. I bring together the molecules of one of my arms until it's almost solid, hurl my fist against his morphing body, and cut hard to the east. The second creature sails straight towards me from behind.

Focusing my vision on a few bright beams, I aim at a row of low hills in front of me. With far less speed at my command than what I had before the days of living on wild sap, the two Murkovin stay right on my tail. At the end of the flat ground, I shoot up a hill and catapult over the crest. As I sail through the air, I see light glinting from the rapids in the distance. Not wanting to get boxed in by the river, the moment my feet skim over the ground, I veer to the north.

I twist my neck to look over my shoulder. Less than twenty yards behind me, both Murkovin are still in the hunt. Returning my eyes to the Barrens in front of me, I yell, *"Concentrate on the beams!"* over and over in my head. At least an hour passes with all of us at full throttle. They don't close the distance between us, but I also don't gain any ground on them.

As I stream over a hill, like a mirage rising in the distance, scarlet light tints the sky. I'm close to the Delta, which means the bridge north of it must be no more than a few minutes away. If they're this close behind me when I come out of my blend, they could easily catch me on the bridge. Tela may have put me in this mess, but the game of chicken she and I have played at least a dozen times on our returns from the Mount might end up saving my life. I doubt the Murkovin have ever tried exiting the light as close to a steel bridge as I have.

When I see the reflections from the bridge, I glance over my shoulder at the Murkovin one last time. They're still on my heels, so I return my eyes to the bridge and aim straight at the corner closest to me. After a search of the land between me and the bridge, I lock my eyes on a rock that's about fifty yards away from the edge of the bridge. That rock will be the last chance I have to retract my particles from the beams.

My other concern is that I'm approaching the bridge at a forty-five-degree angle. The steel surface is only about twelve feet wide. If I transition from my blend to a run too quickly, I could have so much forward velocity that I fly straight over the far edge of the bridge. Even though I'm a strong swimmer, the rapids are fierce where the river forks around the Delta. The banks are covered by large boulders that I could easily be killed by if the waves smash me against them.

As the rock zooms closer, I maintain all of my speed. The split-second I pass it, I suck my particles out of the beams. Stinging like a hive of wasps on the attack, my molecules smack back into my body. The last ray of light evaporates into my skin at the same time my foot hits the steel bridge.

Like a sprinter navigating through a turn, I lean my body to the right. Waves from the rapids cascade off the side of the bridge only a few feet in front of me. I start to topple forward from the force of my momentum and hold in my breath in case go I over the side. When my foot hits the small lip on the far side of the bridge, I lurch off it towards the center.

I stumble while trying to keep my balance, but push off the steel surface with one hand. Pumping my arms by my sides, I finally get my body under control. As I dash up the slight slope towards the arch in the center, I check over my shoulder. The two Murkovin have come out of their blends and are just now reaching the bridge. Even though they're farther behind me than when we were traveling, I churn with all my might over the arch and race down the other side. The moment I reach the shore, I swerve to the south.

After bursting into the light, I reach the road from the Mount in a matter of seconds. I slide out of the beams, sprint onto the bridge to the Delta, and look to the north. The two Murkovin are standing at the center of the other bridge with their eyes fixed on me. When they turn away and head back to the western Barrens, I slow to a jog.

At the top of the arch of the bridge, I stop and drop my hands to my knees. It takes a full minute before I finally catch my breath. With my hands gripping my sides, I walk down the slope of the bridge towards the Delta. Cavu stares at me from above the gate.

The light spilling from the clouds to the crimson hills in the Delta is almost blinding after days of living in black, gray, and sickly purple. I shade my eyes with one hand and watch

Cavu disappear down a ladder behind the wall. After I step into the wall's shadow, I stop in front of the gate.

"Cavu!" I shout. "Let me in!"

"Wait!" he calls out from the other side.

I bang my hands against one of the locked doors. "It's me, Chase!"

"You have to wait!" he yells.

"What is that dumbass doing," I mumble.

It's a good thing the Murkovin quit chasing me or I'd be dead while waiting for Cavu to get his shit together. But as I think that thought, I start to tremble from a wave of paranoia. Did Tela already return to the Delta and blame everything that happened on me?

If Sash really wants to get rid of me, take my daughter and move on with her life, this would be her chance. For all I know, they're plotting to banish me from the Delta at this very moment. Cavu must be part of the plan. He's always looked up to Sash. Why else wouldn't he open the gate for me?

When one of the gate doors finally creaks open, I shove my shoulder through the gap. After barreling through the gate, I look straight at Cavu.

"What the _hell_ were you doing?" I growl.

"He was doing his duty," Larn says from off to my side. "You don't look like yourself."

I snap my head to Larn and clench my hands into fists, ready for whatever comes at me. With tear dampened cheeks, Sash is standing beside him. She crosses the grass to me and envelops me in her arms. Standing erect and still, I don't return her hug. Sash and Larn must be spinning a web of deceit around me.

"I thought you were dead," Sash whispers in my ear.

"Not yet," I say.

"What happened?" Larn asks.

I take a step back from Sash. She drops her arms to her sides and stares at me.

"Is Tela back?" I ask Larn.

"She hasn't returned," he answers. "Where have you been?"

I shake my head and look down at the ground.

Sash reaches out a hand and lightly grips my arm. "What's wrong, Chase?"

"Tela should have been back by now," I reply, feeling increasingly confused by everything that's going on.

"Sash told us that you and Tela went to the flats," Larn says. "When you didn't return, we searched the Barrens in that area but couldn't find you. The other Travelers and Sash have gone out with me to look for you every day since you've been missing."

Sash lets go of my arm. I scuff a foot over the grass and then raise my eyes to Larn.

"After we got our count at the flats," I say, "we were heading back to the Delta. Tela saw something strange, so we stopped. A tree had its branches tied by rope and spikes were stuck in the trunk with tubes leading to a transport. While we were looking at it, a bunch of Murkovin attacked us.

"We got away," I continue, "but Tela went over the side of a cliff. She was too badly injured to make it back to the Delta. I didn't even think she'd live. I found a hidden cavern and stole the transport from the Murkovin. I was able to heal her, but we survived on wild sap."

"Where is she now?" Larn asks.

"I don't know," I answer, immediately deciding to lie about what happened. "We got separated on the way back. A few Murkovin were chasing us, so we split up. They didn't go after her, but stayed on me. I thought she'd be back by now."

I glance at Sash. From the accusing look in her eyes, I'm sure she knows I'm lying.

"What was your path?" Larn asks.

"The cave we were in is about ten thousand miles north of the flats. I aimed straight for the Delta. Tela talked about going far north of the Delta and coming back down the river to avoid them, so maybe it's taking her longer. We have to go find her."

"You look terrible, Chase," Sash says to me. "You need to get the wild sap out of your body before you do anything else."

"We have to find Tela!" I argue.

"You're in no shape to go back to the Barrens," Larn counters. "I'll summon the other Travelers so we can search for her."

"Let's get you to our habitat," Sash says to me.

"I want to see Aven first."

"She's at Home," Sash replies. "I don't want her to see you this way."

"That's not for you to decide!" I blurt out.

Sash kneels to the ground and lays her hand on the grass. "Kyra, please have Aven sleep at Home. I'll pick her up on the morrow."

"I want to see my daughter!" I shout.

Glaring at me, Sash stands up. "You need healthy sap and rest before you do anything else."

"She's right, Chase," Larn says. "If you could see what you look like and realize how you're behaving, you wouldn't want Aven anywhere near you."

I glance back and forth between Sash and Larn. Daughter and father are obviously conspiring against me so that I never see Aven again. As my heart races faster and faster, the veins in my neck bulge from my skin. I aim my eyes at Sash.

"You always have to be in control, don't you? Little miss _fucking_ know-it-all."

"Please stop, Chase," she pleads. "You don't know what you're saying right now."

"I know exactly what I'm saying!" I yell, taking a step towards her. "Everything always has to be your way. It's my turn now. I want to see Aven!"

Larn slides between us and looks down at my face. "You should hold your tongue before you say something you can't take back."

"Shut the _fuck_ up!" I snarl, shoving him away from me.

When I turn towards Sash, Larn pummels his fist against the side of my head so hard that I collapse to my knees. With darkness filling my eyes, I fall face-first to the grass. For the second time in one day, someone knocks me out cold.

Chapter 22

Shaking like a junkie in need of a fix, I open my eyes. The ceiling of our habitat gradually comes into focus. I'm lying on my back on our bed with my arms pinned underneath me. I try to jump to my feet, but rope cuts into my wrists and ankles. I tumble to the floor.

While I struggle against the restraints, Sash walks across the cavern with a cup in one hand and a pitcher in the other. After setting them down on the floor, she grabs me by the front of my shirt and heaves me back onto the bed. Kneeling in front of me, she pulls me up to a sitting position and then picks up the cup.

"Drink," she orders, holding the cup to my lips.

After all the energy I spent outrunning the Murkovin, not to mention being cold-cocked twice in one day, my craving for sap verges on the maniacal. I don't want to give in to Sash right now, but my lips clamp to the steel like a leech on warm flesh. Sash tilts the cup up and I swallow everything inside.

"I want to see Aven!" I spew as she pulls the cup away from my lips.

Instead of answering me, Sash refills the cup and

pushes it against my mouth again. I drain the second cup and then jerk my face away. The pace of my breathing increases until I'm almost hyperventilating.

"I want to see my daughter!" I demand.

"Two more cups," she says. "Then you can see Aven."

Somewhat calmed by Sash's acquiescence, I guzzle two more cups. When I finish the second one, Sash stands up and returns to the table. With her back to me, she sets down the pitcher and cup.

"You said I could see Aven," I say.

She turns to me. "After you sleep."

"You lied to me!" I growl.

I try to rip my hands out of the rope. The more it digs into my skin, the more outraged I become.

"I want to see my daughter right now!" I shriek.

"Go to sleep," Sash says. "You'll feel better when you wake up."

"Go _fuck_ yourself!"

Sash stampedes across the room, crouches in front of me, and grabs me by the shoulders. "Go to sleep unless you want me to knock you out again."

She hurls me down on my side. I roll over so that I'm facing away from her and stare at my blurry reflection in the wall. I should never have come back to the Delta.

Unable to believe how gullible I've been, I close my eyes. Why didn't I recognize the truth sooner? No one in Krymzyn wants me here. Sash just blatantly lied to my face and has no intention of letting me anywhere near my daughter. As soon as I can get to Aven, I'm taking her with me and heading back to the Barrens. Far away from the deception of the

Delta, I'll raise her on my own and teach her how to take care of herself in the wild.

While planning my escape, I drift off to sleep. When I open my eyes again, I don't know if I was out for five minutes, five hours, or five days. I flop over and glance around the cavern. Still keeping watch over me, Sash is sitting at the table.

"Your veins look a little better," she says flatly. "Some of the blue has returned to your hair. Your eyes are still purple, but not as close to red as they were."

"How long was I out?" I ask.

"It's the next day," she answers.

"Will you untie me now?"

"I don't know," she says. "What will you do if I do?"

"I won't do anything."

"I don't want to fight with you," she tells me.

"I think I'm past that," I say.

She stands up from the stool and steps to the side of the bed. "One more day, and you would have been a Murkovin."

"I know. Did they find Tela?"

"Not yet," she answers. "A few of the Travelers went up the river to the north. They just got back a little while ago. The others are still out with Larn. They're trying to follow the path you described."

I shake my head. "I don't know where she could be. We need to help them search for her."

"You need more healthy sap first."

She walks to the table, returns with a cup and pitcher, and sets them on the floor in front of me. After helping me sit up, she unties the rope from my feet and hands. As soon as I'm free, she jumps away from me and clenches her hands into fists. I ignore the cup, grab the pitcher, and swallow gulp after gulp. When the pitcher is empty, I set it on the floor.

"I'm sorry for the way I behaved," I say. "I didn't mean any of it."

Probably deciding that I'm no longer a threat, she relaxes her muscles. "If you said the words, there must have been some truth in them."

"There wasn't," I reply. "From the moment I started drinking the wild sap, every thought in my mind became distorted. We can talk more about it later. I want to see Aven first. Then we need to help find Tela."

"We will." She pauses for a moment. "After you tell me what really happened in the Barrens."

Numbing with shame, I lower my eyes to the floor. So many of the thoughts I had after drinking the wild sap, the false accusations of Sash betraying me, were all lies from inside my mind. As much as I never want to hurt her, I have to tell her the truth.

"Tela was so badly injured," I say, looking up at her, "that if I tried to carry her back to the Delta, she would have died. I found a cavern and then stole the sap transport that I told you and Larn about. The Murkovin were looking for us, so I didn't want to leave Tela alone in the cave. I couldn't come back for help.

"She was in a lot of pain most of the time and just slept for the first few days. By the time she felt strong enough to move, my traveling speed had slowed from the wild sap. I didn't think I could outrun the Murkovin if I carried her. Tela and I talked about what to do. We both agreed that it was best to wait until she could travel.

"Every day that passed, my thoughts became darker and darker. I convinced myself of some horrible things that weren't true. But they seemed real while I was out there."

"Like what?" she asks.

"Did I make a mistake by leaving Earth?" I pause for a moment. "And did you use me just so you could understand all the Earth emotions you feel?"

She folds her arms in front of her. "How could you ever think that?"

"Have you ever had wild sap?" I ask.

"No," she answers. "We're taught as children that it's impossible to control the extreme emotions after a few days."

"Tela couldn't control them," I say. "I could, but only sometimes. It took me a while to get it under control."

Trying to figure out how to explain the rest of what happened between Tela and me, I rub the back of my head.

"Is that it?" Sash asks, unfolding her arms.

"No," I say. "We were getting ready to come back to the Delta when Darkness fell. Everything about the wild sap is stronger during Darkness. A lot of physical desires that are hard to control are released.

"There's a small waterfall in the cavern we stayed in. Tela wanted to clean off before we left. After she got out of the fall, we kissed each other and hugged. It didn't last long because I came to my senses and stopped us before it went any farther. She got mad that I pushed her away, hit me in the head with a rock, and knocked me out. I haven't seen her since."

Sash stares at me in disbelief. "You kissed Tela?"

"It was the wild sap," I say. "I stopped almost as soon as it started. She didn't know what she was doing. The wild sap was in complete control of her. I told her that you're the only person I can be with that way."

Sash's eyes redden. "If she just got out of the fall, did she have clothes on when you hugged her?"

"No," I answer.

"Did you?"

"I had my pants on."

Sash turns away from me and steps to the table. I stand up from the bed and cross the cavern to her. I rest my hand on her shoulder, but she immediately shrugs away.

"Don't!" she snaps.

Although it's not as strong as the prior day, I still feel the effects of the wild sap. I bite the insides of my cheeks while trying to suppress the hostility swelling inside me. I take a few deep breaths to calm myself down enough to speak in a steady voice.

"When you don't understand an emotion from my world," I say, "it takes you a while to learn how to control it. That's what it's like with the wild sap, except ten times stronger. I think the only reason I could get it under control sometimes is because the feelings the wild sap releases are common in my world. I had trouble most of the time. I still feel it now, but it's a lot weaker than it was."

"I can't believe you kissed Tela," she says with her back to me. "You should have been watching out for her. Even though she's been a Traveler longer than you have, she's younger than you. She looks up to you."

"I know she does. She's my friend—nothing more. I did

watch out for her, but I should have been stronger. I just couldn't control it all of the time."

Sash finally turns to me. "No matter what made it happen, it still hurts."

"What can I do?" I ask.

"I don't know," she says. "I need time."

I nod my head to her. "I want to clean off and see Aven. After that, will you help search for Tela?"

"Of course," she replies. "I care about her just as much as you do."

"Thanks," I say.

I walk past Sash towards the waterfall cavern.

"Chase," she says from behind me. "What do I do that makes you think I'm so controlling."

I stop and look at her. "I didn't mean it, Sash. It was the wild sap talking."

"Tell me the truth."

"I don't want to do this right now," I say. "I don't think it will help anything."

"Tell me!"

"Fine!" I belt out, unable to keep the anger out of my voice any longer. "You always insist on taking Aven to Home if Darkness falls. Even if I'm already with her, you come and get her. You know how fast I am and that I can protect her. It makes me feel like you don't trust me with her."

Pressing her lips tightly together, she narrows her eyes at me. "Is that all?"

"And the way you made Tela try to blend her light when she was young."

"She was thrilled to do it!"

"I know she was," I say. "But you made her keep trying until it happened, and she ended up breaking both of her legs. You wouldn't take no for an answer. You never do."

"I wanted her to know that she could do it. She needed to be pushed."

I point my finger at her. "*You* wanted. *You* pushed. You're that way with everyone."

As I lower my arm, she flattens both of her hands on the top of the table and looks down at the steel surface. "You don't know hard it is to have the gifts I have—to be so powerful, to see the future even when I don't want to. What good is it to have those things if I don't use them to help others?"

"You do help them," I say in a much less combative tone. "But you get so caught up in what you think is best that you don't take into consideration what other people might want."

Still fuming, she pops her face up. "When have I done that?"

"When you got pregnant," I answer. "I wanted to talk to you about how Aven should be raised, but you didn't want to hear it. You decided how things should be. The subject was closed until that Darkness at Ovin's tree. It made me feel like you didn't care what I was going through."

"I explained that to you," she says. "I was feeling the same way. I decided it would make it worse for both of us if I told you because I knew there was nothing we could do about it."

"*You* decided."

She lowers her chin to her chest and looks at the

tabletop. "Clean up. I'll let Kyra know we're coming to see Aven."

Chapter 23

"Two Travelers stumbled upon a camp in the southwest," says the tallest Murkovin the woman has ever known. "After a fight with our men, they were trapped in the Barrens for several days. The male Traveler eventually made it back to the Delta, but a young woman fled to the eastern wasteland."

The woman studies the tall Murkovin's eyes. Over the time she'd known him, he'd gained her trust in a way that no person other than her Ovì ever had. The two had forged an unbreakable bond since their first meeting long ago. Over the time that had passed, her feelings for him had grown to what she imagined she would have felt for her Mür had she known him.

"Do you know why the female Traveler stayed?" the woman asks.

"No one knows," he answers. "She was severely injured in a crash while traveling. After the other Traveler stole a transport full of sap from the camp, they disappeared. Even though our men searched the area, they never found them.

"A few days later," he continues, "two of our men spotted the male Traveler on his way back to the Delta. Although they gave chase, they were unable to catch him. On the same day, a commander at another camp caught sight of the female near the Stone Crossing. She had a transport with her, so he followed her trail to the east. After he told me about her, I went to the area to see if I could locate her."

"Did you?" the woman asks.

"I know where she is. I wanted to talk with you before doing anything else."

Knowing that there's no one better at tracking a person in the Barrens than the man in front of her, the woman nods her head. "Can you describe her to me?"

"She's young—shorter than you with a medium build. Legs fit enough to outpace most of our kind. Her hair hangs well over her shoulders, but the blue is now gone. She looks like one of us."

The curious young Traveler I encountered once before, the woman thinks to herself. *The wild sap must have freed her mind from the restraints of the Delta. But despite her strength and speed, she doesn't know how to survive in the Barrens. A fate worse than she could ever imagine might await her.*

Remembering how close she once came to suffering that same type of horror, the woman looks up at the clouds. If not for the man standing in front of her, in the best of scenarios, she would have been killed. She didn't want to consider the other possibilities.

She was still young when it happened, her body still developing. Curves had found their way into her chest and hips, but she wasn't fully mature yet. It was only a few hundred days after her Ovì's death, long before she met the Watcher who became the Mür of her child.

As she often did after she learned to travel, she sped one day through the wasteland to the west. When she reached the hills where the dirt speckled with red, she found a high crest. Far enough from the edge of the Schorachnia's domain that they wouldn't harm her, but close enough that she could hear the music rising from the Eternal Canyon, she sat alone in thought.

She stared at the vines falling over the Canyon's edge in the distance, mesmerized by the rich color of their flowers. She imagined a world filled with vibrant hues, not the drab black and grays of the Barrens. A world where she didn't need to be ready to defend her existence with every breath she took.

While the music caressed her ears, she let herself feel peace. She laid her spear by her side, leaned back to the dirt, and rested the back of her head on her folded hands. As she gazed at the barrier to the Infinite Expanse, the serenade of colors waving across the faraway sky, her eyes began to droop. Her mind drifted into a tranquil state and she soon fell asleep.

She never heard the footsteps climbing up the hill behind her. By the time she opened her eyes, two male Murkovin were already standing over her. She tried to jump to her feet, but one of the men grabbed her by the shoulders and threw her back to the ground. While he pinned her to the dirt, the other brute gripped her arms in his rough, calloused hands. After he bound her wrists with rope, the first man crawled on top of her body.

Squirming on the ground, she tried to buck him off. The man who had tied her wrists together fired a fist to her face.

The man on top of her forcefully clenched a handful of her hair in one hand while groping at the waist of her pants with the other.

"You belong to us now!" he hissed. "You'll do our bidding, or we'll beat you until you do."

Without the slightest sound betraying its arrival, the tip of a spear ripped into the back of the beast's head. As the Murkovin's body collapsed on top of her, his blood splattered on her face. A foot swung over her. With a sharp crack, it crushed the nose of the creature holding her wrists. The same weapon that had killed the first of the brutes then split open the skull of the second.

She looked up at a tall, weathered man standing over her. His face was square and strong, and his hair cut short enough that it stuck straight up from the top of his head. Across one of his cheeks, a thick scar ran from the corner of his mouth to his ear. Rigid muscles bulged from his shoulders and arms. She trembled from the gruesome thought that he'd killed the other two so that he could take their place.

The man leaned down and grabbed the hair of the dead creature on top of her body. After hurling the beast away from her, he knelt by her side. To her surprise, he freed her wrists from the rope, helped her sit upright, and then stood up again.

"Never sleep in the open," he chastised in a low, gravelly voice.

Without saying another word, the tall Murkovin turned away. Fresh blood still dripped from the tip of his spear as he stepped down the hill. The girl rose to her feet and wiped the blood off her face.

"I'm grateful for your help," she called out.

He stopped and turned to her. "Be more careful in the future. You should know better than that."

"Why did you come to my aid?" she asked.

He aimed his eyes at the corpses by her feet. "Like you, I've had people I care about killed by men like them."

"How do you know what's happened to me in the past?"

He returned his attention to her. "My cavern is a few hundred miles west of yours. I often travel through your area. I've seen you from a distance many times over thousands of days. I saw that you buried your Ovì and hung two bodies from a tree. It wasn't hard to figure out what must have occurred. If I'd been nearby when it happened, I would have helped."

"I've never seen you," she comments.

"That's why I'm so tall," he says. "No one sees me unless I want to be seen."

She instantly realized that not only could she learn much from this man, but she could also trust him with her life. "How did you happen to be here now?"

"I saw you travel through my territory. When you were far to the west, I saw two streaks from the north follow your trail. My guess was, whoever they were, they were up to no good. I have no patience for their kind and don't tolerate their existence."

"I owe my life to you," she said.

"You owe me nothing. But let this be a lesson to you. Always stay alert."

"I know," she replied. "I just wanted a few moments of .

. . I shouldn't have fallen asleep."

The man knowingly nodded his head. "If you ever need me for something, you now know the area where I dwell."

He turned away and sprinted down the hill. After streaming into the light at the bottom of the slope, he vanished into the Barrens.

Over the next few days, she found several large branches that had recently been torn from trees. Using a saw blade made out of hard, narrow rock that had once belonged to her Mür, she cut the branches into six separate foot-long logs. With another sharp rock, she hollowed them out to make wooden urns.

Using pumice stones that her Ovì had long ago gathered from the banks of the river, she meticulously sanded the insides until they were as smooth as marble. After cutting round tops for the urns, she used a steel knife that had been stolen during a raid on Travelers to cut grooves in the urns and tops.

Once she was confident that the lids would screw on tight, she chipped away at the latticed shale in the ceiling of her cavern and filled her hands with the thick sludge left behind by grubs. Rubbing it on the insides of the urns, she glazed the wood so that it would no longer absorb liquid.

As soon as the next Darkness fell, she used her spear to open several holes in the trunk of a tree and filled the urns with sap. She could have used the older urns that she and her Ovì had made long ago, but the new ones would bring a better price.

Carrying the six sap-filled urns in a crudely woven backpack, she traveled several hundred miles to the north.

On top of a hill, she spotted a two-foot-high mound of rocks with a dead tree branch sticking out of it. She'd never been to one of the trading posts scattered across the Barrens before. Her Ovì had once told her where this one was located and how to recognize it. After circling once around the hill, she came to a stop in front of a large, oblong rock with a flat top.

Her Ovì had explained the rules for bartering at trading posts, as well as what items could be had. Fabric woven from wooden looms, tables and stools made of wood and smoothed with grub slime as she'd done with the urns, tools crafted out of rock or Murkovin bone, or as much sap as a person could want were all available for the right price. But items made in the Delta and stolen from raids on Travelers always had the greatest value.

Hoping they would have what she sought, she placed the six urns on top of the stone. She knew that she'd be safe during the transaction and her items wouldn't be stolen. The men and women who ran the trading posts earned enough for the things they bartered to keep plenty of everything for themselves. Without a good reputation, no one would ever return to that post again.

As she glanced at the hilltops around her, she assumed there were eight or ten of her kind hiding nearby. She also knew they'd all be armed and as skilled as any in the Barrens at wielding spears. When no one appeared, she loudly called out the name of the item she hoped to acquire.

From behind the rocky crest, a male voice shouted, "They're difficult to come by. The cost will be ten."

"I just made these urns," she hollered. "They're full of sap."

"The cost is still ten," the voice replied.

She looked down at the wooden canisters, angry with herself for not better estimating the cost. After considering her options, she laid down her steel spear beside the urns. Because it had belonged to her Ovì, it was difficult to part with. None the less, she was determined to leave with what she wanted.

"I'll add the spear," she yelled. "Give me a sturdy wooden one in return."

While waiting for a response, her eyes roamed across the hills again.

"We have a bargain," the voice yelled.

As her Ovì had told her to do after a bargain had been struck, she stepped five paces backwards. Two men climbed over the top of the hill and walked down the slope. Several other men and women appeared from behind large boulders far off to her sides.

When the two men reached the rock, one of them picked up her spear and the urns. He checked to make sure all the wooden containers were full of sap. The other man stood by the stone, keenly watching the hills behind the woman in case this was a trick of some kind. The first man finally whistled loudly, the signal to complete the barter. Another Murkovin ran down the hill with the item she'd requested in hand, as well as a wooden spear. After tossing them to the stone, all three of the men took several steps backwards.

She removed her items from the rock, nodded to the men, and then sprinted away. Only when she was out of their sight did she fuse with the light around her. But instead of returning to her cavern, she went straight to the area where the tall Murkovin dwelled.

For a quarter of the day, she stood in plain sight on top of a high hill. The tall Murkovin eventually appeared in a nearby valley and ran up the slope underneath her. As soon as he stopped in front of her, she held out both of her hands. Resting on top of her palms was the item she'd bartered for.

"What is this?" he asked, looking down at her outstretched arms.

"Repayment for saving my life," she replied. "A head on top of a body as tall as yours deserves a soft pillow to sleep on."

The man knew the pillow must be pillage from a raid on Travelers. He was also well aware that it would command a high price at a trading post. Instead of being made of coarse cloth and filled with leaves like those of the Barrens, this one was created with smooth, well-sewn fabric and stuffed with the billowy fluffing that only grows in the Delta.

"I need no repayment," he said. "Take it back."

She shook her head. "It's too late. The bargain has been struck."

From the look of deep appreciation in his eyes, she realized that this was probably the only act of kindness he'd known in a very long while. Also at that moment, she learned that a show of compassion could be as powerful as a spear in the strongest of hands.

From that day on, the two often spent time together. Over many days of practice, he improved her fighting skills until they were as keen as his. After she met the Watcher of the Delta who became the Mür of her child, she shared with the tall Murkovin the steel stakes, rope, and other items that the Watcher brought to her from the Delta.

As more time went by, the tall Murkovin sat with her and the Watcher many times while listening to plans to overthrow the Delta. She knew he disliked the Watcher, but he always agreed with the changes they hoped to bring to the Barrens.

The woman looks down from the sky at the tall Murkovin. "Can you take me to where you last saw the Traveler?"

"Of course," he answers. "She's in a cavern far south of the desert, almost at the edge of the Expanse. I'm curious why you want to see her."

"I've spoken with her before. There's something inside her that wants to be let out. If she's planning a life in the Barrens, she can be helpful to us in several ways."

"When do we leave?" he asks.

"As soon as we can," she answers. "I just want to say goodbye to my child first."

"I'll fetch canisters for us."

After he turns away, the woman hurries in the direction of her habitat. As much as it pains her to be away from her child so often, it can't be avoided—especially when an opportunity like this one arises.

As I thought it might, the woman thinks as she briskly walks, *my first encounter with the Traveler appears to have been more than a coincidence. She'll have a reason to trust me because of the peaceful demeanor I displayed when we first met. I can now provide her with safety in the Barrens and utilize her skills for my own needs.*

Not only can she help me teach others to travel, but she

can also tell me many things about the Delta and the people who dwell there. I've learned much from the stories the Mür of my child has told me, but his views are tainted.

I've learned over time that knowledge is power. The more I have, the stronger I'll be in the end.

Chapter 24

Despite the staggering guilt I feel, I can barely contain my excitement as Sash and I zoom to Home. After days and days of mental torment in the Barrens, all I want now is to feel my daughter in my arms.

When Sash and I come out of our blends in the red meadow in front of Home, Kyra is already waiting for us with Aven by her side. Aven squeals with delight as I sprint across the field. Teetering and tottering through the grass, she runs towards me with her arms waving in the air. I fall to my knees in front of her and smother her in a hug.

"I missed you so much," I say in Aven's ear.

Clutching my neck, she speaks the same words that kept me from making an irreversible mistake in the Barrens. "Wuv-u, Daddy."

"Oh, baby girl. I love you with all my heart."

Sash stops by our side. Aven leans back from me and looks up at her.

"Daddy safe," she says.

The joy I feel from being reunited with my daughter is muted by how much I've hurt Sash. While in the Barrens with my mind devoured by malicious lies, I asked myself a question over and over.

Why did I ever come to this godforsaken world?

The only answers I'll ever need to that question are in my arms and standing by my side.

"You and your mother mean everything to me," I say to Aven.

I reach out a hand and lightly grip Sash's thigh. She yanks her leg away and shoots an angry glance in my direction.

"I'm thrilled you're alive," she says, "but I told you that I need time."

"I never meant to hurt you. I'll do whatever—"

"Wait," she interrupts, holding a hand up to silence me. "Larn just summoned me from the gate." She listens to him for a few seconds. "They didn't find Tela."

With my heart sinking to my stomach, I look at Aven. "Mommy and I have to go for a while, but we'll pick you up at the end of the day."

Making her pouty face, Aven pushes her bottom lip out and scrunches her eyes. "No go, Daddy."

"We'll be back before you know it. Right now, we have to find Tela."

There's no rationalizing with a nine-month-old, even if her maturity and speech match that of a three-year-old on Earth. But instead of arguing with me, Aven's face drifts away from mine and she tilts her head to the side. As though she's listening to something from far away, she gazes at nothing with vacant eyes.

"What is it, Aven?" I ask.

"Help Tela," she whispers. "Help Tela."

"We will," I say. "That's why we need to go. We have to

find her."

After another long hug with Aven, I rise from the ground. Sash and I each take one of our daughter's hands in ours and lead her back to Kyra. As they step inside the doorway to Home, Aven looks over her shoulder at me.

"Tela lost," she says.

"We'll find her," I reply. "Mommy and Daddy will pick you up later."

Kyra swings the door shut.

"She learned a new word while you were gone," Sash tells me.

"Lost?" I ask.

She nods her head. "I told her you were lost in the Barrens. She wasn't the same while you were gone."

"I'll make it up to her. And to you, if I can."

"We should go now," she replies without acknowledging my statement.

When Sash and I reach the Delta entrance, Larn, Nuar, and Roen are waiting for us by the gate. They all have bags under their eyes and their shoulders sag from exhaustion.

"I'm sorry that I struck you," Larn says to me.

"No apology necessary," I reply. "I was out of control."

"The effects of the wild sap may linger for several more days," he informs me. "Pay attention to what you're feeling and keep your emotions under control."

"I'll do my best."

Velt, Jeni, and Kale fly over a nearby hill and soon come to a stop beside the rest of us.

"We still haven't seen any sign of Tela," Larn tells me. "Velt and Jeni searched up the river to the north and returned earlier. The rest of us followed the path you described as best we could."

"Did you find the Murkovin camp?" I ask.

Larn shakes his head. "We saw a few trees, but none of them had rope binding them."

"Maybe you were in the wrong area," I say. "Since the Murkovin were searching for us, she could have gone back to the cavern we hid in. We should check there."

Larn briefly studies the other Travelers. "Nuar and Roen haven't slept. Jeni and Velt had a brief rest. They'll come with us, but the others should stay here in case they're needed."

"You must be exhausted," Sash says to Larn. "Have you even closed your eyes since Chase and Tela went missing?"

"Don't worry about me," he replies. "We need to find Tela before it's too late."

With canisters over our shoulders, spears in our hands, and me leading the way, we follow the same route that I used to return to the Delta. Everyone scans the Barrens for any sign of life during the five-hour journey to the Murkovin camp, but nobody sees a thing.

After cautiously climbing up one of the hills outside the camp, we peek over the crest. The ropes that were securing the branches of the tree are gone. The Murkovin that were here are nowhere in sight. The only remaining sign of anyone being here are the spike holes in the bark of the trunk.

While we walk to the cliff that Tela went over, I describe the fight at the tree and our escape. When we reach the edge of the bluff, I look down at the bottom of the canyon. The image of Tela's bloody, disfigured body flashes into my vision. I grit my teeth so hard from the malevolence swelling inside me and the pure hatred I feel for the Murkovin who did that to her that my jaw hurts. Larn was right, I realize. I still feel the effects of the wild sap.

Maintaining a slow pace to search for Tela, we travel to the cavern. Once we're in the gully, the others wait outside while I creep through the tunnel. I call out Tela's name several times but don't receive a reply. Inside the cave, the all too familiar purple glow illuminates an empty room.

As I look around the cavern, an inexplicable desire for Darkness to fall chews at my brain. I suddenly want to sink my teeth into the black bark of a tree and fill my veins with raw, unrestrained power. Trying to keep the craving for wild sap in check, I choke down the sap of the Delta from my canister.

"Chase!" Larn's voice rings out from the far end of the tunnel. "Did you find anything?"

I lower the steel from my lips. "Nothing," I yell. "I'll be right there."

After inhaling a few deep breaths, I screw the top back on the canister and call out, "Dark." As the light fades away behind me, I hurriedly make my way to the others.

"She isn't here," I say. "Let's go to where I hid the transport."

"Are you alright?" Larn asks. "You look pale."

"I'm fine. Just a few bad memories."

As we speed to the southwest, I try to remember how much I told Tela about where I stashed the transport. I know I said that it was hidden about two hundred miles southwest of the cavern. Although she was out of it at the time, I also told her that it was in a small gully near the base of the tallest hill in the area. If she pieced that information together, the transport wouldn't be hard to find.

When we reach the bottom of the hill, I head straight to the wash where I hid the transport. I'm not at all surprised to find the gully empty. I survey the flat area at the bottom of the hill and spot a fresh wheel track in the dirt. With the others close behind me, I follow the trail for about fifty yards. The line left by the wheel gradually becomes shallower until it disappears altogether. Since it never resumes, the transport must have risen in the air.

"Someone took the transport," I say to the others. "It could have been the Murkovin or it could have been Tela. Whoever it was knows how to travel."

"Does anyone have an idea about where she might have gone?" Larn asks the group. "Her mind obviously isn't clear enough to return to the Delta. What would you do in her situation?"

While we all try to come up with a reasonable theory, Jeni scuffs her boot across the dirt a few times. Even by Krymzyn standards, she's quiet and reserved, but she's the first to answer.

"Maybe she went closer to the Expanse," she says. "Fewer Murkovin dwell out there. That's where I'd go."

Larn turns his face to the west. "That makes sense. Why don't we spread out and travel towards the Eternal Canyon."

Spacing ourselves about ten miles apart, the five of us zigzag to the west. Every hundred miles or so, we each stop on the crest of a different hill and holler Tela's name. After roughly five hundred miles are behind us, I glide to the top of a low hill. Less than half a mile in front of me, a shirtless Murkovin with his spear slung over one shoulder and a backpack over the other is walking towards a valley. While staring at him, I realize he's the same beast that I lured away from the Murkovin camp before stealing the transport.

Before he enters the valley, he looks over each of his shoulders. When he sees me on the hill behind him, he immediately runs away. As I sprint down the hill, my muscles tense with fresh bloodlust for revenge. If I was right about him before, he can't blend his light. I set my sights on him and explode into the beams in his direction.

He twists his neck to look behind him. When he realizes I'm closing in on him, he rumbles to a stop and spins in my direction. I time my exit from the light so that I'm almost by his side. He has zero time to raise his spear in defense before my forearm slams into his face.

The force of my blow lifts his feet off the ground. Losing his balance, he flails backwards until his back pounds to the dirt. Sliding to a stop, I swing my spear over the top of my head. The end of the shaft smacks against his forehead. He tries to lift his head from the ground, but he's too dazed to get up.

After dropping my spear, I leap to his side and roll him onto his stomach. Pinning him to the ground with a knee in the center of his back, I rip the belt off my waist. He tries to get out from underneath me, but I slap an open palm against the back of his head and smash his face to the gravelly dirt. Before he can make another move, I knot my belt around his wrists.

I snatch my spear with one hand and a clump of his hair

with the other. Angling his head to the side, I dig the tip of my weapon into his neck. A trickle of blood runs down his skin.

"Where is she?" I shout.

"I don't know what you're talking about!"

"You're full of _shit_!"

I let go of his hair, pull my spear out of his neck, and drop my weapon to the dirt. After gripping one of his pinkies in my hand, I wrench it to the side. When his finger snaps at the middle knuckle, he shrieks in agony.

"I'm gonna' cut you," I snarl, "and then I'll break another finger. Over and over until you bleed to death or tell me where she is."

"I never saw her again after you took her from the canyon!"

"You're lying!"

I seize my spear in one hand and jump to my feet. As I rear back my weapon, a body crashes into mine. I stagger away from whoever attacked me and wildly jab my spear in that direction. When my assailant blocks it away, I coil with the urge to unleash my wrath on another Murkovin. Puzzled by the face in front of me, I freeze in place.

Chapter 25

"What are you doing?" Larn yells at me.

"Why did you hit me?" I shoot back. "He's one of the _assholes_ who attacked us. He knows where Tela is."

"I didn't see her again after you took her," the Murkovin grumbles.

Never taking his eyes off mine, Larn shakes his head. "Nothing warrants the torture of another living being. You need to get control of yourself right now."

As I glower at Larn, his words slowly sink in. I won't try to justify it as an excuse for what I did to the Murkovin, but I realize that I must have gone ballistic because of the wild sap still in my blood. Suddenly repulsed by my act of cruelty, my lack of restraint, I close my eyes.

When I open them again, I notice Sash standing on the side of a hill behind Larn. Velt and Jeni are beside her, all three staring at me with shocked expressions on their faces.

"I don't know what happened," I ashamedly admit to Larn.

"I told you that you might still have problems with the wild sap," he says.

"That's not an excuse. I'm sorry for what I did and how I behaved. I just want to find Tela."

"Not like this," he replies.

Sash, Velt, and Jeni walk down the hill and stop beside Larn.

"What did you think you were doing?" Sash asks me.

I chip away at the dirt with the tip of my spear. "I was trying to find out where Tela is," I answer. "I went too far."

Larn unclips a flask from his belt and kneels by the Murkovin's side. After helping him sit upright, he rubs a handful of sap on the wound in the creature's neck. Holding his flask to the beast's mouth, he tilts it up for the Murkovin to take a drink.

"Have you seen the female Traveler?" Larn asks him.

The Murkovin finishes a gulp and then pulls his mouth away from the flask. "Not since she was face down at the bottom of a canyon."

"Are you sure about that?" Larn asks.

"I left the area," he answers. "I can't travel. It took me several days to get out here."

Larn stands up and motions for Sash to come closer to him. "Have your spear ready."

Sash takes a few steps forward and raises her weapon in front of her. Larn helps the Murkovin to his feet while Sash keeps a close watch on him. After Larn unties the brute's hands, he tosses my belt to me.

The Murkovin narrows his eyes in my direction, holds his hands up in front of him, and grabs his broken finger. The bone crackles under his skin as he bends it straight, but his face never flinches.

"That's your neck if I ever see you again," he taunts.

Larn holds a flask out to him. "This is yours to keep. Be

on your way."

The Murkovin takes the flask from Larn and shoves it in the waist of his pants. As he grabs his spear and backpack from the ground, he fires a threatening glance in my direction. Without saying anything else, he jogs away from us and heads deeper into the valley.

"I believe he was telling the truth," Larn says.

"The others must have caught her," I reply. "Or maybe they killed her."

"Not necessarily. She's a strong, clever person capable of surviving on her own."

"Then we'll search until we find her," I say.

"She may not want to be found," he tells me. "If that's the case, it may be impossible to locate her."

I shake my head. "I can't believe she'd want to stay in the Barrens."

"Based on how you were acting when you returned to the Delta, she may have passed the point of having the clarity to make that decision. If her mind is trapped by the wild sap, her only thought might be to stay in a place where she can get it."

"Then what do we do?" I ask.

Larn shrugs. "I don't know. She could be fifty thousand miles in any direction by now and hiding in one of many thousands of caverns. A random search by eye is pointless."

"We can't just give up," I argue.

"We're all exhausted," Larn says. "I think Jeni's idea about searching closer to the Expanse is valid, but we need a better plan in place."

I run a hand through my hair. "I just wish we knew

which direction she went in."

Larn bends down to retrieve his spear from the ground. Sash steps to his side.

"You can try asking the Reflecting Pool," Sash says to me. "Ask the Pool if Tela is alive and where she is. Since you were with her, you should be the one to ask."

"Of course," I reply. "I should have thought of that."

"Be forewarned," Larn interjects. "The Pool may not give you the answer you seek."

"Why wouldn't it?" I ask him.

"The Barrens is an immense place. The Pool may not be able to show you exactly where Tela is. She might also stay on the move. At the very least, the Pool could let us know that she's alive."

"It's worth a try," I say.

"Think your questions through carefully," he counsels. "Only the correct one will lead to a useful answer. And even if we do find her, she may not want to return."

"We'll make her. We can use sap from the Delta to change her back."

"That may not be possible," Sash says.

"Why not?" I ask.

"Healthy sap from the Delta won't change a Murkovin into one of us," she explains. "A Disciple tried it once many Eras ago. No one has ever tried with someone born in the Delta who changed into a Murkovin."

"It worked on me."

"You weren't fully a Murkovin yet," she says. "Your hair still had a little blue in it. Your eyes were still purple, not red."

I look out over the endless miles of Barrens around us. "We still have to try. It's my fault she's out there."

"Why is your fault?" Larn asks.

I'm not about to tell anyone other than Sash what happened in the cavern with Tela, nor do I think Sash and Tela would want me to. I also don't think the others would understand, so I resort to a simple explanation.

"I should have made us come back sooner," I say to Larn. "I could have carried her. We were worried that my speed was slower from the wild sap, but I should have tried anyway. I made the wrong decision."

Nodding his head, Larn seems to accept my explanation. "Right or wrong, it's in the past. Let's find her first. Then we can worry about how to change her. We'll take it one step at a time."

By the time we make it back to the Delta, Aven is already fast asleep. Since we promised to pick her up before we went to sleep, Sash carries her to our habitat. When we step inside the main cavern, Aven stirs a little.

"Sleep wif you," she groggily mumbles, reaching a hand towards our bed.

Sash lays Aven down in the center of our mattress and rests her head on a pillow. Our daughter falls asleep in an instant. After Sash and I take turns cleaning off in the fall, we dress in sleep clothes and sit on opposite sides of the table. Sash pours each of us a cup of sap.

"I don't want to make you feel uncomfortable," I say. "Do you want me to stay in an empty habitat?"

"No," she answers. "I want you to stay here. Aven needs you right now."

"I know you need time. I just want you to know that I'll wait as long as I have to. I feel horrible about what happened and want to make things right."

Sash looks across the room at Aven and takes a sip from her cup. As she returns her eyes to me, she sets her cup down and folds her hands on top of the table.

"When I was younger," she says, "I crossed the bridge to the edge of the Barrens with Eval and a few Watchers. We were looking for signs of Murkovin near the river. I stopped by a badly damaged tree that was near death.

"A Murkovin walked over a hill in the distance. Even though Eval yelled at me, I couldn't stop myself from going after him. I wanted to kill him so badly because of the damage to the tree that it twisted my stomach. When I caught up to him, he was hiding behind a hill. As I started over the top, I had a glimpse of the future. A trap was waiting for me that would have resulted in my death, so I returned to the Delta. But more than anything else, I wanted to inflict pain on those Murkovin.

"I know what it's like to feel vengeance that can't be contained. The emotion was new to me at the time, so I didn't know how to stop it. When I saw what you did to that Murkovin earlier, I knew that wasn't you. Something else was in control of your mind. You would never torture someone else, not even a Murkovin. You're not that kind of a person."

"I don't think I am," I say. "I'll kill to protect my life or the people I care about. I've proven that. But I never thought I was capable of doing something like I did. I don't know what happened to me."

Sash looks down at her hands. "After seeing how you were, I think I better understand what happened to you and Tela in the Barrens. I just want you to know that."

Rubbing my temples, I try to figure out how to explain better what happened in the Barrens. Sash picks up the pitcher and refills my cup. I take a few sips and then set the cup down.

"When I saw that Murkovin," I say, "something went off inside me that I couldn't stop. My body acted without the permission of my mind. I blamed him for hurting Tela, for trapping us in the Barrens, and for the bad decisions I made. I wanted him to suffer.

"The wild sap gives a person a sense of power," I continue. "Part of that is the desire to have power over others. That's how some people in my world are. All they care about is power.

"As we grow up on Earth, we learn to control things like anger, jealousy, greed, and revenge—everything you call irrational or extreme. But not everybody in my world learns how. A lot of bad things end up happening to people who don't deserve it.

"I told you that the wild sap magnifies everything to extremes. The longer I was out there, the more a lot of my old fears were revived. But they were ten times stronger than I'd ever felt before."

"What fears?" Sash asks.

"Like, do I belong here? Did I make the right decision giving up my life on Earth? The more I thought about those questions, the more blurred the answers became. I lost my ability to think rationally and ended up getting so mad that I was filled with nothing but rage.

"The only relief I felt was taking care of Tela. It gave me a sense of purpose. I think that's why I gave in at first when . . . when we kissed. All the negative emotions I was feeling were so overwhelming that I believed you tricked me into coming to Krymzyn."

Sash frowns and shakes her head. "How could you ever think that, Chase?"

"Unless you experience it, you can't understand what it does to your mind. I could control it sometimes, but not others. I kept trying to answer a question that I thought I had the answer to a long time ago. Out there, I believed there was no answer."

"What question?" she asks.

I take a deep breath. "How could someone like you ever love someone like me?"

Sash holds my gaze. For the first time since our fight after I got back from the Barrens, her face softens with sympathy. "You saved my life in the river. You've defended Krymzyn against intruders. You've risked your own life to protect me and others. Those are all reasons to respect and honor you, but none of them is a reason to fall in love.

"The first time we went to the Tall Hill, you drew a picture of a sustaining tree in the air. You made sure that I saw a healthy tree because you said the trees seemed important to me. When we sat on the Hill, you asked me if it's hard on me to be the way I am. I told you that no one had ever asked me that before.

"Over and over, you've shown how much you care about my feelings. You're the only person to ever fully understand me. You accepted Krymzyn to be with me despite all that you had to sacrifice. Those are the reasons I fell in love with you, Chase. I've always felt safe with you. Safe on the inside."

"And now I've betrayed you," I say.

"I don't think you betrayed me. I'm angry. I'm hurt. But I still love you. It's going to take time, but we'll find a way to put this behind us."

"Like I said," I reply, "I'll do whatever I need to and wait as long as it takes. Even as messed up as my mind was out there, I never stopped loving you and Aven. That's the only thing that got me back."

After rinsing out our cups in the fall and putting them on the shelves, we climb on the bed on either side of Aven. Sash doesn't kiss me, caress my hair, or rest a hand on me the way she usually does when we go to bed. Understanding that it will take time for her to trust me again, to repair the emotional damage I've caused, I drape an arm over Aven and go to sleep.

Chapter 26

Early the next day, I finally get to spend a little time with Aven. While having our morning sap together, I help her with a simple puzzle consisting of putting the right shapes in the right holes. As the last remnants of sleep fade away, my mind feels sharper than it did the prior day. The long trek through the Barrens seems to have cleaned the last of the wild sap out of my system.

Sash travels with me to take Aven to Home. After baby girl is safely inside the caverns, Sash and I walk together across the meadow.

"I'm going to the Mount now," I say. "Do you want to come with me?"

We both stop and face each other.

"I think this is something you need to do on your own," she answers. "I'll help find Tela in any way I can, but I think you need to ask the questions. You're the one who's connected to her being in the Barrens."

"I kind of feel that way, too."

"Don't forget. Only the right questions will bring answers," she reminds me.

"I know," I say. "I just hope she's alive."

"We all do. I'll let Larn know that you've gone to the

240

Pool. Summon us as soon as you get back."

"I will."

As I turn away, she grabs my shoulder. After briefly hesitating, she reaches her arms around me and pulls me into an embrace.

"I'm so happy you're alive," she says in my ear.

"I'm really sorry about everything."

She takes a step back from me. "I still need time, Chase. But I am relieved that you're back." She studies my face for a moment. "Everything about you has returned to normal except for two things."

"What are they?" I ask.

"You have a scar on your shoulder," she answers.

"A Murkovin stabbed me," I tell her. "What's the other?"

"Your hair is darker. The blue is back in it, but the rest is black now instead of dark brown."

"It must be from with the wild sap," I say, remembering that Tela said the same thing about my hair.

"It's a reminder not to drink it again," she says evenly.

"Believe me. I wasn't planning on it."

Ten minutes later, I reach the entrance to the mountain compound. Not bothering to stop and get gloves and a helmet from the rack by the gate, I jog straight up the tree-lined road to the base of the Mount. Leaving the forest of purple and blue behind me, I stop at the path that snakes up the side of the mountain to the Pool. I immediately sink to one knee and press a hand to the ground.

"Please give me the sign to visit the Reflecting Pool," I whisper.

As I stand upright again, aqua light shimmers from my

palms. I climb the mile-long path up the side of the Mount. When I reach the ledge in front of the entrance to the Pool, a middle-aged, stocky male Watcher is standing guard in front of the closed door. I hold out my hand to show him the sign.

"Do you know the procedure?" he asks.

"I do," I answer. "I've been here before."

He opens the granite slab for me. "No one will interrupt you while you're inside."

"Thank you," I reply with a quick bow.

Before entering the tunnel, I hand him my spear. As I walk towards the blue light at the end of the corridor, the Watcher closes the door behind me. At the opening to the enormous cavern, I repeat the process I learned during my first visit to the Pool. I remove my boots, take off my clothes, and hang them on hooks embedded in the wall.

Inside the cavern, I walk across the firm, spongy stone of the circular walkway that surrounds the Pool and stop at the edge. The small trickle of water that spills down the walls and flows over the walkway tingles my feet. Above my head, the tiny golden Flits effortlessly glide through the candescent cyan vines that dangle from the domed ceiling. Light reflects all around me, creating a ballet of aqua and gold on the surface of the Pool.

After stepping over the edge of the walkway and into the Pool, I ease through the shallow water. I stop at the center and look down at the surface. The small waves from my motion gradually recede until the water is as smooth as a sheet of glass.

"Is Tela alive?" I ask.

While I stare down at the water, a blurred image ripples

across the surface. As the scene slowly comes into focus, it reveals Tela alone in the Barrens. She's sitting on top of a black dirt hill with a decrepit tree behind her. The strands of her hair that were once blue are pure white. Her arms are laced with black veins, and her eyes are fiery red. I let out a long, slow sigh, somewhat comforted by the fact that she's alive.

"Where in the Barrens is she?" I ask.

As though a camera is zooming out, the view slowly widens. Miles and miles of stark hills with no recognizable landmarks around them come into view. But Jeni was right about one thing. Far in the distance behind Tela, the multi-colored cascade of the barrier to the Infinite Expanse tints the horizon. I carefully examine the image to look for any other clues about the location, but I can't find any. She could be in any part of the wasteland that lines the Infinite Expanse.

"How can I find Tela?"

Several of the Flits dive down from the ceiling and fly past my face. Inches over the water, they weave around each other with glittering trails behind their paths. The reflections of the trails in the surface of the Pool erase the image from the water. As the Flits float back up to the vines overhead, the water remains blank. I carefully think about how I worded my last question. Maybe I'm not the one who can find her.

"Is there a way to find Tela?" I ask.

Tiny swells spread outward in the water, leaving a new scene of the Barrens in their wake. I'm not sure what I'm seeing at first or why the image is being shown to me. With her back to me, a girl no older than twelve is resting on her knees on top of a desolate hill. A braid of thick, black hair hangs down her back. It's so long that the end touches the dirt behind her. She reaches a hand to her side, rests it on the ground, and turns her head enough that I can see the profile of her face.

"Maya," I whisper.

It takes me a few moments to figure out why Maya would be the answer to my question. I eventually remember what Sash once told me about her extraordinary sense of awareness. It makes perfect sense.

"She can press her palm to the ground and tell you what any person in the Delta is feeling," Sash once said.

Maya felt my physical pain when I wiped out at the blockade that killed Beck. She sensed the Watcher's death when Balt killed him during the attack near the bridge. What she felt from a man being murdered was so strong that she started screaming from the horrifying experience. I don't know the distance that her powers of perception reach, but maybe she can sense Tela somewhere in the Barrens.

"Thank you," I say to the water.

I turn away and take a few steps towards the side of the Pool. When there's a splash in the water behind me, I stop. My first thought is that someone else came inside, so I glance around the cavern. The tunnel and circular walkway are empty, and the cave is vacant of any sound other than dripping water. As I look at the center of the Pool again, another image waves into view.

I'm confused by what I see since it seems to have nothing to do with the reason I'm here. Sash and I are standing in front of each other, but we're twelve years old. It must be the first time I came to Krymzyn—except one detail is different. We're at the bottom of the Empty Hill, not the top where we actually met.

The light around us darkens and the clouds churn into motion. As raindrops begin to fall, the glaring branches of Ovin's tree whip through the dark behind us. In my first visit to this world, Tork came to us before Darkness fell, and I returned to Earth soon after. What I see in the water never happened.

With raindrops pelting our heads, Sash and I clench each other in a hug. Her face looks so sad that it knots my insides. It's like watching two kids who've been best friends for years and years saying goodbye to each other because one is moving away.

In the distant sky, two of the gray billows spread apart. Through a tiny crack that opens between the clouds, a single ray of blazing white shoots straight at Sash's head. As a snow-white halo radiates around her hair, the image of me leans back to look at her face. In a blinding flash, the scene disappears. I stare at the blank surface of water, wondering what I just saw.

"Why did you show that to me?" I ask.

The Pool remains perfectly still, nothing but a mirror of silvery-blue. I step out of the water, put my clothes on, and leave the cavern.

As I descend the winding path on the side of the Mount, I replay the last scene that I saw over and over in my mind. Why would the Pool show that to me? As far as I can tell, it has nothing to do with finding Tela.

When I reach the narrow road at the bottom of the path, I decide I'll ask Sash about it later. I return my thoughts to planning how to search for Tela.

Wanting to get back to the Delta as quickly as I can, I run down the road towards the gate. As I pass by the clearing where the Constructs work, someone calls out my name. I halt and turn to the meadow to see Wren jogging in my direction. After he stops at the edge of the road, he nervously fidgets with his belt and looks around us.

"Hi, Wren," I say.

He finally locks his eyes on mine. "I finished the soccer goals. I just wanted to let you know."

"I'll get them some other time," I say. "I have a lot on my mind right now."

"I also . . ." He pauses for a second. "Nuar told me what happened. I asked why I hadn't seen Tela . . . you and Tela on the Mount."

I almost can't look him in the eyes because of the guilt flooding through me. I've seen how enamored Wren is with Tela, and he's obviously concerned about her. I try to console myself with the thought that any physical desires that developed between Tela and me in the cave were spawned by the wild sap and nothing else. But Wren is a friend. I feel like I betrayed him. The least I can do now is provide him with some hope.

"Tela's alive," I say. "The Pool just showed me that."

"Do you know where she is?" he asks.

"No, but we'll find her," I answer with a lot more confidence in my voice than I actually have in my statement.

"I hope so. If there's anything I can do to help or

anything you need, please let me know."

"Thanks, Wren. I will."

He bows to me and then returns to the clearing. A renewed sense of urgency to find Tela rattles my nerves. Her mind is clouded by a narcissistic, self-destructive delirium that she has no way of dealing with. I was able to pull myself out of the stupor, but I had years of growing up in a world where we learn self-restraint over negative emotions. I should have been able to suppress them. I should have been able to think clearly for both of us. When she needed me the most, I let Tela down.

Chapter 27

I race back to the Delta and go straight to Home. Soon after I summon Sash and Larn, they soar to the meadow from different directions.

"Tela's alive," I say as soon as they stop in front of me. "I saw her in the Pool."

Larn blows out a long sigh of relief. "Did it show you anything else?" he asks.

"I could see the barrier to the Infinite Expanse behind her," I answer. "I couldn't see the sky to see the direction of the light from the clouds. It didn't show me that. If it had, we'd at least know which side of the Expanse she's near. Maybe that means the Pool doesn't know exactly where she is, or maybe she's on the move. Then I asked if there's a way to find her. That's why I summoned you both to meet me here at Home. The Pool showed me Maya."

"Maya?" Larn asks, sounding mildly confused.

"It makes sense," Sash says. "She might be able to feel Tela in the Barrens."

"Do you have any idea from how far away she can feel things?" I ask.

"We'll have to ask her," she answers. "I don't know that she's ever felt someone farther away than the Mount."

"That's less than eighty miles from here. Even if we know that Tela's near the Expanse, it will take forever to stop every eighty miles."

"Every one hundred and sixty miles," Sash says flatly.

"What?" I ask.

"Eighty miles in each direction. That means we stop every one hundred and sixty miles."

"Whatever," I say. "It will still take forever."

"We should talk to her first," Sash says. "Then we can make a plan. The Pool showed her to you for a reason."

Sash disappears inside the caverns of Home for a few minutes and then returns with Maya and Marc. Once Maya is in front of us, she folds her hands in front of her and sheepishly lowers her eyes to the ground.

"Did I do something wrong?" she asks.

"Quite the opposite," Sash tells her. "We hope you can help us. Did you hear what happened to Chase and Tela?"

"I know they were missing," Maya answers, raising her eyes to Sash. "Aven was very upset."

"Tela is still alive in the Barrens," I say. "When I asked the Reflecting Pool how to find her, it showed me you."

"I don't know I can help."

"Maybe you can sense where she is," I explain. "Do you know from how far away you can feel someone?"

"I've only ever felt someone as far as the Mount."

"Do you know the direction it comes from when it happens?" I ask.

"Kind of," she answers. "I end up turning my face to where it is without really thinking about it. And the stronger something is in the person, like real bad pain, the more I feel

249

it."

"Why don't we try something," Sash says. "If Marc approves, let's all go to the other side of the river. We'll conduct an experiment."

"By all means," Marc replies.

After we're across the bridge, Sash suggests a simple test using herself as a guinea pig. She has Maya and me sit beside each other on the gravelly dirt by the side of the road. Keeping watch on the Barrens, Marc and Larn stand close behind us. Not wanting Maya to see what direction she's planning to go in, Sash asks her to shut her eyes. She also tells us not to worry about anything Maya might feel. Sash then speeds away down the side of the river to the south.

Once Sash is well out of sight, I tell Maya that she can open her eyes. Staring at the rapids leaping from the river, she sits perfectly still with both of her palms resting on the dirt. As I study her face, I realize she's no longer the frail little girl she was the first time we met. Her features may still be delicate—a thin, straight nose, almond-shaped eyes, and high cheekbones in a narrow face—but at roughly the age of twelve, she's starting to mature into a teenager.

After a few minutes pass, Maya winces and clenches her teeth. Her eyes drift away from the rapids and down the side of the river.

"Ouch!" she exclaims. "Sash feels a lot of pain. Straight ahead."

"You know for sure it was Sash?" I ask.

"I sure do," she answers. "I know what she feels like from visiting the clouds with her. That's how I knew you were hurt at the blockade in the road. I could tell it was you because I'd felt you when we visited the clouds."

"Do you know what Tela feels like?"

"Of course," she nods. "She was already at Home when I was a baby. She didn't leave until her Apprenticeship ended. I was around her a lot."

"That makes sense," I say, remembering the bond that seems to link all the children who were at Home together around that time.

"But when the Watcher was killed, he was much older than I am, so I didn't know him well. I felt his pain but wasn't sure who it was." She suddenly jerks her face to the southeast and squints in that direction. "Sash feels pain again, but she's also angry. She's very mad."

"I can't imagine why," I say. "I'll ask her about it later. You're sure it was Sash that you felt?"

"Absolutely," she confidently replies.

"That's great, Maya. Keep it up."

Obeying Sash's instructions, we wait for something else to appear on Maya's telepathic radar. After a few more minutes tick away, Maya's face aims due south again. Shivering slightly, she shakes her head.

"More pain," she murmurs. "But it's not as strong as before."

"What could she possibly be doing?" I rhetorically ask out loud.

"I don't know," Maya says, "but whatever it is, it hurts her."

We sit quietly for another few minutes until Maya closes her eyes. "I think I feel . . . I'm not sure. Something, but I don't know exactly what it is or where."

"Try to concentrate," I say.

She presses her hands more firmly against the ground. A few moments later, she relaxes and opens her eyes.

"I don't know. There was something, but I'm not sure what. I'm not even sure it was Sash."

"That's alright," I say. "What you've done so far is incredible. When she gets back, we'll know how far away she was."

"What is this all about?" Maya asks.

"I asked the Pool if there's a way to find Tela," I answer. "The Pool showed me you. Maybe if we take you to the Barrens, you might be able to feel where she is."

She nervously scrapes her fingernails across the dirt. "To the Barrens?"

"Does that bother you?"

"I don't like the Barrens," she answers. "It's scary out there."

"I know it is. But you might be Tela's only hope."

With a sullen expression on her face, she doesn't say anything else. As long as I've known her, she's been timid and shy. But as I learned when she once insisted that I be the one to transport her to the Mount, she can be confident and headstrong when something is important to her. I decide not to push her now, knowing that Sash has an almost sisterly relationship with her. If anyone can convince her to go to the Barrens, it will be Sash.

Another twenty minutes silently slip away before Sash zooms over a hill. The beams smear into the shape of her body and she coasts to a stop in front of us.

"What did you feel?" she asks, looking down at Maya.

"The first thing was pain from you," Maya answers.

"I'm impressed," Sash says. "That was two hundred miles away."

"Then more pain and you were angry," Maya continues.

With an accusing look, Sash moves her eyes to me. "That was at three hundred miles."

"What were you angry about?" I ask. "You said that you understand now."

"Just because I understand doesn't mean I'm not mad. I'm also upset because I'm traveling around the Barrens and poking holes in my body with a spear. I'm pretty sure that's your fault."

When I glance at each of Sash's hands, I'm almost unable to believe what I see. A round, quarter-inch scab is on the back of each of one. Although the wounds are already healing, probably from sap, they look like they were deep and painful.

"I can't believe you did that," I say to her. "Why didn't you just think good thoughts?"

Sash glances at Maya and then back at me. "Because Maya senses pain much more than anything else, and I doubt Tela has many good thoughts where she is right now."

"I guess not," I agree.

Sash kneels in front of Maya. "Was that all you felt?"

"No," she answers. "I felt more pain on your third stop."

"Four hundred miles," Sash says. "That was my leg."

"I felt something else after that, but I wasn't sure what it was. I don't even know if it was you."

"That was my other leg," Sash tells her, "at six hundred miles. I went farther than that and stabbed my legs a few more times."

"I didn't feel those, but I'm sorry you had to hurt yourself."

"Thank you," Sash says. "We can safely estimate your range to be four hundred miles."

"Is that good?" Maya asks.

"It's awesome," I say. "So it's up to you. Will you help us find Tela?"

Maya scrunches her nose while thinking about her answer, obviously not in love with the idea. Still kneeling in front of her, Sash rests a hand on Maya's knee.

"You have an incredible gift," she says. "How you use it is up to you. If you don't want to go to the Barrens, no one will blame you. But I know how strong you can be. Tela needs your help."

"Will you be with us?" Maya asks.

"Every moment," she answers. "I won't let you out of my sight."

"I'm going as well," Larn chimes in from behind us.

"It could take a lot more than a few days to find her," I say to him.

"We'll take it one at a time," he replies.

"I'll go," Maya announces to Sash. "I want to help find Tela."

Sash nods her head and smiles. "I'm proud of you. If Marc approves, we'll leave first thing on the morrow."

Marc rubs his chin. "I don't know if it will work, but the Pool did show Maya to Chase. Since she's agreed to go, I approve. I don't like the thought of Tela out there either."

"None of us do," Sash says.

Chapter 28

While contemplating the best way to convince the Traveler to join her, the woman observes the distant sky. Her eyes sway back and forth in almost perfect unison with the spectrum of color waving against listless gray clouds. The Traveler showed cunning in her plan to hide in the Barrens, the woman decides. It's no secret to those of the Delta that very few of the woman's kind dwell near the barrier to the Infinite Expanse.

A Guardian might venture far from a Gateway in hopes of catching a Murkovin who errantly steps foot in their domain. The Guardians' lust for sap-filled blood, the desire for a few moments outside the realm of suspended time, had long been a source of fear for those who dwell in the Barrens.

"I want you to go to the Desert," the woman says to the tall Murkovin standing beside her. "Tell my child's Mür that the young female Traveler will be at camp with me. He'll know the one when you describe her. But tell no one else about the Traveler. I want others to believe she's from the Barrens."

"You know I won't talk," he says. "Why do you think she'll go with you?"

"She may not, but I have reason to believe she will."

"I should stay until you know for sure."

Appreciative of his desire to protect her, the woman reaches out a hand and lightly grips his arm. "It will be easier to gain her trust if I'm alone. She might feel threatened if she sees you."

The tall Murkovin begrudgingly nods his head. "I've seen signs of a few others nearby. Stay alert."

"I will," she replies, pulling her hand away from him. "When you reach the Desert canyon, tell him I'll visit soon. He shouldn't show his face at camp until I do. We don't want the Traveler to see him."

"Why not?" the tall Murkovin asks.

"In the unlikely event that she returns to the Delta, it will be to our benefit if she believes he's dead."

"Let the people of the Delta feel secure behind their wall," he mutters.

"Exactly," she confirms. "Go back to camp when you're finished in the Desert. I'll meet you there soon."

"Don't let your guard down."

"I never do," she says.

The tall Murkovin races away across the rough terrain. After he breezes into the light, the woman walks to a narrow gorge between two almost vertical slopes. She stops when she reaches the center of the canyon, sits down on the dirt, and lays her spear on the ground. Less than fifty feet in front of her stands a sheer wall of rock with a crevice in the base. That seam, just wide enough and tall enough for a person to fit through, leads to the current refuge of the Traveler.

For the past two days, the woman and tall Murkovin had painstakingly searched the southeast Barrens where the

Traveler had last been seen. Without the tall Murkovin's uncanny skill at tracking others, the woman doubts she would have located the Traveler. He always notices the tiniest stone out of place, the faintest footprint in the dirt, or the smallest of creases concealed in a hillside. Of even greater value is his ability to think like his opponents. He anticipates every move that enemies might make in battle, and instinctively seems to know where they'll hide if they run.

Even though the tall Murkovin had already seen the Traveler in this general area, they still had trouble finding her. The tall Murkovin finally spotted a faint wheel track in the dirt. Although the Traveler had tried to erase the groove by brushing the branch of a tree over it, they were able to follow the trail to a small gully cut into the side of a hill.

Hidden in the wash was a steel transport, one the woman could tell had been crafted by the Murkovin in the Desert, not by Constructs of the Mount. Since they hadn't recruited Murkovin in this area yet, the woman concluded that the transport had to be the one stolen by the two Travelers.

Well hidden in the rocky terrain, the woman and tall Murkovin laid in wait until the Traveler showed up at the transport. After the Traveler refilled her canister and flasks, they secretly followed her to where she entered the cavern. It's now better to wait for the Traveler to come outside on her own than to risk surprising her in a cramped, dark cave.

After very little time passes, the woman's head begins to nod. During their two days of searching for the Traveler, she and the tall Murkovin had only allowed themselves one brief rest. Fearing she might give in to sleep, the woman stands to her feet and forces her eyes open. Moments later, a silhouette appears in the seam of the rocks in front of her. The person immediately vanishes back into the shadows of the tunnel.

"You're in the Barrens again!" the woman calls out, knowing the Traveler must have seen her. "But it appears you mean to stay this time."

"Why are you here!" the Traveler shouts from the dark.

"I mean you no harm. I want to talk with you."

"I have nothing to say!" the Traveler yells, a growing viciousness in her tone. "How many are with you?"

"I'm alone. I give you my word."

"Your word means nothing!"

The woman holds her empty hands out in front of her. "I've proven before that you can trust me. I'm not in search of a fight."

After a long silence, the Traveler leans her head out of the crevice. She snaps her head to each of her sides to look for others. White strands interwoven with long, black hair whip across her face. Seeing no one else in sight and the woman's weapon on the ground beside her, the Traveler slides her body through the opening in the rocks. Aiming her spear at the woman, she steps down to the flat ground.

As the woman studies the Traveler's appearance, the woman wonders why her pant legs are torn off above off the knees. Other than the dusty boots on her feet, there's nothing about her that would lead someone to believe she's from the Delta.

"How did you know where I am?" the Traveler asks.

"Very little happens in the Barrens that I'm not aware of," the woman answers. "Why are you here?"

"Why do you want to know?"

"I'm concerned for your safety," the woman tells her. "There aren't many Murkovin in the outer regions, but those who do dwell here could find you. Some live peacefully. Others take what they want. You're a healthy young woman. If a certain kind finds you, they'll make you serve them in many ways. Although you'll crave death, they won't grant it to you."

Although the Traveler maintains the grip on her spear, she relaxes the muscles in her arms. "Why do you care what happens to me?"

"I don't tolerate women suffering abuse," the woman says. "Even a woman from the Delta."

"No Murkovin can catch me," the Traveler arrogantly replies.

"You have to sleep. I doubt you know how to secure a cavern the way most of our kind do."

"I can take care of myself," the Traveler grumbles.

She has a decent level of control over the wild sap, a sign of a strong mind, but her temper is volatile. I hope Darkness doesn't fall before our conversation ends. I'm sure the cravings would overwhelm her.

"Is this the life you want?" the woman asks. "Dwelling alone in a tiny cave in the outer regions of the Barrens with tattered pants on your legs?"

The Traveler looks down at the ground. "I just want to be left alone."

What could have happened to make her flee so deep in

the Barrens? If I learn the answer to that question, I may be able to exploit the knowledge to manipulate her into doing what I want. But before I can find out, I have to gain her trust.

"I can show you that life in the Barrens isn't what you believe it to be," the woman says. "I'm teaching our kind to peacefully coexist. I believe you can be of great help."

The Traveler returns her eyes to the woman. "How could I be of help to your kind?"

"I'm teaching as many as I can to travel. In a world as vast as ours, traveling is the great equalizer, but few Murkovin ever master the skill. They're either confined to lives in small regions or aimlessly wander the wasteland as nomads. Trees in many areas are destroyed or damaged to the point that they produce very little sap. Many of our kind have no other option than to kill one another to survive. But as I'm sure you've seen, there are still many untouched trees in the Barrens.

"I'm showing them a way to take sap without killing the trees," the woman continues, spinning her tale of half-truths. "They can bind the trees rather than rip the limbs off them. I'm showing them how to store large quantities of sap instead of barely enough to last a few days. They learn to control their desires because they're no longer desperate.

"I've scoured the Barrens in search of abandoned steel transports, stakes, and tubes from raids on Travelers over the Eras. I'm able to share my ideas with others and provide them with the tools they need to put that knowledge to use. Traveling is what makes it all possible. But I need to teach more of my kind. I can blend my light and show them how, but someone with your advanced skills can be of great help to me."

"What do you get from all of this?" the Traveler asks.

"A better life for my child," the woman answers. "I don't want him to face the hardships I've known. If I'm successful, it will be better for those in the Delta as well. We can live our lives in the Barrens and leave them alone."

The Traveler stares at her without answering, but the woman sees belief in her eyes.

"There was a Watcher who left the Delta," the Traveler says. "Do you know where he is?"

"He's dead," the woman answers.

"Why was he killed?"

The woman had already prepared for that question. "His hatred for the Delta guided his actions. He convinced a few of my kind to join him, but his vision was clouded. He never learned to control what the sap of the Barrens released inside him. He only wanted power over others. When he had nothing else to offer, others turned on him."

"What makes you think I won't be killed if I'm seen by others?" the Traveler asks.

"No one needs to know you're from the Delta," the woman says. "I can guarantee your safety, but only if you answer one question for me."

"What's that?"

"Why didn't you return to the Delta with the other Traveler?"

Narrowing her eyes, the Traveler looks off to her side. "I have my reasons."

"Tell me one," the woman says.

The Traveler hesitates for several seconds before speaking. "He didn't want to be with . . ." She stops talking, clenches her jaw, and turns her face to the woman. "They don't appreciate me in the Delta."

He must have rejected her, the woman thinks.

"There's much you've been deprived of," the woman says. "Someone with your abilities deserves to feel valued. In the Barrens, you can live for yourself, put your needs first, and have whatever you want. *You* define who you are here, not the color of your hair."

As though she's searching for an answer, the Traveler scrutinizes the woman's eyes. "I'll consider it," she finally says. "For now, I want to be left alone."

"If that's what you want, I'll leave you alone. I advise you to change your location every few days. Never stay in one place too long."

The woman starts walking towards one end of the gorge.

"You forgot your spear," the Traveler calls out.

Without breaking her stride, the woman glances over her shoulder. "You keep it. It may come in handy for you to have two."

The woman continues at a steady pace towards the end of the canyon. After a few more days pass, she can try again. Let the Traveler experience more of the harshness that comes with dwelling in the Barrens. The woman can stay close by and keep watch over the Traveler, but it makes more sense not to push too hard now.

"Wait!" the Traveler shouts.

The woman stops walking and turns to her.

"I'll come with you," the Traveler says.

The woman nods her head. "You won't regret it. I can provide you with a cavern and safety with others who think as I do. Strong men and women who want the same things I want for the Barrens."

"Let me get my things from the cave," the Traveler says.

"I'll wait for you here."

After the Traveler slips through the crease in the rock wall, the woman returns to her spear. She reaches down, takes it in her hand, and scans the nearby hilltops to make sure that no others were in earshot of their conversation.

I should restrain my speed as we return to camp, the woman thinks. *Better to let her feel superior in that way. The more she feels needed, the more she'll be willing to help. I'll be able to train the five hundred Murkovin I need in half the time.*

It's unlikely that she'll ever return to the Delta or that they'll accept her if she does. But I wonder if she'll embrace our ways. For the time being, I'll let her think the former Watcher is dead and reveal nothing of our plans. If she's not fully on our side by the time we're ready to attack the Delta, I'll have no choice but to kill her.

I hope it never comes to that. I already find myself growing fond of her. But regardless of how I feel, no one will stand in my way.

Chapter 29

In the golden light of our habitat, Sash and I spend a much-needed quiet evening with Aven. Seated at a small table that we brought from Market for Aven's room, we help her get started on a finger painting. Once she's fully engrossed in the smudges of colors, I spread out a large sheet of canvas on the floor and begin drawing a scale map of Krymzyn. I want the map to encompass everything inside the barrier to the Infinite Expanse so that I can keep track of the areas where we search for Tela.

Seated beside me, Sash helps me with the map by pointing out where important landmarks should go. Although Sash hugged me before I went to the Pool earlier in the day, I haven't seen any other signs of forgiveness from her. She's polite in her communication with me, but I wouldn't describe her as warm. As much as I want to reach out and hold her, give her a hug and a kiss and tell her that I love her, I decide I should wait for a cue from Sash.

By the time we're ready to go to sleep, about a third of the paint that Aven started with is splattered all over her face and body. After showering Aven in the fall, we all climb on the bed. Stretched out between Sash and me, Aven soon drifts into a peaceful sleep. I roll on my side and look over

Aven at Sash.

"I saw something else when I was at the Pool," I say in a hushed voice. "It didn't make sense to me."

"What was it?" she asks.

"You and me the first time I came to Krymzyn. But it was different than what actually happened. We were standing at the bottom of the Empty Hill instead of the top, and Tork never came. When Darkness fell, you and I hugged like we were both really sad. Then a shaft of light shot down on us from the clouds."

While Sash spends a few moments thinking about what I saw, I listen to Aven's soft, steady breathing. "I don't know what that means," Sash says. "It could be an answer to a question you haven't asked yet."

"Why would the Pool show it to me now?"

"Maybe when you need the answer, you won't be able to go to the Pool. Always remember what you saw."

"I will," I say. "It's not the kind of thing I'd ever forget."

Early the next day, Sash and I take Aven to Home and exchange her for Maya. After meeting Larn at the gate, we all slip boots on our feet and drape canisters over our shoulders. Once Maya is secure in a traveling harness on my back, we depart the Delta. Using the bridge north of the Delta, we cross to the western Barrens.

As we glide over the wasteland, the weight of Maya's thin frame is almost unnoticeable. Sash zips back and forth in front of me while Larn stays a few miles behind us to protect our rear. Due to the enormous distance, we spend well over half the day just getting to the area where we plan on searching. We stop on a hill overlooking the Bridge of

Harmony that crosses the Eternal Canyon.

"I want to talk to the Schorachnia," Sash says. "Maybe they saw something. Then we'll decide where to go."

"Do you think Tela would have come this close to a Gateway?" I ask.

Sash shakes her head. "I doubt it, but sometimes the Guardians will go thousands of miles from their Gateways along the edge of the Expanse. They all have incredible speed. They check on their domains in either direction, just like the Serquatine swim the length of the river."

"Why do they do that?" I ask.

"To catch Murkovin if they can. The sap in their blood does the same thing for the Guardians as the sap in ours."

"They're such friendly creatures," I sarcastically comment.

I'm surprised that Sash smiles at my remark. "They serve a purpose," she says. "That's what matters."

Sash runs down the hill towards the Canyon. After I release Maya from the harness, she plops down on the ground by my feet. Her eyes are captivated by the fluctuating colors of the barrier over the western sky. The symphonic serenade of the Canyon spills across the red dirt and flows into our ears. I sit down on the ground beside Maya while Larn stands behind us to keep watch on the Barrens.

"This is incredible!" Maya gasps.

"Is this your first time near the Infinite Expanse?" I ask.

"It is. I've never seen or heard anything like this."

Soon after Sash stops at the Stone of Passage, one of the enormous, scorpion-like Schorachnia climbs over the side of the Canyon and shuffles to her. With his two tails coiled behind him and the pinchers on his two front arms clicking and clacking, the rusty-colored creature has a conversation with Sash. When Maya lowers her eyes from the sky and spots the Schorachnia, she uncontrollably shivers.

"That's the scariest looking thing I've ever seen," she says.

"And to make matters worse, they're not very friendly," I reply.

"Have you met them?"

"I came to this Gateway for my journey to the Expanse," I answer.

She turns her head to me and scrunches her face. "You rode that thing across the Bridge of Harmony?"

"I sure did," I say. "It was an amazing experience."

"Now that I've seen them, I don't think I'll choose this Gateway when I go."

I quietly chuckle. "You've seen the sky and heard the music. That's the best part."

Once Sash finishes speaking with the Guardian, she races back to us. Maya and I stand from the ground and Larn joins us at Maya's side.

"What did he say?" I ask Sash.

"He hasn't seen any Murkovin near his domain in a long while," she answers, "but that doesn't mean Tela isn't near the Canyon. I thought it was worth asking if they'd seen anyone who resembles her."

"What's the plan now?"

Sash's eyes roam the Barrens for a few moments before she answers. "Maya's range is roughly four hundred miles in any direction. The barrier can be seen from about two thousand miles away. If we make a stop straight out from the Expanse at four hundred miles, then two more stops every eight hundred miles farther out, we'll know we've covered everything in sight of the barrier with a little overlap. Then we move eight hundred miles north or south, and we make three more stops in a direct line back to the Expanse. We'll do it over and over until we make our way all along the edge of the barrier. But there's one question we need to answer first."

"What's that?" I ask.

"Do we head north or south from here?"

Sash moves her eyes from person to person while we try to come up with a logical response. Larn turns his head to the north, studies the distant Barrens, and then looks to the south.

"I would say south," he says.

"Are you basing that on anything?" Sash asks.

"I think she'd want to stay as far away from the Delta as possible," he answers. "If she traveled too far north from where she and Chase were, she'd risk crossing the paths we use to the Expanse. I think she'd stay in the southern part of the Barrens."

Sash directs her attention to me. "And you?"

"I agree with Larn, but my reasoning is a little different. The Murkovin were still looking for us and trying to cut off our path to the Delta. Tela suggested that we go far north of the Delta and then back down to avoid them. She knows that I know that, so I think she'd do the opposite."

"You and Tela were about forty thousand miles south of here," she says. "Do you think we should start there?"

"I don't know. We're here now and a lot of the day is gone. I think Larn was correct when he said that we shouldn't be random in our search. Starting here is as good a place as any. If she doesn't want to be found, I don't think she'd stay close to where we were."

Sash nods to me and then looks at Maya. "What do you think?"

"I don't think I should have a say," she answers.

"I disagree," Sash says in a soothing tone. "If you're brave enough to be out here with us, you should have a say in what we do."

Maya glances at me and then looks at Sash again. "I think what Larn and Chase said makes sense. I say south from here. What do you think?"

"It's unanimous," Sash answers. "I think she'd want to stay close to the Expanse with the least amount of risk of being seen by anyone else."

"Let's hope Tela's thinking that rationally," I say.

Once Maya is on my back again, we travel a few hundred miles due west. On top of the highest hill in the area, Larn helps Maya off my back. She kneels to the ground, places both palms on the dirt, and closes her eyes. The rest of us scour the Barrens in every direction looking for movement that might be a Murkovin. A few minutes pass with Maya in deep concentration before she utters a sound.

"I don't sense anything," Maya says.

"It's not very likely that we'd find her on the first stop," I tell her. "Even the first hundred or so."

In less than five minutes, we cover the eight hundred miles to our second stop. We spend another few minutes with Maya on the ground trying to sense something from Tela. We repeat the process over and over, snaking back and forth across the Barrens to the south. As the day wears on, the routine becomes increasingly monotonous, but at least we're covering a much larger area than if we tried to search by eye.

At our twentieth stop, we see a lone Murkovin standing on a hilltop less than a mile away. With her eyes magnetized to the beast, Maya nervously fidgets with the dirt at her sides. The creature disappears behind the hill but soon climbs back to the crest with another Murkovin at his side.

"Can you try to focus on where they are?" I ask Maya.

"I'll try," she says quietly. "This is the first time I've seen a Murkovin."

Sash kneels by her side. "Don't be afraid, Maya. We won't go near them and I won't let them anywhere near you."

The confidence in Sash's tone seems to ease Maya's fear. She closes her eyes and pushes her hands firmly to the ground. After a few moments, she shakes her head and looks up at me with a frown on her face.

"Nothing."

"We should head back now," Larn says. "It's almost time for sleep. We have a long return trip ahead of us and can't keep Maya out any longer."

Maya lowers her eyes to the dirt. "I'm sorry I didn't find her."

"Don't feel bad," I say. "I didn't think there was much chance of us finding her on the first day."

During the trip back to the Delta, I realize what an enormous undertaking lies ahead of us. It took so much time just getting to where we started that we were only left with a few hours of actual searching. With Maya's range, each stop we made took care of roughly an eight hundred mile diameter circle with us in the center. We went through twenty of those, which totals over ten million square miles, an unfathomable amount of space by Earth standards.

I try several times to calculate how many days it will take if we have to search the entire edge of the Expanse. On a stop for sap, I even ask Sash to confirm my math. The number we both come up with—a very rough estimate—is two hundred.

As we near the Delta, one of Maya's cheeks falls to the particles of my shoulder. After it remains dormant there for a few minutes, I assume she's dozed off. My head suddenly aches from all the "what ifs" running through my mind.

What if I'd just insisted that I carry Tela back to the Delta when she seemed better? What if I'd gone to refill the canisters with sap while she was in the waterfall? What if I'd had the decency to leave the cave when she took her clothes off instead of gawking at her? What if I'd come to my senses sooner and realized what the wild sap was doing to both of us?

What if . . . what if . . . what if.

When we reach the Delta, we head straight to Home. Marc takes a sleeping Maya from my back and carries her to her room. Since Aven's already out for the night, Sash and I decide to leave her at Home. We return to our habitat, clean off, and pass out from exhaustion.

Early the next day, we spend half an hour playing with Aven at Home before departing again with Maya. Just as he was the prior day, Larn is already waiting for us by the gate. Before we get our boots and canisters, Sash steps in front of Larn.

"I don't want to sound rude," she says, "but I don't think you should come with us."

"Why not?" Larn asks.

"You'll slow us down. You know how fast my speed is, and Chase has surpassed yours. We need to cover a lot more ground than we did on the prior day."

"It's safer with three of us," he argues.

"We aren't there to fight. Our speed will keep us safe."

Larn looks at me. "What was your count?"

"Three-eighty one," I answer. "But I think I can go a little faster."

"And Tela's?" he asks.

"The same that I had."

He thoughtfully nods his head. "I've noticed how fast you've both become. I'm sorry she isn't here to hear me say this. I'm proud to have served as Mentor to both of you."

"Thank you, Larn," I say. "You can tell her in person when we bring her back."

"I hope I have that opportunity." He looks down at Maya. "Do you feel safe with just the two of them."

"I think so," Maya says. "Sash won't let anything bad happen to me."

Larn returns his attention to Sash. "Her safety is your top priority. Let me know as soon as you return."

"I will," she replies. "Thank you for understanding."

Larn bows to us and then walks in the direction of Market. Considering all his help and how much concern he's shown for Tela's well being, I hope he doesn't feel bad from what Sash said. But I'm fairly certain he recognizes the truth in her words.

"Now it's your turn," Sash says to me. "You need to go faster."

"I think I've got a little more in me."

"You need a lot more than a little. That's why I asked Larn not to come. Do you believe you can go as fast as I can?"

"Of course not," I answer. "You're three times faster than anyone here."

"Do you remember when I helped you go faster by traveling through you?"

"Is that what you want to do now?" I ask.

"No," she answers. "I want you to travel at my speed on your own."

"I don't think that's possible," I say.

"It is possible," she firmly replies. "When I shared my light with you at the Gateway, I had to leave some of it inside you. It was the only way to bring you back from the Expanse. Part of what I gave you is in your spectrum now. If you believe you can match my speed, you'll find the same level of focus that I have and your body will follow your mind."

"Why haven't you told me this before?" I ask.

"You haven't needed it until now," she answers. "Free your mind of the boundaries you impose on yourself and you'll keep pace with me. If you can't do that, you should stay here."

I shake my head. "I'm not staying here."

"Then keep up with me," she demands. "Until you prove you can go faster, Maya will ride with me."

Once Maya is on Sash's back, I follow them to the western Barrens. Soon after we hit the open space, Sash begins to pull away from me. I concentrate on staying right behind her, but she puts more and more distance between us. Tunneling my vision into a few distinct beams, I try to forget about everything else. No matter how hard I try, I can't keep up with her.

When she's almost out of my sight, she suddenly slows until she's right by my side. She drifts towards me so that the tiny barbs of her body bristle against mine. As our molecules partially intermix, she gradually accelerates. I block out every other thought except keeping the feel of her inside me.

Buried somewhere in my body is a gear that I never knew existed. When my mind shifts into that gear, the force of the whiplash almost collapses my lungs. The bite of an arctic blizzard numbs every particle of my body, and I fight with all my might just to suck in one breath. I might as well have straddled a comet hurtling through outer space.

While torpedoing across the wasteland, it's impossible for me to detect any real detail in the terrain. Nebulous shapes warp through my vision. The only sight I can make out for sure is the sparkling trail directly in front of me that I know is Sash. I stay right on her tail.

A blink must be ten miles, a heartbeat twenty, and a breath a hundred. It's almost impossible to judge time at the speed we stream across the badlands. When Sash eventually begins to slow, I broaden my focus until I return to what would have been my normal traveling speed. We both slip from the light and coast to a stop on top of a hill. When I realize we're already on the same hill that we made our last stop on the prior day, I look at Sash in amazement.

"That was incredible!"

Sash stabs her spear into the ground, catches her breath, and smiles at me. "We made it to this hill in a third of the time that it took us to get from here to the Delta with Larn."

Rubbing the sting out of her cheeks, Maya pokes her face out from behind Sash's head. "That was . . ." She pauses in thought. "I don't know what that was, but I want to do it again."

"Whatever you left inside me is pretty incredible," I say to Sash.

"I don't know if that's true," she replies.

"You don't know if what's true?"

"The part about a piece of me staying in your spectrum," she answers. "I made that up."

"You lied to me?" I ask in disbelief.

"I don't think of it as a lie. I think of it as doing what was necessary to make you go faster."

Maya rests her chin on Sash's shoulder. "I hope I'm as clever as Sash is when I grow up."

"I don't think I could handle more than one of her," I mumble.

Sash raises one eyebrow but otherwise ignores my remark. "Now that you've found your real speed, we'll be able to cover three to four times as much ground in a day."

"We need to," I say. "Thank you for doing that."

"All I did was make you believe. You did the rest."

Resuming our procedure from the prior day, we make a stop roughly every eight hundred miles. With my newfound speed, I'm able to stay neck and neck with Sash the entire time. At each location, Maya spends a few minutes on the ground while Sash and I keep our eyes peeled for Murkovin. By the time the day is over, we end up covering over three times the amount of space that we did the prior day. Although Maya never senses anything that might be Tela, we try not to let it discourage us.

During our return trip to the Delta, Darkness blankets the already dreary wasteland. With Maya secure in the harness on her back, Sash travels close by my side. While the rain pounds down and the winds whip across the murky terrain, we both stay alert for any sign of Murkovin.

As we cross the bridge to the Delta, the rain recedes and light returns. Although we arrive at roughly the same time as the night before, Maya is still awake. Her mood seems disheartened, partially from how exhausted she must be, but also from the lack of success at locating Tela. Sash has a brief conversation with her, basically telling her not to give up hope. Once Maya is safely in her room, Sash and I take a sleeping Aven back to our habitat.

Baby girl doesn't wake up during the brief journey to our cavern or stir when we tuck her into our bed. After we quickly rinse off in the fall, Sash and I climb under the sheet on either side of our daughter. I reach an arm over Aven and rest it on Sash's shoulder.

"I feel bad about the time you're spending away from Aven."

"It's what we have to do right now," she says, staring up at the Swirls.

I pull my hand away from her and lay it on Aven. "I

really appreciate all that you're doing. I hope you know that."

"I do," she replies, turning her head to look at me. "But we have to find her soon. The longer she's in the Barrens, the less likely it is we'll ever see her again." She returns her eyes to the ceiling. "Peace."

After the light of the Swirls fades away, Sash almost immediately falls asleep. Despite how late it is and the two long days of searching the Barrens, I lie in the dark with my eyes open. Guilt-ridden thoughts rattle inside my brain, all of them beginning with the same two words.

What if.

Chapter 30

When Aven wakes up the next day, she's so excited to see Sash and me that she starts jumping up and down on our bed. We apologize for being away so much and try to explain the importance of what we're doing. Although her first reaction is to pout, her eyes soon glass over and she looks away from us. As though she's listening to someone in the distance, she cocks her head to the side. Her behavior is almost identical to how she acted in the meadow in front of Home after I returned from being trapped in the Barrens.

"Find Tela," she murmurs to the air.

"That's what we're trying to do," I say.

Her sparkling blue eyes return to me. "I help," she says loudly.

"You are helping," I reply. "If you understand why Mommy and Daddy are gone so much, it will be a huge help to us."

She presses her hands to my cheeks and smiles at me with the faint, knowing smile that I've seen so often from her before. It's as though she knows something important, but can't—or won't—tell me what it is.

While we all have our sap, Sash and I take a little time to play a game with Aven. When we're almost ready to leave our habitat for the day, Eval unexpectedly summons Sash and me to a meeting at Sanctuary. We drop Aven off at Home and soar across the red countryside to the Tree of Vision. With both of us now traveling at Sash's usual speed, we reach the meadow in the blink of an eye.

Eval, Tork, Marc, and Larn are waiting for us when we arrive. Although I'm not sure why she's there, Maya is also with the group. Standing by Marc's side, she stares straight down at the grass between her feet and doesn't look up at Sash and me.

"Greetings," Eval says. "I asked you to join us so that we can discuss the search for Tela."

"We covered a lot of ground _yesterday_ . . . the prior day," I reply.

"That's encouraging. But you can't do this every day."

Wanting to get Larn on my side for this debate, I turn to him. "I know it's a lot to ask, but Kale is good enough at traveling now that he can help pick up my load."

Instead of answering me, Larn looks at Eval. Tightening my jaw muscles in preparation for her response, I return my attention to her as well.

"You aren't the issue," Eval says. "Sash isn't the issue. As we learned while she was with child, the other Hunters can make up for her missing Darkness from time to time. Maya is our concern."

Maya pops her head up for the first time. "I want to help!"

"And the Pool showed me Maya," I add.

"We all know that," Marc interrupts before Eval can say anything else. "But what you're doing is far too strenuous for her. I could barely wake her up this day. Although she's maturing, she's still a child. The long days in the Barrens are exhausting her."

"But I want to help," Maya pleads.

I examine Maya's face and immediately notice the dark bags under her eyes. Her waist-length hair is stringy, messy, and grimy with dust from the Barrens. I have to admit to myself that no matter how desperately I want to find Tela, it's not worth the toll it could take on Maya.

"I'll search on my own," I say.

"No!" Maya shouts. "The Pool showed me to you for a reason."

"Marc is right," I reply to her. "The Barrens is no place for you."

Maya looks at Eval again. "When I was still very small, not much older than Aven is now, I used to get scared if Darkness came during sleep time. I'd curl up in a ball on my bed.

"I knew the Keepers would protect me, but I was still frightened. Even though Marc would keep watch from the tunnel near my room, I hated being alone. Sash used to come to my room and sit with me until Darkness passed, but then she moved to a habitat of her own when she ended her Apprenticeship.

"During the first Darkness after Sash left, Tela heard me crying. She came to my bed and sat beside me. From then on, every time Darkness woke us, she would come to my side. By the time she became an Apprentice, I wasn't scared of Darkness anymore. It's my turn to help her now."

"You're a brave girl," Eval says. "We're not proposing

that you give up the search, but you can't go out every day. Marc has suggested every third day. That gives you time to rest and also stay current on your education."

Maya fervently nods her head. "I'll do that. I'll do whatever I can to help."

"Your courage and dedication are well beyond your height," Eval says to Maya and then looks at me again. "You and Sash can perform your duties as needed on the days Maya isn't available."

Tork has been silently standing by Eval's side the entire time. After taking a step forward, he focuses his eyes directly on me.

"Tela has fallen to the wild sap," he remarks in a bitter tone. "There's almost no chance of finding her. She's part of the Barrens now."

"It's not her fault," I argue. "She didn't make the choice to drink wild sap. It was the only way I could think of to save her life. If anyone is to blame, it's me."

"But even if you find her," he counters, "no one knows if she can be restored to a person of value to the Delta."

"We'll take it one step at a time," I say. "The first step is to find her. Then we'll figure out how to fix her."

"She may not want to be fixed," he tells me.

"Then why would the Pool show me Maya?"

When Tork doesn't answer, Eval intercedes. "I understand your loyalty to Tela. No one wants to lose her or anyone else to the Barrens. But what was the exact question you asked the Pool?"

"I asked if there's a way to find Tela," I answer. "The Pool showed me Maya."

"Unfortunately," Eval says, "I doubt that even the Reflecting Pool can answer the more important question you didn't ask."

"What's that?"

She folds her hands in front of her. "Will you find Tela?"

*   *   *

With a sidearm throw, I launch a small stone down a rocky slope. As it skips across the ground, several dull clacks reverberate up the side of the hill. I look down to see if I disturbed Maya, but she doesn't seem to be aware of anything going on around her. Lost in deep concentration, she's sitting perfectly still with her feet tucked underneath her and both hands resting on the dirt.

Days have turned into what I think of as weeks, and weeks into a couple of months. I've kept track of the areas we've searched by shading them in on my map of Krymzyn. We've covered everything within two thousand miles of the Expanse between the Bridge of Harmony and the southwest corner of the Barrens, about one-eighth of the total space we need to search. We recently turned the southwest corner and began working our way to the east. The process has been moving slower than we first anticipated since we only have Maya every third day.

On roughly half the days that we couldn't take Maya out, Sash and I have searched random parts of the Barrens on our own. Proving again that he wants to help in any way he can, Larn has been willing to have Kale take over my traveling duties on those days. Since Sash can get sap from twice as many trees as any other Hunter during Darkness, missing a few hasn't made a difference in the supply. Although searching by eye is a much slower process than when we have Maya with us, at least we feel like we're accomplishing something.

Maya stands up from the ground. She looks at Sash and then at me.

"Nothing," she says.

"Don't be discouraged," I reply despite the despondency I've felt for weeks. "This is just our first stop of the day. I have a good feeling about this day."

"I'm glad one of us does," she mumbles.

"What's that pile of rocks over there with a branch sticking out it?" I ask Sash. "That's the second time I've seen one of those."

"A marker for a trading post," she answers.

"What you mean?"

"Some of the Murkovin trade things with each other. Things stolen from raids on Travelers or things they make from wood or fabric. We don't want to go near there. There might be nine or ten who run the post. I'm sure they're watching us."

"They actually make things for themselves?" I ask.

"Some do," she answers. "Others just take what they want from the weak."

"Survival of the fittest."

"That's life in the Barrens," she says before abruptly changing the subject. "I don't want to go to our next stop."

"Why not?" I ask.

"I want to talk to the Aerodyne. Let's go to the river."

"That's almost one hundred thousand miles from here," I argue.

"If they've seen her," she says, "that's one hundred thousand miles we don't have to search. They fly from the river to the outer ends of their domain along the southern barrier. If they haven't seen anything, we only lose one day asking them."

"Wouldn't they have killed her if they saw her?"

"Not if she stayed off their land."

"I guess it's worth a try," I say.

Sash glances up at the sky and then back at me. "Darkness is coming. We need to get out of this area."

"Hop on," I say to Maya, turning my back to her and crouching low to the ground.

In a routine we're all too familiar with, she's fastened in the traveling harness in a matter of seconds. As soon as her hands clasp across my chest, I charge down the side of the hill. I can't get into my blend after only a few strides the way Sash can, but I don't have any trouble staying neck and neck with her once we get going.

Before the first drops of rain plummet down, five hundred miles of gloomy wasteland is behind us. What I estimate to be forty thousand miles per hour isn't an uncommon speed for us to reach during our treks through the Barrens. At times, I think we get closer to fifty. I base that estimate on how fast we can reach the edge of the Infinite Expanse if that's where our starting point for the day is. But with the limited light of Darkness, twenty thousand is probably our top speed.

Anytime Darkness falls while we have Maya with us, we weave through open spaces in an unpredictable path. As Sash once told Larn, our speed is what keeps us safe in the realm of the Murkovin, so we never come to a standstill during Darkness. But instead of traveling in a circle around our next stop like we usually do while waiting for light to return, we blaze a path to the east.

By the time the rainfall ends and the murky light of the Barrens returns, we're halfway along the southern barrier to the river. Once bright rays fill our vision again, we cover the next fifty thousand miles in a little over an hour. After I follow Sash over the top of a hill, we come to a stop in a wide-open space at the bottom.

No more than a mile to the south of us, fluctuating, semi-opaque colors tint an otherwise gray sky. Below the barrier to the Expanse, the upper ledge of a cliff extends to the west as far as I can see. Between us and the edge of the cliff, the ground is blanketed by tiny black crystalline rocks that look like they came from the black sand beaches of Hawaii.

Starting halfway between us and the edge of the cliff and spaced about a hundred yards apart, enormous, fern-like plants grow from the ground. The dark-purple plants are roughly three times my height and have leaves that are large enough to wrap around my body. Splattered on the leaves are bright yellow spores the size of peas. The roots of the ferns seem to be almost entirely above ground and extend across and rocky dirt like they're the tendrils of an octopus in search of something. A thunderous whoosh of water resonates across the land all around us.

"What's that sound?" I ask Sash.

"The Great Falls," she answers. "We're not far."

After Maya climbs off my back, I look towards the east. Flashes of light reflect off the waves of the river in the distance. White foam sprays from the frothing water where the river spills over the side of the cliff.

The undulating colors of the barrier to the Expanse stop at the edge of the river closest to us and begin again on the other side. Through the mist-filled air above the Great Falls, seven spectacular rainbows arc high into the sky and curve out over the Expanse. The rainbows aren't two-dimensional lines of refracted color like they are on Earth. These seem to have volume, as though each individual color is a chromatic spotlight that blends with the next.

"The rainbows are amazing!" Maya exclaims.

Sash turns her face to Maya. "I know it's hard on you being out here, but at least you're getting to see a lot of incredible things that many never get to see."

"Is the entire width of the river the Gateway to the Expanse?" I ask Sash.

"The Falls are the Gateway," she answers. "There's no need for a barrier over them. The water drops over a mile with sharp rocks below. Not even a Serquatine would survive going over the waterfall. The only way through this Gateway is to fly on the back of an Aerodyne."

"Is the Stone of Passage near here?" I ask.

Sash shakes her head. "There's not one on this side of the river. I don't want to waste time going all the way up to the Stone Crossing and then back down. I'll try to summon an Aerodyne another way. Follow me and make sure not to step foot in their domain."

"How do we know where their domain is?"

"Do you know what a geyser is?" she asks.

"Yeah, we have them on Earth."

"Once you pass the first geyser, you're in their domain. The ferns all grow close to geyser holes."

"I've never seen an Aerodyne in person," Maya says.

"They're fascinating creatures," Sash replies, "but dangerous. Walk slowly and stay behind me."

As we walk to the south, a few hundred yards in front of us, a two-foot-wide geyser of water erupts at least fifty feet in the air. As the water falls back to the ground, the mist left around the top of the spout forms a winged creature that's almost angelic in shape. Reflecting the colors of light from the barrier, the translucent figure slowly flaps its wings until it eventually evaporates.

Across the half-mile of land between the first fern and the edge of the cliff, several more geysers shoot upward. Each one of them creates a winged creature in flight that soon disappears. The geyser spouts bathe the ferns with water and soak the ground all around the gigantic plants.

"The spores on the leaves are full of nectar that the Aerodyne consume," Sash tells us, coming to a halt about a hundred yards from the first geyser. "Never damage them."

Maya and I stop behind Sash. Hoping to spot one of the Guardians, I survey the sky above us.

"Where are the Aerodyne now?" I ask.

"Somewhere in the sky," she answers. "They fly through the clouds so as not be seen. I'll see if I can get one to join us." Sash looks at Maya. "Have you learned to throw a spear?"

"The Keepers and Watchers have taught us," she answers.

"Let me show you how I throw," Sash says. "It's important to keep your body under control. Never throw too hard and let the spear follow the focus of your mind."

Sash bounces her spear in the palm of her hand a few times before finding the balance she wants. With her hand at roughly the center of the shaft, she curls her fingers around the steel and aims her eyes at the geyser closest to us. One of the huge, purple ferns stands just a few feet past the hole in the ground. When the water erupts from the geyser, Sash rears back her spear. Taking one powerful step forward, she launches her weapon into the air with a graceful but strong throwing motion.

"Never hit a plant or tree that provides for us or others," Sash says to us while her weapon is in flight. "Even the trees of the Barrens."

Neither Maya nor I say anything while watching Sash's spear soar across the sky. At the same time that the angelic shape above the geyser dissipates into the atmosphere, Sash's spear impales the ground. The point punctures the dirt in a tiny space between the outer edge of the geyser and the tip of one of the fern's roots. The vibrating steel shaft sticks almost straight up.

As Maya and I follow Sash towards the Aerodyne's domain, the rocks under our feet shimmer like a field of black diamonds. When we reach the geyser, Sash stops in front of the hole in the ground. She motions with a hand for Maya and me to stay behind her. The tip of her spear perfectly split the middle of a six-inch open space between the hole in the ground and the root of the fern. Sash reaches out a hand, closes her fingers around the spear, but doesn't pull it out of the dirt. We all look up at the sky.

No more than a spec at first, a winged being emerges from the clouds high above us. As it spirals downward in broad circles, I realize that the creature has the body of a man, including arms and hands. But extending out from the center of his back are two wings with a span of at least sixteen feet each. The wings are covered in snow-white feathers, except for a small row of jet-black ones that line the outer tips.

Still a half a mile above us, the Aerodyne suddenly ends his spiral and dives straight at Sash. The swish of air slicing over his wings pierces through the deafening sound of the Great Falls. When he's about fifty feet over us, he vigorously flaps his wings to slow his speed. Moments later, he hammers to the ground a few feet in front of Sash. The terrain around us shakes with the force of a small earthquake.

The Aerodyne immediately aims his eyes at Sash, his pupils a multitude of swirling colors. At least eight feet tall, the shirtless man is built like a world-class bodybuilder. His skin is bronze, absent of hair, and shimmers as though a semi-gloss paint was sprayed all over him. Except for the natural skirt of white feathers that hangs from his waist to the middle of his thighs, he's entirely unclothed. Instead of feet, enormous talons extend from his ankles and grip the dirt.

A crest of long, cherry-red feathers run like a mohawk

from his forehead to the back of his neck, but his head is otherwise bald and smooth. His face is chiseled and handsome—I'd almost describe him as beautiful—much like the famed Adonis of Greek mythology. His tightly flexed muscles and fisted hands leave no doubt how furious he is.

Clutching my shirt with both of her hands, Maya steps behind me. She peeks around my side to look at the Aerodyne as Sash bows her head to the creature. Although Sash doesn't pull her spear out of the ground, her hand remains firmly clenched to the shaft, and the muscles of her arm are rigid.

"Greetings, Chasmatu," she says.

"Why are you in my domain?" he bellows in a voice so deep and booming that it sends shockwaves through my bones.

Chapter 31

Without showing any apprehension or fear, Sash raises her face to Chasmatu. "I'm not in your domain," she says graciously. "My spear is."

"Your hand is touching the spear!" he roars.

"I didn't want to leave something from the Delta in your land." She pulls her spear from the ground and rests the tip on the dirt by her side. "I was afraid you might find it inconsiderate. I was showing the child how to throw a spear, but throwing a weapon isn't a skill practiced much by Hunters."

Considering her response, Chasmatu continues to scowl at Sash. As I replay her explanation in my mind, I realize how carefully Sash chose her words. She implied that it was an errant throw, which I know it wasn't, but never said anything that was a flat out lie.

"What is that creature behind you?" Chasmatu asks.

"A child of the Delta," she answers.

"Not that one!"

"A Traveler of Krymzyn."

Chasmatu shoots a scathing stare in my direction and examines my face. "His eyes are an unnatural color. He was not born in this world. A creature from another plane of existence has no place in Krymzyn."

"The Tree of Vision disagrees," Sash says evenly.

"The Tree of Vision has no bearing on my existence," he says gruffly, keeping his eyes fixed on me. "The Origin's vision for this world is my covenant."

"If The Origin doesn't want him here," Sash says, "The Origin can return from the Infinite Expanse and say so. But the Tree of Vision has made it clear that this man has a purpose in Krymzyn."

Apparently angered by Sash's argument, Chasmatu's wings flutter and the muscles in his arms strain to the point that his veins look like they're about to explode out of his skin. Tightening her grip on my shirt, Maya buries her face in the center of my back.

"I'm Chase," I say to Chasmatu, trying to be polite, "Traveler of Krymzyn."

"I care not what your name is!' he retorts. "Thousands of Travelers have passed through my Gateway over immeasurable time. Names are of no consequence to me."

I want to tell him that I was just doing what I'd been instructed to do when meeting a Guardian, but before I can reply, Sash holds a hand up in my direction to silence me.

"We came to seek your help," she says. "It's a matter of great importance. Your many gifts may prove beneficial to us."

Chasmatu glowers at me for another few moments and then snaps his head to Sash. "What matter?"

"A young female Traveler has been lost in this area of the Barrens, although she probably looks like a Murkovin now. Perhaps you or the other Aerodyne have seen her near

292

your domain."

"I see an occasional Murkovin, but none have stood out."

"You might recognize her," she says. "I know she chose your Gateway for her journey to the Infinite Expanse. Her name is Tela. Larn, the tallest of the Travelers, was her guide to the Expanse."

"Did you not hear what I told the Traveler about names?" he grumbles.

"I thought you might have heard their names in passing," she replies. "It's customary for them to announce their names to you at the Stone of Passage. I know your memory is without flaw."

For the first time since he arrived, probably from Sash's gentle ego-stroking, Chasmatu relaxes his muscles. "I do recall those two entering the Expanse, but I have not seen anyone who resembles her since."

"I'm grateful for your information," she replies.

Sash suddenly looks up as another winged creature descends from the sky. Maya peeks around my side and gazes up at him. With broad, effortless circles, he glides down on fully extended wings. When he nears us, he elegantly flaps his wings until his feet touch the ground with a much softer landing than Chasmatu's. Standing a few feet from Chasmatu, the Aerodyne retracts his wings and bows to Sash.

"Greetings, Hunter," he says. "How can I serve you."

The second Aerodyne's voice, like Chasmatu's, is so deep and rich that it sends tremors through my body. But unlike Chasmatu, his tone is absent of any hostility. I'd describe him as cordial, an obvious contrast to Chasmatu's menacing demeanor. Sash returns his bow.

"We're honored by your presence, Angelicusepte," she says as she returns to upright. "We're in search of a missing Traveler."

"The only Traveler I have seen since the last who journeyed to the Infinite Expanse is standing behind you now." Angelicusepte looks in my direction. The kaleidoscope of colors in his eyes is almost hypnotic. "Greetings, Traveler. Greetings, child of Krymzyn. I welcome you to the edge of our domain."

"Greetings," I reply. "I'm honored to be here."

"Hello," Maya timidly squeaks.

In the same way that the Serquatine all look like sisters, Angelicusepte and Chasmatu are almost identical in appearance. The only distinct difference between them is that the plume of feathers on Angelicusepte's head is canary-yellow instead of red. Just as each of the Serquatine has one of the seven colors of the rainbow illuminating the ends of their hair, the feathered crests of the different Aerodyne must be the same seven colors. Based on how polar opposite the personalities of Chasmatu and Angelicusepte are, I assume these creatures display different dispositions in the same way as the Schorachnia.

"The Traveler may now be a Murkovin," Sash says to Angelicusepte. "She had no choice but to survive on wild sap. You might recognize her since she used your Gateway for her journey to the Infinite Expanse."

"I occasionally see a Murkovin from the air," he tells her, "but few ever venture near our domain. I have not seen the one you mention."

"She may have had a steel transport with her," I say. "I doubt many Murkovin would have one with them."

Angelicusepte looks at me again. "You are correct. Rarely do the Murkovin we see near our domain have items of steel, but I did see something rather curious. It was a female Murkovin with a steel transport. From my vantage point in the clouds, I could not make out the detail of her face, but she had no blue in her hair."

"Where did you see her?" I ask.

"East of the river," he answers. "She was about a third of the way to the eastern barrier and a few miles north of our domain."

"How long ago?" Sash asks.

He returns his attention to her. "At least forty Darknesses have passed since I saw her."

"Your information is extremely helpful," she says. "Thank you for sharing it with us."

"I hope it helps with your search."

Sash bows to the two Aerodyne. "Thank you, Angelicusepte. Thank you, Chasmatu. I appreciate your kindness."

As they return her bow, I reach behind me and push Maya out to my side. She and I bow to the two Aerodyne. After we all return to upright, Sash motions for Maya and me to follow her. The three of us walk to the north.

"Hunter!" Chasmatu calls out. We all stop and turn to him. "I doubt your spear has ever landed anywhere other than exactly where you intended it to."

"Then I'll make sure to never aim it at you," she replies.

The way Sash interacts with the Guardians is fascinating. She's not afraid to stand up to them by fighting intimidation with intimidation, but she's also respectful and gracious. More than anything else, she knows precisely how to speak to them to get what she wants.

Chasmatu walks away without saying anything else to Sash, but as he heads to the south, he glances over his winged shoulder at her. He studies her for a moment with what appears to be approval in his eyes. It's as though he respects her for taking a verbal jab at him, and maybe even for her initial deception to summon him from the sky.

After looking away from Sash, Chasmatu charges towards the cliffs. Angelicusepte sprints behind him across the rocky terrain. Their wings spread from their backs, lifting their bronzed bodies into the air. Side by side, a mirror image of one other, they arc across the sky towards the river. When they reach the edge of the Great Falls, they dive straight down and disappear into the thick mist.

"They are spectacular creatures," I comment.

"Yes, they are," Sash says. "I should warn you, though. Stay away from the black feathers on the ends of their wings."

"Why?" I ask.

"They're as hard as steel and as sharp as a knife. They can slice a person in half."

"That's good to know," I say. "But other than that, they seem pretty harmless."

"What?" Maya asks, not understanding my sarcasm. "Chasmatu is the scariest thing I've ever seen. Even scarier than the Schorachnia."

"He can be a bit frightening," Sash says to Maya, "but as I said earlier, even if this is hard on you, you're getting to experience Krymzyn in a way that only the Travelers can."

Maya nods her head. "I know. I feel fortunate about that. It just upsets me that it's because Tela is lost."

"The person Angelicusepte saw must have been Tela," I say to Sash.

"I think so, too," she says. "Tela could have taken the transport over the Stone Crossing and then gone to the southeast. She knows as well as anyone that very few Murkovin dwell close to the Aerodyne's domain."

"I think we should move our search east of the river," I suggest.

"I agree," Sash replies. "The next time we take Maya out, we'll begin on the other side of the Great Falls and work our way to the east. We don't have time before end of day to go all the way up to the Stone Crossing and back down the other side of the river."

"No," I say. "And there's something important we need to do with Aven when we get back to the Delta."

"What is it?" Sash asks.

"I'll tell you after we pick her up from Home."

Chapter 32

"Happy birthday dear Aven," I sing. *"Happy birthday to you."*

Aven beams a smile at me and claps her little hands together. "Tank-u, Daddy!"

Sitting with Aven on the floor of her room, Sash and I take turns hugging our daughter. Before launching into the song, I'd spent a few minutes explaining to Aven and Sash how we celebrate birthdays on Earth.

At a year old, Aven's hair has grown long enough that it hangs to her shoulders in waves of thick, shiny ebony. Her body is lean and toned, and her movements deliberate and graceful. Any time I watch Aven in an activity, I feel as though I have a glimpse of what Sash must have been like as a child.

Even though Aven's pronunciation isn't always perfect, her vocabulary would be impressive for a three-year-old on Earth. She can only put a few words together at a time, yet comprehends most of what Sash and I say to her. If she doesn't understand something, more times than not, it's because she pretends not to—especially when Sash and I tell her to stop doing something that she knows she shouldn't be doing. Her strong will, for better or worse, is just like her mother's.

"I have something for you," I say to Aven. "I'll be right back."

I walk to the main cavern to retrieve the birthday present I made for Aven. During the months that we've been searching for Tela, I've used the evenings on days we didn't go to the Barrens to secretly work on it. It was the only way I could free my mind of the ever-increasing mental distress from not finding Tela.

As I return to Aven's room, I hide the handmade notebook behind my back. Wren made the front and back covers out of smooth steel plates and used metal pins to secure canvas sheets between them. On the front cover, I carefully painted three words in my finest script—*Aven's First Year*.

"This is really for both of you," I say, sitting down between Sash and Aven. "It's called a baby _book_ in my world. It's a collection of things that serve as a reminder of important events in a child's early life."

After I lay the book down on the floor, Sash and Aven both gaze at it with thoughtful smiles on their faces. I open the front cover and reveal the first page. The sheet of canvas has a black and white sketch of a pregnant Sash standing in front of Ovin's tree. Depicting the scene from the Darkness when I felt our daughter kick for the first time, one branch of the tree rests in the palm of Sash's outstretched hand. Sash's other hand is pressed to the curve of her stomach.

Thumbing through the pages, I show them a series of drawings of Aven over the past year. Each image has a short written description of the various milestones in her life. Aven as a baby in Sash's arms, Aven crawling across the floor of our cavern, Aven standing beside Kyra at the entrance to Home, and Aven taking her first steps on the Empty Hill are each sketched on a separate page.

Sewn to one sheet of canvas is a small lock of Aven's hair that I cut off several months ago while she was sleeping. Intermixed with my drawings, I included a few of Aven's finger paintings and a traced sketch of her hand that I made when she was six months old.

"Boo-i-ful pitchers, Daddy!" Aven gasps.

"I'm really glad you like them," I say to her. After leaning over to kiss her forehead, I turn to Sash. "I'll teach Aven to read the words. I want her to be able to read the _alphabet_ . . . the symbols we use in my world for words. If you want to learn, I can teach you at the same time."

"I'd like that," she replies. "I can't believe how much time it must have taken you to make this."

"I enjoyed every moment of it. Living it first, and then re-living it while making the book."

Sash slips an arm around my waist and lays her head on my shoulder, the first physical affection she's shown to me since our hug before I went to the Reflecting Pool months ago. I reach one arm around her, pull her close to me, and rest my head against hers.

She's been friendly with me over the months that have passed, but I wouldn't describe her interaction with me as loving. We've searched for Tela, coexisted in the same habitat, played with our daughter, and gone to sleep in the same bed at the end of each day. But it's been a purely platonic relationship. I've been waiting for her to let me know that we're on the path to repair. Maybe this is the first step.

Aven jumps up from the floor and throws one arm around Sash's neck and the other around mine. For the first time in recent memory, I feel a genuine sense of happiness.

"I like birfday!" Aven squeals.

"It's your special day," I say.

"Sleep wif Mommy and Daddy?" she asks.

"Of course," I answer.

After looking through the baby book again, we all get ready for bed. Sandwiched in between Sash and me, Aven passes out as soon as the light fades away. I reach a hand over her body and rest it on Sash's shoulder. I'm a little surprised that Sash doesn't lay a hand on mine or react in any way, but at least she doesn't push it away. I take that as a positive sign.

On our next search with Maya, we begin east of the river near the southern barrier to the Infinite Expanse. Feeling like we finally have a solid lead as to where Tela might be, all three of us start the day in high spirits. We use a much slower pace than usual while working our way to the east and allow Maya a little extra time on the ground at each stop. In addition to Maya trying to sense something, Sash and I complete thorough searches of the hills around any trees we see.

Several more weeks pass in the southeastern Barrens without us finding any signs of Tela. The glimmer of hope that we had from Angelicusepte's information gradually fades away. Again and again, I replay Sash's words from months ago in my head.

"The longer she's in the Barrens, the less likely it is we'll ever see her again."

At the end of one day, I finally make another visit to the Reflecting Pool. Standing in the aqua light, I ask the water if Tela is alive. I see the same image of Tela sitting alone in front of a tree. When I ask if there's a way to find her, the Pool again shows me Maya. I also remember Eval's words about an unasked question, so I ask the Pool if I *will* find Tela. The only image the glassy water displays in response to that question is my reflection.

When Sash and I drop Maya off at the end of our search days with her, we both notice the toll it's taking on her. Even with our every third day procedure, the bags under Maya's eyes have become permanent fixtures and her complexion has become increasingly sallow. I'm sure in addition to the physical stress, the mental burden of being shown to me in the Reflecting Pool weighs heavier and heavier on her mind. Although she never complains, her mood becomes more and more despondent. Sash and I try to restore her confidence with frequent praise for her efforts, but I realize that she's losing the last of her hope.

In the same way that I recognize the toll the search is taking on Maya, I see the wear and tear on Sash's face. Although she never says anything, I know the days away from Aven are hard on her.

Almost every day that we don't search the Barrens with Maya, I go out on my own. Larn's spirits were lifted in the same way that mine were by the revelation from Angelicusepte. He's more than willing to have the other Travelers pick up my workload so that I can continue the search.

Retracing ground that Sash and I covered with Maya in the southeast Barrens, I scour the areas around trees and search for hidden caverns. Standing alone on the tops of rocky hills, I shout out Tela's name again and again. The only response I ever receive is the echo of my voice across the empty wasteland.

On the days that I go out on my own, I often return long after Sash and Aven have gone to sleep. It's not uncommon for me to only doze off for a few hours before going straight back out to the Barrens. With me gone so much, repairing my relationship with Sash has been put on the backburner.

After another few weeks of futility, I visit the Reflecting Pool yet again. While staring at the image of Tela in the water, I notice a subtle change. I rack my brains trying to recall if the difference in the image was there the last time I went to the Pool, but I can't remember if it was or wasn't. The sky behind Tela is absent of the barrier to the Infinite Expanse.

I drop to my knees in the center of the Pool and close my eyes. If she's not near the Expanse, she could be anywhere in forty billion square miles of Barrens. Even with Maya, it would take years to cover that much land.

Emotionally and physically depleted, I return to the Delta. When I enter our habitat, Aven is in her room and Sash is seated at the main table. As I put my things away, I decide that I need to tell Sash what I saw in the Pool—or didn't see, to be more accurate.

"I'm sorry I'm so late," I say. "I went to the Pool again."

Sash rises to her feet. "Chase," she says quietly, "you

can't go on this way."

"What do you mean?"

"If you could see what you look like, you'd know you need a break. You're pale and thin. You're so consumed by searching for Tela that there's no room left for anything else. Ever since Aven's birthday, you don't spend time with Aven or me. Even when you're here, you aren't mentally present."

"I can't just give up," I say.

Sash shakes her head. "I'm not telling you to give up, but this can't be your entire life. I'll continue to help as much as I can, but you also have to accept that she didn't want to return. We may never find her."

"Daddy," Aven calls to me from the doorway to her room.

"Not now, Aven!" I bark without looking at her.

Sash takes two steps towards me. Her cheeks flush red with anger. "Do you see what I mean? You rarely see Aven and then you ignore her when you do."

Lowering my eyes to the floor, I don't say anything. The truth in her words hits me as hard anything I've ever felt in my life. Over the six weeks since Aven's birthday, I've ignored everything but the search for Tela, including Sash and my daughter.

"Look at me!" Sash orders.

I raise my face to her. Sash's face is still red and her hands are clenched in fists, but her eyes are watery and red.

"Did something else happen in the Barrens? Did you fall in love with Tela?"

"Of course not," I answer. "She's my friend."

"Then tell me what this is, Chase. Why are you so

obsessed with finding her?"

Trying to verbalize in my mind why the search Tela has completely absorbed me, I stare at her for a few seconds before speaking again. "You know how much guilt I've felt about leaving my family on Earth. Even though I've come to terms with it, I still feel like I abandoned them. I never want to abandon anyone that I care about again. I can't live with myself if I do.

"Apart from you and Aven, Tela's the closest I have to family here. She's like a sister to me. But when she needed me the most, I let her down. I explained to you before why I should have been able to control the wild sap. I just didn't figure it out soon enough. I feel like I abandoned her. It's my fault she's still out there."

Sash shakes her head. "But now you're abandoning Aven and me. You have to forgive yourself. It's not your fault that she chose to stay there."

"It is," I reply. "If I'd done the right thing, she never would have been out there on her own."

"Do you feel like finding her will make up for leaving your family on Earth?" she asks.

"Something like that."

"Daddy," Aven says.

I turn to her and speak in a soft voice. "What is it, baby girl?"

She holds up a large sheet of canvas in her hands. As she spreads it out in front of her, I realize that it's my map of Krymzyn. Gripping one corner with an outstretched hand and squeezing the top seam between her chin and chest, she uses her free hand to point to a spot in the Barrens north of

"Tela here," Aven says.

I walk across the room and kneel in front of her. "That's where Tela is?"

"Yes, Daddy," she answers. "Tela here."

"How do you know?"

"Chees tell me," she says.

"The trees told you where Tela is?" I ask, confused by her explanation.

"Tela here, Daddy," she confirms. "Chees tell me."

I turn my head to Sash. "What do you think this means?"

Sash steps across the room, crouches between Aven and me, and looks me straight in the eyes. "It means first thing on the morrow, you and I are taking Maya north of the Desert."

Chapter 33

With her child perched in one arm and a spear in the hand of the other, the woman climbs to the top of a hill. She stops on a rounded crest and looks out over the flat land in front of her. Far in the distance, three figures of light glide in her direction, the blurs of steel transports behind two.

Near the base of the hill the woman stands on, all three shapes of light begin to slow. As their particles separate from imperceptible rays around them, pale bodies gradually take shape. The female on point, a former Traveler of the Delta, is flawless in her separation from the beams. She effortlessly transitions to her sprint while yelling words of guidance to the other two.

The two male Murkovin learning to travel with transports are awkward as they exit the light. Hesitant and cautious while reducing their speed, they eventually detach from the beams without falling. Of greater importance to the woman, they both maintain control of the sap-filled transports in tow.

With the former Traveler still in the lead, all three ascend the slope towards the woman. Once they stop in front of her, the two male Murkovin drop their transport handles to the ground. As they inhale deep breaths, one of the men bends down and rests his hands on his knees. Stout and broad-shouldered, roughly the same height as the woman, he stares at the dirt between his feet.

The other man, lean and slightly taller than the former Traveler, clamps his hands behind his neck. Gasping for air, he looks up at the overcast sky. Long, black hair highlighted with strands of white falls to his shoulders.

In contrast to the two men, the former Traveler barely breathes heavily at all. With her weapon dangling from one hand, the former Traveler looks back and forth between the two men.

"You both did very well," the former Traveler says to the men before turning to the woman. "After a few more days of training, they'll be ready for any part of the Barrens."

"Their progress is impressive," the woman replies and then addresses the two men. "You two can head back to camp. Relax and enjoy some sap."

"Thank you," the long-haired Murkovin says.

The two men nod their farewells, grab the handles of their transports, and walk down the side of the hill. The young boy nestled in one of the woman's arms alertly watches them as they head towards the nearby camp.

"You have a gift for teaching others," the woman says to the former Traveler. "You've taught them to maintain control of the transports much more quickly than I could have."

"Thank you," she replies. "I like helping others learn."

The woman glances at the two men to make sure they're out of earshot and then returns her attention to the former Traveler. "But you do nothing for yourself."

"What do you mean?"

"You spend so much time alone," the woman answers. "I never see you join the others when the day is near its end. You're usually alone in your cavern or sitting on a hilltop."

"I like being alone and . . ." The former Traveler stops talking and looks at the distant charcoal-colored hills.

"And what?" the woman asks.

"I don't feel like I fit in."

"At this camp or in the Barrens?"

"Anywhere," the former Traveler replies, still peering at the faraway terrain.

"You came here in search of something that the Delta couldn't offer you. Do you regret that decision?"

"No," she says bitterly, turning her face to the woman. "There's nothing for me in the Delta."

"No one else here even knows you're from the Delta," the woman lies, not wanting the former Traveler to know that the tall Murkovin is well aware of who she is. "They'll accept you if you give them a chance."

"They might," the former Traveler says quietly.

"Perhaps if you tried spending time with the others, you'll feel like you fit in. Maybe you'll even find what it is you came here in search of." The woman pauses for a moment, remembering her belief that the former Traveler had been rejected by the male Traveler when they were together in the Barrens. "The younger of the two men you were training is about your height, the man with long hair. His eyes often linger on you. He's the loyal kind and pleasant enough in appearance. I'm sure he wouldn't mind your company when the others gather at the end of the day."

The former Traveler is slow to reply. "He's a fast

learner," she eventually says, "and a decent man."

"If you give him the chance to get to know you, even just an idle conversation, maybe you'll feel a better sense of belonging."

"Maybe," the former Traveler nods.

The woman kneels to the ground and sets her child's feet on the dirt. As she returns to upright, she takes one of the boy's hands in her protective grip.

"Unless you make an effort," she says to the former Traveler, "you'll never know what it is you were hoping to find in the Barrens. Rarely are things given to us, especially things worth having."

"I guess that's true."

"After my child is asleep, I may join the others around the tree. Maybe I'll see you there."

"I might go later," the former Traveler says. "I need to clean up now."

"If I can help you in any way, let me know."

The former Traveler walks down the slope in the direction of her cavern. Although her cave is close to the woman's, on the other side of the same hill, the woman decides not to walk with her. She wants the former Traveler to have time to digest her suggestions on her own.

As the woman had hoped when she first found her in the Barrens, the former Traveler has been a tremendous asset in teaching others to blend their light, especially with transports. But her time of value may be nearing an end.

The woman has made sure that the activities in the Desert have been well hidden from all who pass through the training camp. Only when their complete trust has been gained is more information shared with them, and then only tidbits of the larger plan. Everything they'd accomplished could all be put in jeopardy if the former Traveler were to leave now. If she were to return to the Delta, too many questions might be asked about the woman's activities. No matter what it takes, the woman can never let the former Traveler leave.

After the former Traveler is out of sight, the woman cautiously guides her child down the slope. When they reach the bottom, the boy yanks his hand away from hers and runs across the flat ground. Long, curly locks bounce off the back of his neck. Not yet streaked with the white of an adult Murkovin, the boy's hair is shiny and pure black. The woman jogs after the boy with pride gleaming from her eyes at the speed and coordination her child possesses at less than five hundred days old.

At the valley leading to their cavern, the boy stops to wait for his Ovì. The woman runs to him from behind and slows to a walk. As they stroll towards their cavern side by side, the boy reaches a hand up and slips it into the woman's grip.

"You're already faster than I was at twice your height," the woman says to her child.

The boy looks up at her face. "I want to travel."

"I'm sure you will soon. And you'll probably be much younger than I was when I learned. But be patient. There's no reason to hurry."

Hand in hand, the two weave through the valley to their cavern entrance. As the woman always does, she pauses to look at the top of several nearby hills. Before entering their dwelling at the end of each day, she makes certain that the guards are alert. Only after seeing them at their respective posts does she lead her child through the tunnel.

The woman's loyal female servant and the servant's child are already waiting inside the cavern when the woman and boy arrive. Adhering to their custom at the end of most days, the four sit at a wooden table together and drink sap. Surrounded by the purple light of the tiny grubs burrowed in the ceiling, the woman learns of the two children's activities earlier that day. Her servant, she knows, is well equipped to teach the children the basic skills needed for survival, but the woman takes responsibility for teaching them to fight.

After cleansing her child in the small waterfall at one end of the cavern, the woman lies beside the boy on a large mattress. Running her fingers through his hair, she admires the sleek lines of his face. Unlike most days, she doesn't close her eyes after he falls asleep. Instead, she rises from the bed and crosses the large room to the small adjoining cave where her servant and her servant's child have a bed of their own.

The woman quietly explains that she needs to go out to check on the others at camp. Taking her spear with her, she leaves the dwelling and walks the quarter-mile to the other side of the hill. She glances at the entrance to the former Traveler's cavern but decides not to go in.

She hurries through a broad valley and up to the top of a hill. The tall Murkovin, her most trusted companion, is already sitting on a rocky ridge that runs along the crest. She stops beside him, rests the tip of her spear on a rock, and looks down the slope at the circular flat area below. A lone sustaining tree grows in the center, its upper branches all tied with rope. Stakes embedded in the bark feed tubes that lead to a steel transport. Three more transports reside on the ground nearby, all full of sap.

A dozen Murkovin, an even mix of male and female, sit at the base of a hill on the far side of the tree from the woman. Occasionally drinking sap from wooden cups, they're engaged in light-hearted conversation. The sight of her kind peacefully interacting with one another is one the woman takes great pride in seeing. One day, she knows, this is how the entire population of the Barrens will exist. Those who refuse to adapt to the new ways will die at the hands of those who are loyal to the woman.

In the center of the row of Murkovin sits the long-haired young man who was learning to tow a transport earlier that day. As the woman's eyes scan the others, she spots a man seated a few feet from the edge of the group that she doesn't recognize. Brawny and clothed in worn, crudely-sewn garments, the man's hair is short but unkempt. Sitting alone on a rock with a scowl on his face, he silently examines the others.

"Who's the man on the far left?" the woman asks the tall Murkovin. "I've never seen him before."

From his seat on the ridge, the tall Murkovin looks up at her. "I brought him here earlier this day. He has good traveling skills."

"Where is he from?"

"The far northwest," he answers.

The woman scrapes the tip of her spear across the top of a rock. "The men from that area are often set in their ways—ways I don't like."

"I know," he says. "That's why I'm keeping an eye on him. He's skilled at blending his light, so he's worth a try."

"The two men who once tried to make me their captive were good at blending their light."

The tall Murkovin nods his head. "As I said, I'm not letting him out of my sight until I know more about him."

The woman's attention is drawn to movement at the bottom of the slope on her far left. With no weapon in hand, the former Traveler walks around the side of the hill. Her thick, black hair, a few streaks of white intertwined, flows down her back. She has curves where a woman should, the woman thinks to herself, and knows how to make sure they're noticed when she wants to.

The former Traveler approaches the row of Murkovin sitting at the base of hill. As she walks past the new recruit from the northwest, the brutish man stands to his feet. With a lustful gaze in his eyes, he reaches out a hand and slaps her behind. The former Traveler spins and swings the back of one hand at the Murkovin's face. After catching it in his grip, he forcefully twists her arm until she winces from pain. The long-haired young man jumps to his feet and dashes towards them.

"Stop!" the woman shouts.

The brute releases his grip on the former Traveler's hand. He and the former Traveler look up the hill at the woman. The long-haired young man who was rushing to the former Traveler's aid stops a few feet behind her. At the woman's side, her most trusted companion springs to his feet and starts down the slope, but the woman grabs the back of his shirt.

"I'll take care of this," she grumbles. "You stay here."

Trying to keep the rage inside her hidden, the woman marches down the side of the hill. From their seats near the tree, the Murkovin watch as the woman approaches, wondering what she'll do next. The tall Murkovin stays in place on top of the hill behind the woman, but he primes his muscles and readies his spear in case he's needed.

As the woman walks past the tree, the bulky man's red eyes flame with fury. He's not used to being given orders, the woman knows, especially from a female. Standing a few feet away from the brute, the former Traveler shakes with anger. The woman stops directly in front of the beast from the northwest Barrens.

"Do you believe that because you're a man, you have the right to treat a woman that way?" the woman asks loudly enough for all to hear.

"I've learned to take what I want!" the Murkovin growls.

"That's no longer the way of the Barrens."

"You don't decide the way of the Barrens!"

The former Traveler aims her eyes at the woman. "I can take care of myself. I don't need your help."

"I know you can," the woman says without looking away from the male Murkovin. "I've seen her kill someone larger than you," she says to him. "You'll have your hands full if you tangle with this one."

"I fear no one, and no one stands in my way."

"Does that include me?" the woman asks.

The man glances at the ground behind him where his weapon is propped up on a rock. After returning his eyes to the woman, he assesses her stance, measures the possible strength lurking in her lean frame, and tries to judge the will of her mind. He's plotting his next move carefully, the woman realizes, and not about to back down. She immediately decides that she needs to make an example of this man.

Every person at the camp has seen her compassion and willingness to provide what she can for others. Her servant has told them of the woman's benevolence towards her and her child. The Murkovin at camp are well aware that she intends to improve the lives of all who dwell in the Barrens. But now is the time to show them that she'll always stand up for others. The woman releases her grip on the shaft of her weapon and lets it fall to the ground.

"We don't need spears," she says.

The brute points at the top of the hill behind the woman. "What about him?"

"He won't be involved. I don't need his help or a weapon to kill the likes of you."

The veins in the man's forehead bulge from his skin. She knows how her words must enrage him, the indignation he must feel from being chastised by a woman. His anger, the self-righteous sense of superiority so prevalent in his kind, will be weapons she can use against him.

"What are you waiting for?" the woman taunts. "Are you frightened of a woman?"

He grits his teeth and crouches. Slowly inching towards the woman, he rocks his weight from foot to foot. With her arms limp at her sides, the woman takes several steps backwards. The beast claws at the air between them with one hand, watching to see if she'll react. Her eyes never leave his as she continues to back away.

The beast finally lunges at the woman and aims a fist at her face. She leans forward, almost as though she's falling into his blow. No one watching knows for sure what happens next, but they all gasp in response. For the briefest of moments, no more than the beat of a heart, her body flashes into light.

Brilliant horizontal extrusions burst past the man's side but instantly reshape into her body. Coming out of her split-second blend a few feet behind him, the woman spins towards the man. Before he can stop his forward motion, she hooks one of her legs around his shin and throws her shoulder against his back. As they both fall to the ground, she hurls an arm around his neck and grabs his ear with that hand. After slapping her other hand to the front of his face, she drives a fingertip into his eye.

They slam to the dirt with the beast underneath her. Still clutching his head, the woman pops her knees up to the center of his back. While digging her kneecaps into his spine, she tightens her grip on his skull.

With one sharp twist, the woman snaps the brute's neck. As she continues to rotate his head, the crackles of tearing cartilage leak from his skin. She doesn't stop until his face looks straight up at hers.

The Murkovin frantically tries to inhale a breath, but his broken neck and twisted esophagus keep the air from his lungs. Taking perverse pleasure in the sight, the woman watches his eyes bulge from their sockets. After the final beat of his heart finally echoes in his chest, she clasps a handful of his hair. Standing to her feet, the woman lifts the corpse by her side for all to see.

"If you believe the old ways are best for the Barrens," the woman yells to the group of Murkovin, "you're free to leave now. No harm will come to you. Return to the area of the Barrens you came from and live out your life.

"But make no mistake. A new Barrens is rising. There's no place for anyone who tries to take from others by force. Our kind will learn to live in peace the way we're doing at this camp. Anyone who refuses can live in solitude—or die."

With a combination of awe and disbelief at what they just witnessed, the men and women sitting on the hillside stare at the woman. One female lifts her spear from the ground and plunges the tip down on a rock by her feet. Again and again, she raises her weapon and thrusts it back down, sending loud clacks through the valley.

One by one, the other Murkovin pick up their spears and hammer them back down. As a thunderous boom of steel colliding with stone resounds through the surrounding hills, the woman graciously bows to them.

When the clamor finally recedes, the woman turns away. Out of the corner of one eye, she notices the former Traveler and the young man with long hair walk to the end of the row of Murkovin. They sit on the ground side by side. The woman drags the corpse towards the hill where the tall Murkovin still stands.

After she reaches the slope, she hauls the dead body to the crest. The tall Murkovin expects her to stop beside him, but she continues straight over the top of the hill and down the backside.

"I'll get rid of his body," the tall Murkovin calls out to

her.

The woman stops but doesn't look back at him. "I take care of my own dead."

"You didn't even take a step," he says. "All you did was lean into the light and blend."

The woman turns her face to him, nods her head, and then resumes her walk down the hill. At the bottom of the slope, she hoists the corpse over her shoulder. As she runs to the east, rays of light bloom before her eyes. She only travels for a few moments before disentangling from the beams near the edge of a deep, narrow ravine.

Standing on the ledge of the bluff, she holds the face of the dead Murkovin in front of hers. Her eyes fill with loathing and she spits in his face.

"I've killed your kind before," she whispers. "I'll kill you again. For you, my Ovì."

She hurls the corpse into the ravine. The body pounds to the rocks at the bottom of the gully, shattering the bones hidden under pale skin. The woman stares down at the limp corpse while thoughts of the past whisk through her mind. Memories of her Ovì, memories of so many days of her youth surviving on her own, and memories of the many lives she's taken.

She turns away from the ravine and runs in the direction of the camp. She doesn't bother to blend her light, relishing in the power of her long, trim legs churning across the rocky terrain. When she reaches the base of the hill where the tall Murkovin still waits, she stops and removes a steel flask from her belt. Guzzling the red liquid inside, she immerses herself in the wave of new energy that pumps through her veins. She doesn't pull the flask away from her lips until the last drop has rolled down her throat.

After returning the flask to her belt, she walks to the top of the hill. Once on the crest, she stands beside her most trusted companion. While looking down at the group of Murkovin still sitting in front of the tree, she notices that the former Traveler is no longer with them.

"The former Traveler left?" the woman asks the tall Murkovin.

"A few moments ago," he replies. "The young man with long hair went with her."

"Maybe she's finally found something for herself," the woman murmurs.

"I apologize for bringing the man you had to kill to camp."

"It's not your fault that he was the way he was," the woman says. "Never underestimate how much you've helped me. I've often tried to imagine what kind of a man my Mür was. My Ovì told me that he was a loyal man, a strong man, a fair man. I'm quite certain he was much like you."

The tall Murkovin keeps his eyes stoically focused on the tree at the bottom of the hill. "I'm sure he'd be just as proud of the person you are as I am." He holds a spear out to the woman. "I fetched your weapon for you while you were gone."

"Thank you," the woman replies, taking it from him.

"I'll see you on the morrow," he says.

The tall Murkovin trots down the hill. When he reaches the bottom, the woman's eyes drift to the few remaining people still gathered near the tree.

Perhaps I won't need to end the former Traveler's life, the woman thinks. *Maybe with the long-haired young man, she'll find what she's been looking for in the Barrens. She can finally fulfill the need for companionship and release the physical desires that she's been trying to bury for so long.*

No matter how much I press her, she only reveals tiny pieces of disjointed information about the Delta, nothing I don't already know. But she could prove to have even greater value after the Delta falls.

I need to keep the attack on the Delta a secret from her until after it occurs. Hide her at a camp somewhere in the outer Barrens before the attack, maybe with the long-haired young man at her side.

Once the Delta is ours, I can blame the attack on the former Watcher. I'll tell her that I believed he was dead, only to learn later that he was secretly building an army of the type of Murkovin I killed moments ago. I can tell her that he had others spread the word of his death, but he was actually hiding in the Desert, well out of the view of my eyes across the Barrens. I'll blame the fall of the Delta on him and him alone. She'll believe I was ignorant of the entire plan.

Although we'll kill many of the people in the Delta, we'll let a few of the skilled workers live so they can train our kind. We'll barter the lives of the children with the Tree of Vision for seeds to spread across the wasteland. She could help convince the remaining people of the Delta to put their trust in me, to believe that I'm their salvation.

Chapter 34

"Anything?" I ask Maya.

She remains silently statuesque while seated on the ground. Already knowing what her answer will be, I look at the bleak countryside.

"Nothing," she says.

We left the Delta early in the day, long before the other children at Home were awake, and headed straight to the area on the map that Aven had shown to us. The problem is, when pointing at the map, the tip of my daughter's finger equates to millions of square miles. Sash tried to approximate the center of that point, and that's where we started the search. The entire day has been spent working our way through an outward spiral with stops only a few hundred miles apart. Most of the Delta has probably gone to sleep by now. We appear to have hit another dead end.

"Maybe Aven was wrong," I say to Sash. "Maybe she just wanted to feel like she was helping."

"I don't think so," she replies.

"Even if she can hear the trees, how would they know where Tela is?"

"I don't know," she answers. "Maybe the trees out here can sense Tela and communicate with the other trees across the wasteland. Maybe the trees in the Delta can hear the trees in the Barrens. Maybe the trees in the Delta somehow told Aven what they heard. I don't know how Aven could know, but I believe our daughter."

Looking down at the ground, I rearrange a few rocks with the tip of my boot. I was so excited the night before that I could barely sleep. But as the day has worn on, my initial excitement has withered away. I have the same sinking feeling that I had after getting my hopes up from Angelicusepte's information, only to see it lead to nothing.

"Let's go a little farther out before returning to the Delta," Sash says.

"Sure," I mumble.

Once Maya is on my back, we curve a few hundred miles to the northeast. We stop on top of a particularly steep, rocky hill with large boulders strewn across its slopes. Maya slides to the ground, finds a spot on the dirt, and rests on all fours. After a few minutes pass, she scratches the dirt with her fingernails and shakes her head.

"This hill is a good landmark to remember for the next time we come out," I say to Sash. "We should head back to the Delta. I think we're all exhausted."

Slowly turning in a circle, Sash surveys the weary hills. When she comes to a stop, she focuses her eyes on Maya. Despite Sash's confidence in what Aven told us, I know she must be feeling the same frustration that I am.

"Let's go," Sash says to Maya. "It's late."

I reach a hand down and gently grip Maya's arm. As I pull her to her feet, she jerks her arm away and throws herself to the ground.

"Wait!" Maya shouts.

She squeezes her eyes shut and clenches her jaw. Not a single muscle in her body twitches while she concentrates on whatever she sensed.

"I feel someone familiar," Maya says, aiming her face towards the east. "That way."

"Do you think it's Tela?" Sash asks.

"It has to be," she answers. "It's far away and very weak, but I never sense the Murkovin."

"Let's head east," Sash says.

My heart suddenly races with new hope. I lift Maya from the ground and swing her onto my back. We don't even bother to strap her into the harness. She fastens her hands around my chest and I loop an arm under her leg. With my spear in the grip of my other hand, I bound down the hill behind Sash.

When we reach the bottom of the slope, we sprint towards the east and jolt into our blends. Since we don't plan on going very far, we keep our traveling speed as slow as we can while also trying to stay out of sight. Nervous anticipation makes it seem like hours go by, but no more than a couple of minutes pass before Sash exits the beams. I coast to a stop beside her in a gully at the base of a large hill.

As we climb the slope, we scrutinize the surrounding terrain for any sign of Murkovin. Before we reach the top, Sash motions for me to let Maya off my back. Once she's on the ground, the three of us crawl towards the crest and stop a few feet before reaching the peak. Sandwiched in between Sash and me, Maya lies flat on her stomach with her hands pressed to the rocky dirt.

"I feel her," Maya whispers. "She's close."

"What do you feel?" Sash asks quietly.

"I feel sadness and . . ." Maya pauses and closes her eyes. "And something else. I'm not sure what it is, but it's strong."

"Are you sure it's Tela?" I ask.

Maya shudders as though she's in pain and then blinks her eyes open.

"What's the matter?" Sash asks.

"It is Tela," Maya answers. "She feels awful. She's ashamed and hopeless and wants to die."

"We won't let that happen," Sash tells her. "Both of you stay here."

Sash scoots up to the ridge and peeks over the top. Her eyes slowly roam across the terrain in front of her but soon stop on something. She squints at the distance for several moments and then eases her body back down the slope to Maya's side.

"What did you see?" I ask.

"Glints of light. They were reflections from steel, probably spears. They were about three miles from here and a mile apart. I think two Murkovin are keeping watch from separate hilltops."

"Maybe they're holding Tela captive," I say.

"It's possible. Let's get back down to the gully. Make sure to stay out of sight."

Sliding backwards on our bellies, we descend the slope. About a third of the way down, we rise to our feet and make our way to the ravine. Sash takes a quick drink of sap from her flask.

"Take Maya back to the Delta," she says, returning the flask to her belt. "Don't stop, don't look back, and go as fast as you can. We don't know how many Murkovin might be in this area, so you need to get her to safety."

"What are you planning to do?" I ask.

"I want to see what we're up against."

"You can't fight them alone," I say. "It's too dangerous."

"I won't get in a fight with them."

"You should come with us," I urge. "We'll get more people and come back. You can't do this alone."

She shakes her head. "They could be on the move. We need to know how many there are before we can do anything. It's easier to find out if I'm alone."

"It's way too dangerous. You can't rescue Tela by yourself."

"I won't try to rescue her," she says. "I know how to stay hidden in the Barrens better than anyone else. The more of us there are, the easier it is to be seen. We need to know what they're doing and how many there are before we can make a plan."

I turn my face away for a moment, knowing that Sash is right about her being the best person to spy on them. She's also right that Maya's safety is our top priority.

"Promise me you won't try to fight with them," I say, returning my attention to Sash. "If they see you, you have to run. You need to think about Aven and . . . and after everything we've been through, I can't lose you now."

She rests a hand on my shoulder. "Nobody is losing me. I won't get in a fight. You have to trust me on this."

"Maya and I could wait here for you," I suggest.

"No," Sash says, pulling her hand away from me. "It might take a while to learn what I need to about them. I want to know that Maya is safe in the Delta. Wait for me there. I'll return as soon as I can."

"Okay," I reluctantly reply.

Sash looks at Maya. "I'm very proud of you. We never could have found Tela without you."

For the first time I've ever seen, after months and months of us all being together in the Barrens and all the months I've known her before that, the corners of Maya's lips curl into a smile.

"Thank you," she replies. "I'm honored I could help."

"You're the bravest person I know," I say to her.

In another first—at least since I returned from being in the Barrens with Tela—Sash leans to me and kisses my lips. When it ends, I rest my forehead against hers.

"Please be careful," I say. "I don't want that to be our last kiss."

"It won't be," she says. "Get back to the Delta. Don't stop for anything and go your top speed the entire way. We've put Maya in enough risk."

"I love you," I say.

Sash smiles at me. "I love you, Chase."

Doing as Sash instructed, I load Maya on my back and blaze a trail straight to the Delta. Without ever slowing, I stick to the low ground and avoid going over hills. Maya falls asleep during the return journey and doesn't wake up when I cross the bridge to the Delta. Apart from the Watchers on the wall, everyone else in the Delta seems to be inside their habitats since it's so late.

Outside the caverns of Home, I summon Marc to let him know that we're back. When he meets me at the entrance to the caverns, I tell him that Maya located Tela. Although his face remains as serious as always, he sighs with relief. As I carry Maya to her bed, she wakes up and looks at Marc through half-open eyes. Marc whispers again and again how proud he is of her for sticking with the search and never complaining.

Marc tells me that Aven is already asleep, but I go to her cavern anyway. While sitting on her bed, I gently caress her hair for a few minutes and listen to her steady breathing. I'd like to curl up beside her, but I know that between my anxiety about rescuing Tela and worrying about Sash's safety that I'll never fall asleep. After a few minutes with my daughter, I leave Home and return to the gate.

Even though I know he's sleeping, I summon Larn to tell him the news. He's thrilled to learn that we discovered where Tela is, but I sense worry in his voice about Sash being alone in the Barrens. After our brief conversation ends, I step through the gate and walk to the middle of the bridge.

Sitting on the steel surface at the center of the arch, I raise my knees and rest my arms on them. I stare at the Barrens to the northeast. I don't know if I doze off for a few minutes or just drift away in thought, but I'm startled out of my trance by footsteps behind me. I look over my shoulder to see Larn walking up the bridge. He stops, sits down beside me, and speaks in a sympathetic tone.

"Not being able to do anything but wait might be the most helpless feeling there is."

"It's the worst," I reply, still looking at the Barrens.

"It's the same way Sash felt when you were missing," he tells me.

I turn my face to him. "When I was out there with Tela, I had a lot of horrible thoughts. I thought Sash had betrayed me. I knew it was the wild sap, but I let it gnaw at me more and more until it was out of control. That's why I behaved the way I did when I came back. I thought you and Sash were out to get me."

"It's almost impossible for us to control it," he says.

I vehemently shake my head. "Not for me. All the things it makes a person feel are foreign to everyone born in the Delta. You don't even have words for some of the emotions. But every one of those negative feelings exists in my world. We grow up trying to learn the difference between right and wrong, learning to thrive on good emotions and suppress the bad. I should have been stronger." I pause for a moment. "If anything happens to Sash or Tela, I'll never forgive myself."

Larn lays his spear on the surface of the bridge between us and leans back on his hands. "I don't know if all things happen for a reason," he says. "I think some events in our lives are random and have no purpose behind them. They're completely out of our control. But the one thing we can always control is how we react to them.

"There might be a reason for what happened," he continues, "or it might just be a series of events that unraveled for no reason at all. It's up to you to decide if there's something to learn. For now, have faith in Sash's decision and believe in her."

"She's doing all of this because she knows how important it is to me," I reply.

"She's doing this because of her loyalty to everyone in the Delta. I believe she'll return safely. She has you and Aven to think about."

I don't know what to say in response to Larn's unexpected insight into the emotional bond of a family unit that doesn't exist in this world. He adheres to the customs of the Delta as much as anyone.

"When this over," Larn continues, "I'd like to stop by your habitat sometime. I've never taken you up on your invitation to visit Aven. I think I might find it meaningful."

Even with my concern for Sash, I smile at Larn's change of heart about spending time with his granddaughter. "I think Aven will like that, too," I say. "And Sash. Our door is always open to you."

As the Krymzyn night passes, Larn and I keep our eyes glued to the Barrens. When the Watchers change shifts on the wall behind us, we know that the Delta is waking up for the new day. I fold my arms over my raised knees and rest my forehead on them. Listening to the rush of the rapids below the bridge, I fall asleep.

*　　*　　*

"Chase," Larn says, shaking me awake. "Look over there."

I pop my head up and focus my eyes on the Barrens to the northeast. A streak of light soars over a distant hill.

I jump to my feet and run to the end of the bridge. After emerging from behind a hill, Sash glides to a jog. When she stops in front of me, I throw my arms around her.

"You're safe," I whisper in her ear.

"I promised you I would be," she says.

"Did you see Tela?"

Sash ends our embrace and takes a step back from me. "I saw her and I have a plan. Let's talk to Larn."

We hurriedly walk up the bridge to where Larn is waiting for us.

"What did you find out?" he asks when we reach him.

"Tela is in a camp of Murkovin," Sash answers. "Will you please ask the other Travelers to meet us at Sanctuary? I'll go over my plan with everybody at the same time."

"Right away."

Once the three of us are inside the gate to the Delta, Larn summons the Travelers and Sash contacts Eval. A few minutes later, we reach the meadow in front of the Tree of Vision. Eval and Tork are already waiting for us. After the other Travelers arrive, we gather in a circle.

"Thanks to Maya," Sash says to the group, "we located Tela. She's with a group of about forty Murkovin north of the Desert."

"She's their captive," I add.

"She's not a captive," Sash tells me. "She's there because she wants to be."

"What makes you think that?"

"She came out of what appears to be her own cavern. At the beginning of the day, she was teaching Murkovin to travel with transports. She could have left if she wanted to."

"Why would she teach Murkovin to carry transports?" I ask.

She shrugs her shoulders. "We'll ask her that question if we get the chance. I think I know a way to bring her back."

"If she's not a captive," Eval says, "taking her will be against her will. I don't know if we can sanction—"

"She has no will," I interrupt. "The wild sap takes control of it. She didn't go out there by choice. She doesn't know what she's doing."

Standing directly across from me, Tork scowls in my direction. "Are you suggesting that we force her to return to the Delta?"

I ignore Tork and speak directly to Eval. "In my world, people sometimes become what we call _addicts_. Their entire lives revolve around something like taking a certain substance or being in a _cult_ . . . a messed up way of thinking that takes control of their minds. Some people suffer from mental problems that are impossible to deal with on their own. They can never think clearly. The only way to help them is by forcing them to accept help. They can't do it themselves. That's what the wild sap has done to Tela."

"I fully understand what's happened to Tela," Eval says to me and then looks at Sash. "What's your opinion?"

"I think we should bring her back," Sash answers without hesitation. "I don't know if we can reverse what's happened to her, but we have to try."

"Do you have a plan for rescuing her?" Eval asks.

Sash nods her head. "The Murkovin have a camp situated around several trees in a small area. It covers a couple of square miles. Most of the hills are small and have caverns in them. That's where the Murkovin dwell.

"Tela's cavern is north of the area with the trees. There's

another cavern on the other side of the same hill. Two women and two children share that one, but other than that, only one other Murkovin's cavern is nearby. He's a very tall Murkovin who seems to be in charge of the camp. I saw him giving orders to the others.

"Four Murkovin are always on watch on four different hills outside where the caverns are. The guard on the western side of the camp is about a half-mile from Tela's cavern. The land around the camp is fairly open, but there are a few small hills and large rocks to use as cover. That's how I got close to the camp. If we can distract the guards while the others are sleeping, get them to focus their attention on something else, we should be able to get to Tela's cavern."

"What kind of distraction?" Eval asks.

"Travelers," Sash answers. "Travelers with wagon transports full of steel items."

"Why would Travelers be out there with transports?" I ask.

"When items of steel are worn out or broken," Sash explains, "Travelers take them to the Dunes. When steel is rubbed with the pulp of the cactus that grows there, the steel hardening process reverses. Everything is thrown into the Dunes. The sand gradually wears the steel down to dust particles. They become part of the Dunes."

"But we never go north of the Desert," Larn says. "We travel through the middle of the Desert to the Stone Passage at the Dunes."

"I don't think the Murkovin will think it through that carefully," Sash tells him. "Especially if everything happens fast. But we need two separate distractions. We need one on the northeast of camp and one on the southwest. That will draw all four guards away and leave a gap to get to Tela's cavern."

"We can't require anyone to do this," Eval says, "nor can we risk all the Travelers being in danger at once."

Roen, the second tallest of the Travelers, looks at each of us one by one. Built much like Larn, trim but muscular, he has medium-length, wavy hair that hangs just over his eyebrows. Each time his eyes stop on one of the Travelers, that person nods their head to him. When he returns his attention to Larn, he clenches his jaw.

"We're all going," Roen says firmly. "Tela is one of us. We won't leave her out there."

"That includes me," the Apprentice Kale adds. "I want to help."

"We only need two Travelers," Sash informs everyone, "and they won't be in danger. They'll stop in view of the Murkovin, get their attention, dump the wagons, and then come straight back to the Delta. The other Murkovin at the camp will be asleep. Chase, Larn, and I will go inside the camp to get Tela."

"I'm opposed to this," Tork says. "We put the Delta at risk of losing Travelers."

"I agree with Tork," Eval tells us. Her eyes slowly move to Larn. "But if this is what the tallest of the Travelers deems is the right thing to do, we won't stand in his way."

Larn studies each of the Travelers, including me. No one speaks a word, but the determined looks on all of our faces leave no doubt as to how much we want to take part in the rescue.

"Nuar, Velt, and Kale will stay here," Larn says. "Jeni and Roen will take the transports."

"We should all go!" Nuar argues.

"Our first duty is to Krymzyn," Larn calmly replies. "I also think it will help Sash's plan if there are fewer of us."

"How can that help?" Nuar asks.

"If one Traveler loses control of a wagon and flees, the Murkovin are likely to go after the wagon's contents without calling for help. If they see multiple Travelers, they might call others."

"I had that thought as well," Sash says.

Staring at Larn, Nuar thinks through the plan. "It does make sense," she admits.

When no one else says anything, Larn addresses Sash.

"When do we leave?"

"As soon as possible," she answers. "We should be able to get there by the end of the day. Most of them will be asleep soon after. Everyone should change into long-sleeves so that we blend in with the terrain as much as possible. Chase and I will meet you at Market."

Chapter 35

It would be impossible for Sash and me to leave the Delta without first saying goodbye to Aven. Given the perils that accompany life as a Traveler, I've accepted that whenever I say goodbye to my daughter, it might be for the last time. I know Sash feels the same way since Hunters face risks every time Darkness falls. I've learned not to dwell on it, but it's still hard on me at times. Even on Earth, I guess anyone could die unexpectedly from a car wreck, a work-related accident, or a natural disaster. But the scale is different in Krymzyn.

With only one hundred and sixty-one of us in the Delta and on the Mount, if even one person dies, it's a significant percentage of the population. Travelers, Hunters, and Watchers have the greatest risk to life and limb, but everyone is vulnerable if a Murkovin enters the Delta. It's occurred to me that the ever-present danger in this world may be the reason there is no immediate family structure, everyone living as one. In my short time here, I've seen several tragic deaths that could have resulted in a parentless child.

While Larn and the rest of the Travelers go to Market to prepare the wagon transports, Sash and I speed to our habitat. We hastily change into long-sleeved shirts and then travel to Home. After pulling Aven out of the classroom, we take her to the cavern designated as hers. Sash and I sit on Aven's bed with our daughter nestled between us and our arms draped around her shoulders.

"We found Tela," Sash says. "She was exactly where you pointed to on the map."

"Chees find Tela," Aven replies.

Sash squeezes Aven's arm. "The trees did find her. Maya helped too, and so did you. We're going to bring her back and this will all be over. We'll spend every moment we can with you."

Aven leans her head against Sash's shoulder. "Mommy . . . Daddy. Be safe."

"We will, baby girl," I say. "We love you."

"Love you," Aven whispers, her first time pronouncing the word "love" properly.

After Sash and I give our daughter a long hug, we return her to the Keepers and head to Market. The others are already there when we arrive. Sash suggests that we bring a coil of rope with us in case we need to bind Tela to get her back. I can't imagine that Tela wouldn't want to return with us, but ultimately decide that Sash is right. My mental struggle to get back to the Delta after just a few days of living on wild sap was brutal. Tela has been in the Barrens for over six months.

While Larn and the other Travelers finish filling two wagon transports with spears, canisters, flasks, and a few stools, Sash grabs a sheathed knife from one of the tables. She fastens it to the belt around her waist and tucks the tip of the sheath into the back of her pants so that it won't flop against her when she runs. After realizing that I may need a knife to cut the rope, I grab one as well and place it on the back of my belt in the same way that Sash did. With the coil of rope looped over my shoulder, I follow the others to the gate.

As soon as we reach the wall, a Watcher swings the gate open. With the sound of the turbulent river below, we cross over the bridge and stop at the edge of the Barrens. Jeni and Roen rest their transport handles on the ground and look at Sash for further instructions.

"Follow me through the Barrens," she says. "I'll keep my speed down so everyone can stay close together."

"And then what?" Jeni asks.

"We'll stop a few miles from the Murkovin camp. I'll explain everything else once we get there. It will make a lot more sense when you can see the terrain."

With Sash leading our way and Larn bringing up the rear, we aim to the northeast. If Sash is taking us to the gully where we stopped with Maya, I estimate that it's about sixty thousand miles away. Although Sash and I can cover that distance in less than two hours, it will take us closer to six hours at the other Travelers' top speeds. Since we're leaving in the middle of the day, we should still have a couple of hours when we get there to finalize the plan before the Murkovin are asleep.

Sash and I have only had a few hours of rest over the past two days. I'm running on pure adrenaline and whatever sap I consume, and I know Sash is in the same depleted state that I am. But Sash correctly surmised that they could be on the move, so this may be our best and only chance to get Tela away from them.

As the day wears on, thousands of miles fall behind us. We finally pass the hill where Maya sensed Tela for the first time. Our small caravan of Travelers follows Sash into the same gully that we stopped in with Maya.

After Sash instructs Jeni and Roen to leave their transports in the gully, we all climb up the hill. One by one, each of us peeks over the rocks along the crest while Sash explains the layout of the Murkovin camp to us.

When it's my turn, I peer across a series of low hills covering the three miles between the Murkovin and us. Just past the low hills are two slightly taller ones, one on the northern side of the camp, and one on the western side closer to where we are. While squinting at the tops of the hills, I spot a Murkovin standing on each one.

"The valley beside the western hill leads inside the camp," Sash tells me in a hushed voice. "The valley leads to the small hill where Tela's cavern is. If we can draw the guard on the west side of camp to the south and the one up north farther away from camp, we should be able to get in without being seen."

"That sounds like it should work," I say.

"Two more Murkovin are on guard, but you can't see them from here. One is on the far eastern side of the camp and the other on the south."

After she tugs on my shirt, we scoot back down to the others.

"Jeni," Sash says, "if you go a hundred miles north and then come back down on the northeast side of the camp, crash the cart about half a mile from the guards. As soon as they head towards you, leave everything behind and get back to the Delta."

Jeni nods her head in reply.

"You do the same," Sash says to Roen, "only on the southwest side of camp. That should draw the western and southern guards away."

"What if they don't come after us?" Roen asks.

"Pretend like you don't see them, put everything back in the transport, and walk towards them. They'll eventually come after you, but they might also call for help. Once they're after you, don't wait for us. Leave everything behind and go to the Delta."

Roen glances at Larn and then at me. "Bring Tela back safely."

"We will," I say.

Sash keeps watch from the top of the hill while the rest of us return to the gully to wait out of sight. The time that ticks away is agonizingly slow. We're all pretty amped-up and ready to get the rescue underway, but we have to wait until Sash is certain that all the Murkovin other than the guards have gone to sleep.

While Jeni and Roen pace up and down the gully together, I skip stones across the dirt. Larn sharpens the tip of his spear on a large rock. After a couple of hours pass, Sash climbs down to the hill and tells us that it's time to go. Wanting to fuel ourselves with one last dose of fresh, potent energy, we all guzzle sap.

Just as Sash is about to say something to the group, she tilts her face up to the sky. "Darkness is coming."

"We'll have better cover," I say.

She lowers her eyes to mine. "The other Murkovin in camp could wake up for sap during Darkness."

"It doesn't matter. We'll be fine."

"Why do you think that?" she asks.

"During Darkness, the craving for sap is so strong that it's hard to think about anything else. Believe me. I've been through it. If they wake up, all they'll think about is sap."

"But they're more violent during Darkness," she counters. "If they see us, we can't fight them all."

"They do become more violent," I reply, "but also more irrational. The guards will go after Jeni and Roen because they'll be angry and won't be able to control it. The ones who can blend their light can't go very fast during Darkness. It's hard to concentrate. We'll have the cover of dark to get in and won't have any trouble getting away once we have Tela."

Sash looks down at the ground while thinking about what I told her. "We'll have to trust Chase on this," she eventually says, raising her face to the group. "He's right that Darkness will help us get to the camp unseen."

"What if Tela leaves her cavern?" Larn asks.

"Then we'll wait for her inside," she answers.

As the last word exits her mouth, the clouds covering the Barrens tumble into motion and the light fades away. With almost pitch black surrounding us, rain descends from the sky. The dark soil of the wasteland is soon drenched in water.

"Is everybody ready?" Sash asks.

"Now's as good a time as any," Jeni answers in a quiet, monotone voice that's barely audible over the rain.

Chapter 36

"You two go now," Sash says to Jeni and Roen. "Stop roughly one hundred miles away from the camp so they don't see you. After you stop, give us to the count of two thousand to get in position. Then crash the transports as close to the guards as you can, but make sure you have space to get away. Larn and Chase, follow me."

"Everyone stay safe and stick to the plan," Larn says.

Jeni and Roen step to the transports and grip the handles. They briefly struggle to get their footing in the slippery ravine, but soon sail away in opposite directions.

Sash guides Larn and me up the gully to the east. As we run through a newborn stream, it quickly rises to our ankles. The gully eventually ends at the first of the smaller hills that lie between us and the Murkovin camp. After climbing out of the ravine, we jog around the hill until we reach a pile of large boulders. Sash halts us by raising one hand.

"We'll have some cover along the way," she says. "Much of the time, we'll be out in the open and in view of at least one of the guards. Stay behind me and do what I do."

"Wouldn't it be better to just travel to the camp?" I ask.

"No. It's easier for them to see us if we're in a blend. A few large rocks are in the open spaces. We can stop behind those if we need to. I'll keep an eye on the guards, so watch me for any signals."

"What do we do if they see us?" I ask.

"I don't know," she answers. "That isn't part of the plan, so let's not be seen."

"I like your optimism."

"It may be our best weapon," she says. "When we reach the last of the low hills, we'll wait there until the guards go after Jeni and Roen."

"How far is that from Tela's cavern?" Larn asks.

"A few hundred yards. When we get to her cavern, I'll stay outside to keep watch. You and Chase go inside to get her. Do whatever you have to and do it fast."

"We will," Larn says.

"If she's not there, come out and get me. Are you ready?"

Larn nods his head.

"I'm ready," I tell her.

"One more thing," she says. "Let's try to blend in with the ground."

She drops to her knees and rolls her spear in the wet dirt. Once it's coated with mud, she leaves it on the ground and scoops up as much muck as she can with her hands. As she smears it over the top of her head and down the length of her hair, the scarlet streaks are gradually hidden.

"Hide the color in your hair," she says to Larn and me.

Larn and I both sink to the ground and coat our hair with mud. We also roll our spears around in the wet dirt like Sash did to hide the shiny steel as much as possible. The torrents of rain will soon wash it away from our spears and heads, but the mud gives us some kind of camouflage to begin with. If we need to, we can always add more along the way.

Sash grabs her spear and crawls to the edge of the pile of boulders. Arching her neck, she peeks around the rocks at the northern guard. I don't know how she can spot him through the blanket of Darkness over the wasteland. The hills around us are nothing but almost imperceptible outlines against dark, swirling clouds. Sash suddenly looks in the direction of the Murkovin on the westernmost hill.

"Get ready," she says, tensing her muscles.

Larn and I both coil, waiting for Sash's command.

"Now!"

Staying low to the ground, Sash bolts across the flat area between us and the next tiny hill. With the wind shrieking past our ears, Larn and I follow close behind her. Keeping watch on the guards, Sash turns her head from side to side as she runs, but Larn and I stay focused on Sash. Although we all slip in the mud several times, we make it across the quarter-mile of open space without being seen. When we reach the hill, we hide behind the cover of a steep bluff.

After we catch our breath, Sash leads us around the side of the hill. She immediately decides that neither of the guards can see us, so we sprint across the next span of open ground. Over and over, we repeat the process, zigzagging our way across the flats and hiding behind small hills and large boulders.

While crossing the last of the open spaces, Sash suddenly dives to the mud. Larn and I both throw our bodies to the ground and slide across the wet, mushy dirt. When we come to a stop, we raise our heads to check on the guards. They're both less than half a mile away from us now. I can make out their pale shapes on the hilltops, which means they could see us as well. The northern guard is looking away from us, but the western guard seems to be staring straight in our direction.

Lying in the mud for close to a minute, none of us makes a move. The rain pounds down on our bodies while puddles of water grow by our sides. Dull reflections occasionally shimmer in the wet flats, which is what I hope the guard believes he saw. He finally turns his back to us.

Sash scoops another handful of mud and spreads it over her hair. After Larn and I do the same, we check to make sure the guards aren't looking in our direction. Slithering on our bellies across the black sludge, we pull our bodies with our hands and push with our feet. By the time we reach the last of the low hills, the muscles in my arms are numb.

Sash leads us around the hill to a semi-secluded spot with a clear view of the guards. They're no more than a few hundred yards away from us.

"Be ready," Sash says quietly. "The moment they head towards Jeni and Roen, follow me to Tela's cavern."

While Sash spies on the guard to the north, I focus on the Murkovin standing watch on the western hill. He takes a few gulps from what appears to be a Traveler's canister. After he finishes his drink, he jerks his head to the south. The beast takes two steps forward, studies something in the distance, and then runs down the hill away from us.

"One guard just left," I say to Sash.

"The other one is looking at something," she replies. "It

has to be Jeni."

"We're ready," Larn says.

"There he goes!" Sash exclaims.

She zips into the open towards the valley that leads to Tela's cavern. Trying to keep our footing through the slippery dirt, Larn and I stay right on her tail. When we reach the narrow valley, we continue towards a sheer face of rock on the side of a steep hill.

At the base of that hill, the valley forks around the bluff. We veer to the south, but three silhouettes cross our path about fifty yards away. Glimmers of white shine from their black hair. Slipping and sliding in the mud, Sash cuts hard to her left. With a dull thud, she flattens her body against the side of the bluff.

I lose my footing while trying to follow her and splatter to the wet ground. After Larn slams into the wall of rock beside Sash, they both arch their necks to see if the Murkovin spotted us. Lying face down in the mud, I stay as still as a corpse, afraid to even breathe.

"They kept going," Sash says. "I don't think they saw us."

I spring from the ground and scramble to the cover of the cliff. Sash and Larn step away from the rocks to scan the land around us.

"We're almost there," Sash says. "Let's go slower to be safe."

At a much more cautious pace, we jog the final hundred yards to Tela's cavern. Although we continue to scour the terrain for Murkovin, we don't spot any along the way. The vertical wall of rock beside us gradually angles down until forming the steep slope of a hill. When we reach a cavern entrance in the bottom of the hill, we come to a stop and check around us one last time. Sash raises a finger to her lips to keep Larn and me quiet.

"You two go in," she whispers. "I'll go up this hill to keep watch."

Sputtering through streams of water that flow down the slope, Sash fights her way up the hill. Larn and I wait for her to get halfway to the top before squeezing into the tunnel that leads to Tela's cavern. With me in the lead, we feel our way through the dark passage. The gurgling of a waterfall in front of us becomes louder with each step we take.

I come to a standstill when I feel the wall of the tunnel curve into what seems to be an open space. Reaching out a hand behind me, I stop Larn with a palm to his chest. If Tela is asleep inside the cavern, we can catch her off guard.

"Be ready," I whisper to Larn.

Priming my muscles to leap inside, I wait a few seconds while listening for any movement. It's impossible to hear anything over the spill of the waterfall.

"Light," I say.

The purple glow that I became so familiar with while trapped in the Barrens gradually illuminates a small cave. My eyes dart around the room in search of Tela, but there's nobody inside.

A crude, wooden table is pushed up against a wall on one side of the cave with a wooden stool underneath it. On the other side, a mattress lies on the ground. A small waterfall pours over the uneven rocks at the far end of the cavern. After slowly leaning my head through the entrance, I snap it to the left and right to make sure no one is hiding on the sides.

"It's empty," I say to Larn. "Keep watch on the tunnel in case she comes in."

I take a few steps inside the cavern and then stop to look around. I don't know what to expect in a typical Murkovin habitat, but the room seems bare to me. There's no pillow on the mattress and nothing on the table. Although there's a couple of steel spikes driven into the wall near the bed, no clothes are hanging from them. The only other item that indicates a person might dwell here is a small bundle of black fabric near the foot of the bed.

I walk to the ball of fabric and lift it from the ground. It's a pair of black pants with the legs cut off around the knees. I'm positive they're the same pants that Tela had on the last time I saw her. I toss them to the ground and hurry back to Larn.

"This is definitely Tela's cavern," I say, "but she's not here."

"Let's get Sash and come back inside to wait," he replies.

"Dark," I call out to extinguish the grubs.

Running my hand along the wall, I follow Larn through the tunnel. When we reach the end, the relentless storm is still in full force outside. Larn leans his head out the entrance and looks back and forth a few times. Confident that no Murkovin are nearby, he steps outside. After facing the slope that Sash climbed up, he squints at the top of the hill.

"Sash is gone," he says to me.

Chapter 37

I fly out of the tunnel and look up the hill. Scouring the slope, I search for any sign of Sash in the shallow washes or behind boulders. Through the shroud of dark, I don't spot her anywhere.

"Let's go to the top," I say to Larn. "Maybe she's on the other side."

After a quick check of the valley around us, Larn and I slosh up the steep slope. In the continuing onslaught of rain, we both lose our footing and slip to our knees. Using our hands to claw through the mud, we grapple our way towards the top.

"Sash," I call out in a loud whisper when we near the crest.

We pause for a moment to see if she appears from the other side. Larn glances over his shoulder to make sure no one is behind us and then we scurry the rest of the way up the hill. Trying to find Sash, I immediately aim my eyes down the slope on the other side.

"Chase," Larn says. "Look over there."

I focus my eyes in the direction that Larn points. The backside of the hill we're on slants down to a narrow valley. On the far side of the basin, the ground rises again to another small hill. On top of that knoll, under ominous churning clouds, Sash and a Murkovin woman are locked in furious combat. Each time their spears clash, a sharp clang rings out through the rain. I've seen Sash butcher three Murkovin in a matter of seconds, but in this battle, she can't seem to get the upper hand.

The woman is a little taller than Sash. Other than that, they're built almost exactly the same. The only distinct difference between them is that the woman's long hair is laced with the ivory of a Murkovin instead of the scarlet that highlights Sash's mane. It's hard to tell for sure in the dark, but their facial features seem eerily similar. Every move they make, every attack and block, contains the same strength and agility. They could easily be mistaken for sisters.

"She needs help!" I blurt out.

"Let's go!" Larn says.

We jump to our feet and storm down the backside of the hill. Swinging his head back and forth, Larn watches out for Murkovin while I keep my eyes trained on Sash. She thrusts her spear at the woman's stomach, but the woman bounds backwards and avoids the tip. The woman counter-attacks with a jab of her weapon at Sash's head.

As Sash catapults her spear up to block, she karate kicks one foot at the woman's knees. The woman leaps over Sash's foot, lands firmly in the mud, and fires a fist at Sash's jaw. Sash catches the hand in hers, but a knee to Sash's groin sends her stumbling backwards.

Off-balance on the slick dirt, Sash smacks the shaft of her spear against the side of the woman's head. The woman staggers a few steps to her side while Sash regains her footing. Larn and I reach the small valley below them and race across the open space towards the hill they're on.

Plotting their next moves, Sash and the woman crouch and stare at one another. At the exact same moment, they both lean forward and flare into light. A split-second later, Sash and the woman reappear on the opposite sides of each other.

With our mouths dropping open, Larn and I slide to a stop halfway through the valley. It's almost beyond my comprehension that they blended their light from a virtual standstill. Even more amazing, they instantly came out of the beams after traveling only a few yards.

Now ten feet apart, Sash and the woman whirl towards one another. Although they both coil again, neither one attacks. They're gasping for breath, obviously exhausted from a fight that seems unwinnable for either one.

"Look out!" Larn yells.

He grabs my shirt and hurls me to the ground. When I splash to the mud, Larn pivots his body to avoid a spear that was aimed at my back. As the attacking Murkovin tries to stop, he skims across the wet ground. Larn rivets his weapon into the creature's back. After driving him to the dirt, Larn rips his spear out of the body and then drills it back down into the Murkovin's skull. Out of the dark, a second beast speeds at Larn from behind.

Popping to my knees, I lunge my weapon at the second Murkovin. He arcs his spear over his head and swats the shaft of mine down to the ground. As Larn spins in the direction of the brute, the Murkovin plows his shoulder into Larn's gut. With the Murkovin on top, they both topple to the wet ground beside me.

Larn grabs the Murkovin's arms, but the brute hammers his forehead into Larn's face. As blood spews from Larn's nose, I rifle my spear at the side of the Murkovin's head. Ducking under it, he shoves his weapon backwards at me. A fire ignites in my thigh when he bores the point through the muscle and all the way to the bone.

Cringing from pain, I clutch the shaft of his spear in both hands. Larn bashes a fist to the Murkovin's face, knocking him towards me. I yank the spear out of my thigh and throw an arm around the beast's neck. Clenching his throat, I twist my body to the side and pull him off Larn.

As we fall to the mud, he latches his hands to my arm. He must outweigh me by at least forty pounds, but I fasten my free hand to my wrist and secure him in a stranglehold. Wriggling in the mud, the brute begins to pry my arm away from his neck. Larn gropes for his spear, finally cinches his fingers around the shaft, and hops to his feet. Just as the Murkovin breaks free from my grip, Larn plunges his spear into the beast's head.

"Can you run?" Larn asks, glancing at my leg and wiping blood from his face.

"I can try."

He reaches a hand down and takes hold of my arm. When he pulls me to my feet, pain sizzles through my wounded leg. I desperately pour sap from my canister onto my palm and spread it over the hole in my thigh. The rain quickly washes the sap away, and blood continues to flow from the wound.

"Sash!" Larn shouts. "We need to get out of here!"

I fix my eyes on the top of the hill again. With rain splattering on them, Sash and the woman are still immersed in an unending duel. After a flurry of spears clacking against one another, they both take a few steps backwards. Their chests heave as they try to suck in air.

Sash doesn't take her eyes off the woman or acknowledge that she heard Larn in any way, but she abruptly rams her weapon at the woman. As the woman whisks her spear up in defense, Sash wheels away in our direction. Like the head of a snake striking out of nowhere, the tip of the woman's spear flashes towards Sash.

Trying to dodge the point, Sash flings her hips back. As the steel slices into her stomach, Sash drops her spear and grips the shaft of the woman's weapon in both hands. The woman powers forward, trying to drive her spear deeper into Sash's gut. Larn charges towards the hill.

Using my spear as a crutch, I hobble behind Larn. With her hands locked to the shaft of the woman's spear, Sash digs her feet into the mud. Countering strength with strength, Sash inches the woman's weapon out of her belly. When the woman bulldozes forward, Sash wrenches her stomach to the side. She frees the tip from her stomach, but it rips an even larger gash.

As blood gushes from her wound, Sash keeps her grip on the woman's spear with one hand and whips her other hand behind her back. The moment it slaps to the handle of the knife, she tugs the woman's spear by her side. Still hanging on to the weapon, the woman pitches forward. With a fierce roundhouse motion, Sash slashes the knife blade across the woman's face. The blow stands the woman upright.

Leaping straight up in the air, Sash cocks her knees to her chest. Exploding out of her tuck, she batters both feet against the woman's chest. The woman tumbles backwards and falls behind the crest of the hill. After rolling her body in the air, Sash lands on all fours.

Larn halts in his tracks about halfway up the hill. Barely at the edge of the upslope, I stop and lean on my weapon to support my weight. Sash sheaths the knife and snatches her spear from the mud. With one hand pressed over the wound in her stomach, she makes a mad dash down the hill.

"Tela left the camp!" she shouts. "The tall Murkovin went after her!"

When Sash reaches Larn, he turns and runs down the hill beside her. I look up and down the valley to see if any Murkovin are nearby. Other than the endless torrent of rain, I don't spot anything moving. Larn and Sash grind to a stop in front of me. Sash immediately notices the blood all over my thigh.

"Give me the rope," she says. "I'm going after Tela."

I glance at her stomach. Blood leaks from between the fingers of her hand covering the wound.

"You can't," I argue. "You're injured."

She hands her spear to Larn, tears a flask from her belt, and pours sap all over the laceration in her gut. "The tall Murkovin could kill her," she says. "We're wasting time."

"We don't have time to argue!" Larn yells.

"Give me the rope!" Sash orders.

I clench my jaw, knowing that she's not about to back down. "I'm going with you."

"You can barely walk with that wound," Larn says to me.

Sash grabs the coil of rope hanging around my neck, but as she tries to pull it over my head, she winces from pain and locks her hand to her belly.

"It won't scab in the rain," I tell her. "The water is washing the sap away."

"I'll be fine!" she blares.

"You're the most stubborn person alive!"

"Stop your bickering!" Larn intervenes. "We need to get out of here. Give her the rope or I'll take it from you."

Glaring at Sash, I remove the coil of rope from my neck and hold it out to her. She hangs it over her shoulder and then takes her spear from Larn.

"You might need this, too," Larn says.

He hands her his canister. She takes it from him, twists off the top, and gulps down a big swig. After pouring more on her palm, she holds her hand in place over the wound.

"Get Chase back to the Delta," Sash says to Larn. "I'll stay with you until we're clear of the camp."

"Hop on," Larn says, turning his back to me. "I don't think you can run."

Ignoring Larn, I keep my eyes focused on Sash. "Don't do this."

"This may be our only chance to get her," she replies, surprising me with the calm tone of her voice. "She went to the northeast. I can catch up to her if I go now. I'll deal with my wound when Darkness ends."

Knowing all too well that she won't change her mind, I grit my teeth. "Make sure you come back alive."

"I will, but we need to get out of here right now."

I hand my spear to Larn and then clamp my arms across his chest. After he loops one arm under my uninjured leg, he lopes up the valley to the north. With the muddy ground and my added weight, he has trouble getting any traction or gaining speed. Still nursing her stomach with one hand, Sash runs by our side.

"Get going!" she yells at Larn.

"I don't have enough speed to travel yet!"

Directly in front of us, four Murkovin round the base of a hill.

Chapter 38

As the Murkovin trample towards us, Larn and Sash skid to a stop. After Larn drops me to the mud, I swipe my spear from his hand. Bracing for the attack, Larn and Sash crouch with their weapons at the ready in front of them. On the hill to our left, two shapes of light rocket over the crest and down the slope.

"Two more on our left!" I shout.

Hopping on one foot, I move to the left of Larn and Sash and balance on my good leg. If I can at least slow down the two Murkovin coming down the slope when they come out of their blends, maybe I can buy enough time for Larn and Sash to take out the others. The first four are only a few yards away from us when the two on the side of the hill exit the light. As one shape morphs into the body of a woman, blue glimmers from her hair.

"Yes!" I cheer at the top of my lungs.

Slightly ahead of Jeni, Roen sprints out of the beams. Never slowing his pace, he steamrolls into the first Murkovin he reaches. The beast ricochets off Roen and hits the brute beside him. Both Murkovin sprawl to the ground.

The two Murkovin that are still on their feet screech to a standstill. Jenny immediately crashes into one. As he flops to the mud, he twists and ramrods the point of his spear into Jeni's arm. Using only one hand, Jeni viciously spikes her weapon into the Murkovin's chest. When she yanks the tip from his body, the eruption of blood leaves no doubt that she impaled his heart.

Larn zeroes in on one of the two Murkovin flattened by Roen. Before the creature can push himself out of the mud, Larn's weapon pierces deep into his skull. The other beast on the ground shuffles to his feet, but Roen blindsides him with a spear through the side of his head.

Trapped in the middle of Jeni, Sash, and me, the lone Murkovin still on his feet eyeballs the blood all over my leg. When he bursts in my direction, Sash springs forward and drives her spear into his back. Sash recoils from the impact, doubles over, and cradles her gut in her hands.

The Murkovin flails in my direction. I strong-arm my weapon through his throat and whip him to the ground. Unable to keep my footing with the wound in my leg, I careen off-balance towards the mud. Jeni leaps to my side, catches me mid-fall, and hoists me back up. As I slide my spear out of the Murkovin at my feet, Sash stands upright with a fresh flow of blood from her wound.

"Chase can't travel," Larn yells to Roen and Jeni while squatting with his back to me. "Sash is wounded."

"We need to go now!" Roen shouts, pointing his spear down the valley behind us.

A football field away, a dozen Murkovin thunder towards us. As Jeni heaves me onto Larn's back, I toss one arm around his chest. He loops an arm under my good leg, but we both keep our spears in our other hands in case we can't escape.

"Stay with Sash!" I holler at Roen. "She's going after Tela!"

"No!" Sash wails. "He'll slow me down."

With one arm crossed over her stomach, Sash takes off running to the north. Jeni drags Larn by the arm until we're fleeing up the valley behind her. After sprinting past us, Roen catches up to Sash. He reaches out his canister to her as they run. She grabs it and loops the rope around her neck. Roen glances over his shoulder at the Murkovin.

"They're gaining on us!" he yells.

"Be ready to travel!" Larn shouts at me.

I scrunch a handful of Larn's shirt in my hand. The tromping of feet in the mud behind us grows louder and louder. Grunting while he churns his legs, Larn spurts forward a few times but doesn't have enough momentum to get into his blend. Slowing their pace until they're beside us, Roen and Sash prepare to thwart off a Murkovin assault. On our other flank, Jeni checks behind us.

"Now or never!" she screams.

"Now!" Larn bellows.

With a force that almost throws me off his back, we jettison into the beams. As the wind lashes across my face, I cling to Larn's shirt like a rider on a bucking bronc. Jeni streams to our side, but there's no sign of Sash and Roen. I twist my neck to the rear to make sure they're with us. Already in their blends, they're on our tail.

"No way," I whisper.

One by one, every Murkovin in sight scorches into light.

"They're all traveling!" I shout.

Larn soars past a hill and banks hard to the west. Jeni stays right by our side. As we cross a broad flat area, luminescent figures crisscross in the stormy dark behind us. It's impossible to tell who's who with so many bodies traveling in such a close range.

When two shapes pull away from the horde, I assume they're Sash and Roen. As they close in on us, one veers sharply to the north. The wisps of light gain so much speed in a matter of seconds that it has to be Sash.

As she vanishes in the distance, one of the Murkovin splits away from the pack and follows her trail. Sending a shiver down my spine, the shape torpedoes through the dark with more velocity than any Murkovin I've ever seen. Whoever it is would need to match Sash's traveling speed to cover so much ground in so little time. My first guess—my only guess—it's the woman who Sash fought.

After the long, flat ground gives way to more hills, Larn arcs into a narrow valley. Roen and Jeni stay on either side of us as we weave between the series of uneven hills. Larn aims up the slope of one and slows a little as we near the top of the hill.

"Look behind us!" he yells.

When I check over my shoulder, I see that the Murkovin are still in pursuit. We've put half a mile between us, but they're not willing to give up the chase.

"Still on us!"

Larn sails over the peak and uses the downslope to open up his throttle. With Jeni and Roen close on either side, we forge a path straight towards the Delta. The sting of rain begins to recede and murky rays peek through the edges of the slowing clouds. As Darkness ends, Larn surges forward in a new bloom of light.

After an hour of wasteland falls behind us, Larn navigates towards a high, steep hill. He slows up the slope and comes out of his blend. As soon as we reach the top, he slams to a halt and spins to look behind us. Jeni and Roen exit the beams halfway up the hill. Thankfully, they're the only living creatures in sight. Larn and I continue to search the wasteland until Jeni and Roen stop on the crest.

"I think they gave up," Larn says between huge gulps of air.

"I'll keep watch," Roen replies. "You need a rest."

"Any wounds?" Larn asks him.

"I'm fine."

I slide off Larn's back and land on my good leg. Exhausted from carrying me, Larn drops to all fours and then rolls to his back. While Jeni rubs sap on the slash in her arm, I limp to a large stone and sit down.

"How could you let her go?" I angrily ask Larn and then direct my fury at Roen. "And why didn't you stay with her?"

Roen doesn't say anything, but Larn bolts upright and answers me with the same incensed tone that I used. "Tell me one person who can stop her when her mind is made up."

"Calm down," Jeni says to both of us.

I hate to admit it, but Larn is right. Better than anyone alive, I know how bullheaded Sash can be. I shouldn't have taken my frustration out on Larn and Roen, but I'm so concerned about Sash right now that I'd saw both of my legs off if it would bring her back safely.

"I'm sorry, Roen," I say. "I'm sorry, Larn. That was

uncalled for. I'd be a corpse right now if it weren't for all of you."

"Don't worry about it," Roen replies.

"Thanks for giving Sash your canister on the way out," I say to him.

"There wasn't much left," he tells me, "but it was something."

My eyes wander to the drab terrain to the north. "I can't believe she took off alone."

"She's doing what she thinks is right," Larn says evenly. "Roen couldn't have kept up with her. You know that as well as he does."

I look down and examine my leg. Blood is still oozing from the divot in my thigh. After I pour what little sap I have left on it, the wound finally begins to scab. Since the rain has ended, it gives me at least a little hope that Sash will be able to stop her bleeding.

"It's the Murkovin woman that's bothering me so much," I say to Larn. "You saw them fight. Sash couldn't kill her. That woman is every bit as good with a spear as Sash is. When Sash headed north, one of the Murkovin followed her and was just as fast. It had to have been that woman."

"You need to trust Sash's judgment," Larn replies.

"Maybe we should go after her. She was heading north."

He shakes his head. "You know better than anyone how difficult it is to find someone in the Barrens. We're almost out of sap, you can't travel, and Jeni is wounded. Even if we could find her, I'm not sure we'd be much help."

"How's your leg?" Jeni asks me.

"It'll heal," I answer. "How's your arm?"

"It'll heal," she says.

Larn stands from the ground. "Do you see anything?" he asks Roen.

"Not a thing," he answers.

"I never thought I'd be so grateful for two people disobeying an order."

Jeni stabs her spear in the dirt. "You didn't really expect us to go back to the Delta until we knew you were safe, did you?"

"I expected everyone to stick to the plan," Larn tells her.

"The plan fell apart," Roen says. "Jeni and I had a back-up plan."

"And it was well devised," Larn replies. "You caught the Murkovin completely off guard. Sash, Chase, and I would all be face down in the mud right now if it weren't for the two of you."

"We're honored to lend a hand," Roen says.

Jeni takes a swig from her canister and then hands it to Larn. After a couple of sips, Larn holds it out to me.

"None for me," I say. "You three need it more than I do."

Larn, Jeni, and Roen finish the last of the sap. After helping me stand up again, Roen takes my spear from me and lifts me onto Larn's back. The four of us sail across the Barrens in the direction of the Delta.

As hours of wasteland go by, all I can think about is Sash. When we were trying to get away, the wound in her stomach had an obvious impact on her ability to fight, and she was losing a lot of blood. Even with sap, if she has internal bleeding or damaged organs, she'll need a day or two to heal. At best, she's at about sixty percent right now.

Even worse, a Murkovin version of Sash is stalking her.

After we finally reach the Delta and make it safely inside the gate, Roen helps me off Larn's back. Jeni grabs several canisters from the hooks in the wall and passes them out. We all take several long drinks and then Jeni and Roen say their goodbyes. As they leave for their habitats, I rub more sap on my thigh.

"Do you want me to carry you to your habitat?" Larn asks.

"No," I answer, "but will you to please do me a favor."

"What's that?"

"Go to Home and find Aven. Tell her that I made it back safely but hurt my leg. I need her to stay at Home until it heals. I'll come see her soon."

"What should I tell her about Sash?"

"Tell her the truth," I answer. "Sash went after Tela. But I don't think Aven needs to know that Sash is wounded."

Larn nods his agreement. "What are you planning to do?"

I glance at the gate and then back at Larn. "I'll wait by the bridge until she comes back. If she's not back by the time I can run on this leg and travel, I'm going to the northern Barrens."

"She'll be back," he says. "I don't think it's her time to die yet. You need to have faith."

"That's about all I have right now, but it's running a little low."

Larn looks down at my leg. "Take care of your wound."

"I will. Again, I'm sorry that I yelled at you."

"Apology already accepted," he replies.

"And thank you for saving my life."

He nods his head. "It's what we do for each other."

After Larn heads towards Home, I use my spear as a crutch and walk back outside the gate. I step off the short path to the bridge and make my way along the gigantic marble wall. When I find a spot with a rock large enough to rest my injured leg on, I sit down with my back against the wall. Using both hands, I lift my leg and prop it up on the stone. Silvery-blue waves leap from the rapids in front of me and crash back down to the river, bathing my body in mist.

For the second time in a couple of days, I find myself staring at the Barrens and waiting for Sash to return. But it's different this time. She's not just spying from a distance. She's wounded, on her own in the wasteland, and there's no way for anyone to help her. If that Murkovin woman catches up to her, I don't know that Sash is strong enough in her current state to defeat her.

I look up at the stationary clouds with a new question haunting my mind. If Sash never makes it back, if all that's happened leads to her death in the Barrens, how can I tell Aven that it's my fault? How can I explain to her that if I'd been stronger, if I hadn't given in to the wild sap, if I'd just brought Tela back to the Delta sooner, none of this would have happened?

I already know that if Sash doesn't return, I'll punish myself for as long as I live. There is no absolution for me putting her in this position. But I don't know how I can live with the guilt of knowing that if Aven never sees her mother again, it's because of me.

Chapter 39

Hidden by large boulders clustered on a hillside, the woman spies through a seam in two rocks. She's certain that the Hunter is somewhere in the maze of narrow, intersecting canyons in front of her, but not aware of her exact location.

After raising a hand to her face, the woman traces her fingers over the thick scab on her cheek and nose. The wound will leave a scar, but a scar she'll wear with great pride. It will be a reminder to all who see it that she was the one who finally ended the extraordinary Hunter's life.

The woman and the former Watcher had often discussed the need to eliminate the Hunter. The Hunter's glimpses of the future might somehow expose their plan to conquer the Delta. Now it will be the woman, not the former Watcher, who finally brings death to the Hunter. It will be absolute proof that she is the most powerful being in the Barrens.

She may have led the former Watcher to believe that she needed his aid, but she was never as helpless as she presented herself to be when they first met. For the many pieces of her plan to fall together in a way that would result in victory, she required his knowledge of the Delta and his skill at making items from steel. But the scheme to overthrow the Delta was the spawn of her mind, planted in his spectrum like a seed in the dirt.

He had many clever ideas, including hiding the steelworkers deep in the Desert, but only she could unite the Murkovin. Just as the tall Murkovin would never have put his trust in a former Watcher of the Delta, her kind wouldn't have followed him. The first few Murkovin they recruited to join them only agreed because the woman was at his side. She and the former Watcher soon learned that it was better to keep his true identity hidden, better to let the people of the Barrens believe he was one of them.

Before they ever met, the woman knew that he, a Watcher of the Delta at the time, had been observing her from a distance. She'd already witnessed several of his treks to the Barrens to secretly consume wild sap. When she finally let him see her, she pretended not to notice him. After the first time he spotted her, he searched for her again and again. It was obvious that she had captivated him in a way that no one else could.

On the day of their first meeting, she saw him watching her cavern, no doubt hoping to catch a glimpse of her. She left her habitat with the weathered, wooden spear she'd once bartered for instead of the steel one she'd later taken by force from a man who'd thought he could make her serve him.

When the Watcher approached her at a sustaining tree, she feigned a certain level of helplessness, desperation even, so that he might feel superior. Only after she gained his trust, only after he fell victim to her charms, did she slowly expose her gifts. And even then, never to the extent that he might realize that she's just as remarkable as the Hunter.

She couldn't deny that she'd been attracted to him, and still is to this very day. Although they became close enough over their time together that she wanted to bear his child, she always knew that their time together would eventually need to end. It's the only way for *her* vision of what Krymzyn should be to finally come to fruition.

The woman's ears prick at the faint sound of a rock moving on the slope behind her. Thirty feet? Forty feet? She hadn't seen signs of her kind in the area, but that didn't mean they weren't nearby. Or did the Hunter discover that the woman was on her trail?

She twists to her rear and swings her weapon up in front of her. Instantly recognizing her most trusted companion, she unwinds her muscles and relaxes her stance. He covers his mouth with his hand to signal her to remain quiet and then motions for her to follow him. Without disturbing the smallest pebble or making the slightest sound, she nimbly makes her way down the slope.

As she nears him, he turns and heads down the hill. After they silently step to the base, he leads her to a concealed gorge in a nearby cliff. Once they're inside the rocky crag, the tall Murkovin pokes his head out of the opening. Only when he's convinced that no one else is nearby does he focus his attention on her.

"What happened to your face?" he asks in a hushed voice.

"The Hunter and a group of Travelers raided the camp," the woman tells him. "I believe they meant to capture the former Traveler and return her to the Delta. I fought the Hunter, but she escaped."

"Was it you who wounded her?"

The woman nods her head. "Where were you?"

"Soon after Darkness fell, the former Traveler left camp with a bag of belongings and a sap transport. I followed her. She and the Hunter are both nearby. The Hunter's wound is bad. She's weak."

"Are they together?" she asks.

"No," he answers. "The Hunter is tracking the former Traveler."

"Do they know you're here?"

The tall Murkovin leans his head out the opening of the gorge, briefly studies the terrain, and listens for any sounds. Only when he's convinced that no one is nearby does he return his attention to the woman.

"The former Traveler has no idea that she was followed," the tall Murkovin says. "She hid the transport and went to a cavern for a while. She soon moved to another. A dozen caverns lie in the canyons nearby. She's smart. She's staying on the move and keeping her eyes open.

"The Hunter knows where she is," he continues, "but she saw me as well. She spotted me traveling during Darkness and followed me to pick up the former Traveler's trail. Once I realized she was on me, I watched to see where the former Traveler stopped and then disappeared."

"Does the Hunter know you're still in the area?" the woman asks.

"She suspects," he answers. "She knows how to be careful. She'll walk half a mile or so and then double back on a different route to see if she was followed. How did you find us?"

"When the group that raided the camp escaped, one of them separated and headed to the north. I knew it had to be the Hunter by her speed. I followed her to this area, but eventually lost her. She knew I was behind her. Where is she now?"

"Not far from here," he says. "She's tending to her wound."

As though the Hunter's blade is lacerating her face again, pain seers across the woman's cheek. "We kill her now."

"Not yet," he replies.

"Why not?" the woman demands.

"Keep your voice down," he says quietly. "As I said, the Hunter is smart. When she rests, she only stops on high ground with plenty of open space to escape. She's staying close to the former Traveler, but she's also on alert. If she sees us coming, she could flee long before we get to her."

"What do you propose?" she asks.

"Patience," he says. "She has rope with her. I can only guess that she plans on using it to tie the former Traveler and return her to the Delta. When she goes after the former Traveler, she'll be vulnerable. We can kill them both."

"If we wait," the woman counters, "her wound might have time to heal."

The tall Murkovin shakes his head. "She's lost a lot of blood and doesn't appear to have much sap. She'll need what she has left to travel back to the Delta. Every time she moves, her scab tears open. She needs to act soon and she knows it. If she enters a cavern to go after the former Traveler, we'll have her trapped inside. She'll have nowhere to run."

The woman examines the point of her spear while considering the tall Murkovin's plan. As much as she'd like to kill the Hunter at this very moment, the need for retribution is clouding her judgment. Patience is what has allowed her plan to progress as far as it has.

No living being is as skilled at hunting someone in the Barrens as the tall Murkovin standing in front of her. She decides to trust his judgment.

"You're in charge," the woman says.

"Stay a few feet behind me. Don't make a sound and watch our backs."

He leads the woman out of the gorge and past the hill where he found her. Firm under their feet, the dirt has already dried from the rains of Darkness. They carefully ascend another steep, scraggly hill. When they near the top, the tall Murkovin motions for the woman to stay a few feet below the ridge. After crawling to the crest, he spies through a crack between two large boulders on the labyrinth of narrow canyons directly below. With her back against the rocky ridge, the woman keeps watch on the terrain behind them.

All they can do now is patiently wait for the Hunter to make a move. Once she's dead, the woman's greatest obstacle will be removed. The Hunter's body will decay until it's nothing but the dust of the Barrens.

After the Delta has fallen, she thinks to herself, *the army of Murkovin will learn who the Mür of my child really is—where he came from and what he once was. I'll make certain of that. They'll turn on him and end his life. If they don't, I'll carry out the task myself.*

As I've always known would eventually happen, our time together will come to an end. Although the thought of his death saddens me, it's the only way that I can see my vision for this world come to pass. Nothing and no one in will stand in my way. All of Krymzyn will look to me to guide them.

What was the word I once learned from the Mür of my child—the word he learned from stories of other worlds told by the Disciples to the children of the Delta?

Queen.

That's the word, and that's what I was born to be.

Queen of Krymzyn.

The Journals of Krymzyn

Krymzyn

The Infinite Expanse

A Traveler's Fate

Barrens Rising (release date TBD)

War of The Beginning (release date TBD)

The 8th Purpose (release date TBD)

Light of Krymzyn (release date TBD)

www.ingramcontent.com/pod-product-compliance
Lightning Source LLC
Chambersburg PA
CBHW030546180626
46816CB00005B/1426